The Journey

A Novel

H. G. Adler

Translated from the German by Peter Filkins

THE MODERN LIBRARY
NEW YORK

2009 Modern Library Paperback Edition

Translation and introduction copyright © 2008 by Peter Filkins

Published in the United States by Modern Library, an imprint of The Random House Publishing Group, a division of Random House, Inc., New York.

MODERN LIBRARY and the TORCHBEARER Design
are registered trademarks of Random House, Inc.

Originally published in hardcover in the United States by Random House, an imprint of The Random House Publishing Group, a division of Random House, Inc., in 2008.

This work was originally published in Germany as *Eine Reise* by Bibliotheca Christiana in 1962 and by Paul Zsolnay Verlag in 1999. Copyright © 1999 by Paul Zsolnay Verlag, Vienna. This edition published in agreement with Paul Zsolnay Verlag.

A portion of this translation originally appeared in *Literary Imagination* in 2006.

Library of Congress Cataloging-in-Publication Data
Adler, H. G.
[Reise. English]
The journey: a novel / H. G. Adler; translated from German by Peter Filkins.
p. cm.
ISBN 978-0-8129-7831-5
I. Filkins, Peter. II. Title.
PT2601.D614R4513   2008
833'.914—dc22   2008000072

Printed in the United States of America

www.modernlibrary.com

2   4   6   8   9   7   5   3   1

Book design by Susan Turner

Praise for

The Journey

"Adler is finally getting his due. . . . The translation of *The Journey* is a publishing-world event."
—*The New Criterion*

"Filkins has done a great service by introducing to English-speaking readers an important witness to the destruction of the European Jews."
—*Moment*

"Strongly recommended . . . There is great beauty in this writing."
—*Library Journal*

"After Auschwitz . . . critics believed that literature was no longer possible. Adler believed that it was not only possible, but necessary. Writing this astounding novel, Adler amply proved his point."
—*Historical Novels Review*

"True to the madness of reality . . . For Adler, the lingering effect of his experience is disorientation, and his novel brings that feeling to life."
—*Booklist*

"Bold unconventionality . . . startles like a gunshot . . . [an] extraordinarily ambitious attempt to articulate the unspeakable."
—*Kirkus Reviews*

"There is an old Hasidic saying: If you carry your own lantern, you will endure the dark. And today, as the generation of survivors is almost gone, H. G. Adler's *The Journey*—a reclaimed masterpiece—illuminates their soul and safeguards their spirit. This powerful work, both lyrical and stark, is a rekindled light through the dark of the past, to be embraced as one would an inheritance."
—BERNICE EISENSTEIN, author of *I Was a Child of Holocaust Survivors*

The Journey

Contents

Translator's Note

THE GERMAN TEXT FOR THE NOVEL IS TAKEN FROM THE 1999 REISSUE OF *EINE Reise* by Zsolnay Verlag, which in turn was printed from the plates for the original version, published in 1962 by bibliotheca christiana.

A segment of the translation was published in *Literary Imagination*, whose editors I wish to thank. In addition, I am deeply grateful to the American Academy in Berlin for a Berlin Prize Fellowship, without which this translation would never have been possible. I am also grateful to Bard College at Simon's Rock for a sabbatical leave, and to the Austrian Society for Literature and the Ministry for Education, Arts, and Culture for research grants. My thanks also go to Jeremy Adler for his many patient replies to questions, to Philip Bohlman for his support and friendship, to Bernie Rodgers for reading an early draft, to Tess Lewis for her suggestions, to Chris Callanan for his resourceful help with queries, to Susan Roeper for being there throughout, and to my editor at Random House, Paul Taunton, who appreciated the novel's import from the start.

Introduction

> It seems unpardonable today that I had blocked off the investigation of my most distant past for so many years, not on principle, to be sure, but still of my own accord, and that now it is too late for me to seek out Adler, who had lived in London until his death in the summer of 1988, and talk to him.
>
> W. G. Sebald, *Austerlitz*

I F THERE WERE A DEFINING EXAMPLE OF A "LOST" WRITER, IT WOULD HAVE to be H. G. Adler. Born in Prague in 1910, he grew up in a secularized Jewish family and later studied musicology at Charles University in Prague, where he wrote a thesis on "Klopstock und die Musik," completed in 1935. Like so many of his generation, however, his dream of becoming a professor and writer was soon postponed. Though he made attempts to emigrate before the Germans marched into Czechoslovakia, visas were difficult to come by, circumstances ever changing and confusing, the needs of family and friends too pressing to ignore. Adler was still in Prague when the Nazis arrived in 1939, and after marrying Gertrud Klepetar he was transported with her and her parents to Theresienstadt on February 8, 1942, where he immediately began taking notes for what would become his groundbreaking study, *Theresienstadt 1941–1945*, which he would publish in 1955 to wide acclaim. Adler and his wife spent two and a half years in Theresienstadt, which Adler called a *Zwangsgemeinschaft*, a slave community set up by the Nazis to cleanse the Reich of Jews in exchange for their "safe" passage and the worldly goods they were forced to leave behind. There his wife's father died, while later in Auschwitz, Gertrud would join her mother on "the bad side" as they came off the train in order that she not die alone in the gas chambers. Adler's own mother and father would also meet their deaths in other camps, a total of eighteen family members eventually disappearing into the horror.

As with so many survivors, a combination of good health, sharp wits, and pure luck saved Adler himself. After spending two weeks in Auschwitz he was transported to Niederorschel, a neighboring camp of Buchenwald, and eventually to Langenstein, where he worked in a factory that made sheet metal for airplanes. It was there that he was liberated by American troops on April 13, 1945, returning to Prague on June 20, barely alive. Eventually he regained his health and, after the Soviets moved in, emigrated to London in 1947, where he reunited with a childhood sweetheart, married, and had a son. However, he also remained an exile for the rest of his life, and died in 1988 after having published twenty-six books of poetry, fiction, philosophy, and history, as well as more than two hundred articles and essays on the Holocaust, Jewish history, literature, and philosophy. Never resting, never settling in any one field or genre, Adler described himself simply as a "freelance writer and teacher," preferring to approach his subject matter through both literature and social science in order to carefully detail what he'd experienced, as well as render it in art so that it could be imagined by others.

Though it's customary to begin with the basic biographical outline when introducing an author, in the case of H. G. Adler it's absolutely necessary. Despite those twenty-six books and numerous articles and essays, his name hardly ever appears in the standard works on the Holocaust. You will not find him listed in most encyclopedias of Holocaust writers, nor do most critics of Holocaust literature discuss his writing. Glancing mention is made here and there of his monograph on Theresienstadt, as well as his 1974 study of the systematic structures that set the Holocaust in motion, *Der verwaltete Mensch* (*Administered Man*). Almost nowhere, however, will you find mention of his poems or stories, nor of the six novels he wrote, four of which were published in his lifetime, receiving heartfelt praise from the likes of Heinrich Böll, Heimito von Doderer, and Elias Canetti. Though W. G. Sebald discusses Adler's work on There-sienstadt in the climactic twenty pages of his novel *Austerlitz*, and a 2004 issue of Germany's *Text+Kritik* focused on his entire career, Adler lived to face deep neglect amid the corrosive waves of time, ending up a man who set down his story in numerous works and genres only to see it lost before his very eyes. Only the recent republication of his novels and monographs has begun to bring the kind of attention they deserved in his lifetime.

How could this have happened? What is it about Adler or his work that could have led to such demise? Part of the answer lies in the mundane quirks of publishing, another part in the times in which he lived and wrote. Though Adler's monograph on Theresienstadt received critical ac-claim as well as the Leo Baeck Prize, his literary works were either pub-lished by very small publishers unable to support them with the proper distribution, or not published until years after they had been written. *Eine Reise* (which I prefer to call *The Journey*, *Die Reise* being the title Adler gave it when he wrote it in 1950–51) was not published until 1962. Peter Suhrkamp of Suhrkamp Verlag went so far as to say that as long as he was alive the book would never be published in Germany. Indeed, Suhrkamp died in 1959 and the book appeared from a tiny publisher three years later. Meanwhile, *Panorama*, Adler's first novel, written in 1948, was not pub-lished until 1968, while *Die unsichtbare Wand* (*The Invisible Wall*), written in 1954–56, did not appear until 1989, a year after Adler's death. Two other novels have never been published at all.

Beyond bad luck and the quirks of publishing, something else was afoot during Adler's career, for one can perhaps hear the wall of resistance he confronted in Peter Suhrkamp's categorical ban. The times were not ready for Adler, nor was he at ease with them. As we know, Theodor Adorno's famous pronouncement that literature was no longer possible after Auschwitz was the accepted critical opinion of the day. Adler and Adorno corresponded, and it was on this position that they came to deep disagreement. Adler believed it not only possible to write poetry and liter-ature after Auschwitz but that it was necessary, for only with the full en-gagement of the imagination would it be possible to elicit even a glimmer of the true nature of what had been suffered and, yes, survived. Adorno's view, however, carried the day, especially with the generation of writers, editors, and publishers who controlled the production of literature in German after the war.* Add to this Adler's exile in London, a condition that condemned him to a life lived on the periphery, and one can appreciate what it must have felt like to disappear in plain view, the irony being that this was the very same sentence that he, like millions of others, had seen carried out much earlier.

Neither Germany nor the world was ready for novels about the Holocaust in the 1950s. In fact, the number of novels published by Jews who had direct experience of the camps and lived to write fiction about them in German comes to a grand total of four. Jurek Becker's *Jacob the Liar* is the best known, though Becker was only eight when he was imprisoned at Sachsenhausen. Edgar Hilsenrath's *Night*, a fictionalized account of his experience at a camp in the Ukraine, is another; and Fred Wander's *The Seventh Well* is a third, though it is arguably closer to a memoir than a novel. Adler's *The Journey*, meanwhile, is the only one of the four set in Theresienstadt, that unique combination of a sealed town that would claim a mortality rate even higher than the death camps and the central depot for the transports to the east. Nonetheless, that is all: four novels, and no more, written in German by Jews who survived the camps. Astounding as this may sound, one need only recall that the overwhelming majority of Jews who were condemned to the camps were not of German origin, that numerous German writers wisely chose exile after 1933, and that of course the vast majority who did know the death camps firsthand did not survive to write about them. But *four*. In reverse proportion, it's a number as staggering as six million.

To try to convey in short fashion the complexity and feel of a novel as strange and inventive as *The Journey* seems nearly impossible. Making free use of montage in jumbling its sense of time and place, and mixing philosophical speech with poetic imagery, pointed political insights with oblique imagist renderings, it is the most lyrical of the six novels, or *epische Gesänge*, Adler composed as matrixes of memory and history. *Eine Erzählung*, a tale,

*For a discussion of Adler and Adorno, see Jeremy Adler, "The One Who Got Away" in *The Times Literary Supplement*, October 4, 1996.

was what Adler called it, underscoring its musical nature by attaching the subtitle *Eine Ballade*. However, the irony that lies in the application of such aesthetic terms to a Holocaust experience depends on the immediacy of that same experience being everywhere present in the memory that comes to shape and give voice to it. In this way, *The Journey* is as much about the soul and consciousness of the man who was possessed to write it as it is about the immediate suffering he endured himself.

Like an orchestral suite or tone poem, each separate part is related to all other parts through structural linkages, repeated themes, or even stark contrasts that depend on comparative readings to render the difference that both divides and unites them within the textual score. Composed of multiple voices and themes that at times barely seem to hold together, *The Journey* refuses to allow the reader a secure resting place, its continual change of verb tense and narrative voice keeping us uninformed, devoid of control, and insecure in our understanding of how the story will unfold. Such techniques find strong echoes in the writings of Franz Kafka, particularly in *The Castle*. Their disorienting effect also helps mirror the plight of those who suffered through the events themselves, for obviously to have lived through Theresienstadt or Auschwitz or the Holocaust is not the same as having at one's fingertips the familiar historical narratives we have since developed. Adler's *Theresienstadt 1941–1945* grants a key insight into the sources behind the complexity of his fictional approach when he explains:

> In Auschwitz, there was only the naked despair or the pitiless recognition of the game, and even if there existed a spark of an indestructible vitality, even if the soul managed to escape from time to time into a delusion, in the long run no one could deceive himself, everyone had to look reality in the face.
>
> It was different in Theresienstadt. Everything there could be pushed aside, illusion flourished wildly, and hope, only mildly dampened by anxiety would eclipse everything that was hidden under an impenetrable haze. Nowhere had the inmates of a camp pushed the true face of the period further into an unknown future than here. . . . Only occasionally would the truth arise from the

depths, touch the inmates, and after a bit of fright, they would [go back] into their existence of masks of masks.*

The urge to render an "existence of masks of masks" is what compelled Adler to create a fiction that employs the mythic trope of the fairy tale. Adler's challenge then is how to give shape to an experience that was largely shapeless and unknowable in its immediate sense, and yet which needs to be shaped and made readable in order to be comprehensible. His answer, it would seem, is not to define its shape but instead to suggest one, art's unifying thread of order and composition barely stitching together the various voices, events, places, and people into a unified though precarious whole.

Adler's refusal to be typecast as a fiction writer, historian, philosopher, or poet also shows up in his unwillingness to traffic in categorical identities or referents in *The Journey*, for nowhere in the book (nor hardly in any of Adler's literary works, for that matter) are the words *Nazi, Hitler, Germans, Jews, camps, gas chambers, ghetto,* et cetera, ever used. This approach also avoids the dangers inherent in trafficking in such reductive metonyms and thus masking the lived experience that stands behind them. Instead we are simply told of the Lustig family and the "journey" made by the aging father, Dr. Leopold Lustig; his wife, Caroline; her sister, Ida Schwarz; and the Lustigs' two grown children, Zerlina and Paul. How their journey is recounted, however, is what the "tale" is about. Though in many ways the novel is composed from the perspective of Paul (the family's only survivor and thus a stand-in for Adler himself), along the way the narrative is also spoken by the main characters themselves, the townspeople who observe them, the soldiers and officials who herd them onto the trains, the guards who watch over them, and a narrator possessed of an omnipresent sense of rage at what he pointedly refers to as *Der Abfall,* or the "rubbish heap" of history, which the good Dr. Lustig tends.

Der Abfall, however, also has another meaning in German, namely that of "the Fall," or the descent from God's grace with the election of sin by Adam and Eve in Eden. Amid the rubbish of history, then, Adler

---

*Quoted from Norbert Troller's introduction to his book *Theresienstadt: Hitler's Gift to the Jews,* translated by Susan E. Cernyak-Spatz (Chapel Hill: Univeristy of North Carolina Press, 1991).

weaves a tale of metaphysical renunciation, sin, expulsion, and displacement, the fall and flight from God's peaceable kingdom into human evil
occurring against the backdrop of the Holocaust. The pursuit within such
quotidian darkness, however, is one toward grace, and it is memory that
provides the conduit by which the downfall is overcome. For through
memory not only is consciousness restored and preserved among the survivors, but also the return of justice and its tenuous yet tenacious hold on
life in the face of history.

Similar to the way in which Adler renounces the standard language of
Nazi, Jew, death camp, et cetera, all place names in *The Journey* are fictional, though they indeed serve as metonymic ties to significant portals
along Adler's own journey. The Stupart that the Lustigs leave echoes the
Stupartgasse that Kafka grew up on in Prague; and Kafka's youngest sister,
Ottilie, also spent time in Theresienstadt. Meanwhile, Leitenberg represents Leitmeritz, the town at which the trains unloaded near Theresienstadt, while Ruhenthal, with its biting overtone of "rest" or "peace,"
stands for Theresienstadt itself. Lastly, Unkenburg is modeled after Halberstadt in Germany, but in a deeper sense it stands for the rootless realm
of displacement that Paul later finds himself in at war's end, and which
Adler inhabited as well after surviving Auschwitz and Langenstein.
Through fictional characters placed outside of a direct historical context
and settings that only symbolically connect to actual places, Adler evokes
the mythos that lies beneath the surface of experience, memory becoming,
in the words of his son, Jeremy Adler, "the burning ember that defines the
theme as well as the style."

Take for instance the following passage from early on in *The Journey*
when the Lustigs and other citizens of Stupart are subjected to the repres-
sion that will soon lead to their removal from their own homes, the very
notion of a stable society under the rule of law having been turned on its
head:

> All that had been forbidden in the world now meant nothing, for it
> had never been a law but rather an arrangement that rested on en-
> forced custom. What was once taken in stride now appeared all of
> a piece to the law, which had the last word and did not allow any-
> thing to contradict it. Life was reduced to force, and the natural

consequence was fear, which was bound up with constant danger in order to rule life through terror. You experienced what you never had before. You rejoiced over that which you were allowed, but even this did not last for long, because any such comforts had only to be noticed and the next day they were taken away. Thus the tender juicy meat was taken away since you who are made of flesh need no meat. Then they banned fat, for your belly was full of fat. They denied you vegetables, for they stunk when they rotted. They ripped chocolate out of your hands, fruit and wine as well. You were told that there wasn't any more.

Highways and byways were forbidden, the days were short-ened and the nights lengthened, not to mention that the night was forbidden and the day forbidden as well. Shops were forbidden, doctors, hospitals, vehicles, and resting places, forbidden, all for-bidden. Laundries were forbidden, libraries were forbidden. Music was forbidden, dancing forbidden. Shoes forbidden. Baths forbid-den. And as long as there still was money it was forbidden. What was and what could be were forbidden. It was announced: "What you can buy is forbidden, and you can't buy anything!" Since peo-ple could no longer buy anything, they wanted to sell what they had, for they hoped to eke out a living from what they made off their belongings. Yet they were told: "What you can sell is forbid-den, and you are forbidden to sell anything." Thus everything be-came sadder and they mourned their very lives, but they didn't want to take their lives, because that was forbidden.

Here we see Adler's musical touch in his constant play upon the word "forbidden." No sequence of events leads up to the announcement of what is "forbidden," nor does there seem much logistical sense in forbid-ding things like "shoes" or "dancing" or "night" or "day" except to de-moralize and dehumanize those to whom such edicts are directed. Adler, however, explains none of this, but instead drops us directly into the psy-chological state of the "forbidden" through the arbitrary way it is imposed by anonymous powers for the sake of power itself. Add to this the way in which Adler speaks of the anonymous "you" who experiences all of this in both a first- and secondhand manner and we find ourselves in a kind of netherworld, a place that is not a place, a time that is not a time, spoken by a person who is not a person, but rather the idea or vestige of a person. The result is the "almost futuristic deformation of social life" that the title character of W. G. Sebald's *Austerlitz* cites after reading Adler's study of Theresienstadt. One never quite knows where one is or who is speaking in *The Journey*, and that is much to the point. Such disorientation is meant to convey a society that has fallen into complete dissolution, one where all borders between perpetrator and victim are fluid and unbound, the menace that consumes them a force in itself.

Listen, for instance, to the following passage a bit farther on where Adler now switches from the firsthand "you" that speaks for the "forbidden" to the imperative use of "you" by the officials herding the "forbidden" onto the trains:

> You're being given a sign to move, don't you see it? You have to admit that cross-eyed Herr Nussbaum is certainly on the ball. Everything goes off without a hitch. The assistants sigh deeply, but it's a sigh of relief, for they have done well. Not a single complaint is heard. The heroes stroll and strut the length of the station platform. You sit down, one on top of another, four to a bench, eight to a compartment, like regular, upstanding citizens. But this is no ski hut, there is no snow. No, they are empty train cars. They are narrow, much more narrow than the huts you should have built, but which have already been finished, thus saving you the work. Everything has been taken care of, for they did not want to strain your silky little hands. Who could possibly complain about such sound accommodations? How could you have even completed the job when you have never learned to work with your hands?
>
> You can't be trusted with anything, everything must be arranged for you, because you are a lazy bunch that not even lifting a shovel can change. Like little children, everything has to be done for you, though you arrive at the dinner table without uttering the slightest thank-you. Nothing can be expected from you but your stinking smell. Everything you youngsters need has been taken care of for you, we've made sure of that. We have sacrificed

ourselves for you. If we were a little tougher with you, then you would get all worked up and melt right in the middle of snowy winter. You want snowdrops? We haven't brought you flowers. It's too late. The train will depart before we can get some. We'll send them to you. Yes, everything your heart desires will be sent to you. But you should be off already! Have you forgotten something? That doesn't matter. Just drop us a line, we'll take care of everything. You can count on us. Can't you see it in our faces? Just look in our eyes and you'll see that we can be trusted! Something could happen to you? Who told you that? It's just a bunch of stupid chatter! Not a single hair will be disturbed. Such transgressions are not allowed. Now you are traveling to safety, your new home, just like you always wanted. Is the good-bye hard for you? That's hard for us to believe! No, we can't believe it! The forbidden at last lies behind you for good, and now eternal freedom is waving you on. There you can do what you want. We wish we had the chance to share your lot, but unfortunately that has been denied us. With us lies the responsibility to worry about your well-being, and then to worry about your brothers who are also awaiting the journey.

Again we find several themes at play here. Mention of the "huts" that the "forbidden" were meant to have built alludes to the Jewish work details who were cruelly sent ahead to construct unwittingly their own future ghetto at Theresienstadt. This is countered by the focus on the train cars, as if the latter were luxury travel accommodations about to take them on a winter ski vacation, rather than the same trains that will later transport the "forbidden" to the east and near-certain death. Adler's mix of allusions to the past, present, and future taps the ability of montage to link seemingly disparate times and places such that, again as in Kafka, one place is interchangeable with another amid the nightmare of a seemingly inescapable labyrinth. In addition, an almost comic book–like transparency reveals the bitter irony with which Adler designates the commanders as *"die Helden,"* or "heroes," while his description of the henchman Herr Nussbaum as "cross-eyed" plays off of the vocabulary of deformity and impurity that the Nazis so frequently cast upon their victims. Most sinister of all, however, is the way in which the voice of command and coercion mixes with a disembodied voice of disdain and mockery, leaving us to sort the two in much the same way that deportees were forced to sort through the lies and promises that duped them into signing over their lives in order to gain what they thought was the safe haven of Theresienstadt.

But what of the Lustig family and their individual plight? How are we meant to follow their story while Adler mouths the many voices of the diseased society that surrounds them? The answer is that, in a certain way, their absence from the novel is also a kind of presence. When Adler explores the complex and interwoven relations between the citizens, victims, commanders, officials, and henchmen, our longing, in diminished form, is for the simple human reality of the Lustigs, which they must have longed for themselves. When Adler returns to their story, balance and clarity return to the narrative, though he is also careful to allow this to happen only in the most unreal of circumstances. This way the Lustigs are granted a certain dignity in the handling of their own plight, rather than their circumstances constantly controlling them, however much they are unable to overcome them in the end. Leopold Lustig, for example, may be interned, but he is not a prisoner. He is indeed stripped of his license to practice medicine, but he cannot be stripped of his ability to think and reflect. On the other hand, Leopold's presence is passive, interior, largely unspoken, and largely unknown to those around him. Adler's mission is to make visible the invisible, to excavate that which has been buried, in this case literally. The result is that both Leopold and Adler reach a surprising, if not paradoxical, denouement when Leopold both asserts his own sense of dwelling within this place while also recognizing the forces that have condemned him to it.

Leopold dies in Ruhenthal; Caroline, Ida, and Zerlina pass into the darkness of the death camps; only Paul lives to return. His will be the consciousness, however, that preserves the thought and memory of them, while Adler's own duty is to construct the complex means by which to convey but the slightest glimmer of their being. Adler's own memory of course provided the fuel for the white heat of his tale's content, but it is the cool hand of the artist, Joyce's Stephen Dedalus paring his fingernails while gazing on at the outrage of history, that forges his tale in modernist fashion.

Indeed, if this Leopold reminds us of another Leopold lost in the labyrinth of Joyce's Dublin, the deeper irony is that Theresienstadt is a labyrinth leading to quintessential negation rather than the climactic affirmation of *Ulysses*. At the same time, one would be remiss not to acknowledge the symbolic linkage between Leopold Lustig and Leo Baeck, the spiritual leader of Germany's Jews, who was also interned at Theresienstadt and who also worked on the garbage detail there. Fortunately, Leo Baeck did not die, but survived the war to, among many other things, preserve Adler's voluminous notes on Theresienstadt, which Adler then retrieved after his liberation from Langenstein. Hence, Leopold's fictional death and disappearance among the refuse is countered in real life by Adler's mining of the factual detritus through the assistance of Leo Baeck's act of preservation. That Adler then uses the "refuse" of his experience to create vivid factual and fictional renderings of it is his triumph.

"So what is literature good for?" asks W. G. Sebald in the last essay he wrote, just weeks before his death, a talk titled "An Attempt at Restitution,"* which he delivered at the opening of the Literaturhaus in Stuttgart. Answering this question with a question that Hölderlin asked himself, Sebald inquires, "Am I . . . to fare like the thousands who in their springtime days lived in both foreboding and love, but were seized by avenging Fates on a drunken day, secretly and silently betrayed, to do penance in the dark of an all too sober realm where wild confusion prevails in the treacherous light, where they count slow time in frost and drought, and man still praises immortality in sighs alone[?]" This, in fact, is Adler's question, and the conclusion Sebald reaches also seems pertinent: "The synoptic view across the barrier of death presented by the poet in these lines is both overshadowed and illuminated, however, by the memory of those to whom the greatest injustice was done. There are many forms of writing; only in literature, however, can there be an attempt at restitution over and above the mere recital of facts and over and above scholarship."

---

*Collected in *Campo Santo*, edited by Sven Meyer and translated by Anthea Bell (London: Hamish Hamilton, 2005).

Adler's approach in *The Journey* is ideally suited to transposing Hölderlin's "synoptic view across the barrier of death," thus rising to the standard that Sebald seeks. Through the figurative use of the Lustig family as a stand-in for those who lived, suffered, and died in Theresienstadt, as well as the arch use of the "rubbish heap" and the so-called heroes who watch over the prisoners and sadistically invoke the "forbidden," Adler provides a symbolic frame for the misery inherent to his experience, along with an artistic approach that constantly keeps us off balance as readers as we try to appreciate that experience. Adler accomplishes this by asking us to see beyond his metonyms in order to imagine the experience they represent for ourselves. In this way, Adler's work is both about Theresienstadt and not about it at the same time. Indeed, in some essential way it can never be about the misery endured there, but instead about the imperative for the imagination to attempt to imagine the unimaginable, be it Theresienstadt, Auschwitz, Rwanda, Srebrenica, Darfur, or the next mindless atrocity destined to cross our television screens as we look on, helpless and aghast.

Vitriolic, yet possessed of discipline and artistry; tender, yet refusing self-pity; accusatory, yet knowing the dignity of compassion and forgiveness, *The Journey* is Adler's attempt not at restitution, perhaps, but at the restoration of memory through the fluidity of consciousness evoked through language rather than the fixed edifice of a monument. Only within the music of our consciousness do we connect and reconnect, harken and repeat the disparate elements of our lives, and literature remains the deepest evocation of that process. Through this act of preservation H. G. Adler becomes an "entity capable of remembering itself," as the journey "arrives at a sense of peace." *Die Reise* is the tale of that journey and the apex of Adler's art.

Peter Filkins
December 15, 2007

For Elias and Veza Canetti

The Journey

Augury

D RIVEN FORTH, CERTAINLY, YET WITHOUT UNDERSTANDING, MAN IS SUB-jected to a fate that at one point appears to consist of misery, at another of happiness, then perhaps something else; but in the end everything is drowned in a boundlessness that tolerates no limit, against which, as many have said, any assertion is a rarity, an island in a measureless ocean. Therefore there is no cause for grief. Also, it's best not to seek out too many opinions, because, by linking delusions and fears to which we are addicted, strong views keep you constantly drawn to what does not exist, or even if it did, would seem prohibited. So you find yourself inclined to agree with this or that notion, the emptiness of a sensible or blindly followed bit of wisdom, until you finally become aware of how unfathomable any view is, and that one is wise to quietly refrain from getting too involved with the struggles to salvage anything from the rubbish heap, life's course demanding this of us already.

Thus some measure of peace is attained. It's a peace found in endless flight, but nonetheless genuine peace. It is to be sure not an escape from yourself, no matter how much it may seem so, but rather the flight that consists of a ceaseless progression along the winding paths of a solitary realm, and because you abide in this realm you can call it peace, for upon time's stage everything remains fixed in the present. You're still a part of this. You travel many roads, and in many towns you appear with your relatives and friends; you stand, you walk, you fall and die. You don't believe you're still on the stage, even when you acknowledge you were once on it. But you're wrong, for they took you away and set you back onstage amid the fleeting journey. You didn't escape, even when you seemed suddenly sunk, figuratively and literally.

Yet what happens onstage? Many analogies are sought that often capture something essential, but none serves us better than the metaphor of the journey, which we can think of as flight. But what entity is it amid all these travels that recalls its own essence? It's memory itself, which sets out on the journey and is also dragged along through constant wandering. This entity, however, cannot leave its present location; that's why it acts in the present and finds space enough to unfold upon a single stage, which allows nothing else to appear but this entity capable of remembering itself, and so the image of the journey as flight arrives at a sense of peace, the entity that experiences it having been born in memory itself.

We are often reproached for the passivity of our beginning, of how reluctant we were to bring matters out into the open. But we cannot blame ourselves for our own expulsion, for that would imply that we wanted to give up. Thus we begin our search for a resting place ever anew; driven perhaps by an insatiability that in the end defines us, we are the heralds of life. The previously drawn analogy between the journey and peace becomes nothing but an analogy unto itself the moment we apply it in practical terms, becoming invalid in the world at large, because now everything appears to be in motion and indeed transforms itself entirely through motion. With good reason, one could speak of a passion or obsession that would sweep others along with us insofar as we are able to capture the living breath of our experience in motion. For indeed, we are our own creation; whether we are denied or accepted at our final end, when one must answer for oneself, much more depends, namely the flourishing of a world that, out of its deepest despair and highest aspirations, is called upon to form its own, in a certain sense, eternal countenance amid the destruction of our only meaningful and yet impalpable achievement, one accomplished in and for itself without the participation and help of the world at large.

Thus peace is let go and is gone, though not entirely; its reflection is and remains discernible for anyone who remains aware, amid the fear and horror of each single moment, when all dignity and secrecy are threatened, that an indestructible kernel persists beneath all the terror of this theater of horrors, a center, one which should never be idealized, since its existence is known only to the searching heart. The unmistakable persistence of this center as the last stop on this journey is at the same time your first and deepest memory, yet that is exactly what we are compelled to remember, the center being so distant that it can be described as neither far nor near. Indeed, that is why it becomes obvious that in the flux of our lives memory always remains, and that, much like a memory, we—and thus an entire world—lack a stable, unchanging place in which to live. Thus we remain in flight, there is no rest for us but the interior that we remember; we are travelers on a journey that not a single one of us chose or planned. This we cannot change, the journey has begun, and now it follows its own path; as it progresses, it does not ask for our approval, it does not care if we love it or hate it, yet it stands in our way as soon as we ourselves resist the way.

Perhaps some still expect to hear where we are headed, or that at least some sense of it will be given. Be patient!—for the aim here to try to depict this rather than describe it is the best response. Those who have their doubts can be assured that the destination will not be forgotten, since worries about the prospect of our final destination drive us all; that's why we will always make sure to keep the destination in mind, even if reports from the rubbish heap often seem to believe us.

One thing must be made clear, if we assert that we have suffered, suffered a great deal; by that we cannot and do not wish to set ourselves off from the world, which in itself experiences nothing but suffering, yet in our indefatigable readiness to embrace this suffering, we do not allow ourselves to sink further into the horror through which we cannot help but walk. No, we are not lost, even when we assert our loss, in fact the many losses that we—alone for the most part and with our humble powers—

cannot make up for. But we have set ourselves on the stage. There, as elsewhere, we wish to appear alone, although we are not forsaken. We are never forsaken.

And so we wish to walk on or not walk at all—for whether or not we walk on or make any progress is certainly not up to us nor anyone else. And so allow us to exist; whether it be in the perpetual motion that brings peace, whether it be in memory that ventures toward peace, either ahead of it or behind, whether it be in flight, one speaks of the fleeting nature of appearances, so let us exist in appearances and remain constantly in motion. Indeed, since our eyes are open, and suffering is not all we experience, but also life, allow us to grant this ever-changing existence so full of memory its only proper name—the journey.

The Tale

No one asked you, it was decided already. You were rounded up and not one kind word was spoken. Many of you tried to make sense out of what was going on, so you yourselves had to inquire. Yet no one was there who could answer you. "Is this how it's going to be? For a little while . . . a day . . . years and years . . . ? We want to get on with our lives." But all was quiet, only fear spoke, and that you could not hear. Old people could not accept what was going on. Their complaining was unnerving, such that around those left untouched by such suffering a cold and hideous wall was erected, the wall of pitilessness. Yet the tight-lipped grins remain unforgettable; they survived all weariness and first appeared in the ruined apartments. The apartments were in fact not destroyed, they still existed in regular buildings with roofs that were intact. In the stairwells the ingrained smells, which lend each house its inextinguishable character so long as the building stands, were still trapped.

The everyday existence of inanimate objects can seem quite alluring, but it obeys laws that have little to do with our journey, as long as we don't pick up such things and recognize ourselves within them. True, one speaks of notorious brick walls, but that is only an image for an incomprehensible event, compared to which the visible, the tangible, possesses far more distinctive characteristics. Everything can be left behind, but nothing is cut off from life as long as it remains conscious of itself. That is why buildings stand there indifferent when we abandon them. Then someone shouted, "Go away!" No one actually shouted these words, no one shouted at all, and yet it was declared implicitly, even if no one heard it. But for whoever did not hear it, it meant trouble, because he would crouch in his house as if it were his one and only possession that no one could take from him.

There was a room and other rooms as well. Their solitude was violated, for the doors stood open, though the windows were gently closed and darkened by the black cloth hanging in them. This was called the blackout. The blackout was everywhere, the nocturnal streets of Stupart lay in solid darkness. Yet inside the house there was light. Not in the stairwell outside, no, for there it was also dark. The bulbs were painted an ugly blue color and covered with shades made of black paper which let no light through and only cast down a feeble circle of light. It was difficult for the boots to trudge heavily up the stairs in the dark, but this did not hold back the tireless messengers, for their hurried steps spread a fear before which the lights withdrew. They usually came in late evening or during the night, carrying a message that cast its own terrible light. "Thou shalt not dwell among us!" That was the printed message they delivered. The people already expected the worst, and therefore the apartments were destroyed even before a plane's powerful projectile took pity on them. The planes came much later, cracking open the hollow shells like harvest nuts, but not to avenge the abduction of those exiled from the houses whom they hardly knew of, and who meant little to them when they zeroed in on a segment of the city they wished to obliterate. Each night the raging machines rumbled through the thunderous sky and dropped their murderous cargo on the transitory existence below, which first became aware of them when it burst apart. There were no more apartments that lasted long enough to become ruins, there were only empty brood houses, ransacked shells, or illegitimate goods worthless even to looters. But this happened much later and was never seen by the afflicted, who long before had been told, "Thou shalt not dwell among us!"

Consider well what right you have to enjoy a resting place where you can simply be only because you have the right to be. Ask yourself this when you are in flight and bereft of all your possessions, on your own among the shells of buildings that have become sinister. Once they came after you, be it your enemies or your friends, you can't tell the difference, and they took everything from you. If they only somewhat misled you, they told you to gather up the remainder, because you would need so many things and would be crying out for many of your possessions. All possessions became ridiculous, but nonetheless they remain completely indispensable. The knapsack lies there, neatly packed and readied with care. You cannot leave it behind and now know how important it is to have your own things. You stand up and put your coat on and then let yourself sink back down onto the chair. You decide what belongs to yourself alone. But is that allowed?

"Have you thought it over, my dear Frau Lustig? Tomorrow it's your turn. Off into the wild blue yonder. I heard it's so. I know for sure."

Blissful is the nonbeliever who hides the future's misfortune beneath the protective covering of the present moment, for now everything is obscured by darkness. No one seeks protection when hope and silence alone mark the passing of time and make it believable. But in fact everything is unbelievable, anything that interrupts the horror. Unhappy belief! How unbelievable the bravery, how improbable is belief and all expectation, but in the apartment the remnants of each are gathered. There they find old Dr. Lustig's medal for bravery, the letter from the regiment commander. It's unbelievable, but only the unbelievable can protect us.

"It won't be that bad. One should . . . one could . . . He's done so much good! He deserves recognition . . . credit. . . ."

Words appear amid the horror, like old friends, for the language no longer belongs to us; it slips out, sounding odd, from anyone who attempts to talk. But then the words spill out and seem familiar. Sweet words, words that have floated away, my words, your words, they tear down walls and erect them as well, they weave themselves tightly together, impervious and sound. Yes, the walls are there, and they are known, everything is known, such that one could almost take pleasure in wiping out what feels like a threat. Then the blackout would no longer be feared.

"If you want to make yourself useful, if you . . ."

That's the way it always sounds. Still one must clear away the rubbish, for it so easily gets in the way. The rubbish bin in the apartment is too small and is overflowing before one knows it. In the courtyard the rubbish containers stand by, wrapped in their stillness, and the frame on which carpets are beaten stands there, the circular hooks for the wash line are still embedded in plaster. "That's forbidden!" What's forbidden? Nothing, it's just a wild rumor that disrupts the quiet peacefulness of rubbish with war. Yet all rumors are wild and are regularly done in by the truth. Indeed the truth is often inquired about, the all too earnest asking about it, as well as those who quietly laugh. Even those who display their ignorance with pride cannot ignore this question forever, for it comes to occupy you no matter what.

The intruders stand boldly and arrogantly in the apartment and cast their eyes without worry on a scene they don't appear to understand. Milk is mixed with raspberry juice, the result a new drink. A lot has been done, but nothing has happened, nor does anyone notice. Only sleep is impossible to think of. It was senseless to have made your bed, but it comes from thoughtful consideration, for the hour is come, a glance at the watch you laid down reminding you. In the early hours you pick it up, checking it regularly until the next morning. Then it will be picked up once again.

"Tell me, can't something be done? There's something I have to take care of tomorrow. Besides, I'm completely convinced that it's all a huge mistake."

There is no doubting the mistake, but it lies elsewhere and belongs neither to those who came after us nor to ourselves. It is also not in the house and not on the street. Most likely it is somewhere far off without memory, in the dirges raised against the heavenly bodies. No, it is nowhere to be found.

Don't sit on the sofa, you could squash the cushion. We just finished putting everything in order! Using a soft brush in order to be careful with the fragile fabric, Ida and Caroline have cleaned and smoothed everything. They humbly bent to their task so that everything could look in order, even if they were not certain if they would have any visitors. In a few days Leopold will celebrate his seventy-fifth birthday. Zerlina has used some money and flirted a bit in order to get a couple of cigars for her father. Some relatives and friends are supposed to show up, really they are, for not all have left. They are to quietly ring the bell and gather together for a couple of hours in this room. A cake will be baked, cake and coffee with milk and lots of sugar, especially given the way Leopold likes to shovel it into his cup. Almost everything has been taken care of, even an egg for the cake. Caroline has it all organized inside her head, stubborn woman that she is. Unforeseen misfortune? Not at all, it's just chicanery. The unknown doesn't exist. One only has to stay the course. Leopold pays attention to the law and to nothing else in the world around him. Against injustice one has only to make an appeal. One has only to apply oneself relentlessly, even when it does no good.

"Please, don't make such a fuss, Frau Lustig! Even if you have to leave the house, something that I can't keep from happening, that doesn't actually mean that you'll have to travel farther on from there. Many have left and yet have not had to travel farther. They simply changed locales. There you can set up house just fine."

You hear everything. Nothing escapes your heightened awareness, which is on edge and attentive. Nothing is unclear, because everything is thought through so completely by the authorities that no difficulties arise. Whoever thumbs through the long lists will find all the guidelines. You only have to make up your mind and you are free, if only you submit to coercion. Destiny is now a book written by men. They have their needs just like you and I, and they have worries just like ours. Yet they also have completely different worries, because they are not pleased with their job when they have to strike one of us, something for which their superiors have an excuse, as the case may be, an explanation ready at hand.

Paul's hand stroked the strings of Zerlina's lute before it had to be taken to the depository for musical instruments. That was a few days earlier. He took the lute down from the wall and removed the decorative ribbons, which Zerlina then folded together and packed in a box along with other mementos. Paul then ripped out five of the six strings, tearing open its soul, and with a knife slashed its body. Zerlina shrieked as if witnessing a murder, because the lute was not a piece of junk meant for the rubbish. But now it was; no one would hear its notes again with joy. Finally Paul yanked out a peg and tossed it into the fire. A blatant assault. The night's dark work had begun. Zerlina could not bring herself to strike the lute; softly she reached out for it as Paul tucked it under his arm and carried it off.

The face of the house lady peeked in each evening, a fat round face consumed by barely contained greed. Soon she would no longer have to control her desires. On that day she was there as well, shocked by the strange men. Frau Lischka was not to be trusted, yet with gifts she could be appeased and then she was a trusted soul and there was no danger. Zerlina was startled whenever the house lady stood in her way, but Caroline and Ida were at peace with her familiar ways. Full of chubby contentment, Frau Lischka's greeting spread through the stairwell. "My husband drinks too much. The doctor should warn him about what can happen." She then made the gesture with which she greeted her husband. Yet Caroline said not a word to Leopold, for he was lost in thought and didn't understand what was beginning to happen around him and what had already condemned him and many others who had no idea of the judgment they would suffer.

Everything human involves judgment, which is why it comes as no surprise to say that without judgment consciousness would not be possible. Man is a creature that judges. That's why judgment must be experienced by him and endured until he receives his own final judgment and accepts it. Then the will disappears or is broken. A quarter of an hour passes, then another, as the hour strikes and the great journey begins that marks the conclusion of another great journey, the onset of perpetual motion, this journey being like all others. Everything becomes uncertain; each new decision that's handed down is executed directly by the powers that be who carry it out without seeing the consequences, because even though what occurs later is set in motion on their own familiar turf, how it's been decided and why remains unknown and has to do with the suppositions of the authorities. They themselves have no power; they only shout out the orders they are supposed to and thus bear witness to their faith in the system.

Now they turn their attention to Dr. Leopold Lustig's household, which is to be vacated, though nothing more is sure. Even the officials carrying out their orders have no clear idea of the consequences of their commands as they scatter fates to the wind. A piece of paper brought along is taken out and handed over, the words themselves no longer important. Everything is destroyed, the bottle of raspberry juice falls over accompanied by a shriek as the carpet turns red. A weary hand reaches toward the bottle that rolls away after it falls and slowly lifts it and places it back on the table.

"It can't be all that bad, for it's not so far away, and at least we know where we're going."

But no one can sleep, the night is shattered. The blackout is useless when those in hiding keep their lights on and keep eternal sleep at bay. Yet sleep is not eternal, that is a fallacy, because if it were eternal it would not tolerate any interruption, and the validity of all official orders would be undermined. But for the living who follow the order for the journey to begin, there is no sleep, because everything must be relinquished. The keys cannot remain in the doors and are collected, the IDs that vouch for the names on them are separated from the nameless phantoms, because the permission for them to remain together must be denied, the result being the separation of belongings from their owners in Stupart, the reality of which is committed to paper in long lists. That's what is ordered, and the main office won't worry a bit about what's left when those forbidden to stay leave the gutted houses. No one hesitates when the command is given, since it says in writing, "You are forbidden. . . ."

We are all forbidden because we are not what we wished to become, and we are not what we wished to become because we've been turned into something unwanted. Thus we are nothing more than extra baggage destined to become the tools of obedience, expectant travelers whose weariness is enough to put all of humanity asleep. Still, it's astounding that the messengers are not tired. Only we are overtired. But sleep does not exist for those of us to whom time presents, so to say, an inscrutable and fast-approaching future.

Individual needs can be taken care of efficiently and without haste. Now that we're here, at least they can't take that from us. If we are to fulfill our duties we need sufficient time, as you can obviously see. You are not bad people, and you know that we're not so bad either. In fact it's all a mistake, yet the mistakes are already present and we have to suffer the consequences. Consciousness can practice, and is even capable of getting used to the fact that all experience is betrayed, as well as the need to conjure a tight-lipped smile amid an otherwise emotionless expression. But impatience! Impatience is what does us in. . . .

"Hurry up! Don't stop moving! We have to be there by midnight at the latest!"

That is impossible, for that's not much longer than an hour away. Everything still has to be prepared. Even Frau Lischka doesn't see the need for such hurry. It's still night, and the doctor is so old, and Frau Ida Schwarz has rheumatism. You should just see her hands. There's no way they will leave at night, for that's impossible. But the officials say that they can easily take off with the doctor and Frau Schwarz at a moment's notice. The streetcars are still running and the others can leave, indeed as soon as possible, the bracing winter air will freshen everyone. So get going, get going!

And don't you worry about that fat dog, the house lady can take care of it. What's that, his name is Bunny? A dog named Bunny! Here're some scraps for that hot dog, that should do him, it will only do the mutt good to land in someone else's hands and not be so overfed. It doesn't matter that he's a dachshund; even for a broad-built animal he's still too fat. The looks of him! All this idiotic love of pampered pets, how typical, how useless, what ridiculous sentimentality. Without that, this nonsense would quickly come to an end, for certainly dogs, cats, and canaries will have to be turned in within a few weeks. The Humane Society will take care of them and make sure the critters do not suffer. They'll be in good hands, don't worry, everything will be taken care of.

Alas, everything must be done by hand, even the stones that are still held together await the hands that will rip them apart later. The mortar between the individual bricks will tire of fending off the picks and will begin to crumble into dust. But that's not yet the case, that will take time, that will be put off until later. There's also no need for Frau Lischka to enter the living quarters. The cracks in the wall are not dangerous. Frau Lischka discovers in the living quarters the old flowery porcelain that Leopold's grandmother had received as part of her trousseau. It's all still in perfect condition, without a piece missing; one could even sell it for a pretty price. Yet one shouldn't just barge in, but rather take greater care so that no cracks appear. Nonetheless, Frau Lischka carries off the tureen, gathering up the many plates with pious hands, since it would be such a shame if it was all carted off by the authorities.

Meanwhile Leopold is fitted out. Here he stands, stiff in a winter coat that otherwise he would never wear, a broad floppy hat on his head, demanding the umbrella he always has with him, come rain or snow, as he hurries to see his patients. This time, however, he leaves without his medical bag, for he can see that it will be a long journey, perhaps a return home possible after a number of months, though it could last a little longer, maybe a year, but no longer, everything will be over by then. That's why this time the coat, hat, and umbrella aren't enough; a small knapsack is also packed. Inside are his slippers, as well as whatever is needed to sleep in and to wash, because Leopold needs to feel comfortable. One bag is important, it's not heavy, no, it doesn't press upon his shoulder. There are good things to eat inside: bread with sausage and cheese, apples, and a nice cake.

Leopold, you must leave the house and Ida must go with you. Crippled hands and feet don't matter, the street is dry and there's no wind. So get going, there are no more houses for all of you to hide in. Your tired bones are dismissed. Ida, they spit on you and laughed about your rheumatism. Anyone can have it, there's no shame in that. It's not so bad that your bones are so twisted up, they said, for where you're headed there will be good hospitals with many doctors and young nurses. Just go, Ida; Leopold can't go alone, because he gets confused, but if you're with him everything will be all right. We'll follow behind. Go and enjoy taking the streetcar from Stupart, because there's nothing left in this house that can still belong to you. That makes it easy to say good-bye. —But it was our house. —No, it was never yours, nor anything in it. You took it all, since you paid for it with money that didn't belong to you; it was bribery that allowed you to enjoy the pleasures of this apartment. Four rooms altogether, a dark foyer, a kitchen, living quarters, a bath and toilet, cut off from the outside world because you hid behind a massive door with a flimsy bolt, as well as a dead bolt and chain to quell your fears, and a covered peephole, behind which a bad conscience lurked, climbing up and down the steps as if there were nothing to feel guilty about when away from your loot.

You spent years here and loved to be seen about town. You left your lair together, feeling safe in Stupart, as if it were home, as if you had the right to it, completely unaware because of your greed, not even noticing or questioning what you did. You shook each hand extended to you and said "Good-bye!" yet you thought nothing of it, and so your days drifted past. You thought that you were being sociable whenever you opened your doors to someone, but that only happened because the doctor was treating someone or it was for your own pleasure. You shouldn't complain that it's all gone. Be happy you ever had it at all! No one asked if you ever had the right, which you thought obvious, to hang up a sign on the building and the door of the apartment which read:

Dr. Leopold Lustig
General Practitioner

You were granted that out of magnanimity and you enjoyed every bit of it. Years passed in which you lived among other people who had gathered in Stupart in order to pass their days here. Here there were neighbors and little stores whose doors rattled when you entered and one had to put up with your look. Still, you liked being greeted. People laughed and asked after your health because they loved the money in your wallet, and there wasn't an hour during the day in which you were not welcome, no matter what happened.

But now no one lets you in anymore, and there are many doors you are forbidden to open. Only a few doors are not off-limits to you, and even those are only open for a couple of quick hours in the afternoon so that your insatiable stomachs don't overflow with too much fodder. Others, however, shouldn't have to do without because of you; they want to eat and drink and certainly have a right to do so since, indeed, it all belongs to them. So a little will have to last you, but you'll take it in stride, if only you're able to quell your hunger. You've gotten used to everything, and so you'll get used to the journey as well, for you can put up with anything so long as you are patient with your existence and hope doesn't dry up. Hope never placed limits on anyone, because only you can shut down your own eager expectations. When that happens, impenetrable night descends from which only the forgotten escapes.

But we have not let it come to that. We rise and wander through the night. We have renounced sleep. It's better that the walls collapse; shoes have a harder time keeping out dust than they do stones. It's easy, you only have to put one foot behind the one in front of you, the other foot behind the next. That will help keep you on track, my friend, since where there is no path anything can happen. Illusion shields each of us from our fate. Whoever sweeps that away doesn't know what he'll find, yet he sees things as they are. Inside such a space there is light; there one must confront everything.

"Every bit of damage, every attempt at concealment will be punished!"

You aren't allowed to pack the electric iron. Luckily it's broken. Many things cannot be brought along; much is worn out, much broken, Paul having destroyed not only the lute. Indeed, the authorities will receive a damaged legacy, as well as all its losses. But there is still much too much here. It's not junk! They are precious possessions! They all cost money when we first bought them. It wasn't that easy to earn. There's almost no coal left in the cellar. Frau Lischka took it all away. Everything forbidden is gone, there's nothing more to hide. The mattresses from the beds cannot be taken away. It's written on paper that "Everything must be carefully handled" because it no longer belongs to you. There's no such thing as your property; your property is someone else's property. Preserved goods must stay in the pantry. Others can enjoy the goodies. You've gorged yourself enough. A label is glued to every glass with Ida's shaky handwriting, each one announcing in tidy fashion: RASPBERRIES, PEACHES. There are still eight jars of tomatoes. The plum sauce is from last year and looks black, but it's superb, for no sugar was spared in the making. The sauce is especially tasty on cake.

"Oh dear, the fire in the furnace has gone out! Zerlina, you should have relit it. It would be nice to have it warm in here."

It's not necessary at all. Soon it will be completely cold. The apartment is dead, paper seals carrying official stamps guard the sacred silence of the rooms. There sleep, night, dust, and cold exist. There nothing exists. Not a single memory is there. They took Bunny away. The porcelain from Leopold's grandmother is gone. Now the furnace can remain silent. The ashes will not be taken out. No one is cold in their winter jackets. It just keeps getting warmer under the heavy layers. Finally all preparations are completed. Heavily laden, Paul and Zerlina stand, though Caroline also loads up what her ancient back can carry.

"I don't think we've forgotten anything, Mother. Don't be afraid. We'll be back."

Frau Lischka knows this as well: "You'll be back. My husband will open a bottle of schnapps. Bunny will meet you at the station!"

The strangers know nothing about returning. No one knows if it will happen, everyone hopes it will, none believes so, though no one admits to his lack of belief, not even once to himself, for it's forbidden, and no, nobody lets himself admit such things anyway. Meanwhile, the officials have no souls, they recognize neither joy nor suffering, and whoever is free of feelings only carries out the letter of the law without caring, at an unreachable remove from all others, doomed to their own forms of isolation.

"The suitcases must stay! They will be picked up later. Take only a small bag with you!"

Everything is packed tight, and there's wisdom in bundling everything together in defiance of what's ordered, because one's possessions are themselves an expression of human nature, as only humans can possess something. But possessions are also obsessions, and soon they will be more powerful than those who possess them, since things reveal how they came to be possessed. Once they are acquired, it's hard to part with them. Only when there's a surplus of them does one gladly give them away, or at least without duress, because one chooses to do so. Whether gifts or something sacrificed, they remain gifts that are given of one's own free will, for which the donor never expects anything in return, wanting absolutely nothing to do with a desire for reward or praise. But here all expectations are eradicated, because nothing is exchanged but rather taken. Hence nothing is safe. Yet this flies in the face of what is just. And so we invoke the need for justice.

Oh, what crazy ideas you get, still thinking about justice, as if you were never told that it's already fit and just that inevitably you are ordered about and told to do things that only to you do not seem right. You've never gotten used to the idea of order, that's why we shatter your pride. We will lead you into the desert and say, There, now look for a place to live. —But here is our home, and one can't make a home if there is nothing there beforehand to make it with. One always has to have something in order to exist. Only Bunny and other animals have nothing, they are not the same as people. Only he who can stand up and say, It's really me who's shouting, only he is someone who has something and must have something. —Why do you always have to have something? That's greed speaking for you, the addictive need to always want more and seek it. You have yourself at least.

"Frau Lischka, I have nothing more to say to you. Be well!"

You have nothing when you only have yourself, for this seems like nothing the moment you encounter something else that you *can* have.

"You may no longer . . ."

Yet there is only so much one can do, which the cripple is the first to properly understand, though prison does not represent the soul's strongest possible restraint. The spirit is free, that's what one learns. Does this freedom have no need of space? Is time enough by itself? What's impeded when restrictions are imposed, freedom or you yourself? Why are you dissatisfied? You want the power to control things, yet you never possessed freedom. You are under restraint because the power to control matters has been stripped from you.

The intruders have weak flashlights, which they hold way out in front of them in order to pierce through the darkness of the stairwell. They intend something awful without letting on what it is. They restrict others yet do not know that they are also checked. The intruders are not crippled, hardly even lame, because their prison is everywhere and enjoys the protection of the power that knows no limits, as it can expand its reach farther with every step taken until the illusory feeling of limitless power leads them down the stairs and into the expanse of the darkened streets. The messengers are not afraid of the streets, even though they are cursed as well, but they have badges made of cardboard that they can point to whenever someone protests against the freedom employed during these hours when they also become crippled as they inflict the curse of expulsion. Now, however, their only wish is to stay healthy and on their feet and not to break their necks by falling down the steps. Nothing else worries these men in the stairwell, but this is only a guess that may not be true, for perhaps worries also press at the messengers that are not so apparent.

One of them is a handsome youth. His long hair often falls across his forehead, making him seem annoyed when, with a flick of his head, he flips back the strands, remedying the situation for no longer than a moment. Now he says: "You have to let your father go, there's nothing that can be done." Then he's quiet again and looks down the stairs. A powerful kick would knock him off balance, such that he would fall and injure himself badly. He shouldn't go barging into strange houses, especially in the thick of night. The fact that there's nothing that can be done about it won't save him. His life dangles from a thin thread since he is only following orders. He has sacrificed himself to his duties. Most likely he didn't even apply for this job, but rather was told: "You have to do it. Do you understand?" —"I'll do it. I understand." Then someone handed him a piece of paper and a voice shouted, "Sign here!" He signed the sheet, though with these letters nothing is accomplished to which anyone would grant the least value, nor would anyone be pleased by the signature. Only a name appears, but the sensibility behind the signature is long since lost.

It's hard to understand why you have to sign your name so often. No one should have to sign his name at the end of a letter, for as soon as you do, everything you spent so much effort listing out becomes null and void. Yet everything has a value that can be assessed. Even old bed feathers have their use. They can be cleaned, pulled out, and dried in a warm cylinder that is turned by a little motor. It's clearly stated that one isn't allowed to take bed feathers along. Everything has to remain behind; the luggage allowed is limited to a certain size and weight. Carefully place a piece of paper inside with your name, address, and date of birth. It doesn't matter that you no longer have an address. The worst that can happen is that you don't get the bundles and they are sent back; Frau Lischka will recognize them if you show her which ones are yours. That's when it dawns on them that nothing belongs to them anymore, rather it all belongs to the authorities who transform the anonymous possessions into property once again through simple magic. Outside one can also see the luggage lined up with names, addresses, and the birth dates on them. The suitcases and bags are marked with chalk or have notes glued to them. It's good to have everything ready. Practicality always watches out for itself.

"There, sign here, but make it legible! Why are you letting the pen wobble? You'll end up with a blotch instead of your name. Didn't you ever learn to write! Oh, of course, a doctor! You can write prescriptions. But it never bothered you when the patient died from taking the wrong medicine. As long as the bill was legible. . . ."

Lustig is a name like any other, even when the eyes fail and the voice falters. No healthy person has ever had to consider what it's like to be nameless, for it would never occur to him. Only in graveyards is it customary to give up one's name. If you want complete rest, you not only have to stretch out your legs but also relinquish your name. Only then can you plump up the bed feathers and hope for a satisfying sleep. "Sign your name, so that it's clear you can't do that! Three times, please! In ink, not with a pencil!" Countless hands are stretched out and hold something that needs to be signed. "Here, use my pen!" It doesn't work. There's no ink for the names. Someone must have a bit of ink. Indeed someone, but somewhere else, not here, for no one knows what he should write. "Sign your name where it says 'I waive . . .'" Where there is no name the waiver is meaningless. It strains the eyes too much, and besides, in this blackout no one can see where he should place his mark.

The way down the steps seems endless, because from start to finish you never feel sure of yourself on the stretch of stairs that winds back and forth, living from moment to moment without knowing if the effort will be rewarded. Nonetheless that's where you often went, back when you were a child, whenever you wanted to be by yourself and yet someplace familiar, there where it was easy to pass some time on one of the steps and think about what you were feeling. Once a week the house lady knelt on the steps with a full pail of water next to her, dipping a gray rag into it that she'd fish back out and with both hands wring out with some effort. Then the damp rag slapped onto the stone, the washing having begun, step-by-step.

Frau Lischka didn't like it when someone went up the stairs while she was doing this, and everyone knew that Friday afternoon was no time to invite guests or for anyone to ramble up and down the stairs. Leopold's patients were often admonished and scolded, sometimes sent back down and told to wipe their feet better. Order had to be kept, the building couldn't go to pieces. When Frau Lischka cleaned the stairwell everyone had to stop and wait until the steps were dried with a second rag. "You can use them now, but take two steps at a time!"

Yet the intruders that were now running around, entering each house in search of their detainees, they didn't care about order as they carried out their duties with feebleminded expressions on their faces. The stairs were no longer a sacred place, and the houses were worth nothing; it almost seemed as if they were no longer even there. Yet you could see them, they each had an address corresponding to a name, and they were marked with a sign alerting each passerby that nothing had disappeared, that everything was in its place. You only had to know your way around Stupart and everything became easy.

It was really easy, especially at night, as long as there was no blackout, since then no one had to risk guessing whether you were in a certain or uncertain place. But now you found yourself in an uncertain place. It was not even a place anymore, and perhaps any connection to an actual address disappeared when they took down the sign

Dr. Leopold Lustig
General Practitioner

for now nothing of what once had been was allowed to remain. Thus there was nothing more at all, though memory refuses to accept this, striving continually to give order and shape to it all.

Something can be placed on every step, but Frau Lischka will be upset when she sees how her stairwell has been trashed. The hallway has to remain clear no matter what. The steps are for walking, not for sitting. Just keep moving forward, and no tripping! Whoever takes care reaches out in the darkness to feel his way. The inhabitants are lucky if they know the way, because then they only need to count the steps and they already know where they are. And in like manner memory also counts, the living do not lose themselves carelessly in a present that can be so difficult to bear. To them the past is at their service, ever regressing memory planting its sensation less so in jittery hands than in the feet, which is also why we protect the feet with good shoes. Whoever is afraid of getting lost, which many do, stops on the landing or presses himself against the wall the whole way down, thus rendering the stairwell safe.

Paul closes the door to the apartment behind him and thinks about what he has left behind. Now Frau Lischka no longer has any say and has to keep quiet when her stairs are muddied. Behind the door above, everything has been left behind but not forgotten; it's there, simply there. No one can go back, the stairs will not have their soundness tested again, and who knows whether or not these are the last steps that will be allowed upon them. The rattle of keys when the doors are locked sounds as familiar as ever, it was the same burst of clanging as ever, followed by the feeling of safety; the apartment was still there, we would see it again, healthy and unharmed, ready to receive us. But now the key is pointless, you might as well leave it in the mailbox so you won't have to take it along on the journey. How ridiculous it was when one of the messengers advised Paul to make sure and lock up.

"Apartments left empty will gladly be looted!"

"*Gladly* looted?"

"Gladly looted. But you still have to turn in your key."

The stairwell pressed toward the doors, it descended deeper and deeper as the yelling came down the frightened hallway, *Down, go down!* The stairs yelled out that no one was allowed to climb them. Afraid of break-ins, Frau Lischka had an ever-watchful eye. No one got past her ground-floor apartment without her noticing. "Where are you going? . . . Ah, to the doctor!" Her drunken husband would have let anyone slip through, but his wife never tolerated the door being left unlocked whenever she went out. On Sundays the building remained locked for the entire day, meaning that anyone who did not have a key had to ring the bell. That way nothing could be looted.

The streets were quiet, heartened by the winter cold. The impact of the heavy steps pleased them, for that stamped life into them; otherwise the streets would have been sunk in sadness. They were forbidden streets meant to be avoided in order not to violate their pavement. Thus the streets were crossed out on the maps, no longer existing for anyone. It was too risky, danger lay in wait there, especially at night. But one must not simply accept what is forbidden once you are not worth anything. And so the streets were there again and were much longer and more beautiful than they had ever been before. They rejoiced at being granted life once again and didn't ask to whom they owed their good fortune. Zerlina said earnestly to an intruder, "These streets are forbidden." But the stranger just smirked and rubbed his hands. Because those words, so often repeated, no longer meant anything, for now the forbidden was allowed.

All that had been forbidden in the world now meant nothing, for it had never been a law but rather an arrangement that rested on enforced custom. What was once taken in stride now appeared all of a piece to the law, which had the last word and did not allow anything to contradict it. Life was reduced to force, and the natural consequence was fear, which was bound up with constant danger in order to rule life through terror. You experienced what you never had before. You rejoiced over that which you were allowed, but even this did not last for long, because any such comforts had only to be noticed and the next day they were taken away. Thus the tender juicy meat was taken away since you who are made of flesh need no meat. Then they banned fat, for your belly was full of fat. They denied you vegetables, for they stunk when they rotted. They ripped chocolate out of your hands, fruit and wine as well. You were told that there wasn't any more.

Highways and byways were forbidden, the days were shortened and the nights lengthened, not to mention that the night was forbidden and the day forbidden as well. Shops were forbidden, doctors, hospitals, vehicles, and resting places, forbidden, all forbidden. Laundries were forbidden, libraries were forbidden. Music was forbidden, dancing forbidden. Shoes forbidden. Baths forbidden. And as long as there still was money it was forbidden. What was and what could be were forbidden. It was announced: "What you can buy is forbidden, and you can't buy anything!" Since people could no longer buy anything, they wanted to sell what they had, for they hoped to eke out a living from what they made off their belongings. Yet they were told: "What you can sell is forbidden, and you are forbidden to sell anything." Thus everything became sadder and they mourned their very lives, but they didn't want to take their lives, because that was forbidden.

Once the entire world was forbidden, and there was nothing normal left to forbid, the height of unhappiness was surpassed and everything became easier, no one having to become anxious with lengthy considerations about what to do next. Everyone did what was forbidden without a bad conscience, even though it was dangerous and they were afraid. Yet since you couldn't do anything without feeling afraid, you didn't do everything that was forbidden. Sad and fearful people suffered under these conditions, but others hardly seem bothered, each following his own disposition. If there seems no end to the danger, then it has accomplished its goal already; anything excessive shuts people down more quickly than a discreet act of kindness, through which alone the simple truths of the world can still be perceived. Because one could not perceive this simple truth or at least had no respect for it, everything fell apart. Nothing more could happen and therefore orders were merely carried out.

Their gaze swept over the rows of houses and the street crossings as soon as their eyes got used to the darkness, and soon they were ready to escape, for they knew the area well and there were plenty of good places to hide. An escape was possible; it would not be too hard, since there was no one near or far who would hear them. But steps followed the women and the brave messengers accompanying them, and thus only their gaze stole forth, sending thoughts and memories ahead that thwarted cowardice sooner than weary bodies that, with the weight of all they carried, slunk along in order to avoid their proscribed fate.

Was such servility really due to cowardice alone? Old Leopold and fragile Ida had been taken away and were waiting for Caroline and the children in the Technology Museum. Ida felt helpless and Leopold confused. Both were incapable of handling that which threatened one surprise after another. What could be done for them? There was no clear answer, but one had to stand by them and not leave, because that was forbidden. Disloyalty was forbidden, also reason was forbidden, as it belittled the will to live.

Paul's thoughts hardly went this far, for already he had struggled too long to vanquish the inevitable. After his battle suffered its first and, he feared, decisive defeat, he could no longer worry about every threat that occurred. Paul was extremely tired and smiled at Zerlina, who smiled back. Then Caroline smiled as well. When the others saw this, they cheered up and also began to smile, as one of them said:

"You're right. It's not so bad there. You can eat pretty well. Almost every day there's meat and dumplings. But if they find money or jewelry or tobacco, then you're in trouble and don't get anything to eat."

"It's not so bad?"

"You'll see, Frau Lustig. So many have already stuck it out. Only a few are beaten. But nobody has been beaten to death."

"Beaten . . . ?"

"Yes, but it doesn't mean anything. Only the stupid ones are beaten. Whoever doesn't deliver or hides something forbidden. When they get caught they're the scum of the earth . . . condemned. . . ."

The voices defiled the street, therefore it was better to keep silent and to quietly march on with irregular steps. Legs marched now over the bridges. Each wanted to walk along the balustrade in order to gaze at the frozen river. But here it was particularly dark, and so there was hardly anything to see. Only dirty flecks of foam flickered silver-gray among the dolorous depths, and far off by the dam, where the water never froze, the thundering sound of the raging water could be heard. Here was the island on which Paul and Zerlina had often played as children. There had also been a swimming school that one could visit before such things were forbidden. There had been carts belonging to vendors who ordered colorful drinks for sale, as well as colorful ices and cheap candy, all of it meant to seduce folks with delight and requiring only a small sacrifice of money. Now the island was quiet and empty, certainly no longer ready to receive its regular visitors, and above all not the forbidden ones, especially since the island was now forbidden to everyone. It could no longer be reached, the entrance to it was closed, fenced in with barbed wire because something had occurred there that was now forbidden, and no one should know about it.

Now the island lay behind the wanderers, sunken, an old playground to which no path led any longer. The travelers no longer thought about it, and the bridge was gone as well. Slowly the piers gave way and collapsed, sinking into one another and falling almost soundlessly onto the ice. Then the place was gone, the traffic disappeared, after which there was a long road and everything melted together, and yet another road, gone, gone, everything forbidden now finished, no longer there, not a single memory even attempting to assert itself with a shudder, the forbidden now completely dead behind the gate that was sealed tight and would last and was there and locked the forbidden up for good.

Some halls of the Technology Museum that lay in the adjacent building had been cleaned out, nothing left in them but empty bunks and whitewashed walls. That was the gathering place for those people who were no longer wanted and yet who nonetheless were still there, since anyone who is condemned still exists before being destroyed, just as there must be a place for it all to occur, and so it all began here. Hundreds of bodies lay squeezed tightly together in the darkness that was only here and there broken by the muffled light of an occasional flashlight. But the night was constantly full of the sounds of rustling and groans.

It was impossible to find Ida and Leopold in the darkness. In surly fashion, the nervous commander from the office in charge of new detentions recommended waiting until morning.

"In six hours there will be enough light. You'll find them both then. No one gets lost here."

But all are already lost, and it is necessary to make fine distinctions. Whoever comes too late and has to be taken in should be happy to find a little spot on which he can rest. Now it is night and you have to make sure to find a place to rest. But where? It doesn't matter, the main thing is that you are there. The cross-eyed youth with the service cap aslant on his head smoked one cigarette after another. Wasn't that forbidden? For a commander nothing was forbidden, and he could run off at the mouth. He could fill the reeking hall with orders, as well as with the anger that unconsciously and without restraint accompanied the power conferred on him, and that he could vent on the prisoners in the museum at will.

Those formerly known as human beings now appeared made of wax, but they were still alive. As the morning dawned its gray, they sat upon their bundles and rocked their upper bodies to and fro, though they did not pray. They had no future, nor was the past recognizable within them any longer. "Here you can't remember anything." The cross-eyed youth walked back and forth among the cowering people. He was almost completely dressed in leather. It was forbidden to those whose lives had been snuffed out to wear anything upon their heads inside the halls, but Cross-Eyes wore a leather cap. In his right hand he swung a leather whip with which he could strike whenever it pleased him. And yet he didn't harm anyone, silent threats being enough to satisfy him. Sometimes he murmured: "Soon they'll be here, so order must be kept. No one can be sick."

An old woman next to Ida lifted herself up and stood in front of him: "What will it be like, Herr Commander?"

Cross-Eyes maintained his haughty stance: "Don't worry, don't worry."

The old woman wanted to sit down again, but she lost her balance and fell backward over her bags. Others also sank down. A young woman pulled together some whining boys and girls and distracted them with games. They sang and clapped their hands.

Amid the singing a mad woman howled: "Let me be! The soup scorched my tongue! You can't eat my soup! I want to get out! The pope ordered it! Ha!"

The unhappy woman began to rant. Since no one knew how to calm her down, Leopold stepped in.

"I've been a general practitioner for years. The woman is delusional. Her condition is dangerous. She needs to be isolated and to have a shot of camphor. She can't come along in this condition."

Cross-Eyes appeared out of nowhere. "Mind your own business, old man! She's coming along. Regulations say so. Listen, old woman! Get ahold of yourself! If anyone hears this ruckus, it could mean trouble for you!"

"The soup stinks! I want to get out! Let me go, let me go! The pope called me!"

"Who does the old lady belong to?"

No one said a word. A stretcher was brought out. Two young men loaded the ranting woman onto it, though she desperately tried to fight them off and bit one of their hands so badly it bled. Other attendants rushed to help the young men, and Cross-Eyes ordered them to strap the raving old lady down on the stretcher.

Someone yelled: "That's an outrage! That's inhuman! No one declares war on the sick!"

"Who says so? One can't jeopardize the whole group."

"What do you mean, jeopardize? This madness is what's really jeopardizing us."

"They should be quick and be done with it."

Leopold cried: "That's not right! You should call someone who is in charge so that order is kept!"

"I'm in charge of order."

"You don't bring any order at all!"

"What does it matter to you? Does she belong to you?"

Caroline took her husband by the hand and tried to pull him away in order to appease them, but Leopold was very upset and didn't want to leave the site of the incident.

"It's not right! This patient doesn't belong here! She needs to be admitted!"

Waves of subdued laughter erupted. "Admitted? Admitted? Tell us, are you perhaps free to take care of it?"

"Caroline, this is unheard of! This case needs to be reported to the medical authorities! This is not how you treat human beings. If I had known that such an injustice was going to take place here I would have stayed home and not allowed my family to take part in this journey. The preparations for it are simply miserable."

Leopold wandered off, proud and angry, Caroline leading him away as the laughter grew behind him. Cross-Eyes tapped his head with the tip of his finger three times: "Totally nuts!"

In the courtyard, Cross-Eyes stands in the first light of dawn and is wrapped up in a heavy coat. Nearby are some helpers who for the most part stand by quietly, but who at a sign suddenly start running around like raving madmen before returning to stand motionless again. They are dressed alike, but not as smartly as Cross-Eyes, for not as much leather clings to them. Some policemen plod back and forth and look up at the sky. It's not their concern. They rub their hands. There are also three men in full battle dress with their medals and badges of honor. They are proud men who hold their little heads high with a decisive air. Their legs fidget with impatience. One of them is somewhat small and yawns, blowing a little cloud of smoke from his throat. Another one, who is their leader, calls over to Cross-Eyes, who then stands at attention after he has yanked his leather cap off his head.

"Begin!"

Cross-Eyes gives his helpers a sign, at which the pack fans out. One runs to the entrance and remains standing there as he pulls a list from his breast pocket and unfolds it with great seriousness. After a short while the forbidden people head through the gate in twos, bent over with the weight of their bags. They call out a number and their former name. The helper writes with his pencil and sometimes waves his list back and forth and barks at the swarm: "Faster! Move on!" The forbidden gather themselves in the courtyard and organize themselves in rows of four. Altogether there are a thousand who used to be known as human beings. Cross-Eyes marches in front of the rows, turns over his whip, and strides without a horse slowly along the length of the front row, while with the whip handle he gives every fourth man a light swat on the shoulder, calling out loud: "Four! Eight! Twelve! Sixteen! . . ."

Yet not all one thousand could present themselves, even though there was space enough for a much larger group. Twenty-four members of the traveling group lay on stretchers. Between their legs and on top of them the sick ones' belongings were piled such that they could not move. After Cross-Eyes had also counted the figures on the stretchers, he yanked his cap off his head and strode without a horse as fast as his crooked legs would carry his fat body to the mighty heroes, gathered himself together, and stood at attention.

"One thousand gathered. Twenty-four of them lying down."

"Well done!"

One of the mighty heroes reached for the list and counted the number of those waiting once again. He hardly paid attention to the standing, which he quickly passed by, choosing instead to spend more time among the stretchers.

Across the courtyard a cry rattled out: "Medical report!"

Cross-Eyes yelled: "Medical report!"

One of his assistants charged into the Technology Museum.

The hero barked: "Filthy pigs!"

Cross-Eyes cried: "They'll be right back in line!"

Then the hero barked: "Why aren't they ready?"

Cross-Eyes cried: "Whoever's fault it is will pay!"

Then the hero barked even louder: "Shut your trap, you pig! It's all your fault!"

Cross-Eyes bowed and cried: "Yes, sir!"

Yet the assistant had returned with the list of the sick, wanting to hand it over to Cross-Eyes.

But then the hero yelled at him loudly: "Bring it here, or I'll smack you in the mouth! Nussbaum, you come as well!"

The assistant and Cross-Eyes hurried toward the mighty hero, who began to review what they had written.

"What a miserable typewriter ribbon! Look at this, Nussbaum! Next time I'll break your knees if the report is not typed more clearly!"

"Sorry, we put in for a new one. But no one sent us a new ribbon."

"Disgraceful! There'll be trouble for that."

Cross-Eyes read the names of the ill to the hero, who then ordered that no one should be allowed to lie down who did not have a fever of 102 degrees. Nonetheless, it was obvious that almost all of those on the stretchers were very sick. Only two old men over eighty and a woman who had given birth to a stillborn the previous night were allowed to stay. Otherwise, all of the weak and sick stood in rank and file, as well as the old woman whose attack of madness had so disturbed Leopold. As the hero finished checking the list, he nodded that he was satisfied. The authority's honor had been preserved, and only through an act of grace had the forbidden been transformed into the allowed.

"Load it up!"

It began to snow. Heavy flakes fell from above. They didn't worry themselves about those gathered below. They blanketed the copper green roof of the Technology Museum. If you stuck out your tongue between your lips you could perhaps catch a flake, but it was dangerous to do that since it was forbidden. Zerlina was happy when a flake stuck to her eyelash and hung there. How easily she could have gotten rid of it with a finger or with a shake of her head or with a blink of her eyelids. But Zerlina stood still, making sure not to move. The flake melted and ran cautiously away.

As long as the heroes are there, it's forbidden to move, which Zerlina knew, even if it was not underscored that often. Life is forbidden, something that never quite hits home, because it has not ceased to go on. Even in the courtyard of the Technology Museum no order has been given. They simply have forgotten to enforce what is forbidden, and thus life is frozen and has turned to snow. The same flakes could fall on the heroes or be carried by the wind and drift down outside of the museum courtyard and onto one of the surrounding houses or onto a street. There are no exceptions as to who is part of the moment. There are differences only in how fate is meted out, but not in fate itself, everything now being frozen. One no longer had to forbid movement, for there was none. What you saw with your own eyes could hardly be believed. It was null and void and could only be believed if you closed your eyes. Then the snow melted.

Such was the fabled height of spring in the mountains. The spring runoff could be heard rushing down the slopes. Below, flowers bloomed in all their colors. Here above, winter lived on, arriving toward evening with full force. Then the mountains were closed off by the vixen Frau Lischka, no one allowed to enter them, not even the intruders, no matter how much they knocked and pleaded at the gate. "Sorry, but there's no one home in winter. . . ." Frau Lischka turns away from the entrance to the mountains, but does not worry at all about the troublemakers. She keeps watch over the stairwell and makes sure that the blackout is not violated. All the walls were iced over, and only with the help of ropes could one climb up the stairwell. The tenants sat behind the doors of their apartments and tended the fires in their ovens. Everything was bedecked and looked as if you could lie down in the snow, the flakes having fallen in plentiful heaps. Now one needed only to sleep, for tomorrow winter would be over. The sun will wake you and you can run through the fields.

Exclamations flew back and forth. Anguished cries. No, it was not snow, it was hail. Nonetheless, everything was covered with snow. Snowdrops could be heard. Tin roofs rattled. The crashing sound of pure rubbish. Everything has been brought along, nothing left behind. Frau Lischka no longer needs a doormat. Back home, the patients are safe and dry, only the poor doctor wastes away on a muck heap. What he needs is a shot to revive him, a shot of sun so that he won't freeze. For there is no longer any heat. It is not necessary in the museum. The old machines don't need any oil. The locomotive does not move, but when it breathes, steam rises from its smokestack. Perhaps it will take off. The forbidden ones are hanging upon it. If only they can make sure not to slip on the ice and under its wheels!

A pile of wood should be set on fire in the courtyard. Whenever you drew near you could then warm your hands and feet. Ida would have loved that. Zerlina didn't need it, nor Paul. They were well fitted out and ready for the mountains. The seats were reserved, so no one needed to stand in the corridors. There was no cost for the ticket, for no one was expected to pay. In fact, it was not possible to pay since no one was allowed to have any money, and travel was also forbidden. Now the only question was what the sick would do in the mountains. It would not be possible to carry the stretchers up the sled paths because those who carried them would slip and fall, along with the stretchers. The old people would grow cold. They would die, especially if Leopold was not allowed to care for them. But they were already dead. They just needed to be placed in coffins. But you don't take along coffins on a journey. It's much too costly and the freight is not worth the trouble. Someone cried out when someone else knocked his stretcher. "Please, I just had an operation. I can't take it! I can't take it!" So much snow causes unnecessary cruelty. Much simpler would be to push the stretchers, since they have runners. There are also sleds. The cool air is good for the wounded, for it lets them think of other things.

The sick had the advantage, but they failed to use it since everything was now absurd. Leopold was right, the organization was terrible. The mourners did best to take care of each burial themselves. Even at the cemetery, discipline had to be maintained. Cross-Eyes is much too full of himself; nobody is interested in his sermons, which inspire no one. It would be better to get rid of the leathery fellow, but you cannot have it that easy. If there is only free will, then there would be no suffering, and that would be unfortunate. A little suffering never hurt anyone, as long as one does not feel it in the extreme. What's all the fuss about? No one is ready for winter, though it is easy to see that they will all become so tired that they will sleep standing up. Those who nod off keep in step when prodded on and never know the difference. They are perfectly servile, the heroes are pleased. Each wanders from home to home and no longer needs a doormat. The doormats of yesterday are the men of today.

Paul has to give Zerlina a shove in order to keep her moving. "It's dangerous to move so slow. Be careful!"

"I'm going."

"It's dangerous to talk. Be careful!"

"I didn't say anything."

If you keep your head lowered you see the path better. Ahead of you are feet that also dance without music. The ground is muddy, versus in town where the snow is always swept away and salt is strewn around, while here everything is turned into complete muck. The street sweepers are a useless bunch. If they were sent into the mountains, they would soon be stripped of the illusion that everything must be swept away. For nothing can be. The mud stains never disappear and spread everywhere in town and cause difficulty only for those who carelessly slog through them. Anyone who does not keep his vulnerability wrapped up inside only reveals that he has been pampered too much. People make the mistake of living too closely together. Therefore it's good to be expelled. When you are homeless, there is no resting place. There is only snow and eternal winter. You should come along so that you can experience eternal winter, way off where there is no way out, where no one is even by your side. There you have only your bread bag with you, but supplies are low and as spare as the good-byes you were given when you were banished and others turned away from you with tears in their eyes and snow. And there you stand, empty, trembling, and faint, even though the region has been free of wild animals for centuries. There are no more wolves or bears. Only small animals that flee from you as soon as they catch your scent. Your pockets are empty, and you are hungry. The snowfields through which you wander aimlessly stretch out endlessly in front of you, there being no map to show you the way.

You should give in to the circumstances and play the fool. It's good that you can be laughed at. The old and the weak will leave you in the lurch and run off. You all are nothing more than wild animals. Do you remember that you were once human beings? The gaze of Cross-Eyes meets you at the corner. You're lucky that, because of the frosty cold, he can no longer swing the whip that has frozen into an icicle. He's just glad he can lean on it. He can no longer make any reports and must leave behind Frau Lischka's drunken husband. One day soon she will yank the whip from his withered hand and say that she alone is permitted to sweep away such loneliness. Then you all would be rid of the pest and could confidently dedicate yourself to the belief that if you encounter someone or knock on the door of a mountain hut, behind it will be someone friendly. But you won't be able to say who you are, otherwise they will chase you down the slope and their laughter will crush you. Given the circumstances, they will say they cannot burden themselves with worrying about the needs of a bunch of people on a pleasure trip. If they should ask you your name and origins, tell them you have forgotten everything. If they do not believe you, then explain that your name has been erased, for you no longer really exist. But since you really are standing there in front of them, they won't think that you are a ghost, but rather a refugee no longer forced to remain in the stuffy air of the museum. If they should extend a bit of something to eat, which you take, that will say much more than anything you can say.

But then you must flee. Don't stop, for they will be on your trail and will make sure there is no place where your name can be spoken. Don't flee from the night! Think of yourselves as born from darkness, that what now hangs over you is the need for a light within the darkness, something that earlier was your role to maintain. Fear is piteous, but it spurs no forgiveness, for it spreads terror. The miserable are stepped upon, for that is how others seek to impose justice. That is why you must be strong and find a little spot where you can take shelter from the storm and at night escape the elements. Only, you must believe that it is not so bad. Freedom has been handed to you. The laws of previous societies no longer apply to you. You have been asked to build a home out of rubble with your own strength. How you choose to erect it is how it will come to be.

You're being given a sign to move, don't you see it? You have to admit that cross-eyed Herr Nussbaum is certainly on the ball. Everything goes off without a hitch. The assistants sigh deeply, but it's a sigh of relief, for they have done well. Not a single complaint is heard. The heroes stroll and strut the length of the station platform. You sit down, one on top of another, four to a bench, eight to a compartment, like regular, upstanding citizens. But this is no ski hut, there is no snow. No, they are empty train cars. They are narrow, much more narrow than the huts you should have built, but which have already been finished, thus saving you the work. Everything has been taken care of, for they did not want to strain your silky little hands. Who could possibly complain about such sound accommodations? How could you have even completed the job when you have never learned to work with your hands?

You can't be trusted with anything, everything must be arranged for you, because you are a lazy bunch that not even lifting a shovel can change. Like little children, everything has to be done for you, though you arrive at the dinner table without uttering the slightest thank-you. Nothing can be expected from you but your stinking smell. Everything you youngsters need has been taken care of for you, we've made sure of that. We have sacrificed ourselves for you. If we were a little tougher with you, then you would get all worked up and melt right in the middle of snowy winter. You want snowdrops? We haven't brought you flowers. It's too late. The train will depart before we can get some. We'll send them to you. Yes, everything your heart desires will be sent to you. But you should be off already! Have you forgotten something? That doesn't matter. Just drop us a line, we'll take care of everything. You can count on us. Can't you see it in our faces? Just look in our eyes and you'll see that we can be trusted! Something could happen to you? Who told you that? It's just a bunch of stupid chatter! Not a single hair will be disturbed. Such transgressions are not allowed. Now you are traveling to safety, your new home, just like you always wanted. Is the good-bye hard for you? That's hard for us to believe! No, we can't believe it! The forbidden at last lies behind you for good, and now eternal freedom is waving you on. There you can do what you want. We wish we had the chance to share your lot, but unfortunately that has been denied us. With us lies the responsibility to worry about your well-being, and then to worry about your brothers who are also awaiting the journey.

The engine up ahead gives a pleasant snort, happy that it has been pulled out of the museum. Now it's back in service. Do you hear the jolly whistle? That's not Cross-Eyes. That's the train, or wait, that's the stationmaster who blows his whistle and is in charge of everything. Here he is much more important than the mighty heroes, to whom he doesn't even pay attention. When one of the heroes comes up to him, he gives a careless salute. He believes that the last signal is about to be given. The travelers have been made comfortable. The engineers look ready. In a moment you'll be on your happy way. Officials, nurses, and orderlies will ensure your fate and attend to your every need.

But we don't expect any satisfaction from you, knowing you will just pull ugly faces. It hurts us that you're so nasty, like naughty children, because we're the ones who carry all the responsibility, for we have to pay for your guilt with our innocence. Since we have taken everything away from you, we are your guardians. Your souls are in our hearts, in our laps, in our mouths. We lead you by your little hand so that you can survive the struggle.

Now you are out of the snow flurries outside, wrapped up in your soft blankets, having found peace and joy. We lock the doors of the wagons and place the seal of our blessing upon them. Now you can't get away. Pleasant journey, little sheep, but don't sing too loud and don't shout from the train, because the guards will shoot without warning at a moment's notice. A little caution couldn't hurt. We've secured the route, soon you will reach your destination. Nothing will happen to whoever is obedient. Only the bad ones will be shot. The good will be praised and will get some sugary snow. They are given some before they even purse their lips to ask for it. All in all everything is in place, a safe journey is guaranteed.

The stationmaster lifts his baton. The heroes turn away. Herr Nussbaum turns around and stares with his crossed eyes off and away. Away, away . . . a safe journey and security . . . guaranteed . . . though they will shoot, they'll shoot . . . the house and the steps . . . the beautiful snow, the snowdrops . . . whoever doesn't believe, whoever doesn't believe . . . doesn't believe . . . believe. . . .

The connection we feel to our surroundings is built on belief. Yet Caroline woke up unable to believe where she was, though it also must have been difficult for her to get her bearings, for in the cavernous casemate she could hardly see anything under the single lightbulb that was burning. No brightness came from it, but rather a turbid flickering. She had never seen an electric light quite like it; it reminded her of an oil lamp. Caroline could believe none of it. There was snoring and groaning all around her, the rustling of many little things. It was worms, that was it; they had fought their way through all the impediments, for only worms could thrive in this damp cave. This meant that one couldn't keep any flour because the worms would ruin it and there would be no more bread. And yet it couldn't be worms she was hearing, for she clearly heard someone whisper. It came from somewhere, one minute here, the next in the corner over there that the eyes couldn't make out. So there were people here, genuine people, it occurred to Caroline as she rubbed her eyes in order to see better. Yet that didn't help, the darkness didn't lift and her eyes only burned. This was caused by the gooey flour that had formed in her eyes during sleep. But was there an eye doctor here who could rid her of this awful inflammation?

Caroline sat up in order to see better. She wasn't able to see much more, but she could grasp where she was, and that yesterday they had been locked up here, she and her husband, her sister, the children, and at least a hundred others. They all must have arrived here and rolled around in the flour. No, it wasn't flour made of grain, it was bran, but also not made of grain, rather moldy sawdust that produced an acrid smell, the flaky splinters pressing at you no matter which way you turned. If you stood up and shook yourself off, your neighbors would yell at you to watch out as the bran flew all around and everyone complained. Leopold said it was like being in the army, but outside in the field, not in a barracks, though now it would seem that everyone here was enlisted; you could only make do with whatever quarters you found, making sure that you had a roof over your head and were not stuck in some foxhole full of water. "Look, Caroline, they prepared a straw bed for us so that we would be more comfortable. They even made sure to take care of the lights." It was good that Leopold was satisfied. At home things were never right. Caroline sat and placed her hands on the knapsack in order to better remember. But inside her mind the past was no clearer. She could sense that she had forgotten a great deal, all of which a ringing skull did not help in the least. Was it time for Carnival? Was it New Year's? Had she had too much to drink, let herself get carried away? Or had she been ill and simply been dreaming? Probably she was dreaming, even if it was with open eyes, for only in a dream could such a murky twilight descend and remain so endless.

Caroline thought harder. Then it occurred to her that perhaps she had died, even if she didn't seem dead; it was simply a dying that didn't kill, and that was why she wasn't lying in any grave, but instead stuck in a pantry full of bad air. But how could it be that other people were also here, even her own family? Had they all died? That couldn't be. Only as a result of an earthquake would so many be dead. But there had been no quake. The buildings were still standing, no one had knocked them down. Frau Lischka had locked the door from the inside as Caroline was distracted by the decoys set by others. If the house was going to blow apart, it would come much later, and then the decoys would be angels who would lead the Lord's loved ones to certain safety. In this way the expelled could rest assured, though for those who stayed behind in the supposedly guarded buildings, the final end was already ordained. Between the walls they would meet the enemy and be annihilated by a single stroke.

Were the figures that surrounded Caroline really human beings? They weren't at all, her imagination had simply run away with her as so often happened with the dead, Caroline told herself, and all she needed to do was gather her wits and stare truth in the face. Then it would be clear that Caroline was in the middle of a wax museum that someone had cleaned out and stored for safety inside the casemate. Caroline had been dragged along by accident. She had probably just entered the cabinet of curiosities when the order had come through for it to be cleaned out, a preventative measure that made a great deal of sense. Caroline had become sick as the hands and feet of the wax figures were packed away; she fainted, her face turning a waxy yellow color, such that in the heat of their duty the officials made a mistake and took along the glassy-eyed Caroline and laid her out here in the wood shavings where the undead regained consciousness once again. She wanted to yell in order to get the attention of the guards outside. I'm not made of wax, I can't stand the sawdust, I can't eat it, it's much too cold for me here among these figures.

Caroline didn't have the strength to yell and she could see that things looked bad around her. She could only hope that soon one of the guards would come so that with a sign she could make him aware of the disastrous mistake that had occurred. Yet the prisoner was afraid that she wouldn't be able to give any clear sense of events if the guard, out of fear, wouldn't let her speak. She remembered that simple souls often became afraid in front of automatons. Someone might take her for something like that the moment she stretched out her hand to them. Caroline was not the kind of thing you'd expect to see in a cabinet of curiosities. It was only because of someone's goodwill that she had been included among the chosen figures that had been sculpted by artistic hands. Caroline was an ordinary display model. She stood in the department store and displayed girdles, dresses, and hats to distinguished ladies. No one was interested in her, only what she was wearing. Someone had not been careful while carrying around the mannequin and had broken off some pieces. But no one repaired her and she had been thrown onto the rubbish heap instead.

Here there was nothing more to display. The sad fairy tale had come to an end, the song was over, Paul had kindly removed the ribbons of the lute for Zerlina, the mannequin was not where her dusty little clothes were, yet Caroline had survived everything nonetheless. She lay back exhausted. Since there was no warm furnace, she was almost frozen as again she noticed her surroundings. A door was ripped open. It was not daylight that pressed through, but a glow that didn't come from any lamp. In the door there stood a man who looked young and healthy, who probably had a beautiful wife, almost as pretty as Caroline was as a girl, himself holding his head high and wearing a powerful belt. His voice sounded bright and care-free, almost pleased, as he waved his hand like someone waking the dead and called into the mass grave: "Everyone up!" Many of them quickly got up, some of them propped themselves up, others sat up quickly, yet others jumped to their feet and stood there. They were alive, all alive. Caroline laughed and felt happy, feeling for a moment almost as if she were free.

The sawdust flew about, many sneezed, all of them rubbed their eyes, yet they were alive and could even eat. No automaton did that. Caroline was again herself, she had her family once again and could fuss over them. She was willing to let anyone do to her what they wanted as long as they let her live. Everything would be taken care of. She heard that they had to obey, though it no longer needed to be said, since everyone knew it and it was no surprise. All that mattered was to be able to stand on your own feet. You could then get in line, for there was coffee. The liquid was warm. What did it matter that it wasn't real coffee, since it still got your arms and legs moving and woke them up. Now the mannequins could walk, their little legs hastily shuffling over the winding passageways. They searched around, all of them mixing with one another, mannequins also streaming out of the neighboring barracks, the numbers tied to their chests flapping away. Sometimes one came up to another, lifted the number to his face in order to better decipher it, and then looked at the face itself. Again and again people were overjoyed to recognize one another!

Then came the separation. Numbers were called out and then names as well, for not everyone was used to having a number, and some actually thought that they would not wear numbers forever and would forget them soon enough like so much else, hardly having put any effort into remembering them. But now the numbers were separated and sent here and there. Now there were many good-byes, but only a few felt the seriousness of the moment, and even they felt assured, because the numbers believed, as was solemnly promised them, that the town would not be very large but would be roomy enough, and there you could roam around, allowing everyone to soon find one another again. Man next to man and woman next to woman, thus they were placed together in those first early days; little terror was felt despite their overwhelming sense of surprise. Their faces also betrayed no sense of alarm, everything seemed fine, encouragement and seeming trust revealed in their glances and hand movements.

Zerlina and Ida stood next to Caroline, full of anticipation and laughing at Leopold and Paul, who remained patient in order to make the time pass quickly for the women, whose departure was delayed for one reason or another. Certainly time didn't pass too quickly, but also not too slowly; it was a continual stream that one simply had to trust. Now everything would again be easier than it had been in recent years or had been in the stressful months leading up to the journey. The leisurely pace of life had been restored, the separations made sense. What was wrong with your being forcibly removed if that was not what you felt at the moment? Certainly one day would follow another, each of them followed by night, rules would be followed, the day's rhythms and the passing of seasons would make sense once again.

Caroline waved. No mannequin knew how to wave an arm so delicately; she was no wax figure, that was certain. The milky white of the clouds parted a bit, blue could be detected, sunlight fell on the snow-covered chestnuts in the courtyard and on the arcades in front of the casemate. Things couldn't be so bad. You could open your eyes, only memory could not be set free. Meanwhile Ida had to be held up, though she was brave and happy that her son was alive. She would have preferred to see him die rather than see him caught. The borders were drawn more prominently than ever, but though they were open everywhere no one could cross them. Zerlina lifted all of Ida's bags and laughed. Things would work out, one mustn't despair. Caroline had emerged victorious; no longer was she hallucinating, but rather constructing a future. Where there is a future there is life, and belief is what created the connection between.

Paul watched the departure of the women and did not feel unhappy. He was busy. Next he turned his attention to Leopold, who was also considering many plans for the future. Then Leopold was also led away, which he expected. He said a quick good-bye to Paul. "Now we will all have to get to work." Leopold was firm in his conviction, his belief had not faltered. His advanced age didn't worry him, for a healthy man can also stand quite a lot despite his age. His was an occupation that called upon him to ease the sufferings of others. Here they would need Leopold, his lengthy experience would not be for naught. He left the casemate with some other old men and glanced back at Paul once more with a feeling of triumph. He, too, did not stay long in the casemate and left behind the sawdust that had already been mashed together into a brown smelly paste.

Months went by, a year has passed. Sitting in his room, Paul had often thought that the connection we feel to our surroundings is frequently built on belief. When this belief is violated then the connection is already dissolved and the consequences are incalculable. It doesn't matter whether or not such belief is true if indeed it exists only as belief, for it preserves much more than its possible truth, namely the truth of belief in itself. To the extent that belief is refuted by real conditions it is indeed not enough in itself, but when it fails, nothing is enough. Yet one must be patient. Each rash measure poses a threat and hinders the order of the world. All conditions, even the bad ones, are equal and cannot be changed in nature by merely willing them away. Destructive incursions are a mistake, for they accomplish and mean nothing, even when they lead to annihilation. There are always witnesses left behind whose memory is enough to survive any annihilation and restore the chronology of events even when hidden for centuries or millennia. Then everything reverts back to belief, which the transitory discards, and the past must reduce itself to an apparition upon which not much appears to rest.

In the meantime, sacrifice yourself and expect nothing. Everything will come to you. You indeed approach closer and closer, your every step ordered onward until you are there where your work has been arranged for you, though in fact it is just the opposite, the wall stands before you and demands that you set to work on it. It should be demolished, its history is over. But that only seems so, for walls and histories will be perpetuated through you. You can press at them until you are exhausted, their dust trickling onto you and sticking in your pores. The old bricks rest in your hand, crumbs of mortar clinging to them, though you can't take them away, for they simply remain. Perhaps you'd like to hold on to one and thereby do harm to the edifice in order to stave off history. But the others don't understand you and warn you to keep up the pace. How little you think about your work, and that's for the good, because if you did how easy it would be to stop. Hand over your bricks, pass the next one down the line!

This is the Earth. Once it was on fire, but it has long since cooled and settled into a general state of coldness, the clumps having turned to pieces of ice between your fingers. The sharp north wind blows and leaves you shuddering on your scaffold. The sky is clouded over but contains no snow because it is dry, because your hands have no other work to do but demolish what was once built. The wall once laid down the border between what is yours and mine, but now everything belongs to you, and thus the former border dissolves right in front of your eyes. It could be that the glow of all of the extinguished fires of the world has not chilled. Therefore there must be hot bricks, for otherwise you could not stand here for hours, and your companions would neither be on your scaffold nor the neighboring scaffold. No one would be here, the town would stand empty, and death would cover over anything that dared to live. Yet death does not arrive in order to inhabit us, but instead strolls by. He has chosen the entire land as his empire. His path travels the length of the streets that run past the walls. Not all walls are demolished, not every border disappears; between death and life there is still a separation.

The town is a timeless island of walls. A hundred thousand bricks are baked, bread that is piled into mountains of inhabitable loaves. The town floats on the ocean of time and knows nothing of itself. This is why the town can feel lonesome even when many things are going on within it. If you just take apart the bricks you'll find what has been stored away and hidden. You're interested in such exposure, nothing can hold back your urge to explore. Yet time has slowed, it's become a sticky paste. The fired bricks are crushed, resulting in a coarse dark flour, the bread of the past that no one can chew. Whoever vainly pursues the past will be gobbled up by it. Yet it's easy to chop it up into pieces when one uses a bit of trickery. The hands lift one stone after another and let them fall onto the heap below where the ashlar breaks them up with a dull cracking sound. No one says anything, the old bread is already too crumbly.

A wall is demolished, yet in some empty spots other walls are erected for which no new bricks are available, which is why this wall has to disappear. Thus it means displacement, not salvation, and therefore it's better if many bricks are broken up. One should not erect new walls with new bricks when it can only be accomplished by destroying others.

Sometimes the builder comes by and warns: "Be careful! Don't break any bricks! We don't have any new ones! Wedge the pick between the bricks in order to loosen them. That also makes the job easier. And don't toss any bricks!"

It's easy for the builder to say this, because he doesn't have to take part in the work. Whoever looks on and gives commands stands above matters and walks back and forth in order to oversee everything, though this is impossible, and so bricks get broken. They should clear everything away and remove all the rubble so that there's nothing left for memory to worm its way into. Then maybe a pleasing bit of grass would grow if only the continual steps of the guards didn't trample it. No proper thoughts arise among standing buildings, but rather only misleading ones, though memory alone suits the timeless city. Whatever stands in its way can be cleared away. Then the grass can thrive. When the bricks crumble, no one's will is destroyed. You shouldn't think that the work of dissolution is the same as the work of destruction. Some bricks remain unharmed, especially when handled absentmindedly, which is all the more reason why the builder cannot stand any breakage. But he only gets a few bricks, and there are fewer and fewer as new supplies dwindle and building stones can only be had by destroying old walls. Everything is made of rubble, something stolen from earlier times and not allowed to stand. Rubble is gathered, but that's not good. Whoever wants to begin something anew also needs to provide what's needed to make it happen. As soon as a building is condemned, no concessions can be made and it must be quietly demolished, rather than just stripped of all its components, because that would only fulfill half of the order, thus bringing its validity into question.

The women stand below with half-frozen fingers, cleaning the last of the mortar off of the bricks with iron scrapers. Partial bricks can also be used, said the builder. Anything that's only half done is also thought to be finished; for completion is no longer the goal as long as such shortages remain. The desire to achieve something has been destroyed by the orders handed out. They shoot out like the blows of a whip and no longer move the hearts of men. The will is broken, mere obedience remains, reluctant obedience. Its achievements are fleeting and result in only rubble. The new walls lean and are fragile, they will soon topple. Yet other walls are built, consisting of nothing more than wishes. They tower above and require no scaffolds in order to be erected, nor do they belong to any building. They pop up so fast and collapse so quickly that there is no joy in their accumulation, these false edifices, these moldy loaves of the soul. The living go hungry because the bricks can't feed them.

Sometimes the bricks are lined up and counted. Then rifles are brought out and a voice yells: "Move!" The bricks begin to walk because they have grown legs, followed by swinging arms and finally heads. The bricks walk between the walls that are still standing and the walls that are already demolished. These walls want to be taken along with them, no one prevents it, so more and more bricks join the march. At last all walls are left behind, then a muddy path appears into which the bricks almost sink, though no one grants them any rest, an order transforms them into wheels that must turn. Yet the wheels cannot make their way through the mud. It doesn't help that the children push them forward with canes, for the wheels are not toys. Someone should have strewn sand on the path so that the wheels can go forward, but now it's too late. No cinders are to be found because there's nothing more to burn, only bricks, and the ovens have not had any fire in them for ages and are now lying in pieces. Only blackened chimneys indicate that these buildings were once heated, themselves now nothing more than memorials to apartments that once were, lodgings ready to serve one's bidding.

Then a voice struck by a cane screamed: "Nothing is real anymore!"

"What isn't real?"

This question found no answer, yet another voice rose up, its tone much harsher than all of the other voices: "It's all over for you."

Perhaps it was a thought that was stronger than the ruins that were stuck in the mud, since that's the way things seemed as soon as the wheels could not move anymore, life having come to a standstill. Then it was up to the spirit alone whether or not one rotted there and died without finding someone who would even remember what had happened. Everyday life is over, and no new arrangement replaces what was lost.

Suddenly the path begins to climb up out of the mire again, the clumps of mud drop off to the left and right as the wheels get hold of themselves and begin to move again with a feeble rattling. They feel like singing or whistling, but that is not allowed; they are only supposed to gasp for breath and not enjoy themselves. As a result of the stress from the way they are handled, they gradually come to their senses and remember they have eyes. They look around and they are no longer wheels, but rather pairs of crutches with heads stuck on the top. They are heavy heads that wag back and forth, human heads that look like those of horses, though the crutches are neither made of wood nor metal, but rather of stone dust that has turned into cement.

Everything has turned heavy and cannot move by its own strength alone, but nonetheless they are driven onward, the shouts spilling out continuously, yelling at them to hurry as long as the heads are still upright, craning themselves with their last strength, if only to protect the spirit's shrine, even if the heart has long since rotted and dried up. Heartless pillars of concrete are chased toward higher ground. All that's needed is a strong reminder, the crutches jumping at the ready with a powerful lurch, making sure only that the heads don't fall off. A careless lurch would mean something could happen to your head. No one would dare bend down to save you. Who could afford to lift up a head and set it back on top of its crutches in the middle of such haste?

Yet the heads also change, because they have to think about flight and ascent, while their usual wishes and desires are eradicated. Thus they become bird heads with bristled feathers, darting glances, and protruding crooked beaks. Around each head grows a bright feather ruffle that appears vibrant against the backdrop of the bleak concrete. The beaks are sharp and open themselves now and then as if they want to bite, but then they close again without snatching a morsel.

The untouched splendor of the fields and meadows is trampled by the reckless strides that hurry to climb the heights. We are men, these wild monsters think; we are erect ants, we are warriors who have been called to battle. We are surrounded by enemies whom we do not know, and who don't know us, neither having ever done anything to the other, but that's war, in which we do nothing to one another. We know nothing about you, you know nothing about us, yet between us seeds of hatred are strewn by which we are both ruined. Orders fall upon us like a hail of stones, and we squawk like crows and peck out one another's eyes. And yet we have no idea whether it will come to this, as we never meet up with one another, but instead hop on and sharpen our beaks. If you should happen to be armed, we are lost, doubly lost, for no one has entrusted us with weapons or trained us. We've only been gathered together out of the rubble, the women having scraped off the mortar from us. We were pieced together from the walls that were demolished, put together like we once were, like we still existed, and now we are put to work once our will has been broken. Now we are nothing more than implements of an endless journey, having long ago said good-bye to our own natures once there were no longer any buildings left.

In the air a rattling and whistling began to rise; perhaps it was little birds, sparrows buzzing above our heads on the tail of the wind. Instead it was the all-powerful voice of command, and everyone fell down without knowing why. Then a new transformation begins. The head bends forward, but there are no more crutches on which it wobbles, but rather an extension, an appendage that is quite flexible as it twitches and twists. For now they are snakes with endlessly long tails. The poisonous fangs have broken out, and there is poison within them and they have to drink it. They soon feel awful and experience pain that had disappeared when they stood erect. And yet the snakes have become immune to harm. They are consumed by burning pain, and yet it does not affect them.

What are soon in danger are the changing voices that tirelessly shout their commands; at least this is what the snakes believe who do not know that the commands prevail even when they encounter enemy fire. The commands can be pierced, but they cannot be brought down, for unknown powers maintain their timelessness. As long as these commands do not yield, freedom is denied, even power's own freedom, for there is no longer any sense of power, it exists without any sense of itself. But where all feeling dwindles, freedom loses all sensibility and turns away from reality. Freedom is unknown, a dream from a golden age, man having erected powerful memorials to both time and freedom. Yet along with time, freedom has been absorbed by them, the memorials themselves unable to resist the all-powerful onslaught of the passing years, and so everything is absorbed within them, such that not even memory seems believable. Now only blind reverence maintains their abiding artifice, for they are not freed of their duty.

But you all want to continually ask whether or not there is anything left of you that is recognizable, because if there is something, then the flames of your will must still exist, you would not have become snakes, but rather remained birds, and your crutches would turn into feathered wings. Then freedom would exist once again, reality no longer contradicted by unreality. So it would be. So it would be for you. You could still reach for it. You believe you still know it to be there. You are insatiable, your desire fills the cold emptiness until something is there. You have not sworn that you will deny everything. Instead you are always ready to see it; you believe that you can observe it before it is ready to be seen. But this can happen only when you do not notice that even this has been taken from you. And so any question about reality is worthless.

You always want to reply that at least the question is still there, that reality will be conjured again as a result, the question alone not enough in itself once it is asked. Then the end would be defeated, the last threat of danger overcome, and a beginning launched through whose vast gate everything must pass once more in order to gather before lewd looks and hands. That's how it should be, you say. But something is missing! What should be simply is not; you cannot begin again that easily. Remember that nothing is, and nothingness disavows even itself. There is always a "no" that hollows out every subject, and absence doesn't answer back. Indeed, only the humiliated think that it does.

Everything is a mockery, the snake's cunning circles back on itself. If there is nothing, then there is really nothing, but even that is a lie. Belief in that leads to despair and a destructive madness that can crush an army of apparitions, while what is essential flees it and repels every approach. The misery of such deep disturbance is already enough in itself to refute such destruction. For then nothing more will come to harm, all that is fleeting is restored, the world in its inseparable twining of the beautiful and the horrible rises anew and carries on. You slippery snakes, however, have your part, and if it's miserable, then so it is; that changes nothing about the truth of life, the course of history remains undisturbed. It's up to you all whether or not you know to call it a blessing or a curse.

Yet you don't know what to say because you are the reflections of our helplessness, and therefore you are doubly and triply ridiculous in your own helplessness. Yet the snakes do not sense what others think of their weakness. They've reached the top of the hill, from where they can look down in order to better observe what is being destroyed. They lift their heads and sway back and forth, for now they are not afraid. Below, towns have been built in which things do not go so well, even though they contain fenced-in buildings separated into apartments, broken up into rooms and chambers, which have been leased by many people who have no idea what is to come. They themselves have the right to move about and to leave their apartments. Without asking permission, each of them leaves home to head out and take care of his business and pleasure. No one lurks, full of jealousy, watching every step, and the living are not treated as suspect. Yet perhaps that's an illusion, for it could just be that they're allowed to walk around because the authorities are careless or the guards on duty too lazy or because there are so few guards. It could seem to them that people enjoy a certain amount of freedom and go along their way undisturbed. Why should they care about the law through which the authorities impose their own commandments? They can escape such traps, they are also snakes, though blessed with more luck than the snakes up above.

That's why it's better not to look down at the snakes in the enclosed towns, where in the narrow confines of wretched streets they are almost lost in the dirt. The heights, however, grant you awareness of the depths from which you have climbed. Now you can recognize which path you took. That was the journey. You and yours traveled and were led on. Joining the journey happened out of your own free will or by force, and yet it occurred, such that you could wave good-bye, so much having been left behind. In the vases at home, flowers still stand that need fresh water, yet you forgot to turn their care over to someone reliable. The stalks have rotted, the leaves and blossoms dried up.

Consciousness has split itself into two wings that have fallen from the body. Now the wings flutter on their own, sadness in their beating, yourself unable to control them. Now one, then the other, then both, sometimes neither, but you have to put up with them, whether they pester you or not. You want to get rid of them, and you point in dramatic fashion at your chest and say: "I know. I exist. I don't lack consciousness." That's foolish. Don't you really feel that you know nothing and are possessed, such that you know only half of the consciousness within you? That's the way it is since you set out on your journey. It would have required courage to retain your consciousness; you could not have set out on the journey if you did. Now you will need even greater courage in order to withstand the journey. It won't be easy for you. Whoever remains at home can gather together again better than whoever launches out on an adventure. Don't think that you'll succeed in finding any place that's safe, where you can stop to recollect yourself and restore your undivided consciousness. Even if you should finish this journey without being left behind along the way, you'll still be disturbed. In essence you will feel cut off from the world, you'll want to set your hands and feet on your own turf once again. But don't think that far ahead! That's the future, which you must continue to fear for as long as you live.

So you departed and were never allowed to look around. Or you were curious to spot the back of Cross-Eyes, rubbing his hands as he left the train station. Herr Nussbaum certainly didn't go looking for that empty building in order to cheer up the lonely walls. Departure weakens vanity but strengthens character, which casts away the mask of fear. The scent of the invisible blossom of decay strikes the nostrils. There is no avoiding it, even if you don't want to choke on the smell. The necessary journey is always one that is imposed. Since no one is asked whether or not he'd like to come along, understanding is never even sought. The departure only requires that you hurry. Travel fast so it doesn't last. Yet why is it all so confusing? Why must one lose one's sense of free choice, itself always having been a part of arriving at the truth?

The journey had already begun the moment you thought about whether or not the decision about making such an impending journey was worth serious consideration. Cultivating freedom is fine as long as you still don't know how dispensable it will become once your decisions disappear in a stream in which you realize you are dispensable while looking back at the journey you were ordered to take. You are not your own guide; you are swept away even before you have ordered the tickets, the authorities having purchased your seat, which is for the best, for it would be much more aggravating to try to get a seat when others might want to leave you behind. Then you would have shouted and demanded that you become a passenger, though doors would be shut before you everywhere: "What's that, a seat, and you're in it? You're not a passenger. The one whose seat it is must be off somewhere. Away with you!" You would have then fought your way through in order to figure out how to make the proper connections so that you got the proper travel permits despite the imposing obstacles placed in your path. Exhausted, you would have collapsed and sunk into the rubbish that was brought along on the journey because it was already too late. In this manner you would have found no peace, and the potential agony of the subjugated remains always small when compared to the agony of the lone wolf who never knows what will happen from one moment to the next.

And so you looked at the inhabitants of Leitenberg who wandered around the streets of their town naturally uncertain. You and others marched four abreast between the rows of buildings and across the market square. You were not allowed to stop nor to step onto the platform at the station, but were forced to hurry across the tracks as if you yourselves were a train waiting to serve its master's every wish and desire rather than its own volition. Essentially what awaited you was an open question, for there was nothing you had to worry about. To the extent that you were buried in your own cares and worries, you were aware of no one else but yourselves, the worries themselves superfluous simply because you had not yet learned to give up your dear old sense of normalcy.

Even if it wasn't quite right, Leitenberg was nevertheless indifferent to your plight. It was a town through which you were led like so many times before, this being perhaps not the last time either. What strange fate awaited you that perhaps you were not aware of? A town, fine, a town—but there are plenty of towns. No curious onlooker claps the restless, runny-nosed traveler on the back to help him breathe better. No sooner did you reach a town and you left it behind, so it was no use tossing pebbles at a window to try to find out the secrets to some stranger's home cooking. The severe penalty you'd have to pay for such a misdeed would not have been worth whatever unlikely relief you might have gained, and the penalties might have meant your own end, one of pure misery.

Leitenberg is not your town, no matter how many times you may have been led through it, for it offers you no view of itself but the backyards of houses on the outskirts that for years you quietly passed almost every day on the train. In the dark, or even in your sleep, it's enough for you to think that you'll soon be there, just a little longer, just another half hour before you reach your stop, the one meant for you alone, and so you stand and move on, almost home. You could also wander through Leitenberg with your eyes almost closed, or you could lower your gaze to the ground and count the paving stones and your steps. Soon you will know, having passed the last houses and reached the open field. Leitenberg is only a dream, or no, an accident, which you can no more avoid than the train can leave its tracks; only by jumping the tracks could it plunge into the strange town and disappear.

Only certain views meet certain faces. Everything else remains hidden and buried in impenetrable murkiness. At first you wander along a river valley where there are poplars and vegetable fields. The land is wet and lush. Its owners are unknown to you, unknown also to you is how they tend the fields and nurture the fruits and vegetables. You've no idea if there has been enough rain or sun this year to guarantee a good harvest, because you know no one who will enjoy the yield, and it's even questionable if there is indeed anyone who takes care of what grows here. Seeing the blossoms on the weeds makes you happy and would continue to do so if you were allowed a brief stop. You're just happy that it's not raining, for your shoes are rotted, the puddles of mud make your steps difficult. Quietly your gaze takes in the plants that required such incredible toil, the kind generated by either great hope or bitter need. A hailstorm could destroy it all, bursting the soft melons and battering the cucumbers, the harvest crushed.

Keep moving! You're not allowed to stop here and while away the hours. No one prepared this harvest for you, none of it is for you, no matter how much you may want it. "Look, a tomato! It's almost ripe!" It's better to chase away all such thoughts before they start to cause you great pain. Keep moving! Out in the countryside already you pass the surprising somberness of individual houses covered with vines and surrounded by overflowing gardens in which productive hands and nature's powers vie with tender plants and bushes. Who will win the battle between them? Meanwhile you pass barns, workshops, small factories, dumps, and sheds, all of which announce the presence of anxious owners who must live nearby, their need or greed serviced by these facilities. You're not allowed in, you're not allowed either to take care of anything or destroy anything, because no one is allowed in who doesn't have the right to enter already.

Only the inn called The Golden Grape heartily invites anyone in, but it is empty and quiet. The door is closed, the windows of the dining room gray with dust. Ridiculous are the musical notes painted on the walls, ridiculous the sign and the inscribed lead plaques with all of their advertising slogans, which are already rusted and no longer mean anything. Still, you read them.

SHADE GARDEN

LEITENBERGER BEER

COFFEE AVAILABLE

Yet you don't believe them, since they are a joke. The powers that be had called for a war that no one wanted and that put everyone in debt. That's why the beer became scarce and finally dried up, coffee also disappearing from the planet. At the very least there was no way to stock The Golden Grape, and so sadly enough the inn is closed and dirty. Perhaps the innkeeper had been taken away and it was closed for good.

"My dear sir, you've tapped kegs and served up beer for free long enough. It's time to leave it all behind. If you don't wish to die, then it would be better to come along now in order to die later. In any case, here you'll have nothing to do for the foreseeable future. The magistrate and the citizenry of the town of Leitenberg will gladly confirm that."

The innkeeper was a portly man who bowed respectfully to all authorities and never raised a peep as long as things concerned himself alone. On the other hand, it seemed to him unfair to close the inn as a result of his—as he hoped—temporary departure, since there was still a wife and some daughters, along with a maid, who could keep things running.

"Look how many there are . . . ," as he made one sad gesture after another at the members of his house. "Look how many there are who can cook and serve, who can carry booze back and forth. My business won't fail. There's plenty of customers."

"That's where you're wrong, Herr Innkeeper, or at least you've only partly grasped the truth. You're right, your business won't fail, for the statutes don't forbid your wife from running it. But the times are against you, and that's what is shutting down your garden and cozy booths."

"You mean the war?"

"That's right. You have to understand that there's no more beer and wine, no sausage, no cheese."

"But there are still allotments! Smaller, but they still exist! If there isn't enough of one thing, then there's enough of another. It just keeps changing. Not everything disappears all at once."

"That's right, it doesn't disappear, but is redirected and shipped elsewhere. Only a few important restaurants are still open, and even they have to limit what they can serve. Here outside the town, where at most wagoners stop or on a sunny day good country people come to enjoy your shade garden, business has to be sacrificed until the victorious end of the war. The business must close."

"My inn doesn't matter? Nor the wagoners or good country people?"

"They're not important. The drivers will disappear no matter what, and as for good country people? Herr Innkeeper, open your eyes!"

"Don't mock an honest man! My inn is important, I say, important, for I and my people live off what's left over after taxes."

"None of you need live any longer. It doesn't matter if you do. Just think of our new anthem!"

" 'Everything will soon be over, everything will soon be finished'?"

"Why do you say it with such a questioning tone? The anthem is simple and clear. It's meant for those on the journey, yes, for the journey."

"But the wagoners, even if they no longer trot along with a team of horses, but barrel along instead, sir, they travel nonetheless! They need their beer, yet another drop appearing out of the bottle. . . . I always poured a full glass for free! Twice I'd fill it up! I'd sacrifice my own profits for the beauty of a well-poured pint. I gave away good beer."

"Travelers can drink water, it's also bright and clear. We need sober lads if we're going to win."

"And the Sunday guests?"

"There aren't any more! Days off have been done away with!"

"Good country people. I know a slew of them!"

"There's no such thing. They've been done away with!"

"Why should my wife and children suffer?"

"We all must suffer! That can't be helped! Everyone has to pay the price!"

"Yet people say . . ."

"Lots of things are said, but everything is different than what you hear. Words mean nothing, they can easily be taken back. What is still of value will be so because it is what is willed."

"My people shouldn't have to starve!"

"No one wants that, Herr Innkeeper, at least as long as it can be avoided. Though many in history have starved. But it won't come to that. There are means of support if you need them. Nothing will happen to anyone. In general the prospects are good, there's no need to worry. Especially if your wife and oldest daughter volunteer to work. Everyone is needed. It's been ordered. That's the way it is. If there are no extenuating circumstances, there are no exceptions."

"How about my family . . . ?"

"Not reason enough. There are families everywhere. There are no grounds for exception in your case. The world is big. Your wife is strong. Your daughter is able. We must win."

"And so I must leave house and home?"

"Yes, you must leave everything. No one can stay who is of no use. Here you are of no use. Everything will be taken care of in this manner, because it's for the best."

"And the little children?"

"The local authorities will take care of them. You have our word. You can leave them behind."

Then the innkeeper was gone, taking along only a pair of kisses and a packet of snuff in his pocket. On his way, over the mountains, into battle without beer or coffee. With the last pint poured, the keg is empty. All the other family members are gone as well. Only traces of them remain, but they are not apparent to anyone who can read them, since the memory of them no longer exists. The inn stands empty and listlessly waits for the time when it will return after much has changed, that is, if it hasn't already been destroyed, its bricks having crumbled into sand scattered to the wind.

Yet you're still here, despite having been so transformed that your displacement can be brought off painlessly. None of you want to sit in the shade garden of the inn, since you would be afraid and wouldn't even know how to sit on a proper chair. If the innkeeper's wife came herself she wouldn't serve you, rather she'd be frightened and would implore you to disappear. You wouldn't be able to stand this request, it would remind you of ancient prohibitions. Whoever articulates this within his thoughts allows death to awaken. You are like yellow chickens lined up once again, and the dust that covers you no longer offends anyone, because you are not who you are but rather are led through Leitenberg like strangers. The bridge that spans the wide river already awaits you. The moment you cross it another wish is fulfilled; you are transformed yet again. No one will recognize you.

The town stretches out before you and is magnificent. From the bridge it offers up a pleasant view that has existed and been loved for centuries and is steeped in history. Happy people pass by. They are tired from a long walk and ecstatic with the knowledge that they'll soon be home safe. Their eyes are free to roam in wonderment and they celebrate the happiness that has come to them. You, too, can look around just as long as you keep moving. The one thing you can't do is stand still, for that will disturb the travel plans. Misuse of the emergency brake will be punished, as well as the continual transformation inherent to your own being. To the right and left beneath you there stretches the ribbon of river, silver and deep blue. Several boats lie anchored, some move along the surface.

But before you lies the town that rises from the banks and stretches off into the distance where peaceful mountains rise above Leitenberg. There in their lush green live the thick forests that can only be killed but not transplanted. They are unfamiliar woods that stand before you, but you could know them and walk through them and wander among their shade if you saw how close they were. Many paths tempt you, soft, compliant ones, yet they only lead to the free outdoors that you may not use because it's been designated as free. From the moment a foot steps toward the forest, it must keep to fixed paths, for the fields must be protected, since they are owned by strangers and bear crops that are handled by many hands that transform their labor into food. Meanwhile the woods remain inviting with their shady embrace cooling the sweat of your fear, the trees towering above you that no human step can harm. Now you are no longer bound to certain trails and can explore curious paths known only to the game warden. Now everything has become a forest; the light is muted, the shade provides protection, and the crunching of leaves beneath you stops, everything peaceful and still.

Yet the forests remain far away and unreachable, occupying an impassable area that is cut off, only inquisitive glances allowed to enter as shy guests. It's for the best, for these woods are undeveloped and it's easy to lose one's way, a network of many paths running between the trees, their destination unknown despite the promise they offer you. Only those who sustain their solitary ways by walking through the woods know where the paths lead. They know where they are and where they are headed and don't want to be subject to the eyes of strangers. That's why you have to remain chained together. You make up the band that crosses the river, a train that sways left-right, moving onward step-by-step, always a little farther, obedience not being a condition you chose for yourself, freedom of choice having been taken from you instead.

You have been inserted into an overpowering machine. You can't ignore its reality, even if its construction and purpose are not clear to you, since the chief operators to whom you are mere tools never reveal or review what will happen to you or even to them. Everyone becomes blind as soon as they are pressed to say how things look from their position at the moment. Don't cause trouble by asking questions! Your bewilderment, your disillusioned empty gazes will only bring you harm, only more trouble can come of it. As for you at the end of the bridge, you who walk through the city's Gothic gate while in the distance the forests cause you to lower your eyes, these bailiffs in army gear with their weapons hanging loose know nothing about you, the individual links to the chain that wanders on, no, they know hardly anything about any of you. The soldiers are only following orders.

"Go to Ruhenthal and pick up the three hundred prisoners that the guards will hand over to you there! Make sure to count exactly how many there are; you're responsible for anyone who escapes! If anyone tries to escape, don't call after them, just shoot! Your weapons should be clean and at the ready! You'll march through Leitenberg toward the Scharnhorst barracks, where you'll report, then onward to the firing range at Dobrunke!"

The corporal listens to the order and takes along a private and ten soldiers, who pick you up. Now they drive you onward, young, strong lads who don't know you and will not know you because they don't speak to you since that is forbidden. They see you, but they don't look at you, their shyness immense, their appearance fragile and empty, childlike embarrassed sadness hiding within their faces. They walk confidently and place their leather-clad feet firmly on the ground, one step after another. They are not part of the chain, but their stride is as human as your own, just a bit less tired. They stride powerfully, leading you on in your own powerlessness. Only rarely do they make eye contact or with a few spare words cross the divide that separates you and your guards. If they did decide to disobey the strict regulations, they nonetheless could learn little about you, because there are too many of you, there wouldn't be enough time, nor would there be any trust between you. On top of that, there's too much to do as you march, work, and march again, the day soon over.

At midday, when there's an hour's rest from work, the guards change shifts. These soldiers also have their orders to take you back to Ruhenthal early in the evening and hand you over to the guards after carefully counting you. Orders alone artificially hold you together and in a few hours divide you again, it all taking a short while. Only a set of gestures and understood signs unites you, there being no way to relate to one another on a deeper level; everything that transpires happens in an inhuman network that consumes all of us. Yet we plod along as well, our participation not in earnest; no one can think he truly knows anyone whom he's glad to meet but hardly knows. No, no one is for real; that is the fate of those who journey, those forced to take a ticket. So get going, for you still have to reach the prescribed destination, no matter how tired you are. Quietly the will prods you on in order that suffering doesn't erupt in all of its destructiveness, denying each questionable existence.

"What a pain you are when you rant and complain! Cheer up!"

"How can I cheer up? Nothing will allow it. What has happened to me may seem right to you, but it's unbearable to me."

"You can bear it. Try counting the steps. Maybe the soldier over there is doing the same. He looks like he's just looking on absentmindedly."

"But why doesn't he absent himself altogether? He could desert. He has a weapon. He could do it a lot easier than you or I. He doesn't have to do what he was told. Open rebellion wouldn't sit well at all with him, for he lives under irrefutable laws, but he could desert! That's for certain!"

"Yes, sure. But if he bails out, there will be another one to replace him.

And if that one leaves, then there will be another after him. And so on for eternity, and because of that it never stops."

"Isn't that always the case? There are always more. The guilt just shifts from one to the other, it doesn't go away. No one is himself. Each is the other one's ape. If someone has a problem with that, then he's replaced. That's the way it more or less is and will always be."

"Don't you want to see any meaning in it at all?"

"Do I want to . . . ? You're a fool! The desire is there but it's like an untouchable flower, one that is always visible and yet which always remains out of reach."

"I misspoke. I don't mean if you *want* to make sense of it all, no, I mean whether you can see *any* sense to it."

"Why do you mislead me with questions about secondary matters when I am forced to live life firsthand? It's what's happening to us firsthand that matters! And what's happening firsthand is not necessarily for the best. Rather, it's enough that it is. Any meaning it has, and there indeed is one, has been so eradicated that at best you can only collect your thoughts. Yet given the state of necessity in which you live, you don't want to see what you're a part of."

"Isn't that then the meaning of it?"

"If that's the case, then you are reducing meaning to something inessential. That then would place it outside of the operation that controls us, and also therefore outside of our own essence."

"Yet our essence is not this operation. These are only the outward conditions that we are forced to suffer."

"There's no such thing as outward suffering felt by each of us as well as by me. We are a community held together by suffering, and that is essential."

"But there is suffering that you don't experience. A stranger's suffering is not your suffering."

"Any suffering is my suffering. You know, if something is treated as inessential it is still my concern; it doesn't matter whether I wish to recognize it or not. Suffering exists in and of itself, whether I feel it or not. I can always feel it, always it is right next to me, even when for a moment I don't feel it and don't have to bear its entire weight myself. But I at least have to see it, hear it, feel it, even smell it, for it continues to spread its thick mist."

"But how about meaning? Doesn't it exist as such, yet in a much more ungraspable, much higher sense? I'd even go so far as to say, as a much higher form of meaning?"

"You play with the word *meaning* by placing it in uncertain terms in one instance and certain terms in the other."

"You're picking at my words and ignoring their meaning!"

"I don't want to joke around and pluck bare your heart's innermost desire, since you are also speaking of my desire. Meaning is what we desire."

"And desires truly exist!"

"But as desires. Don't you see the difference? Suffering exists. It's there, and it's not desired. No one desires suffering, or at least not his own suffering, that is, if he isn't so disturbed as to take joy in his own suffering. But many, if not all, desire meaning. Desires are intentions that can sometimes be attained, but often they are unattainable. Meaning at its most basic level is an unattainable desire."

"Since it floats before me, it also materializes somewhere inside me; thus it exists within me."

"That's right. I have nothing to add to that."

And so what remained silent was what could further be said about meaning, for it cannot bear up under constant focus if it is to cohere to what we believe and think. Sometimes the moment calls each of us up out of the depths in which we linger or think we linger. Such moments can simply pass, but it can also happen in such a way that what follows them grants no reality to suffering. Then usually that's it, everything that once seemed to break all bounds becomes the everyday.

Lucky is he who doesn't have to wait for this because he already knows the sentence that's been handed down against him. Though he awaits his execution, it's certainly not a surprise. The surprise attack meant to disorient him is known well beforehand and is a dependable and trusted companion. The other passengers are only there for a while and frequently disappear before they are even missed. Only a small, albeit sudden surprise can upset the inertia of one's feelings, which themselves always want to cling to normalcy, since within that exists a protection against overwhelming suffering. It's true, whoever needs to protect himself ends up feeling doubly disturbed at any change, for normalcy is invoked as a means to scare away loneliness. Yet because normalcy doesn't find the truth to be sweet, truth always wins out, thus normalcy can never be certain that it will continue to exist. One may always like to think of it as reliable, but it is clear to all that though it may be nurtured for long periods of time, in the end it always abandons human beings without fail.

The truth is merciless, and it is always victorious, always to people's surprise, for nothing is as deeply mocked as the final victory of truth, even when its story involves countless insults, though never a final defeat. The truth is most terrible for those who never risk it, something that upsets them more than mockery or disdain. Truth allows no escape and readies itself for the pursuit that presses through its every pore until it conquers the resistant heart. Thus truth is merciless to him who tries to lock it out of his heart and is forced to accept it nonetheless. But it is never cruel, and only lies try to cast it as so by binding it up with something awful in order to battle the truth and delay and prevent its victory until the very end. This victory occurs when normalcy breaks out again, even if it's the last part of normalcy, namely life itself, even though it may know its own end, yet can never fully believe it.

The moment will strike you when nothing else stands between you and the truth. Then all false images fall away. Yet this is going too far; it is not up to life to show the truth in its final form, for its own execution does in life as well.

Whatever then could possibly survive or remain would be the truth itself.

That's probably so, but let's keep our wits about us so that we can indeed exist and serve the truth perpetually. That way we certainly cannot escape ourselves, but we do not need to run away from ourselves, but rather must get hold of ourselves and say to everyone that we are the ones who rest while we journey and who journey while we rest. As long as we are ourselves, everything that is not us will pass, and in the same way everything is in the midst of a journey, everything passes which is not us, the ones whom all that is strange just passes by.

Yet, full of fear, we court the strange and seize hold of it in order to own something for the first time, because it is difficult to believe in yourself when you are not master of something that stands for yourself, thus confirming that you exist through what is yours, though in the end it's still only a part of yourself. This touches upon the fact that you yourself are so little, it being difficult to even know if you exist at all when you in fact possess nothing. All power, all fame, and all greatness love to be displayed through symbols of power or at the very least wealth. The history of mankind is a history of power and wealth, its fairy tales and proverbs have been shaped by it as well. The face of the Earth, as long as man has prevailed upon it and transformed it, is nothing more than a scarred field created and abandoned by such madness.

Leitenberg is a wound, a superficial ulcer that owes its creation and existence to the greed of men. Each one says: "This is mine! A house, a yard, a dog! This I call mine! Mine! Mine! These I grant my will and a name, which I think is a good thing. I chose them myself. A house, a yard, a dog! I need my possessions!" And so Leitenberg was founded and grew. This and every other town struggled for dubious rights through grim means and used coldhearted power to dupe those who didn't know anything, didn't want to know anything, and who were continually done in by human intentions. And so it came to pass, the deadly battle raging back and forth, an undeclared and thus maddening war.

In the name of justice, injustice is installed, defying the condemnations that want to destroy the visible signs of greed. Yet the monuments have long since superceded human power with their own power, and so they remain as someone passes by who is being taken away and has been dispossessed and sent into exile to survive there as long as he can until the day of his final dissolution, when he is nothing more than a dead animal, the horrible image of which he remains for only a few hours more, and which he had become even before the truth was completely revealed to him.

Those who live on create special memorials to the dead, whom they call the departed, wishing still to possess them or to appear to possess them, though they also turn them into rubbish or refuse, which is easier to abandon when necessary. And so gardens are set up, fenced in and tended with care, where in locked crates the former owners pass on through the observation of certain customs and morals. In the gardens narrow holes are dug and filled, around which gather the living with heavy hearts, shedding tears as they stick the crates into the ground, tossing their murdered flowers after them and shoveling them over with earth until the holes close up. But the ceremony doesn't satisfy their pride, and so they create a mound above each hole that is planted with flowers and decorated in order to satisfy their belief that the former owner will not disappear from the memories of the new owners.

The mounds in this garden are lavishly decorated, and each is named. That's something special, as workers drag in special blocks of granite that require great effort as well as expense. With chains the blocks are lifted and placed above those who can do nothing against the fact that the stones are set directly above their skulls. But there's comfort in this strange custom, for now the dissolute once again possess something that, at least in the imaginations of the living, cannot be taken away. The dead are condemned to silence, but the stones must have pity on them and, amid all the ornamentation, proclaim the wonder of their names for all to see.

Whoever has a name enjoys his simple existence and has not left the society of whatever world in which the slightest hint of a name still brings him joy. "All ye rejoice, for we have a name!" Holy choirs sound beneath the ringing of bells that swing to and fro and that do not shatter. For that would mean existence is endangered, there being nothing to denote it with gusto. The dead are not erased, rather their names are instead proclaimed far and wide. Their legacy outlasts their contempt, their misery, and all sadness. For existence has erected a monument to itself that towers above them.

Existence is all that remains, an almost incomprehensible collection of the detritus left over. The one who lives, who cannot live there, feels like a helpless stranger. He is someone who is led past and then through. He still has eyes and can see, he's not dead, even if he can do no more than express what he observes, thus becoming a ghost imprisoned and dressed as a living figure. The dead man made of stone is not absent for long and needs no outward shell, since he has one and is one. The ghost newly transformed is added to many other ghosts of his own kind, all of which appear in similar manifestations, possessions being one of them, even though there may be few left, or few that are allowed or granted by higher powers, versus the power of the wrongful owners who have ensured their own control over existence and make no distinction as to whether what they have seized are things that belong to the dead and are what remains of them, or indeed if they belong to the living who want to own them for themselves and make their claim to them. However, the living cannot do so, since after the creation of the laws that caused them to cease to exist, they are not what they really are, having instead become goods that have been taken, which, since they are not things and therefore do not exist, can no longer be proprietors that one can either count or recognize as people, but rather are ghosts clad in different forms whom the unbelievers retaliate against whenever they make themselves visible, harming them in ways that any of us can suffer but that one should never be forced to bear.

The chain of people driven on through Leitenberg consists of ghosts because only a few inhabitants of the town have the ability to see them, their own eyes having practiced looking deeply into the eyes of people whose essence they recognize but who are not essential at all. And so the inhabitants run around, mostly women and children who busily move and jump about without thinking. Their eyes are either closed because they possess the countenances of dreamers, or their gaze wanders, looking straight, though not entirely through what is not completely alive. Nonetheless they look at a specter that to them is not real, though they don't lash out at objects they are not accustomed to seeing, their gazes drifting off endlessly. Gazes that see clearly become few and far between, because once they become empty of thought they are fleeting and no longer exist. They represent something that cannot easily be controlled, even though the otherwise helpless are provided with free security, presumably only through the merciful desire to maintain, amid totally collapsed or never achieved order, some kind of legal structure, though not through the will of the secured or the power of the guards, each member of Leitenberg participating in it, as well as all of those outside the town, no matter where, as far as the world reaches.

It doesn't matter whether it is so or not so. It either looks different to you all or you don't see it at all. In any case it will pass and you will pass on. Or you'll simply stand there unable to move and everything will pass by you. But it's not as if you have not experienced any of this; none of you is so shut down that you feel nothing pressing at you from outside or within. None of you is free of this fate. Indeed, none of you can stop it, which is why it's called fate, yourselves voyagers journeying toward a specter that appears everywhere. Should anyone bother to try to find out what happened, it will already have passed. And so everything passes.

Even though things continue, they also fall apart, and thus nothing survives.

This or that is picked up along the way and lifted up to be assessed for its worth and placed together symbolically with similar things that have been collected, different relationships drawn between them, the unexpected possessing its own inward reality and attesting to the fact that something else indeed still exists. Distinctions become obvious as soon as the symbolic power of objects ignites as effigy and meaning is gradually restored to them in the movement of the flames. Entire worlds can indeed be destroyed, which the thinking person appreciates—thought is nothing more than memory, which is why thought is also a kind of memorial, and so its content is always outstripped, its desire being always to exist in the present, among whose thick webs it presses on into the endlessly pressing gaze of the possible, which is the future—and yet nothing remains of thought, because whatever is thought has already passed, time having already passed, namely into the helpless past, the realm of all that remains of what has flowed into reality as manifest desires that have now come into being, though through their becoming they have forfeited their essence and their truth.

Only because thought takes pity on the tiny bits that remain is there something on which everything rests and that can be relied upon. There are some who easily say it is so, and with some measure of hope. For then people would have sufficient reason and excuse to accept everything as is, to construct it before themselves, to build it themselves. How long it lasts depends on the strength of the builders. Usually it lasts for a long time; the fear that results in protracted endeavor sees to that. An endeavor is a concern that tries to protect itself and that doesn't want to let itself turn into a satisfied effort, whereby the continuation of real relations is realized amid total flux.

The sinister is buried or, without anyone noticing, is thrown out with the rubbish that the town hauls away once a week and dumps onto open ground near the Scharnhorst barracks in Leitenberg. There all despair is tossed away and forgotten, for so much intense disgust is associated with the useless that the community has decided as one to block it out of their immediate view, and in exchange for pay for this equally important and despised task, they let the unfortunate people cart it all away, away, away so that it is out of sight, out of mind. Only the rats love what's normally thrown out, as well as those rarities that they are not shy about. Thus near the camp, the rubbish lies there and rots, unobserved by most, despised by those who must look at it or who see it by chance. The plants themselves thrive, growing fat and lush with spreading leaves and tiny buds, shamelessly indifferent to the rubbish that nourishes them.

Today it is much quieter in Leitenberg than when the hauling away of rubbish was a sacred ritual and taken care of with loud fanfare. Back then a man moved from building to building with a handbell, stepped into the foyer and rang loudly, the sound echoing joyfully up through each floor. What it said was: "Listen, people, and be happy, for right behind me the garbagemen are coming to haul away your rubbish!" Many impatiently waited for the herald, while whoever had forgotten today was the day had the chance to be saved by the envoy's bell. Then all the housewives and maids would run out of the apartments with buckets and boxes and gather before it building's front door. Vigorous chatter erupted as they kept a lookout for the expected wagon. And indeed it was only a little while before it lumbered along slowly yet steadily, the cart swaying as it passed over the cobblestones. Two powerful horses were hitched to the wagon, the driver never having to yell "Halt!" since they knew their task so well that they stopped at precisely the right spot in front of each building. The sign to move on was given with only a casual click of the tongue.

Soon the wagon reached your own building, all of the women running out to it with their full containers that two men gathered in with open arms. Their practiced hands emptied the containers in one sweep, pounding hard twice on the bottom to make sure nothing stuck inside. Then the men casually handed back the crates and buckets, which were taken in by the expectant hands reaching out to them. Clouds of dust rose from the wagon, as well as ashes and tiny grains of dirt, now and then a bright piece of paper dancing impishly on the wind. Whoever stood next to the wagon could breathe in the stench of rotting scraps and cabbage leaves, but it was never a single smell, for it contained both burning smells and sharp smells alike. Meanwhile the horses moved on, and quickly the women and girls headed back into the building with their empty containers. The doors of the apartments closed, buckets and crates were placed firmly back in their spots, ready to receive the garbage of the coming days.

No longer is the whole process carried out in such good spirits, nor is the glee involved in getting rid of the rubbish either enjoyed or looked forward to or perhaps even fathomed. Now in the courtyard some large metal cans stand, into which at any hour you can dump what you no longer want to keep, and once a week, without prior notice, a huge wagon appears with two men in overalls with rubber gloves that look like fins. The men walk into the courtyard, confident and indifferently cool, lifting one can after another, emptying each coldly and in a professional manner so that no dust rises, not a word is said, the empty cans rolling back into the courtyard as if it all meant nothing. Once the wagon is full it travels as fast as it can out behind the Scharnhorst barracks, its contents dumped with a simple tilt of the wagon's body. Sighing and gasping, the rubbish sinks into the field, then the wagon rushes back to the city in order to clean out more streets and suck up more victims into its monstrous stomach.

All of this is entirely different in Ruhenthal, the town of visible ghosts, who also have a ton of rubbish. But since everything there is in shambles, it's difficult to distinguish normal rubbish from abnormal. That's why it only becomes noticeable once it has filled every corner and the courtyards are overflowing with it. Then at last it's gathered up by tired souls and, amid complaints, is thrown into open barrels that stand on an out-of-service funeral wagon. These wagons have neither motors nor animals, but instead are slowly dragged away by ghosts who shuffle along in baggy clothes. It all happens with hardly any noise but for a low hum, some squeaks, and a muffled growling, as the wagons rumble roughly along. Their suspensions—which were not made for such heavy loads, but instead for a corpse's wary journey into the unknown—have long since broken down. The cobblestones are also broken and sharp, or composed of thick fat shiny stones so rounded and uneven that the high wheels of the hearse wobble back and forth as they bump along down the street.

Here Leopold, the old doctor, keeps busy and looks completely satisfied. He doesn't have to strain himself too much, for the funeral wagon is accompanied by a crowd of men and women who, though none of them are young, still have enough strength to carry out their task casually but with discipline. Leopold also doesn't have to load the rubbish, the group having dispatched two young women to take care of that. As the oldest, Leopold is given special consideration he's completely unaware of. He believes the task is easy, certainly much easier than taking care of grumpy patients. One gets to travel around the neighborhood, seeing this, hearing that, and taking joy in the extra slice of bread one gets for the day's work. Sometimes he instructs his fellow workers and tells them about various illnesses they could get from what they're handling, or better yet how to guard against them. More and more he sinks into himself, standing and walking along next to the wagon, which sometimes stops while he keeps walking on absentmindedly, unaware of what's happening around him. Then someone yells, "Hey, Doctor!" Leopold snaps out of it and mutters something about why didn't anyone say something earlier, then all right, all right, as he slogs back in good spirits and with a grateful smile.

Leopold has time to think things over. He is here because he has to be. It's because of the war. It's the same as being in the army, and he's the surgeon major. He's not really here, for he's only passing through. It's an extended summer vacation, but the accommodations could be better. There's no butter and the coffee is terrible. The service is slow and irregular. Things need to be better organized, but Leopold is not asked to do so. He's too old, although that's not true at all. It's just not right. Caroline can't stand to watch. The women don't understand any of it. Leopold came here because he was ordered to, but the day is coming when such an order will no longer mean anything, the war will be over, someone will pass out bars of milk chocolate and restoratives to build strength, Leopold writing the prescriptions for the best preparations before he heads back to Stupart, from which he was dragged away like a condemned criminal meant for Devil's Island. Leopold won't spend a single hour more than he has to in Ruhenthal. The suitcase will be quickly packed, Zerlina helping him, since she does it best.

Frau Lischka will be shocked and astounded when Dr. Lustig returns with his family, but Bunny will be happy to see them and will get a huge sausage as a reward. Politely the house lady will come along and open the door wide. At first she'll be dumbfounded, but then she'll remember her duties and will remind the doctor to wipe his shoes because of all the mud still clinging to them. Yes, that's right, everything in Ruhenthal is filthy, the shoes so rotted that they can no longer be worn. Yet that will all soon change, Frau Lischka, we'll now buy new shoes. Yet what's unfortunately still true will remain no more than a moment, a war memory. Just wipe it away and don't ask any questions so that one can just forget! Everything bad is gone, and only the beautiful past remains. Doctors are always needed. Many in Stupart will be happy when there's someone like Leopold around again, someone who has learned and experienced a great deal, and who always gives his best effort. Leopold is happy to tend his patients with steadfast care. He has saved many, and there's no giving up on anyone in good conscience until they are dead. Many cases are quite serious, but none are hopeless. One must try to heal the sick and never give up hope as long as they are breathing. Miracles indeed don't happen, but nature has limitless resources, you only need to find them and tap them. Then something can be done.

The sick call on Leopold, mothers arrive full of worry and frantically say, "Doctor, my child has a fever. Please, come quickly!" And he says, "Make sure to keep him in bed! I'll be right there! It won't be long. I just have to finish with my appointments. Or is it that pressing?" —"No, hopefully it's not that pressing, but please make it soon, dear Doctor, please hurry!" —"I'll be there soon!" Or at least as soon as all of the patients in the waiting room have had their chance to complain about their pains and be examined and taken care of, as Leopold washes his hands once again, cleanliness not only being the better half of healthiness but also the better half of medicine. The washstand is old and its style outmoded, but it always served its purpose well. The basin is held by two brackets and can be tipped with a simple push of the hand, though care must be taken, for the bucket behind the wooden stand fills up quickly with dirty water and can overflow. Then Dr. Lustig complains that things are not being looked after properly, and then Caroline gets angry at Leopold for not paying better attention to the water, saying that he should keep an eye on it and let Emmy know when it's full so that she can carry out the pail before it runs over. Leopold is simply annoyed, for how many times has he not said that someone should come into the examination room from time to time, or at least once an hour, and make sure everything was in order, because he had patients to take care of and had too many other things on his mind to bother about such small matters. The doctor grows just as angry whenever Emmy forgets to fill the tank above the basin, as such annoyance brings the practice to a halt when Leopold turns the faucet and only a few drops run out followed by nothing. But if the water tank is filled as it should be, such that Leopold can wash up, then he quickly dries his hands, sticks all his necessities into his medical bag, and scurries into the foyer, where, summer or winter, he dons the same light gray coat and large black floppy hat.

As soon as Caroline hears these familiar sounds in the foyer, she comes out of a room or the kitchen to ask, "When can we expect you, Leopold? When should I have lunch ready?"

"Caroline, how many times have I told you, a doctor never knows when he'll be back. The patients need me. Between one and three. I'll be here as soon as I can. You can keep the food warm. Take care!"

With dignity the doctor leaves the apartment, hurrying on his way to his many patients, all of whom are waiting for the good doctor. He examines them thoroughly and considers each condition seriously, giving the proper diagnosis and writing prescriptions so that everything is well again soon. Leopold struggles against illness, and being a doctor is for him a sacred occupation, one that he chose because he wanted to help people, which is why he must take care never to underestimate the severity of an illness. That's why it's also necessary that the patients do exactly what the doctor tells them. He cannot stand objections, it being nothing but a waste of time, though who would dare try it? One glance and the patients shut up or nod their heads in understanding. If they don't want to do what they're told, Leopold scolds them by reminding them of all the possible complications and dangers that can threaten one's life. If they don't want to listen then he simply says, That's it, you had better find a different doctor, or, Sorry, but I have to be at the hospital. But it rarely ever comes to this, because no one ever wants to leave the good Dr. Lustig.

Then usually everything goes well and the convalescents or the healed come to the office to thank Leopold and praise his care of them. At the end of it all they ask what the bill is, but the doctor is quite generous and the patients soon breathe a sigh of relief, after which comes more thank-yous, as they feel blessed and close the door behind them as fast as politeness allows. Leopold doesn't earn much, nor is there much left over for savings. In the Lustig house the budget is tight, as things have gotten ever more expensive, when the doctor stops to consider. However, he has no idea of the value of money and never asks what is needed to run the house, or what Caroline and the children must live on. As a result, every couple of months Caroline has to sit him down, but he doesn't quite understand what's being asked of him; he works the entire day and complains that he can't just steal money like a common thief.

"I can't charge as much for my services as can a dress designer for a fancy dress. No, Caroline, I can't do that. Forgive me. People also need money and they take no pleasure in being sick. They have to be helped. It's enough that they have to pay for expensive medicines. Illness is a misfortune off of which I don't want to get rich. I won't have anything to do with something so unjust and would rather be poor, that's certain."

"And the poverty of the doctor and his family is also a misfortune. . . ."

"You talk too much. Have we not always had plenty of bread and butter? Have we not had a good life for ourselves?"

"It didn't come from your earnings, my dear Leopold."

"Where from then? I've given you everything, almost everything!"

"You always gave it, Leopold, but it was always too little. Do you hear? Too little!"

Leopold keeps on talking, but Caroline doesn't pay any attention and leaves the room, thinking that she will never get through to the man because his head is always in the clouds; reality doesn't exist for him. All he thinks about is his work, not about others, not even his wife or his children, nor in thirty years of marriage has he ever had a notion of what really goes on in his house. No, he knows nothing other than his medicine and his patients, both of which he lives for and sacrifices himself. He has never been hard to please, all he needs is his own comfort, meaning good food, his clothes cleaned and ironed, and a well-tended office. How hard is it to fill these desires, how much could it possibly cost? Yes, but the family also has its own desires and wants to be taken care of, and that all costs money, my dear Leopold. Where are we supposed to get that if the father of the house doesn't take care of it himself? What the children earn hardly amounts to anything. How is Caroline supposed to earn extra money even if she does have certain skills? No woman should have to work for pay, thinks Leopold. But how would we manage if Ida didn't help her sister out? No one should accept money from others, not even from a sister who is herself a sickly widow. The family shouldn't rely on her. Meanwhile, so many patients are so grateful that they are not satisfied with just paying their bills. At the end of the year they send some wine or other valuable gifts. Yet how expensive they are! As a housewife, Caroline knows the price of things and should figure out what such things are worth. But it never occurs to her to do so.

And now Leopold is no longer a doctor. The world into which he came with all of his industry and thoroughness slowly grew ill and died. It had to do with an affliction that the doctor at first did not notice and then later never completely understood. Above all he did not see that this sickness had to be fought off with powerful medicines, for there was nothing about it in his thick medical books, nothing in his journals. Indeed it was a different kind of infirmity, against which no amount of rest, no diet, no radiation worked, not even the healing powers of the almost forgotten and yet so comforting mustard plaster. No, this was no case for that part of medicine that Leopold knew well, namely general practice, which involved internal ailments that one had to carefully tap and listen to, or childhood illnesses that Leopold recognized at a glance. Instead, it was an affliction without cause, undetectable by eye or ear, though the affliction was nonetheless there, overpowering and quickly spreading, a part of psychology, something for which Leopold had never had much use. You couldn't do much for someone suffering from mental illness except to secure the environment in which he was isolated and give him sedatives to keep him calm whenever he became a danger to himself or his keepers.

The sickness had crept out of nowhere without a sign to alert the medical world before suddenly everyone fell sick. It was the first epidemic of mental illness, but no one recognized it as such, neither the patients nor the doctors. No one told anyone he was sick, for as a result of the epidemic everyone was crazy, and once they finally recognized what was happening it was too late. Therefore the afflicted neither came to Dr. Lustig's office nor asked him to visit them. He would have given them a talking to, yes, he would have, yes indeed. . . . But also the psychiatrists, these charlatans who were of no use, because they knew nothing about medicine and were only considered doctors out of a sense of tolerance he could not understand. "When you're not capable of anything, that's when you become a psychiatrist!" Leopold often said. Indeed, if only the condition had made itself known then they could have warned others about it and continued to publish information about ongoing case histories, but all sense of duty was abandoned, the spread of the epidemic was not thwarted, appeals to the authorities went unanswered, no warnings came from the medical associations, even the professors of the medical schools remained silent. Nobody had a clue, not even the public health officials of the Ministry of Health had done the least thing to try to stop the spread of this threatening disease.

Once the unknown epidemic spread throughout the country it was too late. Now people noticed something was wrong, yet they still didn't grasp what it was, not even Leopold, for no one had allowed him to examine or treat them, which would have allowed him to report on the type and nature of the illness. "Totally crazy is what they are!" But that is not a clinical diagnosis, rather layman's terms that undermine the authority of serious medicine, and sadly the hand lets the stethoscope fall, no sounds are heard, only twanging sounds, the patients perhaps having no lungs or heart. What Leopold had accomplished as a doctor suddenly meant nothing. That's why Leopold took it especially hard when he was stripped of his right to practice. Sadly he read through the decision of the medical board, though he understood completely what it meant.

Dear Dr. Lustig,

In compliance with the order handed down by the Minister of Health on March 23 of this year in regards to the protective measures concerning the classification of the entire health service as set down in the applicable statutes found in Section 2, Paragraph 1, I am writing to inform you that your right to practice medicine, whether for financial compensation or not, will be officially revoked as of July 1 of the current year.

Failure to comply with the ban outlined in this letter will be subject to the penalties set down in Section 4 of the ordinance quoted above, which we are giving you full notice of here. The right to treat immediate members of your family (as mentioned in Section 6 of the aforementioned ordinance) will remain exempt from the overall ban on further practice.

Because the jurisdiction of the aforementioned ordinance (Section 5, Paragraphs 1–3) clearly applies to you, no recourse to this decision will be possible.

With sincere greetings,
Dr. Kmoch
President of the Medical Board

Leopold had only to see this to understand that the sickness had become much more powerful than he had ever imagined. There was no recourse against this condition; the sickness had spread so wide, leaving behind weakened tissues, metastasis, and a radical condition whose prognosis was no longer even within reach. Caroline had to ask Frau Lischka to have Herr Lischka take down the sign next to the door of the building, for there was no more Dr. Lustig the moment his license had been revoked, the patients heading off down the street without having been tended to because the medical board had ordered it so. Leopold, however, packed up the instruments that would soon be confiscated, though of course he was given a receipt for them, all of it taken care of officially, followed out to the letter, indeed everything carried out the door in proper fashion, perhaps carried off to the medical board, perhaps to Dr. Kmoch's apartment, the examination couch the only thing left behind, since it was probably too old and wasn't worth anything, and oh yes, of course, they also didn't take the washstand, it remained behind, though it was no longer filled with water. For who was there left who could do that since Emmy had been let go, something that the ministry itself had ordered. Meanwhile, eighteen months later Leopold began his journey to Ruhenthal, the city of prisoners.

It was then that Leopold said to Zerlina, "You know, child, I will be needed there. Prisoners also get sick and have illnesses like normal people. They'll be happy to have an experienced doctor and a former surgeon major among them."

But when Leopold arrived, they laughed at the old man as he repeatedly and stubbornly insisted, "My dear sirs, I am a doctor! I have practiced medicine for forty years. I'm healthy and can be of help to you."

"We already have plenty of young doctors here who are of no use to us. We could plaster the walls with them. There's already too many!"

"But I'm experienced! I'm a good doctor! Perhaps you might even find some former patients of mine who will attest to how I have helped them in the past."

"Ridiculous! You're no doctor to us, you're just an old man who has seen his better days and is used up and done for! Go ahead, rest on your laurels!"

"Even when they're old many realize their greatest accomplishments!"

"That doesn't matter to us. First of all, we've already told you that we don't need you, and second, no one here who is older than sixty is allowed to practice medicine. Do you understand?"

Leopold, however, understood nothing, though he heard every word. It hurt him deeply that no one wanted anything to do with him. Clearly the people here were also afflicted with this unknown sickness that forbid a doctor to be a doctor. When there's a sickness that prevents doctors from practicing, then medicine is useless, it having collapsed and become nothing more than a fable from the good old days when there were still doctors who studied, graduated, and did their residencies, after which they set up their own practices, placed a sign next to the front door, and then worked for as many years as it pleased them or their health allowed. No one could revoke their right to practice as long as they took their work seriously and practiced it in a knowledgeable manner. Only criminals and frauds were expelled from this noble profession amid scandal and shame, but this seldom occurred, because fortunately there were only a few certain individuals who grossly insulted the honor of the profession. Standing in front of the Ruhenthal officials, Leopold pointed silently to the stethoscope he had saved and managed to carry with him through all his travels, pointing to it proudly and boldly, as if challenging the officials, though they looked on keenly and laughed loudly as one of them grabbed hold of the stethoscope.

"You don't need that here, Doctor. Still, our doctors will be glad to have it, for we're running short of stethoscopes."

Leopold stood there looking pale, a tear falling from his eye. When the official saw that, he responded in mock compassion.

"Hey now, take it easy! It's easy to get sick here, because people much younger than you get sick, and then a young, talented doctor will show up to take care of you. He'll hold your stethoscope in his hands and will be able to tell right away what sounds your heart and lungs are making. Here it's important that one gets a good diagnosis, for there's hardly any medicine, and we have to save what we have. But at least we know what people need and what's causing them to die."

"I can listen without a stethoscope, young man, but you have to have medicines available. You have to! Otherwise nothing can be done!"

"We don't have any, or at least hardly any, Doctor, and yet we manage."

"You mean to say you heal people here only through diet, bed rest, and physical therapy?"

"Diet and bed rest? What are you thinking of? And you want to be a doctor! Here it's death that does the healing when nature isn't able to help on its own."

Still laughing, the officials left, Leopold surrounded by laughter all around him, Caroline laughing as well, just like everyone. Only Leopold remained serious and rigid and stared hard through the murky room.

"Do none of you have a clue, or are you all mad? Diet is important, but that's not enough on its own!"

Leopold should not have had to work, for normally someone his age was freed of such responsibility, yet in return the old ones were expected to give part of their rations to the other prisoners. This was what was simply expected of them, though there was no interest in hearing what they had to say about it, they were expected to just accept these measures. The authorities in Ruhenthal had given the order: more for the young, because they will live, and less for the old, because they will die! This was the normal run of things in Ruhenthal. Human wisdom confronted natural law and sped up its course. Die, Doctor, die, you are not needed! There's hardly any bread, and so one doles out a few hard crumbs, which don't harm the digestion. Also the long overdue return of justice is helped by such clever distractions, for the day-to-day boredom of life simply won't allow itself to continue. The state has a stranglehold on the people and like a leg they fall asleep. Die, Doctor, die, and lie down on the rotten straw! Everywhere the human race has secured a victory with hardly a struggle. A new age of inventions is here, die, die, the state has tightened its bandage around you! The destruction and care of the Earth has been handed over to mankind, the compress in place, the state thrice blessed, dear Leopold! So die, for the stethoscope is broken and your hearing has failed!

No one can bring about something in the world without encountering certain problems in its structure that have been unavoidable. Thus those who are dissatisfied begin to gather together and disturb the image of perfect unity that exists in society. What they want, contrary to all reasonable rules, is to keep other options alive, though the only option that's given them is the right to work. Whoever doesn't work doesn't eat! That's fine. But whoever works should be able to eat! Work or death are the choices, dear fathers and grandfathers! Honor the young, who came up with the idea! Leopold, there's no need to die, your tired old bones are not a day older than seventy-five. You're healthy, you can do it. But old folks shouldn't desire to speak openly or have any say in matters, for silence suits the old ones, as well as a modest spot under the sun, frugality the order of the day because—watch out!—the old ones can't have all the wisdom for themselves. The old ones should be happy with their lot, a teeming heap of rubbish, for there they can wait patiently until they are dragged off, though if they don't want that, then, indeed, there are plenty of small jobs by which such creatures can make themselves useful. Get away from the rubbish! You've had it too good for too long! Now try sauntering through the city and showing the young what you're good for!

It was a clever idea to gather together thousands of old folks in Ruhenthal. They were a group of volunteer workers among which there was no woman under sixty and no man under sixty-five. The thousands of old people were used everywhere they were needed. Old people hauled coal, water, bread, and bricks. They cleaned the toilets and swept the streets. They pushed funeral wagons and wheelbarrows. They made sure no provisions were stolen, that no break-ins occurred.

Leopold also has asked to be put to work and is now on the rubbish detail. It's pleasant and healthy work. The job just takes care of itself and is not so rushed as in Leitenberg, all of it happening at a leisurely pace. Now and then a voice barks out an order, but it doesn't mean anything. Silent laughter is the proper response, each one thinking to himself without being especially upset, Sorry, we can't, we're doing the best we can. And so the work moves constantly along from building to building. Quiet talk full of memories and hope accompanies it, helping to keep disdain for present matters intact. Eight to ten buildings are taken care of before noon, followed by the same number in the afternoon. When the three barrels on the hearse are full, the group pulls and pushes the wagon slowly along toward one of the roads out of town. Continually they have to stop in order that the old ones can try to catch their breath. Then they lean on the barrels, regardless of the dirt; it feels good to rest and it's the one happy part of the job.

Leopold stands there and closes his eyes for a while. Sometimes he thinks of nothing at all, then he remembers how important it is to the inhabitants of Ruhenthal to have the rubbish cleaned out of the courtyards where the blue flies buzz. The rubbish lies there for weeks before it's hauled away, for the hearse is not available to take care of things each day, yet there are many people living in each building who always have something to throw away. But if the prisoners want to live, they have to empty their buildings of filth and junk. This the former doctor knows and tells them so, whether he's asked or not. And as soon as a talent is discovered it is put to use, its value appreciated, each profession having its function, nothing done in vain. Those who laugh at this are wrong. Taking care of rubbish deepens one's relation to the stuff we use. That's why, if we are indeed thankful, we love rubbish; it doesn't matter that it's what we no longer need.

At last the group of ancient garbagemen reaches the outskirts of Ruhenthal with their wagon. The group leader leaves his place on the shaft and tells the guard how many companions he has with him. Then someone walks out from the guardhouse with lazy steps and counts the people three times over, hands the leader a note, waves, the barrier is raised, and the old folks slowly start moving with their wagon, the barrier lowering behind them.

The path is not far off, it takes only a few minutes before they get to the dumping spot. Now there approaches a difficult moment, for the heavy barrels have to be emptied. But it's not that hard as long as there is enough strength to take care of the task. The leader has a rope that is tied around the last barrel. Two of the women in the group and the leader are young. The leader gives the order, the young women grab hold of the ends of the rope, some old guys place themselves on the other side of the wagon and push or at least make it seem like they want to help. The leader then yells "Heave ho!" and the two women pull hard on the rope until the barrel tips over. It empties out with a loud rumble and usually falls from the wagon, although that's not supposed to happen since it's easy for the staves to burst. Whenever a barrel is done in, it's the leader who gets into trouble.

"You're banging that barrel! Do you think I can just fix it? Watch out! It will be a month before I can get hold of another one that good!"

But everyone yells that nothing has happened to the barrel, it's only rolled off, and the ground is not that hard. Because the leader is really not a bad man, he only scolds them for a while and then calms down again once the barrel is lifted back onto the creaking wagon with a great effort. The tipped-over barrels do not empty out entirely, which is why the leader bangs them with a shovel until all of the rubbish is out. One barrel follows another. Once they are all empty and are placed back in their rows, the rubbish still has to be spread out so that there is enough space for the next load as happens in any properly run dump.

This place is not sad, it's a garden of freedom where everything that is dead is given over to itself. No longer does this place have to suffer through the presence of misery's sweat, or the greedy looks that like to peer out between rotting crusts or keep on the lookout for the sticks that poke and digging hands that grab hold of something that no one wants anymore, reducing it to despised possessions once again. Instead, such residue is free of all greed, humiliation done away with, all that is left is sun, wind, and rain, which are offered in peace to the useless treasures that the earth takes into its arms with an almost undetectable rustling. All power fails when the unalterable law of nature completes its unconscious work. No one looks on any longer, everything becomes still and discovers itself amid silent reflection.

Time also stands still, a healing measure. Leaning against the wagon, the old folks rest. They feel the first early warmth of spring, which takes away their hunger as if it had never existed. The air is light and free of every nasty rumor, for it is gentle and blows from a distance from which it has gained fresh strength. Perhaps it's blowing in from the nearby mountains that you won't come any closer to, something that makes their dark brooding quality seem even sadder. Perennials and weeds grow on the slopes and don't worry about a thing since they live without knowing. No one scolds them for thriving, because their undisputed prerogative is that they neither hate nor are hated. On the other hand, whoever does something nasty to them does so without bad intentions; whatever is done to the stems and leaves is done unconsciously. They remain unaware of the state of mind of whoever destroys them, since such intent simply drifts away over the open countryside, unless they grow ever more thin, conquered and calmed by the stillness of the meadow, disappearing without a trace.

The will to destroy is directed essentially toward people and their works; everything else remains off to the side, only grazed or accidently swept up. Indeed nature's resilience is its salvation; whatever bends straightens itself again. But destruction's fury, which culminates in death and never can hold itself in check, is nothing other than a sick and twisted form of greed that prefers a peaceful, versus a violent, control of things the moment sinister war breaks out, during which owners lose the balance and security of normal lives and orderly relations, the seemingly irrefutable right to ownership suddenly being suspended. Then they die or become despondent if they don't do something bad out of the fear that causes them to do terrible things. Then they turn into hordes that are hard to control, everyone joining the march or urged to join in the uprising. Everyone is sent forth and given the charge to spread trouble, which is wicked, but even more wicked when it is done on the sly. For that's how a fiend spreads trouble, who then is only satisfied when it leads to an orgy of destruction that swallows up everything in its reach. That, however, is when the rubbish blows about! And it blows around as well what is not yet rubbish, but will be! It has to be stepped on and kicked out of the way, its memory left to rot! Murder and fire and terror wander among those who unleash them, though they themselves will also be consumed by such force and will be pulled under by the misery they instigated.

Yet this race that eventually leads to self-destruction is rarely apparent to the minds behind it. The horror behind the flickering flames and tinkling shards of glass remains hidden and protected by secrecy, both the rampagers and the victims of the day remain unaware. Whoever outlasts such events and looks back at them as judge or victim shuns the light and doesn't want to know in order that silence absolve the sins. Forced to speak, the participants claim that is not how it was, or at least not how it was supposed to be, fear's dirty euphemisms smoothing things over with clever sayings that gladly conceal what they carry. However, the sadists listen to whoever among the escapees finds the courage to force himself to speak and are barely able to contain themselves before such fabrications, though it's not long before their patience bursts and, mixed with obviously bored yawns, the crack made in hatred's facade closes up again and new wounds are inflicted upon old open wounds, laughter soon following, then disgust, and finally suffocating forgetfulness. If the accuser, however, still cannot prove the charges, he must continue to press and threaten, for only that will bring him peace. If that fails, then nothing more is heard; no accuser is clever enough or strong enough to jump over or knock down the wall of willful deafness once it's erected. Then the accuser must go hungry and thirsty, every exit is blocked, the desert in which he initially cried out simply disregarded, or it's simply too far off, no one having any idea in which direction it lies, the journey leading from one desert to another desert, though the right desert is never reached, everything having been in vain.

What is destroyed never really was, and that which is in vain never came to be. And so they are one and the same, soon indistinguishable, and soon gone. From withered fingers the last drop of dust has fallen, and they are dry, brittle brushwood that collapses upon itself. Yet when everything appears to be over, when the past means nothing at all, what should have been will again be known by those who come after, all the rest now gone like a last giant breath of air one tries to take while dying. It would be useless to try to find the dust that's blown away in a huge new sigh, for that won't work. The hope that it will still be there leads to a rare new beginning, but in the face of the rubbish heaps it collapses. This time all the barrels have fallen from the wagons, the dust rises high, the old men are terrified, the group leader is upset and yells louder.

Go outside and stand in front of the gully in Ruhenthal, but don't think about why you have been allowed out. Instead be happy that you have cold, damp noses that you can touch with your fingers. You're alive! You're alive! The bittersweet odor winds around you and makes your eyelids heavy, yet that is good. At least you know that you're alive. You are counted off. All noses are gathered together, present and accounted for are the long snouts of the dogs. And don't blow your nose if someone presses it! —Ouch, my nose! —Don't scream! The nostrils take a deep breath and suck in air that tastes good to you whenever it's not rancid. Hair grows long in the noses that bend over the spots where others have died. Just think, you noses, it didn't take much to seduce you into a dream, one that you hardly could have imagined would turn out this way! Now you root about in mud and muck. But now off with you, for the leader has to call the tired noses back to the barrels and the wagon. Easily the empty wagon rumbles over the gravel on the way back to town.

Go to the dump that's half the way to Leitenberg and behind the Scharnhorst barracks and stand in a long row. You can say a blessing over the past, but then you will no longer know what really has happened, how you got here and why. Only because you are tired will you stand there satisfied that you have been granted a moment's peace, you noses on long legs. Your eyes have been allowed to stare, their gaze comprehending where recently, perhaps yesterday, the bellies of the wagons were emptied, where weeks ago, months ago, and already years ago, there where gradually the earth resettles, it no longer looks so bad because the rain has smoothed out the ashes and mixed them into the earth. The blessèd wind has also spread seeds. Pointed, jagged weeds have sprouted and dare to display their colorful blossoms. When the gaze can free itself of disgust and can take in the healthy little patches of color, then it turns toward renewal and doesn't have to know that here misused, betrayed, and eventually tossed away goods rest, which in good-natured fashion no longer resent the harm done to them.

With effort and some tender care the beds of the most beautiful gardens could be transformed. If the Leitenberg Beautification Association could recommend anything, it would recommend that its field of concern not be focused on the castle gardens, in order to restore certain views and other enclosed spots, but instead here. Indeed the members would have to sacrifice their weekends in order to shovel, sift, smooth, and roll the earth, clear clean paths and set up beds with rose trellises and decorative bushes, build a hard-packed through road and place benches everywhere that proudly would carry labels that say:

Leitenberg Beautification Association

The money for this work could come from public donations. Young girls would have to stand on street corners each Sunday, offering paper flowers for sale and calling out:

Listen, good people, to what we say
We want the rubbish and rubble hauled away
So spend a penny, maybe two or three,
So that such dreck no longer will be!

The local authorities, as well as the military authorities, could provide a subsidy so that such initiatives could begin without delay. Architects, building firms, and gardeners would hurry to provide advice and skill, plans would be entered into vigorous competitions, tools and steamrollers placed at one's service for free, and Captain Küpenreiter from the Scharnhorst barracks could make sure that there would be enough soldiers and tools to take care of it all.

But nothing comes of it all. Meanness, avarice, misunderstanding, and the inertia of the heart resist such well-meant undertakings; people are fed up with such efforts and turn away. Indeed your efforts at such beginnings are even seen as a madness that in the end will cost you. Such useless dreams can only occur to people who have nothing better to do, that's what is thought, and therefore it's good that no one ever gives you the chance to express your wishes. It's a waste of time to bother yourselves with rubbish, a miserable sensibility that shows a lack of will to accomplish anything. That's why it's appropriate that you are strictly controlled as long as your suggestive natures still exist. Only because you are miserable are you sad about the stinking rubble that is the mirror of your own un-questionable hideousness, what you yourselves are and what you still don't wish to recognize, though it's the despair within yourselves that makes you long for the help of the Beautification Association.

No one hears what you have to say, for it is wisely arranged that no one is allowed to speak to you. In much the same way that people in houses keep away from you, so you are kept away and it becomes true that you are not allowed any longer in houses, according to our wishes, and that you may no longer inhabit them. You are rubbish, but the kind that is not allowed between table and bed, between chair and cupboard. Rubbish mixes with rubbish, and sin with sin, all of it a disgusting gruel that is only good for the vermin that help it to rot even further. People said good-bye to you and wrung their hands over you, but they didn't wave; on the contrary, they raised their hands to ward you off. Souls washed themselves in the waters of guilt as you were uninvited and the doors were closed in front of you, commands barked behind them as they snapped shut, for they were ordered not to look at you. Meanwhile, con-cerned mothers went even further than any command as they carefully closed the windows and drew the curtains so that the little children wouldn't see you or the sight of you cause them harm. "Mommy, who are all those dirty men there?" No, such a question the mothers hated, for then they had to lie—"They're poor men!"—and that would not be enough and they'd have to say "They're no-good devils!"—though that didn't work either.

And yet you don't give up. You are given a few minutes. You are told that you should take care of your needs. You can open up your pants and piss on the rubble. If there is nothing else available, you are allowed to go down into the ditch so that you can pull your pants down. You are your own graveyards. You should be buried under the weight of your own de-spised possessions. It's not meant out of hatred, but rather pity. Yet you still long to get away from the rubbish; you still long to be elsewhere, which only demonstrates how disingenuous all those ideas are about beau-tification floating around inside your head. Stuck in the weeds and squat-ting down, you look around and sniff for anything that might be of use. You want to have what no one has any longer, but you cannot take it. In-deed, the warning says:

Public Waste Disposal

as well as:

All Forms of Rubbish Left Behind by Private Citizens Are Strictly Forbidden

And yet removing anything from the dump is also not allowed, because it all belongs to the authorities and therefore is still not free of owners. Thus there is nothing left in the world that doesn't belong to someone; all goods are divided up and cause pain to those who have nothing and don't want to have anything. It's to them that the warning on the sign against entering is directed. So it is only thanks to the corporal's good nature that you're allowed to squat out here in order to ease your aching intestines. What you're allowed to do here is indeed permitted, but it is against the general decree and is only allowed because the authorities are comfortable in the security of their own rights, though they are not generous enough to take the care to put an end to such a command.

Moreover, the town fathers don't believe that anyone would want or take anything from here. With the stinginess of an owner who doesn't give anything away freely, they calculate what something is worth, especially since a higher office, namely the Ministry of Commerce, has already staked a claim to the free acquisition of all that was useless, since whatever one didn't use the state can always use. Long memos were sent to the local authorities: You must save, save, and save some more! Thriftiness spells riches to the victor! Whoever values the worthless is certain of riches! Save old glass! Save old copper, iron, and sheet metal! Save whatever one can bend or weave! Save old bones! Save paper! Save, save everything! The state doesn't sneeze at what its citizens no longer love, and thus the rulers stand humbled before the ruled, forwarding a shining example of self-denial. That's why next to the trusty rubbish cans in the courtyard of every building in Leitenberg there stand special containers into which everyone tosses whatever glass, metal, rags, bones, and paper they no longer have any use for. Everyone tosses it all away for the sake of the state; everyone tosses away what is worthless and sees the state transform it into something of worth once again. The dross of life itself is redeemed and repatriated through a renewed sense of its own worth, since all of it served a shared purpose, retrieved from mud and muck only to be dusted off and restored to a bright luster.

The same thing happened to the consignment shops as had happened to The Golden Grape. They were taken over and told they were no longer needed. You are out of business, because officials from the Ministry of Commerce will now handle your business, as well as take control of the stockrooms of all dissolved firms. Only a few secondhand dealers were still able to apply their expertise. Even though they were just servants and underlings, they still stood a rung higher on the social ladder since they were now civil servants. This allowed them to wear the glorious emblem reserved for those who are paid servants of the state.

A large part of the work was not the concern of the former rag dealers. The people's pride wouldn't stand for that. Instead, the responsibility for gathering and saving was reserved for those who were better suited and brought more spirit to the work than the cool, calculated nature of salespeople. New people were tapped who slowly, from hour to hour and year to year, attained their full potential in service to the state, climbing from the fallen on the lowest rungs of the ladder to the holy desk of the front office at the top. The Ministry of Commerce approached the Ministry of Education to help spread the feeling of general well-being, and so schoolchildren with their clever heads and tender, diligent, restless hands were enlisted to gather monthly from the houses of Leitenberg all the useless items thrown away. Whenever the children found nothing or almost nothing in a courtyard, they knocked on the door and reminded those inside, "We're from the War Brigade for Recycling. Don't you have any bones?" Then the people would bring the children some gnawed bone or another, the young hands snapping it up like young dogs and running away without so much as a thank-you or good-bye.

The consequence of this relentless recycling is that less and less is tossed into the dump. What is brought there is a somewhat uniform kind of rubbish that doesn't look nasty at all. For the most part it consists of ashes mixed with scrapings, potato skins, and cabbage leaves, as well as broken pottery, pieces of wood, and nearly unrecognizable refuse. Yet whoever dared to poke around a new blossoming heap of rubbish could find rusting iron pots and kettles with holes in them or underneath a rotting shoe worn right through, a faded hat, a coat with no arms, and numerous other treasures that the wild beasts who wandered the hunting fields of what had been publicly abandoned would gladly gather up, provided that the booty was not so ruined that nobody knows how to restore its dignity or save it from further decay in order to alleviate the poverty of the ghosts of Ruhenthal. Now and then a hand lifts something up to eye and nose, and whenever it is something that could be easily hidden—a small can, a nail, a little piece of leather—it disappears into a pocket. Yet if it is something larger, you can't take it, because the soldiers would notice immediately and shout.

"Are you completely nuts? Throw that crap away right now!"

Then the precious rag is tossed back, its fate sealed forever by wherever the wind will take it.

"Fools like you who steal from rubbish heaps ought to be taken care of for good!"

The words are barked out, but they do no harm. Only actions still matter, no longer words, for they make nothing happen. The power of the word has disappeared or is hidden away, language having lost all meaning. Indeed, what is said is not that different than in earlier times, but it no longer carries any weight. Gravity rests in actions that can be completed right away. Fate waits for nothing. Hardly is something ordered, a wave being all that it takes, and it's done immediately. Life without sacrifice is no longer possible, while at the same time caution is thrown to the wind. It can no longer even be picked out of the wasteland of rubbish. It exists only in each single step taken by the chain of ghosts. Left right, left right. The symmetry of the steps is not something arranged, but rather only the result of fixed habit.

The soldiers have no problem with this, but in fact look on pleased, because it corresponds to their own sense of habit. They have good boots and walk left, right. They thrust their legs forward, and it feels good to do so, the arms following, a four-footed creature that has been so well drilled that it can stand up and stomp the earth on just its hind feet, though it cannot conceal its origins, having maintained the swing of its front legs. The ghosts, however, are not as capable as the striding animals, but nonetheless they keep trying and sway left, right. Their ragged, torn footwear creates no pounding, but rather a quieter, more uncertain sound, a scraping, left, right, perhaps a stiff-legged dance that moves along the streets in wretched fashion. Some of the ghosts don't want to settle into "left, right," but instead want to slide across the earth, rocking back and forth as they scrape along, slinking, shoving themselves forward, wanting to roll, some even wanting to hop along silently, though the other ghosts spoil this game because they want to seem real to the Leitenbergers, so that at least some of them can say, "I saw it myself. It's really true. We witnessed it ourselves."

And so the ghosts continue trying without success. What they attempt to do cannot be accomplished, namely to get the Leitenbergers to think of them as real. If the ghosts were to think of themselves as real, that wouldn't amount to anything, because the townsfolk would still not consider them real. Even if this difficulty were overcome, it still wouldn't mean anything, because the Leitenbergers would still not believe their own eyes. Such people would only mutually agree that there must be something wrong with their eyes. This would only remove any last doubt that in Leitenberg one cannot see what one does not believe.

Because of their number, the existence of the ghosts was not plausible. Left and right, those are not ghosts. Left and right are only sides. Left and right, those are the streets of Leitenberg. Everything is left or right. Everything is based on left and right. Nothing is left and nothing is right if it in fact does not exist, and therefore there are no ghosts on the right or the left, they can only exist in general, and because ghosts have been abolished they no longer exist, no, not anywhere. The ghosts are not clever enough to realize this, because they really want to seem human as they shuffle along left, right. And so they carve their path forward, pressing upon the surface of the stony pavement, even if it's with the soft flesh of the knees, left, right, onward, onward, though unlucky are those who cannot keep up because they have blisters on their soles and their shoes hurt, some of them having to hobble along and thus disturb the remaining ghosts, right, left.

The small streets climb uphill. The rows of four across almost fill the street, a sidewalk on the left, a sidewalk on the right, each seeming so close and yet so far away. No ghost can step upon them, because the long curbstones have banished anything impure, anything that would harm the health of the souls of the pious owners. How confidently the few people stand on the two-colored mosaic of the sidewalk and have no idea how small the distance is that separates them from the swaying ghosts, themselves simple people who do not like to stray too far from their lairs in order not to lose touch with their familiar smells. Only reluctantly do these loafers step forth out of their shelters when it concerns their jobs or their needs, and then they quickly turn back. They all push open their doors easily with one hand, take a whiff of their own houses and sniff each curious stain.

Already the street is absent one man. It's Ambrose, who clambers up the stairs that lead to the upper floor and his apartment, where he slouches in a chair next to a large table. Ambrose has been expected and everything that he needs after his brief outing is set for him. The wife stands ready, her face flushed, a clump of hair having fallen from the knot as she places the tureen of soup on the table. No requests are necessary, it only takes a glance and whoosh! the bowl is filled with vegetable soup brimming full right to the rim. Ambrose bends his back and stoops over the table with his nose pointed straight down. Left lies the spoon, which is picked up and transferred to the right hand. Then it splashes into the bowl and disappears into the steaming broth, though that's not enough in itself, as the spoon swishes back and forth through the broth in order to fish out a slice of potato and a carrot cube. Then the spoon is lifted up a bit and the nose sinks down quickly, while from down below an extra bonus appears, a chunk of meat that swims up from below and touches the lower lip. Then the spoon is lifted and disappears in a flash into the mouth that snaps shut around it. A faint gurgle can be heard as some drops fall from the corners of the mouth and back into the bowl. Ambrose lifts his nose, testing the soup with his gums and then swallowing. Then he sets the spoon down once again.

"Once again it's gone cool, Katie, and no salt, not enough salt."

"I put enough in. Otherwise it would be too salty, and you'd complain some more."

"It's not enough. It should be hotter. That's all I ask. Only some more salt."

Katie reaches for the saltshaker with her left hand. The spoon sinks lazily back into the soup and is let go of as Ambrose's right hand grabs the saltshaker, turns it upside down, and shakes it once twice, once twice, once twice. Grains of salt fall from it in thin strains.

"The salt is damp, Katie! Some things never change!"

The saltshaker now in his left hand, his right hand grabs the lid and turns and turns, once twice, once twice, once twice, until it's off. He reaches for the fork with the right hand and pokes down to the bottom of the hardened salt. Then the top is screwed back on again, worked by the right hand, the left hand. Salt is shaken into the soup, more soup is eaten. His hunger is enormous, yet he still fills his stomach, left then right. The bowl is emptied, then is followed by another, and then a third bowl is emptied. That will do it. Ambrose is full and at last feels himself a proper man, and that Katie is a good wife, and that all residents are good because they are holed up in their own houses or houses they rent, in which they take care of their bodies when the times are good. The bodies stretch out and are covered with warm blankets, soon getting hot and sweaty as they grow quiet and sleep as all good people do. That's what they learned as children, but because they have been so good, they never have to change anything, but rather repeat the same thing day after day, night after night, left right, left right, afraid only of the law and wanting to uphold their sense of responsibility.

The residents gather together and agree on what is good and to the right, while that which is bad and to the left they want nothing to do with and toss away. They feed themselves properly and digest their food as they have always done. They listen to the doctor whenever there's a problem with the seamless running of their metabolism until once again they are healthy. If the doctor cannot heal the body, then the doctor looks them in the eye sincerely, and then behind their backs laughs and shrugs his shoulders. Then comes the notary, followed by the undertaker, and everything is complete. Other proper souls move into the emptied rooms, generation after generation, right and left, as far as one can see.

Yet on this particular day nothing is known, everything is the same, not even a closet door is opened. Today is never fully known, something is always bound to be happening elsewhere. As long as it doesn't intrude on matters then nothing changes. The journey doesn't seem real, there is always just Leitenberg and the streets, this house, and here Katie and Ambrose nestle and lounge about and get up and gnaw away at bread and beets. Not much waste is produced, nothing but ashes. The days repeat themselves, once, twice, one after the other, whether or not the ghost train wanders by or not. It's always the same, the noses sniff, nothing bothers them, nothing gets on their nerves, because ghosts are strange and must atone for the fact that they are still there even when they are not welcomed in this house. If there were no such ghosts then there would be peace in the land and the sons of Katie and Ambrose would also be at home and not marching left and right in the wide world.

Then Katie called out, "They're coming!"

No, not the boys. Which is why Ambrose doesn't even look up and has no interest in his soup. He is tired, much too tired; rest is the wages of work. Ambrose wants nothing to do with this horrible yapping. Digestion is all the salvation one gets.

"They're not coming, Katie! Stop thinking that they are!"

Ambrose, however, doesn't consider the banished, whose scraping feet can be heard on Bridge Street. He sees his boys before his eyes and knows that they will never again walk down the streets outside. My boys, my boys, yanked from their home, whisked away, though for a good cause, for the war, the country's security, the peace of the citizenry, as well as applesauce, the tax on consumption, glory, and soup. So it's for the good! The victory palm already stands in the vase beneath Grandpa's picture. One can't be quite as sure of the good Lord, but almost, for there must be one, though without a beard, and there will be peace in the land, here beneath His long nose, as they march left and right through the applesauce of the good Lord watching from above, amen. Amen! Then the journey will be over. Garlands will hang from the bridge. WELCOME TO THE GOLDEN GRAPE, SERVING COFFEE AND WINE. Katie, wouldn't it be wonderful to march with them? No more ghosts. No more paper, just my dear boys. We wouldn't throw anything away. Not even bones, we could grind them into a fine flour instead.

"My dear, you're sleepy. Go to bed."

"No, no! I'm not at all. Just a quick nap. And now I'm fine. I just barely dozed off. But it doesn't matter. Not at all, Katie, I swear, most of all to you."

Without war there can be no victory. That's what Ambrose had been told. *The Leitenberg Daily* had written the same thing. The result being left, right. That's the way it was. Written words are sacred, because you can hold them in your hand. You can throw them away, but they don't disappear from the public library. That which is written down speaks the truth, which is the most sacred thing of all. On each little cube it says, "I am Vita-All. Just add me for extra spice and nutrition in your soup. Katie, toss me in; Ambrose, left right, will love it! Since he already likes having gruel and soup, it will also help his terrible teeth!"

Everything is a mess. The boys who will never walk the streets again, the ghosts of Ruhenthal who march on by, it's all a mess, even Katie is a mess, and Ambrose is a mess, the potato soup with Vita-All is a mess, and then whoosh! the brimming spoonful disappears between the rotten teeth, swishing around the left jaw, the right jaw, then down the middle and into the stomach, into the pit, buried, everything covered up, thrown into the rubbish where it boils and bubbles. Tasty sauces bubble up in order that Ambrose can rise and shine once more. For he's there again after his winter's sleep, going up and down the steps. Then he takes to the streets. He sees soldiers passing by, carrying out the pleasurable business of guarding the ghosts in order that they do not run away. Though they've been forbidden to do so, that won't do any good if one isn't careful. The riffraff from Ruhenthal are only afraid of the cold bullet in the belly. They all have a little tummy that has grown thin and dirty, because they are pigs who don't wash, their women nothing more than hollow straws full of thin soup. How it would spray about if one peppered the pack with shrapnel! Then the voices of the ghosts would scream loudly and croak on the spot, Bridge Street full of rotting corpses, the war on, the result a bloody mess and no applesauce, the remains needing to be thrown onto a wagon with pitchforks. Then off to the dump and away with them! Let's have at it! Into the pit with hip-high boots! Roll up your sleeves! Dig those graves! Cover them over! But that's too much work. There's a better way. And so the gasoline is brought out and lit, a huge hygienic fire billowing. Then ashes are all that's left, which can just be spread about.

Ambrose smiles with pleasure. He stretches and lightly dreams, but he doesn't sleep, no, he doesn't sleep. Katie has moved the easy chair next to the window and into the sun so that the man of the house can sprawl out with his legs spread wide. He is a little tired, yet he feels completely fine, for he's feeling fine, and because of that he can digest his meal in peace. Potatoes and carrots swell the belly, yet Ambrose has to eat them if he's to get his fill, since there's no meat. Katie must do everything she can in order to have enough to feed Ambrose, because a hungry husband in the house is a problem and will only lead to trouble for the wife. But Katie always managed to bring it off because she loved her Ambrose, and love was more inventive than necessity. Because of that Ambrose is nearly satisfied and only grumbles a bit. Things could be better, certainly, but after four years of war it's bearable, you get used to it since you only live once. If one were to consider everything that happened under this foolish heaven, then it would be unbearable, which is why Ambrose doesn't want such things to trouble his head.

Whatever happens will happen, meanwhile the soup is served. First the eyes take it in, then the belly senses it. Sleep, Ambrose, sleep on! Ambrose hears his mother's voice. It sounds so warm and friendly that he cannot imagine how such a charming voice can call from the grave, but that must be because the Leitenberg Cemetery is so beautiful. There is not a more beautiful garden in the entire town, not even the one by the castle, and for All Souls' the cemetery is filled with endless garlands and bouquets, the entire landscape smelling of damp earth and ruffled late autumn blossoms, of flickering oil and tallow candles, Masses sung in all the churches, *credo in unum deum, credo, credo,* done in the third conjugation. After four years of high school at least some Latin still remained, and there is still a God in heaven, everyone knows, though He doesn't have a beard, the pope having said so himself. With a little Latin one understands a lot more in life than uneducated commoners, *plebis plebis,* that being the third declension, not to mention that one also has a credit line and a savings book for the First National Bank, the Leitenberg branch. A worry-free old age is ensured, *credo in unam sanctam,* for there is always enough to go around if only the currency doesn't depreciate still further.

But when the currency becomes worthless paper then you can burn it. To hell with credit! The coal is almost gone, yet Katie must still heat the house and light the oven. The cinders are emptied out. The coal shovel scrapes its way into the expended remains of the burned-out coals, a soft sound, as the crumbs are tipped into a dented bucket. Katie sprays water on them so that the ashes are not so dusty. Ambrose carries the bucket downstairs and tips it over, spilling it all out. Only when it snows are a part of the cinders spread on the sidewalk in front of the house so that people don't slip. Otherwise they could fall and break a leg. That's punishable by a fine. The town can't be icy. Better that it be covered with cinders, but tidy, because safety is the first demand. So says the First National Bank, and so had Ambrose learned in school. Everything in the world since the first days of creation had been aimed at ensuring safety for everyone. It is the prime aspiration of the state and the public at large, it is the aspiration of every citizen. For then commerce and trade flourish. Anything unsafe is cleared from the sidewalks, that being the first law, *dies irae*, and so away with that awful snow, the massive broom sweeps it all away, the cinders cure the dangers of winter.

The streets are cleaned throughout the year, for even in summer danger can arise. Horses and dogs soil the pavement, papers and trash fall to the earth. Then come the sweepers who push with a gentle swaying motion the little dustbins in front of them. Once they have gathered up enough, they load their cargo onto a shovel, all of the street's woes stuffed into handcarts that the sweepers busily push through Leitenberg. Each morning they show up on time, going about their daily work in peace and with care, for which they receive a weekly salary. It's light work that serves to spread the peace. Which is why no street sweeper ever seems to apply himself as vigorously as he should. Instead, he takes a break and takes out a sandwich from his pocket as a way of relaxing in the face of his endless sweeping.

And so Johann stands guard next to his handcart, his broom and shovel leaning against it, as he noshes on what he leisurely lifts to his mouth from his pocket. The mouth is opened, the sandwich is shoved into the cleft, then the lower jaw lifts the front teeth and presses the sandwich into the upper teeth. Immediately the teeth slice through the porous mass, the hand holds the sandwich and pulls it away from the mouth once the bite has been taken, lowering as the tongue, gums, and saliva work together to accomplish the ravenous swallow as the moistened bite is choked down the gullet. Then it occurs again, until it's all gone. Meanwhile the street is forgotten, the broom is forgotten, the daily tasks full of dust and trash are forgotten. After the snack the flat metal flask sneaks out of a different pocket. The cork, attached by a thread, is yanked out, the flask lifted high, the head tilted back, the mouth pierced as it opens small and round, the teeth recessed in order that the flask's neck settles into the opening. It all happens fast. The cool, sugary chicory coffee with milk flows into the hole until it is full, the tongue itself between the mouth and the flask's neck in order to stop the flow. Then the mouth is emptied after a series of hefty swallowings, more coffee follows until the last drop has disappeared. The flask is then corked before sinking into a jacket pocket.

When the meal is finished the broom is taken up a bit more joyfully. Happily the broom sweeps away as Johann goes about his work eagerly and with satisfaction. It bothers him somewhat that some people are pigs and make such a mess of the streets. Each day Johann arrives at an inn, outside of which it's always a complete mess. It's been that way since at least the start of the war. Today it's a little better, but most every day one can see the results of hard drinking in the bar, each morning the street outside covered with puke spewed out amid uncontrollable laughter. The bellies having been filled up inside, they then spew it all out again in disgusting, thick streams. Johann's broom sweeps it up as though it doesn't bother him, the street soon clean again and gleaming in the light of day.

Johann is afraid of neither wind nor cold, he protects himself against each. Only when it rains too hard does it annoy him, because his coat gets as soaked as a sponge and heavy, such that it doesn't dry out overnight. But Johann barely grumbles about it, because he is shrewd and knows that every job has its unappealing sides that one has to take in stride, Johann being quite happy to put up with them. Other people had to slave away much more and couldn't help but complain. Their situation is much worse and often much more dangerous. The sewer workers, for instance, never had it as good and would jump at the chance to trade places with the street sweepers. Johann doesn't want anything to do with having to stand up to his thighs in such filthy slop. It wouldn't even be worth the high rubber boots issued by the town. Nor was Johann tempted by the ration card for heavy laborers that allowed them access to horse meat and real meat sausages. Better to do with a little less and yet live a better life as a street sweeper, as free and happy as the sparrows who are hardly afraid of Johann's broom, but instead happily peck at nourishing bits of grain in the horse droppings on the street.

Life on the street is healthy and not as pressing as the drudgery of the munitions factory, where three other street sweepers have been seduced into working rather than remaining in the open air and seeing different things each day. People and cars pass by in a hurry, both familiar and unfamiliar, providing lots to think about and look at. That's what keeps Johann feeling young. Even after many years he will still be able to work, no matter how long the war lasts, along with its need of able men. If there were peace, then Johann would probably already have been sent away into retirement. Now, however, nobody gives it a thought, the community at large is only too happy that he continues on. At the central department for street cleaning and rubbish collection, they told him within just the last couple of weeks:

"You're right, Herr Pietsch. The fatherland can make good use of your broom, but might you think about munitions?"

"Please, I'd rather stay on the street."

"How good of you, Herr Pietsch! There, too, the fatherland can use you and is grateful to you. How long have you actually worked for the town?"

"Forty years it will be come January. Wait a minute . . . yes, forty years indeed! I'm sure of it."

"I'll recommend you for a raise, Herr Pietsch."

"Thank you, Inspector, thank you!"

"Faithful service should be rewarded, my friend. That's how it is here in the fatherland. You will also get a certificate of appreciation, you'll see, signed by the mayor himself."

Praise from the inspector is nice, and a handwritten letter on behalf of the fatherland is even nicer, but Johann doesn't need any of it. The raise, however, is another matter, for that is certainly pleasing. It would be nice to be paid a bit more for his contribution, as that's the best token of appreciation of all. Then the dirt is swept away by the broom as the ghost train passes right in front of his face. Johann steps to the side, scratches an ear, and remains standing quietly, the broom at rest in his left hand while his right tugs at his chin. Johann stares ahead and thinks to himself, What kind of heroes are those who are being led by? Maybe they are prisoners of war, since they wear a symbol on their breast. These days all kinds of people are brought here from far away and sent off to work in order that they pay for the fact that they raised a hand against the fatherland. Perhaps there is a street sweeper among them whom Johann could show how one swings a broom and shovel in a strange country, since other countries no doubt had other ways. But there's dirt everywhere, and it all has to be cleaned up. It's the same in France as it is in Russia. But then why do people go to war? Everyone should just take care of their own streets at home. Street sweepers can get along wherever and work together to clean things up. Johann only needs to look into the faces of these prisoners, for there certainly are good fellows among them, not just "nothing but villains" as it said in *The Leitenberg Daily*. Those indeed are tired stallions with empty stomachs who would much rather be home than here, not knowing why they have to work for some other fatherland. Certainly they have wives and children at home from whom they've received no letters for quite some time. Johann imagines to himself the worry they must feel when they hear nothing from home. Back there is everything they have and love, and yet there is nothing they can do for their families. But things will once again be good, one only has to not lose heart. Everyone has his own broom to sweep, and if you just throw yourself into it everything works out eventually.

One day, yes, one day the higher-ups will have had their fill and will say: "That's it! The war has gone on too long already!" The people in charge will sit together in a castle and confer with one another. Oh, it will take forever! Then a special edition of *The Leitenberg Daily* will appear announcing peace at last. Peace, people! and everyone will display his flag, there will be parades across the square, brass bands will play snappy marches, all the houses will be decked out, one two three, the bakers will bake special cakes, the town will ready everything for the return of the soldiers so that they will be properly welcomed. Then all of the streets will be full of people, one next to the other, the people will leave behind a ton of trash, though it won't matter, for that's also part of victory and Johann will happily put in the overtime so that Leitenberg is clean once again, if only it means peace, finally peace. In the cathedral the organ will roar, the bishop himself will read the Mass, and everyone will sing a *Te Deum*.

That will also be a day of celebration for these prisoners. No longer will they be led off to work, but instead they will be brought to the train station, the boys wearing green leaves in their buttonholes as they quickly climb into the train cars. "We're going home, boys! Be happy, Mama awaits us!" Johann wanted to say it all out loud, but he was afraid to, because it would be dangerous. It would mean consorting with the enemy. High treason against the fatherland. That's why it was forbidden to so much as say a friendly word. One could not give even so much as a wave. Which is why Johann says only three words to himself.

"Mama awaits us!"

No one heard it because he said it so softly that no one was able to hear it and thus report it. If someone did, then Johann would be thrown in jail, having been hauled off by both arms, bound, and fitted out with green overalls. Johann damn well didn't want that, stuck there with the bedbugs in the holding pen of the district court, for he'd heard nothing good about that at all, and it would only mean adieu to every last bit of freedom. Quickly they would get on with the trial. They always have a couple of witnesses on hand who know everything, even what never occurred, and are ready to say what the judge wants to hear until there's no way out of such a jam. That's why it's better to remain silent, but nonetheless he can look on a bit at these poor fellows, and if he happens to laugh at them there's nothing wrong with that and is considered quite all right. Perhaps the boys will understand that Johann is not really laughing at them, but rather that he means well, which might make them happy and realize that among the street sweepers of Leitenberg there are nice people. But should an informer see Johann laughing with them and consider it a crime, he will not be afraid and will calmly say: "No, I wasn't laughing with anyone! I was only laughing at them because of the mess they're all in. They thought to themselves that they would be the victors marching into our fatherland, yet we caught them all! And so it's over, away with them!"

But everything is all over. The wandering ghosts sense it and hope for nothing from the people of Leitenberg, who indeed don't want to help them and couldn't if they did. The street sweeper there need not strain so with such a grin, for no one recognizes that it's well meant, nor is he even noticed. To them he is nothing but an empty mask, just like everyone else in the town who walks along the streets bored or afraid. Life has been drained from the townspeople, although they still want to appear lively, even though they have been dead a long time. Only out of habit do they thrust a leg forward. Paul looks out over them and is only curious to see that there are still buildings and not everything he remembered has disappeared. And yet it's already finished, the town having become a beautiful stone corpse. All towns and cities are corpses that will soon be reduced to the rubble that they will bury. To contribute to this natural sequence of events, in fact to hasten it, was the only sensible thing that Paul could think to do.

Paul is tempted to whisper some of these thoughts to the man next to him, whose name is Fritz, but Fritz pokes him in the side with his elbow in order to remind him that between the bridge and the Scharnhorst barracks all conversation is forbidden. Leitenbergers are not supposed to know that the ghosts can speak. And so Paul remains silent and lost within his thoughts and walks on, left, right. Yet looking about is not forbidden, otherwise that would force the soldiers to have to lead a chain of blind men consisting of nothing more than a set of noses hanging down from hollowed-out eyes. Only hands and feet would sway as they dangle, lead ropes needing to be stretched between them in order that the train could feel its way tentatively. Or one would have to chain them all to one another and blindfold their eyes, using blinders like on horses, turning them into blind cows. Only the eyes of those in the front row would need to remain uncovered, since they could do nothing more than watch the path and tread carefully upon the earth. The others would just shuffle along behind, their hands upon the shoulders of the one in front of them, a mute ghost train in no need of tracks to run on, moving ever forward with uneven breath, whether it be day or night, each limb of the train taking a halting step, though still wanting to feel everything there amid the withdrawal of all friendly relations deep within the incommunicable and abysmal, almost entirely lost.

Were this to happen, time would be erased. The journey would have only a direction, but no destination. It would continue and yet lead nowhere. Senseless would be the question about when you were born, for the day of your death could come long before the day of your conception. Have you never noticed how in a turbulent time everything falls apart? What you take for granted today can suddenly disappear, each of your false dreams no longer a certainty, savings now being a necessity since there would be no interest or compounded interest, since you would know nothing of calendars, nothing of dates, yourself having to roll along among the dreary masses, everything the same and fitting a single mold, though in other ways not, there being no such thing as together or apart, but also neither going nor staying, both the cause and the effect made meaningless. Instead of causality, something that is eagerly attested to and yet never manifests itself, there would remain nothing but the dumped detritus of lost things, which cannot be collected because you wouldn't know when to collect them, their worth having been destroyed and dismantled before they were able to convince anyone that they needed to be saved.

From this point onward there is no such thing as time. And yet what exists from this point onward? Senseless talk. When there is no time, there can be no talk nor will there be, for without verbs language is destroyed, everything scurrying along higgledy-piggledy on the wretched journey. Ridiculous is the First National Bank, as ridiculous as it was the day it was founded. The frost is just dampness when there are no seasons. Ambrose has no credit. There is no bank account, the bills are left unpaid since they are never written in the first place. It's difficult for him to spoon the soup. He cannot find his mouth and cannot eat. Mutsch the cat jumps onto the table and licks the sauce and eats up the strands of meat. Mutsch isn't blind. The animals can still see, for time has not abandoned them.

The animals take control of the town, because once time is taken away from the people, the animal age begins. They storm the bank, and the people devoid of time get the short end when the animals destroy everything after they find nothing in the bank to feed on or satisfy them. Mutsch the cat whips her tail about with angry gusto and roars like a lion: "Everything is rubbish!"

The street sweepers are continually kept busy. They can't keep on top of their duties because the animals' claws mess up everything. The endless stream of rubble overwhelms the street sweepers. They try to battle against it with snowplows while trying to clear a path through it. Yet it's useless. They can't make any headway and remain miserably stuck. Steamrollers are used to try to push back the mass. With senseless haste gears groan and wheels turn, but the rollers remain stuck, valves that have become useless now whistle sadly. Plows and rollers are driven into the ghost train, but the drivers take no notice and only curse that someone has put water in the gas tank, though that's not true, and so they shout, Full steam ahead! as they shake their fists and pound on the motors while master keys are fetched and massive pliers and crowbars, though nothing helps, the town transports remaining stuck in a vise against which the technical staff of the community can do nothing despite all its skill and strength.

Thick and sticky is the ghost train that stands in the road. Locusts surround them that can't be chased off. What good does it do to try to shoo away an irritated swarm? No good at all, and so be patient and wait for the locusts to disperse on their own. That can take forever, especially when the clocks refuse to tell the time and time no longer wants to exist. There is no order for the hour, everything has come to a stop, despite there being no cease-fire for the weapons that are thrown with increasing fury against the unknown in combat. And so you must wait, wait, until the locusts destroy themselves. Perhaps then time will exist once more and the town clock will once again have mercy and move its exhausted hand so that the hour will announce itself, and as it strikes will say with a clocklike voice, *a quarter past, half past.*

But when will the hour finish striking? No one knows, not even if time exists for you again, because no one has any insight into anything. In vain you strive to achieve real insights. But nowhere can you find them. Which is why *The Leitenberg Daily* has to form them for you. The printing presses no longer work, the gears are rusted, the rollers no longer turn, the ink is dried up, rows of type have been turned over by Mutsch the cat, the letters lost. The filthy paper is scratched to bits and stinks. The editor's office is occupied by unknown animals that have nested there and armed themselves with brushes and scissors in order to let no one in. The publisher's office has turned into an odious dump. Someone has forgotten to chase away the young lady who sits at the window where the classified ads are delivered, which is why she still sits in her chair, though she's gone completely mad and says that she is following policy and is strictly authorized to accept only obituaries. The millimeter-high printed line that has been shrunk eight times costs an amount that has been raised eight times over as well. Every now and then the young lady shouts and demands the money needed for a new obituary, yet no one comes. Perhaps the cost is too high for those who remain behind, or the citizens are too proud amid their grief to announce it publicly. The Leitenbergers gnaw away at grief, perhaps because they don't want grief to gnaw away at them, or rather, maybe it's just because they have nothing left to eat. Mutsch the cat and her troupe have polished off everything.

Only the local reporter Balthazar Schwind still works. He is tireless. He is capable. He draws his pointed dagger and writes. He first came into his own at the start of current events. He rides a wobbly bike that traverses every impediment with ease and easily maneuvers with every ghost train and locust swarm. On the fly he reaches the middle of the market plaza. He quickly scrambles up the steps that lead to the gilded aura of Saint Rochus that crowns the column erected as a memorial to the plague. The reporter has already endured numerous battles, and his sharp eye and even sharper camera don't miss a thing. Herr Schwind has survived the end of time, and for him it still exists, and he still records it as one of its new creators. Which is why Schwind will also survive this battle in which he will be the only one to lift himself out of the rubble that he will cling to and glorify for all of eternity. He lifts his convex lens toward the sins and photographs the downfall of time. Herr Schwind sits at the apex of the end of history and is happy. Any reporter would be happy to be there and be able to see it all happen. Something beats in the reporter's breast, and that's the heart that beats *a quarter past, half past,* though it never strikes the full hour.

Still the stony old witnesses stand by unharmed, left, right, not stuffed full with shrapnel, not eviscerated by a bomb. The holy cathedral, the town hall, the old guildhall with its green cupola, the baroque townhouses with their ornamental arches and attendant porticos. The reporter looks on at the disappearing order whose undisturbed framework waits and waits, revealing to him the town's history, which he knows all too well. For him, who still has time, the past has also not disappeared. He doesn't need the folios full of brittle documents, nor does he require the yellowed chronicles in which are depicted those years gone by when men and things still maintained a comprehensible relation and everything was joined one to another and augmented everything else. Schwind knows it all, yet in the face of imminent death it all threatens to disappear, even as a memory that cannot be preserved. No one will know how it all was born and passed on, because soon the stones placed one on another will no longer hold together, even though it won't require a brutal conqueror to bring them down. The stones and bricks will separate from one another by themselves, and no mortar will hold them together, nothing remaining but rubble broken to bits and pulverized, and no one will be there who can save the town archives from Mutsch the cat.

Balthazar Schwind greets the antiquities across from him, lifting his right arm and smiling, and all the buildings send back earnest and cheery greetings in return, towers and tin roofs bow deeply and display a dazzling and glinting array of decorative lights. Today marks the celebration of the eight-hundredth anniversary of the founding and incorporation of the venerable town of Leitenberg. For this a special edition of *The Leitenberg Daily* should appear, but because of present circumstances it must be forsaken. There is not enough paper, as well as contributions, and the local reporter can't do it all himself. In the end it becomes obvious that the town fathers and the citizens have at the last moment forgotten this memorable day. Schwind sat himself on his bike and set out to find people willing to talk. After a quick greeting he told them that he was from the daily paper in order to overcome the grim silence of the grown-ups and the timid fear of the little ones. Then he posed his questions.

"Excuse me, what do you think of the eight-hundredth anniversary? What do you think of the past, present, and future of Leitenberg?"

These questions were met with surprise, if not even disturbance. Mayor Viereckl needed to excuse himself for an important council session in which new emergency measures would be discussed, and therefore said:

"I'm afraid you've caught me at a loss for words. I have no idea how old the town is. I thought it was always just there and has hardly changed over the years. Similarly, I expect it to change slowly in the future, our best hope being for an end to the war, which the clear and imminent emergency measures will bring about, making even more certain the victory that we already anticipate today."

After this forthright explanation, which Viereckl had barely comprehended on the margins of his own understanding, he collapsed into himself and wearily fended off the earnest and somewhat confused reporter with skillful parries by dropping useful bits of news, out of which Herr Schwind could only extract the words *emergency decree*, after which the intrepid newspaperman undertook a further investigation and climbed some steps to land at the office of the town's archivist. The archivist greeted him with a friendly face and responded to the reporter's every wish.

"You know your way around the archive much better than I do, because I hardly ever bother with the past these days, mainly because of the way the present presses at us. You know how I am ready to help you with any information at my disposal, though you must understand that you'll need to find what you need for your article by yourself among the old papers. Right now I have no assistants. Because of this I also need to ask that, should you pull out a file full of documents, make sure to dust it off your-self, and after you're done, place it back in the same spot in order that things here don't descend into total chaos."

The high school principal was so busy running the school that it took a series of long explanations before he understood what the reporter wanted. However, when the principal understood just what he wanted, his interest was sparked by the visit. "How wonderful that you thought of us when it comes to the pride and honor of this town. I can only tell you that our high school is nearly three hundred years old. It's no surprise that so many young men have graduated from here. You also went here, Herr Schwind. We have inhabited the present buildings some fifty-seven years, a long, lovely time. I've been the principal here for some eighteen years and will most likely retire after next year, if the war has been victoriously concluded by then."

"But the town, dear principal, the town!"

"Yes, of course it's much older, no doubt of that. But I don't know much about it. I wasn't born in Leitenberg, but what I'm referring to are the noble ideals that have turned our young boys into able men, a venera-ble tradition that can still be found within every single member of the fac-ulty that stands behind me and with whom I share the same unified spirit."

"Permit me, please, to press a bit further . . ."

"The town, my young, impatient friend, certainly existed long before the founding of the high school, and I can imagine how poor the educa-tion was here before a Latin school was erected."

Schwind, however, was not allowed to see the bishop. Only a canon received him and explained with professional courtesy that the present leader of the diocese was the seventeenth Bishop of Leitenberg.

Schwind winced at the poor results of what he found out from asking educated professionals, but when he asked the common folk, he encoun-tered equally meager results. The reporter met a portly man of roughly fifty on Bridge Street, who, yawning, had just emerged from his house.

"Forgive me, but I'm from *The Leitenberg Daily.*"

"Fine, fine, but who cares?"

"I wanted to ask you some questions about our town."

"I don't know anything about it."

"But wait until you hear the questions first! You don't even know what I want to ask you. What is your name? Your occupation?"

"Are you from the police?"

"No, I'm from *The Leitenberg Daily*."

"Then I don't have to tell you anything. I only have to answer to the police."

"But I don't want to interrogate you. I'm a reporter. It will be in the paper! People will read about you! Just imagine, the special edition! It's supposed to be thirty-two pages. It will be a huge edition. If you could just tell me your address—I assume you live in this beautiful house—then you'll get three free copies. So what's your name, please?"

"Ambrose Budil."

"How old?"

"I was fifty-two in June."

"Occupation?"

"Accountant for the electric company."

"Married?"

"Yes."

"Children?"

"Two sons in the army, somewhere on the eastern front."

"Very good, Herr Budil, very good! Everything is going to work out fine! The future belongs to us! What do you have to say about the eight-hundredth anniversary?"

"Pardon?"

"The coming celebration. The town is celebrating its eight-hundredth birthday."

"My gosh, the town is that old? I never would have thought so. The time, it goes so quickly."

"It's been written about in *The Leitenberg Daily*. Aren't you one of our readers, Herr Budil?"

"Yes, I read it all right, but I didn't see anything about a birthday. So *The Daily* covered it, you say. . . . How interesting! Everything can be found in the paper. In my occupation I hardly see anything. We're also talking about a long time. I know for sure that my grandfather, whose name was Vincent Budil, no, not Vincent . . . that was my great-uncle's name. My grandfather was called . . . wait a minute, I've almost got it, he was called . . . he was called . . ."

"That's perhaps not so important, Herr Budil. Anyway, your grandfather . . ."

"I've got it now, he was indeed called Vincent; my great-uncle was Anton, I'm always mixing them up. Anyway, what was I saying . . . ?"

About your grandfather . . ."

"I know now. My grandfather was born in Leitenberg in 1824. But his father, or so he always said, came from Ruhenthal, the town that they've now closed off. Over there. You know what I mean. He would have been amazed to see that today you're not allowed to enter it! The times sure have changed. Moreover, what an outrageous scandal, for even though there's a shortage of apartments everywhere, they've turned over an entire town to the civil service and the inmates who have been brought there! Are there no penitentiaries? Or can't those crooks build barracks for themselves? You need to appreciate the fact, my good sir, that I have to look on every day as these loafers are led by a military honor guard along Bridge Street right past my nose."

"That's another matter altogether, Herr Budil. What I want to know is what do you think about the past, present, and future of our town?"

"Me? I don't have anything to say to that. I have nothing to do with it, I have no say whatsoever. Leitenberg is certainly old and beautiful, but there's a war on; who knows what tomorrow will bring? I've no idea, my good sir, none at all! You'll have to ask other folks. We all just have to grit our teeth and hope that everything comes out all right. It has to!"

Then Balthazar Schwind spoke to a street sweeper, who, after having just taken a bit of a break, pulled a red handkerchief out of his pocket and blew into it hard. He found it easy to get Johann to talk.

"My goodness, eight hundred years already! That's almost too many to count! But things have always been good here. We'll soon see how it all comes out. Then our great-grandchildren can say how it is after yet another eight hundred years."

With such similar responses the reporter could do very little, it soon becoming obvious that there was little else that could be used as well. Therefore there was nothing left to write about except the flight of Saint Rochus atop the column, who had guarded the town since the plague of

1680. Rochus had also endured the cholera epidemic of 1866, but the people of Leitenberg had not erected any more columns dedicated to saints. Amid the old buildings, Rochus towers upward out of the ruins in lonely fashion. The reporter sits above and cannot take any photographs, and is saddened when he begins to worry whether or not he can develop his pictures. There is still a darkroom, but hardly any more developing fluid, and there most likely won't be any more anytime soon. Undeveloped rolls of film are like unborn children. All too briefly does light touch them, then they must rest in their dark containers until they are brought to life under the shimmering red, though it still takes a bit longer as the new pictures bathe in the flat pans that are gently rocked back and forth. Then they at last see the light of day. Only hopes and silent wishes accompany them in the urge that they fulfill what today is nothing more than a dark promise.

"Someday it will happen!" Balthazar Schwind said aloud as he grabbed onto the stony nose of the saint and looked down into the rubble and the ruins that proclaimed the end of Leitenberg, something that was certain and unavoidable once there was not a single inhabitant who knew anything about the history of his town.

Captain Küpenreiter, an officer from the Scharnhorst barracks and a foreigner from far-off Unkenburg, could never once say for certain what town he was in, it always being just a place where he was commanded to do his duty. From the drawer he pulled out a strategic map and picked up a compass with which he measured distances on the map. After a heavy sigh, Captain Küpenreiter said with relief:

"Look here, Schwind, we're located some three hundred meters west of this contingent—you recognize it, don't you? Here is our barracks. They can hardly be defended in an attack, unless you put too many men at risk, at least more than we already have in the garrison. A strategic retreat here toward the north, where you see the marked path that runs along this undulating slope, that would certainly be the best choice under certain conditions, most of all if we assume the enemy is not able to attack this highly advantageous position and control the path through a continual barrage. Should that occur we would have no choice but to hand over this side of the river without a fight and dig in on the other side. There are woods there that can provide good cover, even from aerial attack. The supply line for ammunition and provisions could be maintained along that road. That's where we'd have to go, although unfortunately that would mean losing the barracks. Besides, they'd have to shoot up the place themselves, and this town here, that's right, the place you call Leitenberg—that's right, just have a look, Schwind, the name is right here on the map—Leitenberg would also be lost. All that would be left would be a wasteland of rubble. It won't be easy, but it will fall to the citizens to have to build tank traps and dig themselves into the streets in order to stop the enemy. You have your doubts, Schwind? You shouldn't! With a bit of courage from the citizenry one can inflict a fair number of casualties on the enemy, even if one cannot stop them in the end."

"But, Captain, the front is two thousand kilometers from here."

"That may be so. I've never actually measured it, Schwind, but we have the strategic map here at our disposal in order to ascertain it precisely."

"You can't mean that the enemy will invade our fatherland, can you?"

"My job is to protect the fatherland! My good man, I am a soldier! For me, the possibility of an attack or the need to defend always exists. I love the country that has asked me to serve it."

"From a military standpoint, is the situation that bad?"

"A soldier does not have opinions, but only assesses the situation according to orders."

"But, Captain, we're talking about eight hundred years of Leitenberg, the homeland, the people of this beautiful region, the citizens!"

"That's all well and fine, but it is of no concern to me. They are, after all, nothing more than hindrances when forwarding the war."

"But you must have a home yourself! Think of your mother, of the house in which you first gazed upon the light of the world!"

"My home—that's another matter altogether! But in any case, one has to forget all that when you're a soldier. Look at this map on the wall. *That* is my home! Look at all the pins in it. The ones with the little white flags mark our positions, those with the blue are the enemy's positions. Our regimental staff prepared it for our next maneuvers. Everything will work like clockwork. Almost like the real thing. In the next few weeks we will lead operations across this terrain. My good man, this will be something that you'll have to see for yourself! In one sector there will be intense fire, and for people's safety we'll have to clear out a village for a couple of days. It's the village next to the firing range. You can see it here on the map,

Schwind, there! It's called Dobrunke. There's no real danger, mind you, but the townspeople are always curious and incautious, so it's easy for something to happen. We officers never like to see something like that happen, because it can make the military unpopular, especially when someone is hit by a stray shot for which any soldier normally would congratulate himself in battle."

Balthazar Schwind says good-bye to Captain Küpenreiter and is sad that the officer of Leitenberg knows nothing about the town, even though so many good soldiers have come from there. Yet no one knows the place any longer, neither the natives nor the strangers. The reporter thinks about who else he can interview. If those who were healthy knew nothing, then perhaps there was a slight hope that the sick would still know something of the town's history. One would think that the head of the hospital, Zischke, would certainly be well informed, but indeed he had no idea either.

"The question that you've posed is far outside my concerns. We have three hundred and twenty-seven beds and twenty-seven spots in the emergency room. At the moment we are completely full, and there's a long list of cases that are waiting for us to tend to them. It doesn't matter to me where the cases are from. We only consider the urgency and the place on the list. No one is allowed to remain in the hospital longer than six weeks except for pressing reasons. For the most part, patients either get healthy in that amount of time or they die. For longer-term illnesses, it usually involves in-home care, the patient either rallying or dying, thereby making it unnecessary to keep him here. The only exceptions we make are for the war wounded. There is normally no special medical reason to support this, but it has to do with remaining humane, for we have to find some way to reward our heroes. National law not only demands this but also the gratitude of the people. However, it would be hard to say what influence the hospital could possibly have on the past and future history of Leitenberg, for in principle, these days all hospitals in the country are alike. Since they are no longer privately run, the differences between them have practically disappeared. Because of that, any further developments in the hospital's running have much more to do with advancements in medicine than the future of the community of Leitenberg. Remember, of course, that we don't belong to the town. We are national. The name 'Leitenberg Hospital' is a holdover and causes confusion. There's a history behind it.

It would please me to see the eight-hundredth anniversary help spread this useful bit of information among the population."

"Many thanks. Would you mind if I asked a patient what he thought of the anniversary?"

"Unfortunately that's not possible. There's no possibility of that happening. Interviews have been banned in the hospital according to a clear policy made by the director, who happens to be me."

The local reporter broods. He feels just fine sitting atop his column, but he also appreciates that it's a last refuge. Below on the pavement everything is already unsafe, because this pavement will not hold up and no longer has any history ever since it has been overrun with locusts. The stones say nothing, they being nothing more than dumb witnesses, since no memory attaches to them. Nobody here can even have such a memory. The old parchments in the town archives are of no use as long as nobody reads them nor can read them, for whoever is still alive is overwhelmed, while the only ones free are dead. What does it matter that the street sweeper Johann Pietsch swirls around the column with his broom raised high when for him the slippery pavement is nothing more than a surface on which to pile up rubbish, one as good as any other, though at the moment Johann wants nothing more to do with it since he's just doing his job. He himself has no idea that Mass was once served in front of this column. Each year, on the name day of the saint who guards against the plague, people gathered here and held a Mass under an open sky. Masses are no longer celebrated. At least not here. There are no people here who would want to hear them, no consecrated priest who can pronounce the creed, no *gloria in excelsis deo*. What is there left to praise? The heavens no longer exist ever since the sky has been occupied. And where there is no heaven, there is no earth beneath it.

Leitenberg has disappeared, but there is no special edition announcing it. The last edition of *The Leitenberg Daily* cannot be delivered. The locusts have made it impossible. There are no subscribers, no one to take out an ad. Birth announcements and obituaries are no longer published. Even the young lady at the front desk who devoted her career to handling these has turned to stone. Everything has marched off to the dumps in long processions, though the locusts are not accompanied by church dignitaries. Mindless legs attached to noses hobble along. Miserably they shuffle along, left right, left—stop. The corporal cries out in a rage, because the procession doesn't move right along but instead scrapes and creaks along, left-right-right-lo-cust. Outside on the teeming heap are wriggling insects, spiders, and worms. Mutsch the cat looks at the mess and raises a threefold ruckus against the Beautification Association. The locusts think it's an anthem marking the sudden appearance of Mayor Viereckl, and so out of respect they remove their hats. They are wildly happy and continue to buzz.

Amid its chilly, golden solitude the plague column remains. It stands tall above the compost. It is made of petrified wood, an ancient tree with mighty knots and bloody boils amid sunlight, a monument to itself that is imperishable. Balthazar Schwind smiles as he looks on at the endless ghost train that stands before him. The ghosts bow and lewdly wobble their rabbit ears, though perhaps it isn't lewd, but rather out of the fear and horror that the ghosts feel when the chorus of locusts chirp their dissonant fugue. The reporter looks down at the sunken spirits of the rabbits and doesn't know whether their mute reverence is directed at him or the saint that he towers above. Most likely it is him, because together the ghosts lift their noses upward toward him, rather than staring at the locusts, nor would monuments to saints mean anything to ghosts. They want the life that they no longer have. They want to be photographed in order to create verifiable evidence that they are there. If it were true then the incorruptible film would provide proof, because that which does not exist cannot be photographed. Schwind would be happy to oblige them, but the rusted apparatus prevents it. Vainly the reporter tries to turn the crank in order to forward the film, but the black box only crunches its worn-out gears and cries out for mercy.

"I can't take a shot of you. It's forbidden. It's the last roll. There's no more film. One quarter, half, I'm afraid it's all gone. My dear rabbits, or ghosts, the good old camera is broken."

"Please, take a shot! Only that which is forbidden can save us! We ourselves are forbidden. What will become of us if you don't acknowledge that we exist?"

"I allow that you're here, but I'm not allowed to allow that you're here!"

"But there's no one here to stop you, to prevent you allowing that which is not allowed. Dear reporter, high up on your column, be brave and don't shy away from the impossible!"

"Your appeal almost moves me to tears. Yet what you claim is not true. The unallowed has been forbidden. I have received the strictest instructions for editing. Perhaps you don't understand why because you no longer know what's going on, but you must believe me! I could be suspended from the fatherland's press corps, be censored, or receive some other penalty."

"There is nobody to ensure that such deadly orders are complied with. We won't betray you, for you are one of us. Don't deny us any longer! Pull out that black thing with the long handle! We insist! Take a shot, right now!"

"I can't turn the film, I already told you. If I pressed the shutter you would appear as a double exposure and that would be poor evidence for your unknown existence."

"Mere excuses, Herr Schwind! We exist wherever one can take a shot of us! It may be a double exposure, but take a shot! We only need to be seen, and that you can do if you are a good reporter."

"You're wrong, for I want to! But I can't do whatever I wish. You should know in your hearts that I have always wanted to report on you. But unfortunately nothing ever came of it, at least since the start of this war. The moment I wanted to do something it was over, and then I could only perceive the pain of the past. But not as having passed, for the pain was there. It's still there, and is incessant. I also wanted to do a special edition on the eight-hundredth anniversary. But the hell surrounding us wouldn't allow it. The fading away of Leitenberg got the best of me."

"But we're still here! You could do a wonderful issue about us! Take our pictures! After the war the Americans will pay a load of money for them. If the problem is that there are no people around, we can fill the gap. So let's just start a new life, and we'll bring you along with us. We are building a new future for ourselves in Ruhenthal. Come along with us to the other side of the river. There are deep woods there that prevent one being seen, making it perhaps even safer from aerial attack. We'll name you the editor in chief of a new newspaper, which we'll call *The Ruhenthal Prospect.*"

"Thank you for this honor, but I'm afraid I can't accept it. The ban is still in effect and will remain so as long as I'm around. I'm alive and real here upon this column where you see me, that is, if you can see me."

"Quick, take a shot! Develop it and come along with us! Ruhenthal awaits you! Ruhenthal will welcome you warmly and take care of all your future needs! You'll have your own special accommodations, a proper bed for yourself alone, a loaf of bread each day, and a double portion of soup for lunch."

Schwind wavers amid his indecision and wonders if he shouldn't give in to the ghosts. He thinks of old ballads about the water carrier who wanted to entice his victims to cross the river. Maybe it wouldn't be so bad to go along, since after the destruction of Leitenberg there will be no more hometown to live in. It is completely possible that he could also preserve himself amid the bewitched realm of the prisoners if he only chose the other shore. And yet, though Balthazar wants to take a shot and presses his thumbs against the camera case, his strength fails. The reporter realizes this is no game and is startled. He wants to lift his legs from the stony head of Saint Rochus, but he can't. Schwind has lost the feeling in his legs and therefore calls down to the ghosts hesitantly:

"I'm afraid I can't do it unless one of you climbs up here and takes the shot for me before helping me down from my lonely perch so that I can join you all amid the muck! But make it fast!"

But no, Balthazar Schwind cannot be helped, because the expectant and extended rabbit ears can no longer hear his voice since he can no longer speak, his voice having dried up. Thus he has to hold fast and follow orders, whether or not he recognizes those orders or not. He is now a part of the column itself, an idle and monstrous piece of fruit that is welded to the trunk. He is caught up in the inevitable and titanic fate of the born reporter who must fulfill his responsibilities whether he wants to or not. To always be there when something happens, that's what the reporter's code states, and Schwind now feels the guilt of his failure. He thinks of his ancestor Prometheus. He was indeed the one who gave humankind the gift of the newspaper, something for which he suffered for eternity. And now all it amounted to was to be welded to a plague column, to wait there and not join up with the ghost train, as in silent agony their offer had to be declined.

The reporter looked on with empty eyes as the train began to again move off into the unknown with no sign of sympathy for the one welded to the column. Only Johann Pietsch still stood at the base of the column, appearing undisturbed by all of the events and remembering his duties as he worked on without worry, battling against the immense piles of rubbish with his broom. It was a touching reminder that in this world there was still a clear sense of purpose and responsibility. But after a few strong efforts the sweeper realized that it was impossible to take care of all the dung and dirt. Johann looked up at the column as if Balthazar could provide some kind of illumination, but the reporter was suddenly no longer up there. Most likely he was free again after having thought about disobeying the rules, and now he could once more take his photographs and make his notes in order to write up a snazzy article about life in the town for his paper. To this end he had left his perch on the column, climbed onto his bicycle, and scooted back to the comfort of his office.

The times had once more become humane. Peacefully the big hand of the town clock followed its proscribed course. Refuse is still strewn about, but the locusts have taken off and there is no trace of the ghosts. Peacefully the sun shines on the gaudy sign of *The Leitenberg Daily*, whose publication is no longer in question. There people stand in front of newly displayed pages and nurse their thirst for war and their hunger for news about the latest events in the city. Above, on the first floor, in the safety of Schwind's brightly lit office, the otherwise impossible is first born, the story having just been finished, which now tenderly rocks in the security of the newspaper's offices before, a little while later, the people gratefully learn what's happened. Schwind looks at his secretary, slaps his forehead in amazement, and realizes that though everything in the story had happened, it existed no longer, it was over, and therefore could be printed. If he hasn't expended every last beat of his heart while pounding on the typewriter, then perhaps he'll last another quarter hour, even a half. The newspaper is time's bandage and shows how things can heal. Read it and you'll be healthy again! The voice you hear is your own, it's a success. Time is also back on its feet, the high point of happiness having been scaled, because the newspaper is back, appearing punctually and available everywhere. No longer can events just flutter away, they are gathered and remain, turned into paper and taken care of for your benefit. Numerous copies end up in the rubbish, but certainly not all of them. Some survive and will still be around to tell your grandchildren the truth.

Thus the newspaper's words prevail over you. The ripened pages are carried out in flexible bundles, the word of the day is finally offered up, still smelling of ink. Carriers run through the city with satchels and thick bundles, paperboys call out loudly with chirping voices on every corner: "Here it is! We don't have to tell you what's happened, because it's folded up four times and printed, it's now dry, it's been saved!" The pages are handed over to people walking by in exchange for small coins as addicted eyes sink into the latest events of the day, though none exist any longer. And so it endlessly goes, souls drinking in a perpetual yesterday, which they are granted as if it were their own. Each recognizes it for himself for just a few moments, feeling blessed by the powers of the editor to reveal the innermost secret of existence, but the words can hold on to it for only a short while, in fact for just a few moments, because even when it lasts for a quarter of an hour, a half, or even a whole hour, after a single day everything is simply over with, an unappeasable desire pressing at the poor townsfolk as *The Leitenberg Daily* unleashes once again the fury of transitory life.

Except for a few copies, each day's edition is done away with when, after an array of fates, the copies meet their end when tossed into the rubbish. The butcher Alexander Poduschka regularly collects old newspapers to wrap his wares in, for he doesn't want to give his customers the officially allowed allotments of meat, sausage, and fat in their naked, natural state. Poduschka blesses each day's printed pages, his faithful customers bringing them to him quite happily since they know he can't get any other paper. And so the victories of our heroes, the disgraceful acts and lies of our enemies, as well as the hardly noticeable article on the special new tax measures are carefully wrapped around thin slices of sausage. Then the headlines become damp and greasy, the clear print blending together in dreamlike fashion. With some effort one can still make out the words, yet nobody likes the melting together of current events, as each yearns instead for the bland food within, crumpling up the useless paper without a thought and sticking it in the furnace in order to light a fire. Such is the fate of the headlines among the people. Soon nobody remembers anything of them. Once more all effort is for nought. What exists is consumed, everything is consumed. No crumb is wasted, because the need for each is immense, and there are many unlucky people who would be overjoyed to have strewn before them the crumbs left behind by naughty children who don't want to eat them. Mother, the teacher at school, everyone had said that one had to be grateful that all of the needy had been so well taken care of during this war. There were no longer rich and poor, only justice existed for a just people. What was taken from the ghosts was given to the people. Everything was the same for everyone. In huge letters, what Mayor Viereckl had told the schoolchildren on the eight-hundredth anniversary appeared on the front of the offices of *The Leitenberg Daily:*

YOUR NEIGHBOR'S SUFFERING IS YOUR OWN JOY

The ghost train has arrived at the Scharnhorst barracks. Leitenberg is behind them. Paul only remembers being led through the streets and the marketplace. The prisoners can once again speak openly, for talking is allowed here as long as it isn't too loud. And so questions and answers shuttle quietly back and forth.

"Did you see at the marketplace that they . . . ?"

"No, I didn't notice it, but when . . ."

"They live as if it were peacetime. They don't have to go without anything but . . ."

"It's easy to feel jealous, yet their day will come, and maybe sooner than . . ."

None of it is true. The prisoners have seen nothing. They have indeed seen a great deal, but what they glimpsed has told them nothing. Everything has become impervious, making strained conjectures useless. The headlines in the vending machines of *The Leitenberg Daily* offered no clues. Despite sharp eyes trying to read the dense columns, nothing was gleaned from them. The war has not ended, imprisonment has not ended, the slaughter goes on. Only belief ventures to penetrate the impenetrable through wishes that soon turn into wild rumors that appeal much more to the dazed than do plausible hopes.

Paul turns around. The town is obliterated. Now it was lost to the depths, a gray cloud of smoke floating above it. Near the barracks it is quiet, because here there are only a few houses with large yards that no longer appear to have any connection with Leitenberg. The streets are unpaved and meander off into neglected cart paths. The sidewalks are marked by long curbstones, but they are also unpaved. Grass and wild weeds spring up among the sand and do not sense the gravity of the nearby town in which freedom no longer exists. There might also be people living here who keep their curtains closed, leave a broom leaning against a wall, or forget a little wagon in the yard. Should it be that there really are people hidden behind these walls, they nonetheless know nothing of the town's oppression as long as they can remain holed up in their quiet neighborhood. Here they have retreated and remain protected from the danger of streets trampled by people who for good or for evil are heaped together. Public announcements are also made here, but they mean nothing, their clumsy earnestness greeted by a supple tomfoolery, causing the edicts to hardly ever expect that anyone will pay attention to them.

The red mailbox is ignored, everyone having lost confidence in the mail, such that it remains empty of all news. Probably there is a yellow notice plastered to it on which one can read: MAIL WILL NOT BE COLLECTED FROM THIS MAILBOX UNTIL FURTHER NOTICE. The power of the town officals to fill this lost neighborhood with nervous haste and disquiet does not reach this far; the normally brazen municipal envoys become shy here and hesitant when stepping up to make an announcement on behalf of the authorities. Who knows if these streets have ever even been swept?

It's unusual for barracks to be located right here in this neighborhood. Usually the army likes being a bit cut off from the town because it can go about its business without anyone seeing the nasty things that go on. In order to be completely certain of protection from prying eyes, every entrance is completely shut, and even in front of the main entrance three guards are stationed. One soldier stands motionless in a guardhouse, one marches with a loaded weapon back and forth, a third stands in the middle of the entrance and denies entry or exit to any unauthorized person. Here one has to have permission to do anything. Yet only a few are permitted, and only under very specific orders, which cannot be violated. Whoever might still want to try anything forbidden will pay for it. Because everyone knows this, that which is not allowed never occurs. Everything is kept strictly in order and therefore nothing really happens, it all just goes according to plan. No one can really say how it all happens. Proceedings simply run right along according to unalterable orders that are fulfilled reluctantly, but without complaint. The proceedings take forever, though they are carried out in herky-jerky fashion because they have been practiced only once. The preservation of the future is guaranteed as soon as the instructions are handed out. Captain Küpenreiter has given them out, he himself not having thought them up or issued them at his own bidding, for he is only here to execute the will of those in the know, though he is not simply a tool of obedience. When Küpenreiter says something, it's clear to everyone and it gets done.

The sentry who stands in the middle of the entrance suddenly shakes his head. This is an agreed-upon sign that the prisoners can move through the barracks entrance. They have earned the right to do so. The slaves enjoy the rights of their masters and are better off, despite their powerlessness, than those who live freely in reduced circumstances. "Grab those shovels and picks!" They're allowed to do so, even if they must do so. The slaves are free. They can listen and obey. They drink in the commands and are allowed to follow them. The soldiers can also listen and obey. The slaves and the soldiers. Everything is arranged, and thus it just happens. The route across the open yard is well known. The experience has been imprinted. One after another like a row of ducks. The citizens of Leitenberg have to remain outside, even Mayor Viereckl himself. The slaves move along on their own feet through forbidden terrain. They enjoy the air of the closed-off district. Together with their masters they share a similarity that allows them to live a shared life. If you're not allowed, then you can't. That spells freedom, Fritz! You're free to do what you must. You must, because you exist. The journey happens as it is supposed to. It follows the itinerary that was prepared beforehand. You see Küpenreiter, who for you is unapproachable, and yet you also sense his closeness. You belong to him, not he to you. He can yell at you, but you can also listen to it because you have such beautiful rabbit ears that can hear so well. Just be careful! You must. Whoever is not allowed will be locked up. Küpenreiter doesn't like to leave his soldiers, because when he screams at people in the town it means nothing. They are not part of the army like you are, Fritz, for only you enjoy the complete and unmediated freedom that disturbingly slips in between the order and its fulfillment. Only those who remain in bondage perpetually feel the inevitable power that hangs cryptically over the free.

The prisoners step one after another into the familiar sheds. They recognize the place, although the room appears to be shrouded in darkness after they come out of the glaring light of day. They know where the rifles are stowed, which they are not allowed to touch. They also know where the picks and shovels rest, which they are allowed to grab. They may take them and place them on their shoulders and cross the yard once again, their eyes blinded by the light. Now they hold in their hands something strange that has been created by the efforts of unknown others. The prisoners arrive by themselves, and by themselves they leave and head back out to the entrance and out of the barracks. The sentries let them pass undisturbed and never once worry about the shovels or the picks, because the prisoners have a right to them. That's why they move along unafraid and march confidently through town. They have a clear conscience, for they are only doing what they've been ordered to do.

They don't have to show their papers, and for that matter they couldn't if they wanted to, since they don't have any to show. They are trusted because they've been rounded up, and they have been rounded up because they are imprisoned. That's why it's all right. If one permits something or orders it, a trust also evolves that forms a set of assumptions that prove true, even if they are not the only assumptions formed. Each single instance cannot be reviewed, Fritz, yet in the army hazy dreams disappear, because here pure essence is realized. You are not just pretending, you are it, a pure essence. That's why you should not worry that no one knows who you are, because you are known, even more than you know yourself.

And so the gathered prisoners leave the barracks through the entrance through which they entered only a few minutes before. No lengthy hospitality has been extended to the men in these hallowed halls, yet what good would it have been if it had. Pure essence and pure purpose won't stand for any delay. You're on top of it all, Fritz. Nobody seems to worry that the youths with tools hurry on through or might become unruly. The ringing sound of the blades being sharpened is seen as harmless. Nothing out of line occurs, nor is one's faith in one another betrayed. Willingly the prisoners fall in together as they gather before the barracks without anyone needing to order them. Such willing cooperation anticipates each command, thus paving the way for the freedom of the trains. The head of the train company must be very pleased. Whenever it pleases him he can see the trains headed just where they're supposed to. Nothing can come as a complete surprise. Everything is there and in order, just as on the first day of creation. Any deviation is out of the question, because it is not accounted for in the plans. No one should think anything special if he hears a train. It's not hard to refrain from certain anxieties if you are hauled off. You only have to come along, which anyone can do. Each single train car is a component of the willing allegiance of the entire fleet.

You want to know where you are headed? That's not necessary, because you'll know soon enough. Everything has been set up without even disturbing you. There will be a whistle, just wait there. Your suggestions and objections are too late, there can be no allowance made for them any longer. If you think that it would be any better in Leitenberg, you've got it wrong. The magic order also rules there. To the same degree. It's better if you don't know too much about it. Abandon yourself to your dreams, if that comforts you, but you shouldn't believe them! Beware of curiosity! It only lays the ground for fear and anxiety as soon as it's satisfied.

The break is over. Everyone get up! Paul walks on, Fritz walks on. All three hundred men walk on together. Even some of the uniformed officers just coming out of the barracks. They all walk on together. They all certainly have a destination ahead of them, because that's the way it is. And so it comes to pass. So it was said in the beginning, and so now the only thing remaining is for it all to be fulfilled. The path falls steeply down away from the dumping grounds. Onward, left, right! Just get on the train. The journey has already begun. Is Captain Küpenreiter waving at the train? Whoever travels along does not look around and therefore does not know. Whoever refuses to travel will immediately be shot, and with good reason. Here foot traps will be set! So forward! Stay in line! No one will hesitate to shoot! Warning! Rattraps have been laid out! No stopping! Watch it! *È pericoloso sporgersi!* So move it! . . . That's written everywhere because so many dangers are lurking. *Latet anguis in herba!* That's what the Romans have already posted in their parks. Everywhere there are warnings against loitering. Vermin are unhealthy and will be spit out in reams. But to spit openly in the train car is forbidden because of tuberculosis. Shooting someone is much more hygienic if there is lime available. The town's plans for disinfection are to rid Leitenberg of dreck. In Ruhenthal it's no different. Cleansing takes place everywhere, and for the same humanitarian reasons is everywhere forwarded, endured, forbidden, and directed. The train is directed toward its destination, and therefore cannot lessen its pace. Leaning out of the windows is dangerous because of the engine smoke, and therefore it is forbidden. The loss of the right hand leads to serious bodily injury. One recognizes a dog by its muzzle. According to the law, nobody has the right to choose his own end. Stopping is forbidden because the journey has begun. If there is no travel, there is no way to pass the time. For proper execution, shake and mix fifteen drops in a glass of water. Not by the trains but rather through human indifference shall you recognize them! Credit and safety above all! A general insurance society versus executions and legitimized assaults.

The train slowly chugs through the colorful morning landscape. It climbs. To the left and right larkspur and scabious and other flowers grow out of the dust of the streets and do not shrink away from the people passing nearby. The street shrinks to a narrow pass that is bordered by fences, behind which plums and apples can be seen. Then comes the freedom of a street that opens out beyond the narrow pass as they slowly move on with their cautious feet, left and right and left and right. Don't look around, like in duck-duck-goose. Whoever travels last, travels best. Caroline always said that it's always better to ride in one of the middle cars, because in any train accident the risk to one's life is much less there. The window has to be closed in order to guard against the engine smoke. Otherwise kernels of soot can become lodged in the cornea and one has to then carefully wipe them away. But above all, travel on. It's not so steep now, and the engine runs along freely. No one had better pull the emergency brake! Any mischief will be punished, because it will disrupt the traffic, as well as cause danger. Take express trains that only stop in a few stations. Enjoy the luxury of a dining car. It's an endless journey that no one should have to finish. Fritz, the passengers should get on well with one another! Children need to be kept on a leash in the train. Exceptions are only tolerated in especially dangerous conditions. The journey's final destination needs to be reached on time, and everything must be executed punctually. That's why the soldiers have brought along their rifles. You take part in the journey at your own risk. Orders are only followed, fear is superfluous. No using the facilities when the train stops in a station! The fruit gardens, the vegetable fields, it all can begin to rot. No, let your fear fall by the wayside; it should have gotten off at the last stop, it's a blind passenger, a lost piece of luggage that no one inquires about. Fear will be auctioned off by the stationmaster and sold or stowed away behind the impenetrable fog, or in the river that flows into Leitenberg and passes by. Eventually fear will be swept into the sea in which everything is lost and through which it will be transformed by the sharp corrosiveness of salt. The execution is over, but what it leaves behind will merge with all fears and be carried to the grave.

The mortuary in Ruhenthal is empty. Stamping merrily, the horses wait outside in front of the transport wagon onto which the bearers slide the coffins. The dead have attained the peace they deserve. They have not sought their death, but they have attained it. It does not matter where the end has been fulfilled. What matters is that everyone has met his end even before the journey commences. Sorrow is slight when vanity is not allowed to adorn it. Once summoned, the forbidden find it easier not to exist. The fulfillment of a command is no longer expected. The briefly held services for these dead are not decked out with memorials. Death announcements are not mailed off. There are no funeral clothes. Somber faces do not hang around. The ancient prayers and farewell songs are performed, but with marked hurry, certainly not because there is just one, but rather so many to say good-bye to. Time is pressing. It's very cold in the hall. Two weak lightbulbs cast a murky light. On each coffin there is a note. Otherwise those left behind, who have shown up pale and half frozen, won't know where they should put them in the half hour they have to serve life's transience.

"Where is Father?" Zerlina asks in an even tone.

"I believe he's over there," Caroline answers woodenly.

Paul bends over to inspect the writing on the note cards. "No, Father is here."

Then they walk over and stand there. Leopold is dead. He didn't want to die in Ruhenthal, but he didn't make it and was taken away before he could go home, which is what he always wanted.

"It's not so bad here, everything is all right, though it could be better. I want to get away from here. A doctor belongs in his practice. I'll go to the Ministry of Health and give Dr. Kmoch a piece of my mind. The patients are waiting. I need to help them get well."

Leopold is sick. He lies in his narrow room on a rough wooden bed-stead. In addition to him there are seven other old people. None of them has any strength. They cough. They are sick, but they will recover. That's what they have promised themselves and said to one another. Nurse Dora doesn't disagree. She is impartial. She comes and brings soup. She brings a bedpan. She brings bone char. She carries away the spittoons. She takes the broom and wraps it with a damp cloth when she sweeps so that the sick don't cough as much. Once a day the doctor comes. His name is Dr. Plato. Leopold had asked for his help. He had asked that a proper diet be pre-scribed. But here the doctor prescribes nothing. Dr. Plato has no time. He hardly listens to Leopold's recommendations. In many such cases fresh air would be recommended. Chronic cough calls for it. But if you open the window here, only dust flies in, and it's much too cold. Here there's hardly anything but aspirin and bone char. That's not enough to handle every-thing, and bed rest alone is not enough. There should be no more than three patients in this room. When the window is closed there's an awful smell. The diet contains too many fluids. The preparations leave a lot to be desired. Dr. Plato has no idea of the requisitions that should be made available to any modern doctor. The new generation has learned nothing, even though their education has been extended by two years. It's madness to just keep giving people thin soup. The heart and kidneys can't stand it. If you just prick them, water will come pouring out, but why have so much going in in the first place? Besides, it would only help their state of health, but as long as the general approach does not change there is no help that will last. One shouldn't be surprised that illness in Ruhenthal so often takes a fatal course. It is the task of medicine to use all available materials and the latest scientific understanding to cure all illnesses, to handle all possible complications in a timely manner, to extend the life of each pa-tient, and to warn the healthy as soon as possible before the onset of real pain. But there can be no talk of that here. Has Dr. Plato never heard of the Hippocratic oath? It doesn't appear he has. Which is why injustice prevails, positions of responsibility fulfilled by nothing more than good-will. Nurse Dora cannot do it all by herself. Someone will pay for it some-day. A Dr. Lustig is forced to haul rubbish, but a young greenhorn . . . ? Leopold does not want to dwell on it too much, yet he is annoyed that the most basic responsibilities have been disregarded.

"That's unheard of, Zerlina, that never happened in my time! One would be ashamed for anything like that to occur. They should let the newspaper know about it!"

"There is no newspaper here, Father."

"Yes, how unfortunate! When there's no paper the public fails to get the necessary information. A healthy press can call attention to a number of problems. The government becomes more attentive and leads an inquiry. I've often seen it. There was a case . . . a case . . . I don't recall now, Zerlina. Have you seen no newspaper anywhere? What's the news?"

"Please, Father, don't talk so loud!"

"I can talk as loud as I wish. Treading softly doesn't suit well my sense of academic honor. I am a free man, do you understand? Nurse Dora understands better than you do."

"But Father, no one says that you are not as free as one can be in Ruhenthal. But look, there are others around you who want their peace and quiet."

"No, Zerlina, that is too much! I am amply considerate, that I know. The patients are fond of me. I was always against having so many patients in such a small room and amid such unhygienic conditions. Dr. Plato doesn't want to listen to me. You can't blame me!"

"Take it easy! I'm not blaming you, but please, please, don't shout so, I implore you! There is no evil intention behind there being so many in this room. There simply is no room."

"What do you mean there's no room? If there's no room, then one indeed has to find some! If people do right, everything will go all right. Otherwise not even all of Ruhenthal will do any good."

"Please, Father, try to understand! People do mean well, at least Dr. Plato does. But—are you listening?—it's the ones who sent us here that don't."

"Ah, yes indeed! You mean . . ."

"Yes, them. Which means we must be patient. Things will surely get better. That's for sure! Soon we'll be on our way home! That's what I heard. Paul said so. Many others as well."

"I did ask you, Zerlina, whether you had seen a newspaper?"

"No, I haven't. But someone told Paul that there have been bombing runs done under cloud cover, but for real. Supposedly *The Leitenberg Daily* wrote about it."

Leopold smiles happily. Zerlina straightens up his bed and props up the pillow. Leopold stretches and says cheerily, "Thank you, Zerlina. I'll soon be back on my feet. Nurse Dora completely agrees. I'm half a doctor, but the good half. Lying down so long has weakened me and is not conducive to the lungs. I need to practice standing and walking."

"Soon, Papa, soon! Just be patient a while longer."

"You always say 'soon' . . . ! What a strange child you are, Zerlina! Tomorrow I will get up. I've no time to lose!"

"Good, Father, tomorrow we will see how you feel."

"Nonsense, we won't see anything! I'm fed up with waiting. Whoever lets himself go goes to hell. Next week I'll go back to my job again on the garbage detail. And next month we'll go home. I will write down my experiences from here and publish them. About the hygiene in a prison camp and about the prevention of a lice epidemic. I have it all here in my head. Bring me a paper tomorrow, Zerlina, and a pencil as well. I want to make some notes now. As long as I am still of service, any free time has to be made full use of."

Zerlina promises. She had promised something each day for the last year, for the last eighteen months. Caroline promises. Paul promises. Dora and Dr. Plato and everyone promise. They promise Leopold and one another the impossible. They promise it to themselves. They are white lies, unjustified hopes, unfulfillable wishes. Borrowed dreams that will come to nothing before reality sets in and demands that the false premises on which they are found are acknowledged. Ruhenthal is an impenetrable thicket of loaded questions and warped promises offered up from loose mouths. Everything is overheated and unhealthy because of the widespread proliferation of rubbish, which the garbage detail can no longer keep up with. Piles of rubbish fill up every courtyard. Foul odors rise from sewers and toilets that can no longer be cleaned. Darkly clad figures wearily creep through the rotting slime. Complaints of lost riches stumble exhausted over the sticky drains.

"At home everything was different. We were rich. Regular guests at Semmering and Cortina d'Ampezzo."

"We weren't that rich, but we lived well, I'd say. Once a week we went to the theater or the movies! In summer we sometimes went to Fuschl, sometimes to Pörtschach, or traveled around."

"I don't miss the movies that much. But the Sunday drives to Spessart and in winter the walks in the countryside. It's good that I brought my winter clothes with me, because the weather here is nearly always bad."

"The weather isn't actually that bad, but the hunger is terrible. I wouldn't give this soup to my dog."

"One shouldn't continually think about food, for things go better then."

"That sounds fine, but only if one can stock up first."

"We always took the six twenty-one train from the central train station and by eight o'clock we were in the open countryside. I always packed a knapsack with some tasty items. In the middle of the forest we'd find a little place with a bit of meadow and some golden sun above us. Then we'd lie down and get comfortable. We rested, then Rosa would unpack the provisions. We gobbled them up and then closed our eyes and sunned ourselves. In the evening we'd come back tanned and refreshed. Most of all we were happy when the entire day was beautiful, making sure toward evening to head back and get home just in time before a thunderstorm let loose a cloudburst and it poured. Usually we didn't eat anything more, though Rosa always had fresh salad and stewed fruit ready, and naturally we were very thirsty. A lemonade tasted wonderful then."

Leopold listens to it all and now and then says something in reply, but for the most part he talks only about medicine, about patients, about new therapies and unusual cures. The frail men in the room talk to one another about the riches of the past, for they are of the temperament that simply does not want to talk about Ruhenthal. They also say that everything will soon be as it once was, if not better. Only a little patience is needed, but that is not hard, because they also survived World War I, and back then they were not in the safety of the hinterlands. The old men also wanted to know from Dr. Lustig what he used to do on his days off.

"On Sundays I visited only the most pressing cases. That I did in the morning. In the afternoon I went to the Café Bellevue, where all the newspapers were brought to me because I knew the owner. I could always be reached there, because who knew when it might be something important. A doctor who goes on vacation when it's not absolutely necessary is unprofessional. One always has to be there and should never let someone stand in for him, if at all possible, in order to best follow the patients' course of recovery. At least that's one thing good about Ruhenthal, the doctors can't go anywhere."

Then Leopold stops talking about his practice, as he steadily gets worse. The day passes slowly for the sick. He waits for the nurse, for the doctor, for a visit from his family. Leopold listens for steps. Sometimes he tries to take his pulse, but can find none. He blames it on the clock. The second hand doesn't work. The clock needs to be fixed. Leopold wears a yellow nightcap. His white hair is unkempt, yet he does not want Dora to comb it. Only Zerlina is allowed to do that. Little gifts are brought to the old man. A slice of apple. He should swallow it down, but it would be better if it were pureed. Leopold has no idea how bad off he is.

"That's only due to being weak, my dear colleague, just temporary weakness. I need something to build my strength! As soon as my condition gets better, I'll be back at work. But I'm not going back to the garbage detail! I'll be a doctor again and push through pressing reforms in Ruhenthal. Nourishing food, my dear colleague, will buy me time! But not that raw barley that won't pass through and clogs up the small intestine. You should give me chicken! Only the white meat! Or veal!"

Leopold no longer speaks. Only the others in the room speak, but with muffled voices, because the old doctor will not live much longer. His limp hands nestle into the gray blanket as he dozes. He no longer bats away the fleas that jump upon him. He hardly reacts anymore when his wife and children visit him. They stand there helpless and want to say something sweet. Caroline holds a small bowl of gruel made from rice that she begged for, but Leopold doesn't even look at the gift of love. Mechanically his hand grips the spittoon. He can't lift it to his mouth; he holds it upside down, the cover opens and the disgusting contents drip out before Zerlina can help. Nurse Dora washes and whisks it all away with a cloth. The mucus annoys Leopold. He can't cough it up, he can't spit at all anymore. Leopold is propped up, but it does no good. His breathing becomes heavy, his mouth hangs open, the lips are slack, his eyes large and glassy. Dr. Plato scurries by and knows there is nothing he can do to help. Only out of courtesy does he stand there for a while. The nurse sees that the end has come. Everyone knows it. Zerlina calls to the old man as his consciousness flickers in and out for a short while.

"We'll soon be home, Papa! Do you hear? Home! Everything's fine. Maybe even next week! Then we'll have a party with roast goose!"

Leopold's lips whisper in a monotone. "Roast goose . . . that will be a triumph. . . . Little Bunny . . . he'll get meat . . . not bones. . . ."

The battle with death lasts a long time, through the night and into the next day. The man in the next bed is quite religious. He hardly ever lets his prayer book slip out of his hand. He turns the pages, he hesitantly calls out the holy names and reads aloud many passages in a low voice.

"That helps. The Lord giveth and the Lord taketh away. Praised be the Lord! Forever and ever, amen!"

The color empties from Leopold's face, the rattle in his throat is quieter and less frequent, his breathing is weaker and more superficial, his breast barely rises and sinks. The fattened fleas creep around and out from under the blanket and gather on the wall like a band of troops. In Ruhenthal that's a sure sign of the arrival of death. Even a feather hung before a mouth hanging open no longer moves. Everything is still. Only the pious neighbor has sat up in his bed, his lips moving expressively as he prays very quietly and very fast, his head moving softly back and forth. Caroline closes the eyes of the dead. Nurse Dora closes the jaws and binds them. Paul takes off the yellow nightcap that sits crookedly on his father's head and shoves it into his pants pocket. Zerlina strokes a lifeless pale hand.

"Father is gone. He was the most scrupulous person I ever met. He never understood the ways of the world, but he knew his patients like no other. He was an innocent fool. They murdered him here. They let him starve to death."

"We certainly did not, Fräulein Lustig! I have constantly portioned out food fairly, and rather than short any patient I've even given them some of my own portion."

"I certainly don't mean you, Nurse Dora! Don't you realize the truth? Have you no heart at all?"

Paul and Caroline go back and forth about it.

"No, it wasn't the nurse, nor anyone in the room, but those above them, the murderers, the violators of all souls!"

A last look at the deceased. Then the nurse pulls the sheet over the head of the corpse. Caroline yearns to see him once more.

"It's better not to look again. Take from his things what you can use!"

But Caroline doesn't want anything, nor do Paul and Zerlina. They stand there silent. Then Paul gives a muted sign. Caroline understands and takes Zerlina by the hand. They slowly leave the room, exhausted, anxious, and hungry. The neighbor continues praying incessantly. Then he looks around in earnest, but furtively, and waves toward those left behind as if to assure them that he will follow through with the recommended prayers to the end. Then it's all over. In the dark street a dreary rain begins to fall. Night has fallen earlier tonight. The passersby whisper intensely and in a muffled manner. Work is done for the day. Life begins. Today there's nothing happening. A pale blue desk lamp furtively turns on. Feet slog unwillingly through cold puddles. Ruhenthal gasps amid an uneasy slumber. Only the mist from rubbish rises in hidden pits. The chorus is silent. Above the small podium appears the gray beard as it casts a long shadow over the numerous coffins. Then the voice is heard.

"And so we think with gratitude on our dearly departed, because they are a part of us and we are a part of them. All of them who have passed on have fulfilled their responsibilities as fathers and mothers, as sons and daughters. They have all accomplished something imperishable in life and that is more comforting than all the grief we feel. They were all true children of their people and worshipped the eternal. We, however, we who are gathered before these coffins, have the responsibility to humbly bear our loss and to not be swallowed up by our own pain, but rather to think of the example that the departed set through their works, and courageously face the coming days, since from us further accomplishments are expected, from which we may not shrink with a good conscience. If at this moment we do not know by what means to conquer our loss, we must also not despair in saying farewell, but rather let us say as one, remember us, Lord, Thou who created us, of whom it is written, the Lord giveth and the Lord taketh, praised be the Lord. . . ."

The last oily hymns are poured out. This makes cleaning the streets easier. The dust is knocked down and sealed in. Easily and elegantly the broom glides over the pavement. Tar is poured out. It has been warmed in large pans. Now it flows slowly over the street, coaxed by broad wooden spreaders, a dark syrup, blood gone black, honey of the dead and their inextinguishable memorial, poured out from large drums and pressed into an iced cake. Consecrated hymns of execution turn into a celebration of innocence. Merry hangmen in white robes have imposed the verdict. Farther and farther the pitch flows and is spread by long squeegees that spread it directly onto the low arches of the cobblestones before it sets and hardens forever, now already composed and hardened, no longer answerable to the fire that melted it amid death's drunken gurgle. The men who have been awarded the honor of this work stand by in dignified manner, because it is good work that they are doing. No day without a good deed. The former professor of theoretical philosophy agrees. To oil the earth is good. The air is clearer, the buildup of mud in bad weather is greatly reduced. Pavement means dryness, peace, security. No one sinks down when walking upon it, because each step is secure only when there is a road that will hold one's footing. Dangerous roads are closed off and forbidden. Only the workers are granted access. They apply themselves to the strange and transform it into the familiar. To break through to new worlds is the job of the philosophers. Whoever can, does; the good deed is accomplished without complaint.

Fine macadam is spread upon the tar with flat shovels, and then soft wide squeegees evenly distribute it. Once more orderliness has won the day. Now the steamroller effortlessly completes the task by reducing the stone and tar to a uniform smoothness. Proudly and slowly the heavy machine passes back and forth. The motor rattles, levers and wheels move much faster in preparing the way for the dignified entrance of the steamroller. The macadam is tamped down, embedding itself completely in the tar. The path is rescued, the dust banished forever. Out of friendly hoses water is sprayed, now the street is ready for everyone. No one should be forbidden from using it again. The philosopher takes a modest bow: now the job is done.

The dead know nothing of this. They can take no joy in the changes that have indeed occurred. Defenseless and without fuss the corpses allow themselves to be coffined and carried off. The whip snaps, the transport driver sucks harder on his pipe, the horses move forward with a hard jerk. Slowly the funeral train begins to move as it sets off as the last escort. The living like to follow the dead as far as possible. Gratefully the living follow behind as long as the wagon continues to roll along, but when the cargo reaches the barrier they are suddenly prevented from fulfilling their responsibility. A sign informs the funeral train that it has reached its final stop. And so it stands there. It cannot follow along, though it can watch the process that then unfolds. Two policemen look at the wagon that sets off slowly, their eyes asking, You dead, do you have anything to declare? Only their eyes ask this, not a word is spoken. The policemen look on with their dark brown eyes and smile in knowing readiness. The last honor of the dead. They are allowed to leave without a pass, the coffins never once being counted. The barrier lifts high, the wagon pulls ahead, duty-free and as free as a bird. The dead have nothing with them, nor does anyone question that they do. Their death, their honesty is not questioned. No one demands, "Open all your coffins!" The horses pull more vigorously and Ruhenthal's load of human freight sways across the sand-based macadam and tar. The barrier falls, the farewell is completed. Merrily lurching ahead with sprightly speed, the funeral wagon rumbles along.

But why did the policemen wave the coffins through? Why didn't they call out to them? The authorities wanted to avoid the accusation that their orders are not carried out promptly, for the dead only understand action, and no longer words. The authorities are humble and wise, they don't interrogate the dead and content themselves with proudly presenting their indifference, so that only the aura of the secret magic of power can be resented by the living. Through fear and anxiety the shame-faced execution is brought about quietly and slowly, but also knowledgeably, for once the state has done its duty it retreats to the guardhouse by the side of the road next to the barrier. Bon voyage, you dead, but you the living are here, that is, until you go to hell!

The mourning party stands still, the heads stretch forward slightly, the eyes longingly gaze past the barrier, the wind causes a few tears, the funeral wagon already has turned the corner, no longer visible, the hammering of horse hooves echoing. Everything is kept hidden. All the details following each execution are taken care of. Each hanging is practical and quick. The cut fruit lie there, already cleaned, still warm, crisp with distorted eyes, the gallows rope wrapped around their throats. Nicely arranged, ready to be sold in a Sunday market. They were only criminals, not people. Villains who have fallen to the level of rubbish. Military honors are denied them. Bored, Captain Küpenreiter removes the blue-and-white flags from his map. The press photographers are allowed in, Balthazar Schwind is granted a new roll of film. Everyone has to wipe his shoes first, since the prison administration does not trust that the freshly tarred road is indeed dirt-free. Each has to be inspected for lice and aphids, since the prevention of contagion must be maintained. Left or right, it doesn't matter, both arms must be lifted, then both legs. Plague has broken out, but the serum from the Institute for Infectious Diseases has arrived, the authorities tracking as ever the course of the epidemic. After an injection the dead pose little danger. Thanks to the barrier, the inoculations are kept to a minimum.

"And here we have the executed! Use the fleeting nature of such sins to create a horrifying example that will do your readers good. You may look at the executed goods from all sides and photograph them, but under no circumstances are you allowed to touch them. No mementos may be plucked either, neither hair nor whiskers nor nails! You are in the presence of death. Control yourselves. Exchanging bodies is out of the question. The names on the attached foot tags are guaranteed to be correct. Copying any of them will be severely punished."

The press photographers stand there rigid and are busy with their cameras. Each snaps a few pictures. Floodlights are turned on. The dead enter the dark grave, rolls of film head to the mortuary. There it will be developed, the Institute for Infectious Diseases having provided a good developer, not even the butcher Alexander Poduschka having a better one. The pictures turn out superbly, the spitting image says someone, and are developed on white, shiny paper, then enlarged painstakingly, almost to their natural proportions. Wonderful materials for study. The dead look so alive, almost like the originals. The city archivist has sealed them so that they neither get moldy nor are eaten by insects. It's such a pleasure to look at them. The high school principal asks for a few of them since he finds them so useful to look at in class. The butcher Poduschka doesn't get any because the readers of *The Leitenberg Daily* cut them all out. He has to pack the sausage into the holes in the paper, though it's not his fault. The corpses are secretly cremated, but the photographs remain there in eternal infamy. Throughout the land one can buy them, carry them home, and put them in the family album. There is now an excellent artificial glue for photographs that is made out of tar. And so the memory remains, set down for all of time, though the meaningless dead are long gone.

The mourning party turns around and breaks up into smaller groups that trail off into the wind. Ruhenthal takes in the living once again, the execution is called off and done for the day. It will be continued, yet nobody thinks about it for the moment. There is no time for grief, for life wants its own due, and for that reason the cadavers are taken away from Ruhenthal. The crematorium situated on clay soil in the middle of the meadow works well and reliably, and there hasn't been the slightest complaint about it since it was opened. It works fast and is free of dust. The ashes are filtered and crushed and converted from morsels to crumbs, which are then spread upon tar and quietly pressed into it.

As soon as everything is finished and the remaining mourners have withdrawn, Caroline lets herself be helped by her son and daughter, though it deeply hurts her to do so. The husband belongs at the side of the widow at all times, not the children. But what happens when the man has hidden and run off? No good husband does that. Was Leopold a good husband? He was never there when you needed him, for indeed he was a person devoted to service who had no notion of love, or at least responsibilities toward loved ones. Slowly she shuffles along the path and says not a word. Caroline feels weak and is happy that the children are at her side, as they carefully lead her by the hand through the town. Then suddenly the gray silence is too much and the mother must say something.

"Now we are alone. We will all die here. There is no point in having any illusions, those were for your father. Soon our hour will strike as well. My hour, not yours. You must not remain here. Both of you can go back."

"Mother, don't talk that way, please! You know that I read *The Leitenberg Daily* from the day before yesterday, and in it they wrote . . ."

"They've written that for ages. That has nothing to do with us, us most of all, no, nothing at all! They've been writing that for two years already!"

"But one day it will be true."

"Who knows what the real truth is? It's all humbug!"

"You can't talk that way, Mother. You have to control yourself, if only for us."

"What for? There's no longer any point. You're both grown-ups. Wasn't the old man right after all?"

"You're upsetting Zerlina. One has to believe in something in order to keep on. Good never dies. Evil will meet its end."

"Evil never dies either. For us it's just begun."

"Stop bickering! I need to go make my little boxes and I don't want my head full of such worries. I can't stand it anymore! You keep yanking me back and forth! It's enough already, really enough! Moreover, Mother, we still need to give something to Nurse Dora. I want to give her my colorful scarf with the small narrow edging, or half a loaf of bread. Also a bit of bread for the roommate who said prayers."

"Give, give, nothing but give! They've all gotten something already! We just don't have enough to keep giving!"

"I'm fed up! Ugh! I am completely fed up!"

"Zerlina, of course I'll give something, my child. Get a hold of yourself, please, at least in front of the people on the street! What will they think of us? I will give them bread if I have any to give."

"I don't care what others think. I'm fed up, that's what I said! They let the old man starve! We didn't do enough for him. . . ."

"Don't say that! We did what we could. We went hungry ourselves in order to save a bit for him. As a result I'm a wreck. And I don't even want to tell you how you look. In any case, it would be best if you didn't look in a mirror."

"They killed him! That's what I told Dr. Plato. They executed him! I know it. They could have saved him. He could have saved himself if he stole like the others, but instead he let himself be robbed."

"You're talking nonsense, Zerlina! What happened has happened. We should not fight on this day of mourning. Paul, what are you going to do today?"

"Nothing. Tomorrow I'll go back to the firing range."

"Good, Paul, let's walk Zerlina to her boxes."

"No, no! Please just leave me alone! I can't do it. So please just let me go and be merciful! I have to go my own way alone. I have to be by myself and think other thoughts. As long as you are at my side, that's not possible." Zerlina kisses her mother. "You are a poor devil, Mother. There's nothing you can do for me. But you don't understand. You will never understand, but that I wish you from my heart. It is better, a thousand times better, if you never grasp it. To forget, and never to know what can't be forgotten. In times like these, that protects the soul from misfortune. Be well! Paul, be well!"

Zerlina breaks loose and goes her own way. Paul looks after her, observing her hasty feet, left right, left right, her feet hurrying and her nose cold, feet hurrying, unhappy feet. But one must never look into the future, the plague memorial is already too old to even have a future. One can only wait, just as the street sweeper waits for fresh trash. Leitenberg will surely continue, left, right, in the future. Ruhenthal, however, will descend into sleep. A different sleep than now, a sleep beyond sleep, not just a deep sleep. Paul takes his mother under the arm and brings her to the front door of her building. His mother lives there; Paul is quartered elsewhere. Perhaps something was said along the way, though Paul cannot remember precisely what. He had to look down at the ground in order not to stumble, left and right. Before the front door he hears the brittle voice of a stranger. Perhaps it was Katie Budil's voice.

"Thank you, Paul, thank you. You've helped us so much. You are a good son. Please let me be now!"

Paul walks off, a tall, thin youth, his legs heavy and clumsy, feeling lifeless. It looks as if he is counting each step. Caroline looks after him for a good while. Why is he so sad? It can't be only because of the father. Paul doesn't belong here. Young men don't belong in the city of the dead. Old people can stand that for a while, and when they die it's not that tragic. The young should be elsewhere or should hide. Here among the old they are lost and can do nothing to help them. They don't want to believe the worst, because they simply cannot, and yet that's the way it is. Their faith is only the courage to have faith. Through that there is a future despite all else. And so the days roll on, as if blown away by the wind. If Caroline can just go to sleep, that is good, but it would be better if she did not have to wake up the next morning! A life lived by arbitrary grace. So you live without living, only the eyes bring pain. Yet you can't be so serious. You forget with time. Above all, forgetting is the forward course of life, for there's no such thing as remembering more, nor do you become more clever, for all that happens only in school. Yet you are easily fooled and then do not see how things really are. You are diminished more and more through life's changes. At the beginning you are deceived, then later disappointed, meaning that the deceptions fall away like powder after a fancy ball. There are no hopes, when Caroline thinks hard about it, because instead there are only deceptions that you wear like makeup, as life goes on pleasantly and all its many unpleasantries remain hidden from you in order that they not be discovered all at once if you were to stand in front of a mirror. Whoever cannot hide anything will soon be unhappy and will stand there with empty hands. Everything is taken away. People will go after anyone who has something. Then comes flattery, beseeching, and begging, though Caroline would go crazy if she gave away anything. Zerlina is the complete opposite, which is why there is nothing left of her but her naked soul. That doesn't go far in Ruhenthal. Here you are not given anything, and most certainly so if you give too much away. Caroline is clever. She leaves nothing in the open. The money is well hidden. Many times her place has been searched but nothing is ever found. The thug who was led around by cross-eyed Nussbaum had looked at her hard and demanded the truth.

"Hand it all over! If you tell us straight off where everything is you can go scot-free!"

"I don't have anything. How then am I supposed to produce it?"

"You have two minutes to think it over."

The thug whistles and looks at his watch while Cross-Eyes looks at her as if he were ready to bite her head off. Time's up and the fool screams, "We'll search through everything. If I find anything, then you . . ."

"I don't have anything. I swear it."

They then rummage through everything. The contents of her bags fly out in arching bows. Every piece is minutely inspected. Curious onlookers gather around in circles, the family also stands by, worried, though everyone is chased away eventually.

"Powder! Where did you get powder? You're already white enough and certainly don't have to powder your nose."

"Indeed, my nose is always so shiny. I have always powdered it."

"Shut your mouth or I'll have you up on charges before you know it."

The powder is dumped out. Perhaps a piece of gold could be hidden in the powder. Underwear lies crumpled on the floor, food could be wrapped up in between. The cake has been cut into small pieces. The heels of shoes are banged. A needle is used to poke into the cover of a suitcase. Fingers probe the seams of dresses, looking for money that's been sewed into them. No success, all effort has been wasted. The thug becomes enraged: "I haven't found anything! You must be hiding something!"

"I don't have anything. I'd be happy to give you something, if I had anything. But I'm afraid where there is nothing, then . . ."

"What's that? Shut your mouth!"

Even the body search turns up nothing. Caroline knows better ways to hide money. Whoever tells the truth loses. And so you have to be clever. Which means talking only when it's of use, just as in cards. First you bid, then you pass, and then you trump! Everything can be taken out of its hiding place, though one has to be careful. Whoever goes too far will pay for it. You'll be locked up and beaten. Above all, you have to hide your thoughts and feelings, otherwise you will give yourself away and stand there with nothing left. How hard that was for Zerlina! Without that, no one can be helped, and all that's left is disappointment. Given the way of the world, Caroline has to meet it head-on. Only fools want to make the world better. In the end such idiots are the laughingstocks; that is the only reward their goodness deserves. One just has to be happy to survive without being stomped on. Leopold is dead, whom Zerlina takes after, though less so Paul, who is somewhat different. The song is over, the band has stopped playing. Caroline had not always sung along, for the tune was often too difficult to carry. Leopold was a good man, but still he only thought of himself. It never occurred to him to think about what a young wife might need. Caroline didn't need much, certainly not luxuries, and she certainly didn't need to be pampered, but a bit of care and attention would have been good nonetheless.

Leopold was blind in both eyes, for he saw neither wife nor children. Only the patients. "Caroline, you don't understand. Women have no sense of professional responsibility," he had yelled when she dared to disagree. Leopold kept everything hidden inside. They all do that, one after another. His candor was made possible only through a naïve game of hide-and-seek that he played with himself. He had cut himself off and didn't know himself, but rather only a few basic principles. He had lived by them for decades. If you asked him something, you knew in advance what the answer would be. He was a child whom Caroline had to take care of without getting anything in return. Nor had he ever worried about Paul and

Zerlina. Of course he had been happy when, as children, they looked so sweet and wore such pretty clothes, but it was Caroline who had always taken care of it all, Leopold never having worried his head about any of it. "Children are women's business. A man cannot busy himself with such stuff. The patients are waiting." What were they all to him? Certainly not people, only patients! But everyone is a patient, even when medicine knows nothing of their ills because they are so deeply embedded that they cannot be found.

Which was why Caroline had to come to grips with it all on her own. Now that Leopold is no longer alive, there is less for her to worry about. He had lost nothing as a result, for he had little idea of what one really had to endure in Ruhenthal. It is better for him now. Paul will quickly find the desire to go on. Men don't mourn as deeply as do women. For Zerlina, clearly such desire is evil. Her mind is set. She sees too much, but what she should see she does not. She judges Caroline, because she supposedly did not do enough for the old man. That is nonsense. Caroline had never been angry with him for being so neglectful. On the contrary, she had made his life easy, even here in Ruhenthal. Here most of all. If she had not econo-mized so well, producing hidden money again and again as if by magic and trading bits of clothing for food, she could not have made Leopold's soup tastier and cooked extra dishes for him. Which is why she has been reduced to skin and bones. She has sacrificed herself because she did not want to be at all responsible for the old man's collapse, nor did she want to constantly have Zerlina's reproachful glances before her eyes. He certainly did not starve to death, he always had something to eat. The entire ward envied what he had. Every day, no matter the weather, Caroline visited him at least once, if not twice. Like a little hungry dog he waited for what she brought with her: "Show me, Caroline, show me what you brought! Hmm, that's good, that tastes good! Bring me some more of that, if you have any left!" But where she had gotten it, where she was supposed to get more, Leopold never thought of that. It was all obvious to him, just order it up and stick a napkin in his collar, just like in the days of peace. Not even once did he ask whether Caroline and the children had enough to eat. Though that was only half true, Caroline had to admit. With sincere yet clueless eyes he had often asked: "Do you all have enough? Certainly you do, Caroline!" She didn't contradict him, but neither had he pressed the matter.

Just before he died, Leopold began to withdraw. "You live on the moon!" Then Leopold grew angry and said no, much like a child who has been asked whether or not he is there who then quite innocently answers from his hiding place, No, I'm not here! Such a person does not suffer much, one in whom everything is buried and never sees the light of day. It is easy to be a good man when you let all of your worries roll off you and, whatever happens, you take it all in without comprehending. No, he really did not suffer. Zerlina must not say that he did. There are poor devils much worse off than him who have nobody here and are wretchedly hungry because no one makes sure that they get what they have coming to them. But that's the way of the world, one gets something, another gets nothing. When there's little, one has to make do. Hunger is a mean commander, which is why Caroline is not surprised so many in Ruhenthal had become disreputable. Who indeed can be trusted and does not take from his neighbor whatever he can grab? If you don't join in, you end up with the short straw. Anyone can remain above it all as long as he has a surplus. In a pinch everyone is as bad as the next. No one should think himself capable of setting an example for others. Anything can be bought for a piece of bread, but you can also sell your soul for it as well.

Whoever takes things as they are can come to terms with it all and at least carve out a bit of happiness for himself. Caroline will live differently now that she no longer has to worry about Leopold. Then it suddenly occurs to her that she can no longer visit him. Indeed it's all gone, the day asserts its rights. There's not even a cemetery where one can tend a grave. During these times there is nothing left of the dead, sentimentality having disappeared. Memorials have been deemed out of style. Caroline almost has to laugh when she recalls that there even was such a thing. If she really thinks about it, she really has to concede that the piousness and care required by graves were only an insincere bit of comedy that had to be played out by family and friends. Here no such theater was played anymore. Instead there was just naked life, rather than drama upon a stage. There were no longer disguised feelings. They were all made clear, whereby it also became obvious that everything was a complete sham.

Caroline grew up in the upper middle class. The walls were almost completely covered with paintings. Throughout the entire apartment you could not see what was behind them. In the salon there stood a bulky piano with an embroidered silk doily and numerous figurines upon it. A boy strangling a goose, a child pulling a thorn out of his foot. They were all very beautiful, but also impractical, made out of white alabaster, or maybe it was only plaster. All of the children took piano lessons, but none of them actually played. Soon the piano lid was shut, the keys were at rest. The instrument was never touched again and darkened over the years, a monument that was always in the way, each day gathering dust that really needed to be wiped away. Back then everything was hidden, hypocrisy burying the truth, much more so than later, because in general everyone was doing well. If Caroline were now a girl of marrying age, she could turn down Leopold's proposal. There were younger and handsomer admirers whom you could choose from at your leisure. But only Leopold was there back then, no doubt the marriage having already been arranged. He didn't ask much and he didn't say much, and soon the parents were in agreement. Caroline was presented with the facts. And so the marriage was sealed.

Caroline could have resisted, yet she would have been too ashamed, so she did not protest. Her parents explained that Leopold was from a good family, a doctor, an educated man with a promising practice. There was nothing to decide, Caroline was still young and had hopes for the future. What could she have said when, after a year, the disappointment set in? Absolutely nothing. Divorce was not yet the order of the day. It would have been a scandal throughout the entire town. Many years later Zerlina blamed Caroline for not wanting to separate from Leopold. She would have done it, but by then it was really too late, for it seemed heartless to leave a helpless old man. Today everything is changed and nothing matters. Life is a mess. Ruhenthal is closed off and hidden from the world. Old people here know nothing of the world and can go no farther than the barrier at the edge of town, and even then only when there is a burial. The barrier, however, is still raised for the young. If only Paul would decide to escape! The countryside is huge, there are many little villages to hide out in. But Paul is a good-natured, wishy-washy person. He fritters away every chance and never seizes the opportunity. At his age Caroline would have been long gone over the hills. Paul's indifference is worse than laziness. Events just sweep him along, and he just goes along without a fight. Caroline cannot depend on him. Zerlina, however, is nothing more than a bundle of nerves. She is too stubborn and always has her neck in a noose.

Then Zerlina wonders why she can't catch her breath. Staunchness only makes sense when it is joined with courage and skill. The girl is too excitable, and that's why she overdoes it. Early on Caroline had hidden too much, but Zerlina hides too little. According to her, whoever immediately spoke the truth had no burden to carry. Yet every little thing need not be brought into the open, for then you die a day at a time and suffer agony. The girl is just hysterical. If I didn't keep her in line constantly, we wouldn't even be here. She'll be the end of us by constantly confusing her dreams with reality. Ruhenthal is no summer vacation.

"You have to finally learn to keep what you think to yourself a bit more."

"Things are different for you than for me. Do you know, Mother, it would be better if you stopped lecturing me. You're not going to change me. Nothing will change me. You should have sent me away before the war even started."

"You didn't want to go away. I suggested it to you and Paul again and again."

"You're the one who said so . . . ! Because you knew that I would never leave you both. I am what I am. I've come to accept that, and that's why I'm asking you to let me be as I am."

"You're making yourself miserable, child! You're not helping yourself at all. I don't want to talk about me and the others."

"You're not talking about yourself, but you only think of yourself. What do others matter to you? Look, Mother, I know what you're like, I know exactly what you're like. And yet I've taken it upon myself to stick by you and the family."

"Worry less about the family and more about yourself!"

"You say that, but as soon as I go my own way you turn to look at me accusingly and are cold to me. You make it seem like I'm being egotistical. But let's not go into it!"

"You've got me wrong! It's wonderful when people stick together, but one also has to think about oneself a little. You accomplish nothing with your self-sacrifice. You only put everyone on edge. For it's something that is easier said than done. You keep accusing me, but you're a lot like your father. One has to keep an eye on you, otherwise you'll be in a mess before you know it."

"You don't have to worry about me. I've never demanded anything for myself. The old man . . . let's not talk about him. You stayed with him, which is your own doing. You can let me go in peace. I can take care of myself."

"You can take care of yourself all right! If I didn't keep a watch over you, you'd be in fine shape now! There would no one to take care of your things, to warm up your food, to darn your stockings, and yet you have doubts whether anyone loves you, that nobody thinks about you, that nobody cares about you."

"Please, don't do anything for me! I've always gotten along just fine. But since we're on the subject, is it really all that much, what you did for me? It was nothing at all, and you know that yourself. It's miserable to even waste words on any of this!"

"Please, don't get so upset! I'm only stating the truth, a part of the truth, which you love so much. Zerlina, you need to remember, no one accomplishes anything in this world if all you do is bang your head against a wall! You have to have reserves that you don't tap until the very end, something hidden, secrets. . . ."

"I have no reserves. I don't want to have any! Where has your constant carefulness and caution gotten you? Here we sit in Ruhenthal, Frau Lustig! What a beautiful destination, our dreamed-of fairy-tale castle, our gingerbread house! What else do you want to deny while someone has you by the collar? You can deny all you want, but no one will ever let you go free again."

"Okay, we're trapped, we're trapped! But . . ."

"There is no 'but'! Everything is finished! Caution and frugality and denial no longer have any point, so to hell with them! The song is over, Mother! Do you hear what I'm saying? Whoever doesn't live life to the full now has never lived!"

"You always live life to the full, and yet it is no life that you live! Zerlina, you've exhausted life! And whoever isn't careful now will be finished!"

"We're all finished, dear Mother! It makes no sense to fight against it. We'll get through as best we can, but each has to go her own way, you yourself and I myself."

"And Paul?"

"And Paul has to go his own way."

"Paul won't make it. He relies too much on you and me because he is so weak."

"I won't talk about Paul with you."

Caroline tries to come to terms with it all, but she sees that it is hopeless. Now that Leopold is gone, everything is falling apart. It cannot be helped anymore. The more pressure there is upon people to keep them locked up, the more any sense of togetherness dissolves. Life has become full of holes, great gaps have opened up, spaces between tiny islands. No one knows anyone else. What one says and hears never coheres into one view. You still think that you stand on solid ground until all of a sudden you fall into a hole. When you finally realize that you have fallen into a hole and are lost, you can yell all you want but nobody comes. Should someone happen by, he either doesn't see anything or has his hands full or doesn't have the time to help. There is no such thing as family life, for here there is only hell. You keep on as if there is no such thing as love or care, but rather only the agony that people suffer. Caroline is too weak to resist giving someone the shirt off her back. Any talk of togetherness is nothing but lies, much like the silent piano that the dust motes shower dust upon, though nobody has the nerve to haul off the old crate.

Since Ida is gone, Caroline has only her roommates to talk to. Ida and her crippled hands have left. Whenever Zerlina comes in and behaves as if Ida will sit down next to Caroline at any moment, she can hardly stand it. It's unbearable when Zerlina greets them both. It's crazy. What would Ida think of it? Each should meet her fate alone, but that's not what happened to her. One day they were told that two thousand people had to leave, strong men and women ready for work. Sort them out from among yourselves, you're forty thousand people in all! Anyone under twenty for sure, you won't mind it at all, such a small bloodletting won't hurt at all, so off with you! Off with you! Don't ask the reasons why, or where you're headed. What matters is: we need you! Don't say anything about already being prisoners and that should be enough. No, that's not enough, we want more from you and think it fine if we throw you all together. Prisoners should travel, the world is wide and bright, you should see some of it!

Here you're so packed in one atop another! You complain that the rooms are too full? We're happy to assist you and provide Ruhenthal with a little breathing room!

Why do you all hide? Whoever hides will only be discovered, and he won't like the journey from there on out. You're all free to go. Report! Off with you! You don't want to go? Okay, then it doesn't matter if we force you to take a journey. We're telling you what the law is. It's slavery. It always manifests itself when it's not wanted, that's its nature, because otherwise there would be no slavery on Earth, and people could rest easy. Step forward if you want to be condemned to slavery! That amounts to self-condemnation, in which the strong are victorious and the weak are defeated. All of you, get ready! We will take you on the journey. Each of you can bring yourself along as well as some bags, though not too many, because otherwise the journey will be uncomfortable, and you still have to be herded together. We just wouldn't feel good about it, trains that are too full are bad for the railroad.

Onward a little farther. Maybe even backward. Leopold had often wished for that. After the war . . . that's what he always said. That is not necessary, for even during the war one can travel. It does one good and enriches oneself to experience the wide world, for it nourishes life. You all can see for the first time how many towns there are in the countryside. There's plenty of room for you, for you don't need much. The horizons of travelers are broadened, and you always valued education so much. Can you appreciate the fact that we're doing all of this for you for free? All we ask for in return is your life, thus the price is cheap, for what is your life worth? Used up and worth nothing! No one would think of buying it, and so it belongs to us, and we're shipping you off. You have nothing to lose, and only something to gain. Whoever doesn't know how to help himself otherwise, just go with the flow! Get yourselves ready and don't be late, because in three days we'll be picking you up. The song is over.

And so they selected Ida. She is a widow on her own who can travel. Nobody will miss her since she has no family here. A sister with children doesn't count. —But Ida is so sick and helpless. —Doesn't matter! —The terrible rheumatism that's gripped her hands. —Doesn't matter! —It says only those who can work. . . . Ida can't because of her hunched back! —Doesn't matter! —She can cook. She's been darning stockings for years. —One can't just sit around quietly patching clothes in Ruhenthal. Off with you! Ida is number twenty. During the war small intimate bonds are ripped apart that no longer can be patched together. It's not bad luck to have to leave. Soldiers travel, and so can Ida. —Where to? —The soldiers don't know. —The course of the war can change. —Ida won't die in battle, at least as a prisoner she'll be looked after. —No, that's not so. She can only die. —But anyone can die anywhere. With a knapsack on their back and a rifle. —Ida doesn't know how to shoot. —Doesn't matter! Anyone can learn. —She might keel over because of her hunched back! —It's good when one bends one's back. The bullets fly over and then she won't die. Only the twentieth one dies. —But Ida is the twentieth. —But not out of those who die, only out of those who journey on. —Ida is not very fit. —We'll turn her into a canteen woman. —That's inhumane! —No, the war is very humane.

Be brave, Frau Ida, be brave. Back home there will be a welcome awaiting you when it's all over, yes, back home. You say that you can't imagine greeting anyone again? Don't be ridiculous! Life begins at sixty. Your neighbors will take care of you. Does that mean you'll be looked after? Why, of course it does, which is why we're taking you along, in order to better look after you. —But Ida can indeed be taken care of here. . . . —No, that can't happen. Whoever is looked after must willingly accept such care. But Ida doesn't want it and bristles at the idea, needing to be coaxed like a young girl as she cries and complains. She doesn't want to be hooked up to a freight car, she doesn't want anything to do with a cold, heartless train. She loved the man whom she married, not like Caroline and Leopold. No, Ida most certainly will not travel, she has a heart condition, she isn't up to the rigors of the journey, she is not even curious, she is handicapped, she has no interest whatsoever, none, really, it would please her much more to stay in Ruhenthal. —That's nonsense, how can she just say that when she isn't even convinced of it herself! Is it really all that nice here? —Of course it isn't, yet she knows what she knows; unknown happiness hurts more than familiar pain. —Enough of this useless chatter! There it's completely different, and Ida at least has the chance to make the comparison. After the war, after sharing her greetings once again, Ida can say what it was like back then and there, and what she found to be the nicest part.

Ida concedes that it's a trap, a bad business with no good intentions involved. If it were not bad, they would not keep secret the journey's destination. If one can get along here, what need is there to be elsewhere? There's no reason for it, this journey is a waste of time. . . . —Useless considerations, Ida, for it's better to just give in, because then you won't worry your head about it all to no purpose, for nothing clever ever came of that. If we really did have bad intentions, as people assert, then the journey wouldn't be necessary, the evil deeds could be done much more easily in Ruhenthal, for the fortress graves are wide and deep enough for all of the prisoners to fall into after being shot. No, there is no danger threatening anyone. The journey is taking place in order to answer the most pressing questions. Everyone who remains behind should be grateful, and even more thankful if they travel on, for they will have it much better. The table is already bedecked with white linen. The flowers stand in the vase giving off their scent. Old folks homes with silky gardenias. Sanatoriums with community rooms and numerous good doctors! Parks with comfortable benches on which to rest in the sun, in the shade, however one wishes. It will be a new home, comfortable, friendly, and healthy.

But where will it be, sir? —No, that we can't reveal to you. —We're ready to get away from here, we love the train station. Best would be if you just let us go free. Come on, just tell us, where is this long journey taking us? —It's a surprise, dear children, a journey into the wild blue yonder. Soon you'll be there and will see it all. Just get in here, for it will be a long, long train with an able locomotive placed at the helm. It's whistle will howl out your song the whole way through so that every switchman and stationmaster will understand, Attention, attention, they're coming, keep all tracks open in order that the train is secure and has a secure escort. Nothing can stop it. Our trains are reliable and have the lowest accident rates of any trains on the planet. The automatic signal system brings any train that is going the wrong way to a stop as soon as possible before any catastrophe occurs. Everyone knows this, of course, for even before this our train system was renowned. —Yet the question still stands, who knows where we're headed? Someone has to know! You can't just send us off into thin air, into just nothing! —How many times do we have to repeat what we've told you? Into the wild blue yonder, into the blue! Okay, that's enough yapping, just get ready for a surprise! The final destination will please you all!

Ida got her little piece of paper. The messenger had not even knocked. He just stood there as the light was quickly turned on, because it was the middle of the night. There was nothing on the piece of paper except

SCHWARZ, IDA—6/1/1882

That was all, and yet it made her cry. Caroline also wept. Everyone in the room wept. They are so sad in the middle of the night and cannot sleep, although nothing has happened. Just a piece of paper. Ida is exactly the same as everyone else in the room, one among twenty. What would happen if there were only nineteen? Could you hide out in the attic for three days? In the cellar? Sickness will certainly save you! For sick people the journey into the wild blue yonder is not healthy. Then the doctors show up, they look at the thermometer, look down the throat, they take the pulse, they do everything that doctors are supposed to do. Then they say: "Be patient! You will hear from us!" Ida should hide out among the dead. Being dead for three days is not too long. If you are not alive then you don't have to leave. Then the journey is postponed and postponed once again. But Ida cannot die, because she is alive and there. She will have to take her own life, but that she does not want to do. And so she lives and will journey on, because the doctors have said that she can travel. Her life is not in danger; all she needs is some powder to take along the way, yes, the same powder that Dr. Lustig had ordered for her and which always helped. Certainly, as soon as she arrives she will have to be placed in a doctor's care, though she will be looked after, for she can take a written referral with her so that one can be informed about the condition of her heart, excessive strain to be avoided at all costs, though they can do what they need to since there are good doctors everywhere who know their craft.

"It all depends on the choice of doctors, my dear sirs. Here I'm satisfied and am used to the ones I have."

"That's your mistake, dear Frau Schwarz. Whoever gets too used to things in these times must suffer."

To wander is the miller's joy. —That's right, but a journey all the way to Jutland seems a bit much! —Who told you we're headed to Jutland? —Supposedly Lippe-Detmold, a lovely town! —No, maybe Strassburg, by chance. . . . But that can't be! Innsbruck, I must leave you! Ruhenthal, I must leave you! Oh world, I must leave you! Don't leave anything! Take it all with you! You'll need it. I must travel, I fear, and say good-bye to my true dear. Singing is not allowed because of cramped quarters. Will you, my dear boy, come with me? I'm not a boy, I'm Ida Schwarz, widow, sister of Caroline, Caroline Lustig. Will you, Ida Schwarz, come with me? I don't want to go; the song is over. I might catch cold. Impossible, the journey happens in sealed cars. This prevents any drafts. You can sit such that your heart points in the direction of the journey. Otherwise one sees nothing at night. The journey's direction leads straight into the future. Only in large stations are there any lights, but only a few, because for the most part there are just freight cars. Even a heart condition does not allow you to lean out. So stay inside the car! Duck your head! Beware, high voltage! Touching wires, even by the downfallen, is dangerous. Keep your skull inside! The butterflies are flying around, though they're actually moths. Don't turn on any lights, otherwise they will burn their wings.

Whoever is cautious journeys the longest. The Italians know this already, *chi va piano va sano*. No, no *piano*. That creates dust. It's forbidden to bring along musical instruments because they disturb the peace. Whoever stows away a violin will be thrown out, the song is over. —If it were a journey to Italy I'd have no trouble traveling without a piano. Sun and seaside resorts help my rheumatism. —Yes, but they're supposed to be bad for the heart. —Excuse me, but will we be allowed to send mail from there even if it's not Italy? —No, it won't be necessary, because you'll have everything you could ask for. —As a child, Caroline collected postcards. —Nonsense, she is not a child. —Fine, but she still needs to know how I'm doing. —There's no need, no one will feel lonely! —But not to be in touch by mail is horrible! —You can live without mail. Just think of yourself as dead and the appeal of correspondence will soon be lost. —But you're mistaken, I'm not dead. Which is why I was shipped off. —Yes, of course, that's right, pardon me, I forgot that. . . .

"Excuse me, Frau Schwarz, sorry to bother you, but now you really need to think about packing!"

Ida and Caroline get up. They realize that this day's journey can no longer linger in a dream. Maybe Ida will still be able to stay if a miracle occurs. But one can't count on that, and so it's best to get ready. Ida must not overexert herself. She must above all take care of herself, and mind her hands. Yet she still has to sort through all her things. It's lucky that they can still talk. Only the orders shouted into the room are a disturbance, but afterward it's quiet again for a little while and one can catch one's breath. Ida needs to eat regularly. No, don't give anything away!

"So this frock can stay here, Caroline, you can have it. Maybe Zerlina can alter it if it doesn't fit you."

"No, Ida, take it with you! You'll need it, especially when it rains. It will be very damp there."

"The suitcase is too full for me. I can't carry that much. I'm wearing what I need most."

"Fine, but the frock hardly takes up any room, so you can surely pack it."

"I most certainly won't need it there. You can exchange it for some bread in order to have more for Leopold and the children. It's made of lovely material. Just feel how soft!"

"No, Ida, that's a practical piece to have with you, you look so lovely in it! You also need to have something beautiful to wear in order that you don't look like a poor beggar woman. Maybe you'll have even better luck bargaining for something there."

"For bargaining I already have my silk shirt and my boots. They're very good ones."

"But they take up a lot more room than the frock. Take my advice, Ida! You also need to hide something away for yourself. As well as a supply of food."

"I prefer to have that in my pockets so that I can have it with me on the train. You never know if you can keep your suitcase with you. I like to have everything right on me."

"You're right. And don't forget your medicine, the drops for your heart."

Paul runs around. Zerlina runs around. They want to prevent it all from happening. It is also said that the journey will not happen. That it will at least be postponed. There were still no wagons waiting. —But they will come. —You can't say that. As long as they're not here there's still hope. —There's nothing to hope for! —Whoever just gives in to his fate might as well let himself be buried. —That would probably be for the best. —Please, be patient! Maybe the war is over. Miracles do happen. It's not so rare after all! —No more miracles will happen today. They're long over. —There are black flags hanging. They seem to be mourning something. The war is going badly for them. They've lost another thousand aircraft. —That doesn't matter. It's all happening a bit late for us. That's why it doesn't matter who wins the war or who loses, because we have already lost it. —But there are still so many here in Ruhenthal! —Only for a while longer! Soon they will come for us. They're just waiting for the schedule. By the end of the war nobody will be left here. Only a fool would think otherwise, no one will escape. —They just need able workers. —That's a joke, for they're only sending away people who are really sick. Ruhenthal is not a safe place to hide.

"So, Paul, what have you heard? Have you arranged anything?"

"No. Nothing for sure, yet. But maybe. I spoke with someone. If he can, he said he will."

"Have you promised him anything?"

"I have. In fact quite a bit. I don't even know where I'll get it all. I've set something aside. I told him I could get the rest to him after the war."

"That won't mean anything to him. Anyone can promise something after the war. Here and now is what matters, Paul."

"I'll take my chances. But he says he's not that way. He believes me. But he's also afraid."

"He's only afraid if there's too little in it for him."

"What you've given me is a lot. But unfortunately not enough. Yet I know he'll trust me."

"Go, Paul, I beg you, now go!"

Then he's outside and looking for him. He tells him what he can give him. He gives him what he has. It's not enough. Paul ends up with nothing. Only promises. If it's possible. He swears on it. Not easy. Dangerous. It could easily go wrong. Paul is much too weak. One has to be up to it. Zerlina is more up to it. But she won't pay such a price. You cannot give up your sense of honor. You simply have it. It's a part of your skin. You don't carry it to market. No one can demand that you do. Decency cannot be bought. There's nothing he can do for his dear aunt. Also nothing for his mother. Zerlina won't even consider it. She'd rather get on the train. Here decency means nothing. And thus Ida has to get on the train. Caroline has made her some nice soup. The last meal of the condemned. Ida needs to build up her strength. She is still here. One roommate donated some noodles. Another, a teaspoon of dried vegetables. A third, a teaspoon of real fat. No, not just margarine. Such good soup warms you right up. Ida also receives a bonbon and half an apple. Dessert. Caroline refuses the quarter portion offered her.

"We're so sad to see you go, Frau Schwarz. It's the least we can do. . . ."

But after the war. Soon it will come. Everyone is waiting for it. From there it's just a bit farther to home, but one can still travel back. First class, which is only fitting. Though Ida has never traveled in anything higher than second class. But then it will be time for first class. That will be wonderful. For we are the victors. We are picked up and brought back in triumph. The trains are decked out like young girls. It's a celebration. The song begins. All the cars are full of gifts, namely those who have been saved. They are given lipstick and powder in order to get themselves ready. They still don't look so good. Soon they'll be better. They're given everything. They marry. Good men are brought along. Each chooses the right man. Bright banners and colorful letters. WE ARE FREE! Everyone can see us. We're not nuns. The veils have been tossed away. The children play. WELCOME HOME! At every station refreshments are laid out. Free buffet. The prettiest girls have been selected. Cute little dresses. The girls approach the train carrying cups of hot chocolate with fruit tarts and wrapped-up little gifts. Ida eats until she is finally full.

All fear has disappeared from the world, no one has to hide anymore, nothing has to be hidden. Jewelry is worn again once more. Freedom, freedom, to sit in one's own apartment! How nice to sit next to the furnace. Just feed it another shovelful. There's enough coal in the cellar. The curtains are drawn. No one can look through the window into the room. How wonderful it feels to sit so nestled in! Bunny the dog is back. He's never wagged his tail as much as he does now. At last the dear lady is back. Everyone is here. Now Bunny can go for a walk. At last everything is right, and no one speaks about the old complaints. What you suffered the day before is no longer bad today. The journey is over, no one says anything about it. Parties go on for an entire month because peace has returned. Indeed, everything is much more wonderful than it has ever been, for only now is freedom truly valued.

Then the Society of Ruhenthal Veterans is founded. Every week they get together and play cards. Each dresses well and tells stories. Each member wears a badge that has the Ruhenthal coat of arms on it. Reunions are arranged, one weekend a year in Ruhenthal! Caroline will lead them. Everyone will come. The railroad will offer reduced prices. In Ruhenthal there is music and many speeches are given. Poems are written, the newspapers will cover it all. Everyone will say that he was there when it was so bleak and no one believed it would end well. The times change. No one will hide his joy. Most of all, Ida will laugh.

Caroline looks up. Ida looks at peace, almost pleased. She has slept for a little while. She is not as anxious about what will happen, but concedes that she can also get along there. You only have to maintain your patience, you cannot give up your courage and will to live. Ida promises Caroline that she'll keep her will to live, there is no need for her to worry so, for it won't do any good. Then the women see what Paul and Zerlina have done. Zerlina arrives and announces what she has heard, namely that the old people will indeed not be taken away, which means no one over fifty, because only really able people are needed there, not any sick ones, new guidelines have just been handed down. Everyone breathes a sigh of relief, the danger is gone.

"Ah, children! Now, that's better! You'd think they could have told us sooner!"

It appears to be true, not just a rumor, everyone talks about it openly, Ruhenthal is full of good news. No one will have to go who is not really suited. No one wants to kill us, they only want us to work. Just as Paul picks and shovels away on the Dobrunke shooting range back in Leitenberg, so many of us will end up doing the same. Not everyone is needed in Ruhenthal, there are no factories here. They will have to go off to the countryside, and where one works is where one also meets other people. There our young people will not be so cut off from the land, so they won't have to worry about sustenance. Caroline wants to unpack everything, but Ida resists doing so.

"I haven't seen it in black and white yet. No one can be certain until the departure happens."

No, nothing is certain. Additional news spreads. Everyone must go. Everyone must go who originally was supposed to go. The healthy will work, the sick will be taken care of. Thus Ida is saved, for she doesn't have to work, though she has to go nonetheless. But that can't be so bad. The journey won't take that long, a day, then a night, maybe two days, three at the most, certainly no more than four. In any case it must come to an end sometime. As long as you are on the train, you only have to sit there and not worry about anything. There's no getting off. That's the advantage of the special transport. You get on and you get off. In between nothing happens, the train just keeps going. Afterward everyone can rest, especially the sick.

The travelers must gather together. Ida cannot remain, but she is still there. She can take a little while, no one will mind. No one will miss the train. It will wait for all of those who are traveling. Until the departure she will still be there, nothing will happen to her. She can remain there, she can indeed. She can laugh and cry, she can feel happy or sad, whatever she wishes. Ida can hardly walk because her feet won't do what she wants. But the sick stand there waiting. The luggage is taken away. "Have you made sure to mark everything correctly?" Yes, everything is in order. With soluble chalk the name and date of birth have been scrawled onto the top of the suitcase. Anyone can plainly read it. This suitcase belongs to Frau Ida Schwarz, née Schmerzenreich, who first saw the light of this world on 6/1/1882.

Back then she was suddenly there. She left her hidden sanctuary and screamed for the first hour of her life. She was taken care of and her first warm bath was prepared. The midwife was a capable woman who understood her job. "It's a girl, Frau Schmerzenreich!" she called out joyfully. And Caroline now had a little sister. The child was named after an aunt called Ida. She was a darling child, so good-natured and cheerful. The parents were overjoyed with little Ida. She grew up and was soon big and as beautiful as a flower in a poem. She went to school, learned how to cook and sew, she sang and danced, fell in love, got engaged, and then she got married. It went off in splendid style, for all the relations approved. The wedding table was decorated elaborately and looked even more beautiful than when Caroline was married. There were many guests, each with a flower in their buttonhole. Some had come from far off just to be there. All of them had brought gifts. Caroline and Leopold gave them a marvelous coffee service for twelve, white with a wide gold rim. Ida was taken aback and touched by the many expensive gifts and cried, as young girls often do. Soon Ida would be very spoiled, which suited her just fine. Her every wish was fulfilled. There was money in the house and it was transformed into decorative goods or jewelry. Lovely clothes were sewn and acquired, anything Ida's heart wished for. A son was born, named Albert, and he grew splendidly. Then, unexpectedly, came a difficult time when she found herself a widow. Her husband died suddenly after dinner. He just stood up from the table, gave a little cry, followed by a heavy thud, a heart attack; he was already gone by the time Leopold arrived. Yet Ida was well looked after. There was a large building with a wonderful apartment, some savings, and a large insurance payment. Ida lived for her Albert and was happy, for the son grew tall and was good.

But one day it all came to an end. The good son suddenly took off for the haven of America. There they needed a talented photographer. Ida, who loved Albert above all else, was glad that he had left. Soon Ida had to move out of her luxurious apartment and in with Caroline. That was not too inconvenient, because Leopold's waiting room stood empty and he could take her in, even if she wasn't a member of his immediate family. That's the way it was and no one could tell Leopold any different. Yet after a year had passed, Ida had to travel with Caroline and family to Ruhenthal. The good son was in America and could not know. As soon as the war is over, Albert will come back; a good son doesn't let his old, sick mother wait an extra hour. That will be the loveliest day of Ida's life. Yet she hardly talks about it, for just mentioning his name fills her with worry. Also, Caroline's children can easily get upset, and Ida is careful around them. One talks about what is nearby and thinks about what is far off. Ida hears her sister say, "It's good, Ida, that we are all still together. At least you're not alone. Together we can better get through it all." Ida agreed. She didn't carry along the good son with her to Ruhenthal. He should not have a thing to worry about. She will never say his name until the war is over. Whatever will come to pass is inevitable. It's only lucky that she can share such danger and privation with her next of kin, because a widow on her own in this world . . .

"We will never be apart, Ida! We won't let oursleves be separated!"

"No, Caroline, a thousand times no!"

"Certainly not us!"

"No! No!"

And yet Ida is off. And you, my dear, remain here. You must, I must. There is no other way. Should we let Albert know? It would be too hard on him. She doesn't pass on her greetings, instead she will see him again one day herself. The journey is inevitable. America is off in the wild blue yonder. Only in the blue. An invidious song. And even that is over. Leopold is so old. It will be hard on him. At least it's fortunate that he no longer understands. The poor man. No, Ida has it much worse. One has to plead that she be allowed to stay, to do everything possible at the last moment. It's never too late to try. The entire family can go with her. Certainly. There's nothing to it, nor would it be too much of a sacrifice. Leopold is over seventy-five. No one will take him. Only up to sixty. Almost the very same age at which Ida must still leave. You can't plunge an entire family into trouble just because of one person. But it's not trouble! Who said anything about trouble? No, it's not trouble, it's orders. It can't be helped. There is nowhere to hide, and that's disappointing. You expect everything to be all right, but soon you find that bad things happen fast. You don't get up. Better to just pull the blanket over your head, for that's also warmer.

The suitcase is already gone with all of its goodies inside. Memories for a better day. Why better? All right, of earlier days. All days are alike. They pass. They crawl out of their caves and then they are there, then they creep back under the earth again. Only man remains. He runs along throughout the day and knows nothing. Or do the days run through him? How about the mayflies? They don't outlast the day and remain caught within it always. They don't see that the sun rises and sets; thus they live in an eternity. To them the sun appears eternal, eternal is the light. They are the happiest of creatures, creatures of fable. Something like Zerlina. Each moment is full of tender life, without any worries about food or drink, then comes a gentle death that harms no one.

Ida holds her bags in both hands. From her shoulder a large bag hangs and a small knapsack is attached to her back. Everything is precisely labeled. You can read IDA SCHWARZ from any direction and know immediately how old the lady is who is traveling with you. Notice in particular the birth date, you dear fellow travelers, for then on the first of June you can congratulate her. It won't be too long before the date rolls around and a couple of sweet words will make Ida happy.

"But how do you all know that it's my . . . ?"

"We saw it on your bags and that's why we brought along flowers. It's so hard to get flowers here, yet what we won't do for you!"

"That is so sweet of you! I will never forget it."

Yet Caroline will not be among the well-wishers, nor the children, whom Ida loves as if they were her own. Nor Leopold, who rarely came around, though he was always there for her birthday. Meanwhile her dear Albert is safe in America.

"Where are my family members?"

"Holed up in Ruhenthal. They would love to be here, but it rained too hard and because of that they didn't catch the train."

"That's not very nice. They should have arrived at the station an hour earlier."

Caroline cannot stand the guilt she feels. You don't allow a sister to travel alone, at least not in this war. Ida is gone and so are all the others. Separated from one another. The song is torn in two. Different train cars. The railroad does with people what it wants, no one is never allowed to complain. Please don't forget to send a telegram. Arrived safely. Lovely here. Weather like at home. Healthy. Luggage unharmed. Excellent accommodations. Five meals a day with a wide choice of menu. A comfortable room in the hotel with a view of the lake. On the balcony, lounge chairs with umbrellas to protect against the sun. There you can lie low in comfort. Pleasant company. Charming staff. Running water, central heating. Nearby is the spa where the band plays from morning to evening. Overtures to Martha, Martha who disappeared. Nice relations here. Everything just like home or even better, since you don't have to worry about anything. The cook and the housemaid do everything themselves, no need to hassle them. Everything works without a hitch. The hours for meals are fixed. There is nothing to eat. No, there is something. But it's pretty bad. The potatoes are black and hard. There are only peels. That's why it costs nothing to stay. No need to pay anything, not even the luxury tax on spas. One would only like to know just where the money for such luxurious expenditures is coming from. It makes no sense. This new social order is perfect. The oppression and enslavement of people has stopped, they are all perfect ladies and gentlemen, each as happy as the next.

Therefore no one needs to worry about Ida, given how well she's taken care of. Caroline, Paul, and Zerlina accompany the passengers who are ready to board. Ida says good-bye to her housemates. "Head high, dear Frau Schwarz! It won't be so bad! And then we'll see each other again after the war, it's a promise, so good-bye for now, for now good-bye!" Then they're gone. Only Leopold is not there. He is too weak and is lying in the sickroom. Why bother disturbing the old man as well? He says that it's not fair, but he doesn't understand. It would also bother Ida to see Leopold there. He was in agony as he spoke to her when Ida went with Caroline to say good-bye.

"Well then, Ida, you're off. Safe journey! Be brave! Write us as soon as you can! If you really like it there, we'll come join you. I'll talk about it with Paul so that he can make the arrangements. But if you think it's better here, don't let anyone tell you otherwise and come right back as soon as you can! Paul will pick you up. And be careful, Ida! You can't be too careful when you travel because there are so many shady characters who especially like to take advantage of women traveling alone. Never let your bag out of sight! Also, remember your rheumatism! It's important to stay warm on the trip! You're so easily distracted, but engine smoke is poisonous to you! Keep your legs wrapped in a blanket, and wear your wool gloves, Ida! And don't forget to use your umbrella as soon as you get off the train!"

Caroline was beside herself. He would never get it. All this about Ida getting sick! He's crazy or he's putting on an act by behaving as if the world had not turned upside down.

"Let him be, Caroline, it's what he needs! He hasn't changed a bit, only the world has, and he doesn't see it."

Then they leave the house. Paul and Zerlina grab the luggage, Caroline takes her sister's arm.

"You must be brave, Caroline. I'll make it after all!"

Now they are by the gate, beyond which no one is allowed to accompany the departing passengers, who spend their last moments in Ruhenthal guarded only by the train attendants. Paul and Zerlina drape their aunt with her bags. Caroline laughs with tears in her eyes. The aunt also cries and laughs.

"Take care of yourself, Ida!"

And then she is gone. Those left behind look on as she slowly shuffles across the dirty floor, but Ida no longer looks back.

"She's gone."

Caroline is alone and has let her only sister be hauled off. What would her parents have said? Siblings stick together through thick and thin. Once we sat together at the same table. You in a little dress, me in a little dress, you a little doll, me a little doll. The doll is gone, the dress is gone. The sister tossed away as well. Betrayed and sold off. Not enough packed away in her bags. Tossed into the unknown like a piece of rubbish on the rubbish heap. No one by her side. Released to the dark depths of Hades and with only mementos packed in around her. Caroline had seen the same in a museum, the things that are given to the dead in order to release them, particularly the Egyptians. They heaped up treasures for the dead. But Ida had nothing more than a bit of stuff that she pressed to herself. She cannot carry it all, but she will take it all with her. "What do you need that for, dear lady? Give it here, dead is dead! Unburden yourself and your conscience!" The suitcase is gone for good. It is yanked open, everything is strewn around, the empty suitcase thrown onto the rubbish heap. What good are the large white letters now? The Egyptian graves have been broken into and robbed, yet the thieves are made famous by their theft, write books about it, and are celebrated in the newspapers for their misdeeds. But the thieves are not made happier by their violation of the corpses. The ancient curse has caught up with them, they die like flies, though the treasure is stacked up in the museum and no one feels any shame over such a scandal.

What will happen to the treasures of the departed? Everything is displayed in glass cases after it has been cleaned and conserved, the neat writing explains everything. Burial goods for Frau Ida Schwarz. Knit stockings and a piece of soap. The little nightcap whose band is somewhat damaged, and the coffee cup with just a small crack. The glasses in the open case. The photographs of Ida's husband and her dear son behind the glass on a wire stand. The teacher leads the children into the museum and has to explain everything in detail.

"Stand still and behave, dear children, and pay attention to what I have to tell you! What's here once was. This woman was once alive. We don't really know anything about her, but isn't it amazing that we indeed do know so much about her because of advances in science? Back then everything was gathered up and sorted out, then wrapped in cotton matting and sent off to the museum. Here it was carefully unwrapped and cleaned up as good as it could be. Then everything was set in order and described exactly. There are thick books written about all of it. When you are older you can read about it sometime. In the school library we also have a thick volume with many colorful pictures. You'll find everything there described in detail. We will be writing an essay about this, so pay close attention! If you look closely at everything here, then you won't need the book at all and can write your own proper description. The child who does the best work will be honored by the museum director. No pain, no gain. So all eyes here! Those are the shoes that this woman wore. They're made of leather. How well preserved they are! You all can imagine what it was really like, even though it was at least a hundred years ago that this woman was sent off on her journey along with many others. Yes, those were great days, when people could still be shipped back and forth, though I'll say more about that next time!"

Most of the schoolchildren are well behaved and press their noses to the glass and lick the corners of the case. Only some misbehave and giggle, poke one another with their elbows, don't care about the noteworthy goods, and hide behind the display cases.

"I thought you would all be nice in the museum. Just remember that this is sacred ground. Only because they have so much to teach us, no one buried these mementos, but instead displayed them so that we could learn by looking at them. Remember that all these people were once alive and went to school like you, even Frau Schwarz here. Just try to imagine that it is quite possible that this woman had children, just like all of you here. This photo here, for instance, in the opinion of scholars, can only be of a son, and no doubt this boy and his siblings cried once they no longer had a mother. Don't be surprised if you find yourself experiencing a shudder of deep fear here in the museum. These are powerful and precious memories."

"Excuse me, teacher, but where are the bones and skull of this Frau Schwarz? Why are they not in the museum as well?"

"The bodily remains of Frau Schwarz are not here. It could be that the corpse was somehow lost and no one has found it yet. Nonetheless maybe someday it will be dug up, since everywhere so many interesting discoveries are made these days. However, it's also possible that the earthly remains were cremated, thus making it difficult, first, to find the ashes and, second, to prove that a pile of ashes contains the remains of Frau Schwarz. When something is not known for sure, dear children, then it's not suitable for display in a well-organized museum that plays an important role in the scientific community. That's why you all have to be satisfied with the burial goods that have been carefully gathered together here. It's indeed a miracle when something remains of a person. But now you've seen enough, we have to move on."

Only Caroline remains standing in the museum, because she cannot pull herself away from what she's looking at. Who knows whether these things belonged to her great-grandmother or even her mother back then? Everything looked so familiar to Caroline. She is sure she has seen these things somewhere before. But that was a long time ago, when the piano still stood in the parents' living room. But Caroline could also be confused, because all of the contents of the museum look remarkably alike. The Romans also had central heating. Nothing has changed. People also supposedly wore shoes in the Ice Age. Glasses already existed in the Middle Ages. But these things are not that old. Hardly any of them were made by hand, except the nightcap. Everything else is factory-produced, just like those made and sold today. Yet that doesn't matter so much. Such things also did not belong to Caroline's long-lost ancestors, much less a woman who had been saddled with a fate as overwhelming as one endured a hundred or even a thousand years before.

Caroline is frightened at the thought that such a thing could also happen today. The times don't change at all, they just pass by. Just as the world looks when a child first gazes upon it, so it is right up until death. This woman did not die a natural death. It was an accident. Zerlina couldn't prove that she starved to death. A train tipped over, and as a result there were so many dead that the bones couldn't be sorted. Only the bag survived in part. Now it's here. The children had minded it and made sure it didn't disappear for good. Frau Schwarz had no idea what would happen when she got on the train with all of the other passengers. She in fact was happy about the journey and looked forward to the destination, and yet there came the sudden end. How many tears the newspaper must have caused to flow back then! We regret to inform our readership about the sudden death of a special long train. In lieu of flowers it is requested that donations be made to the Technology Museum; drop off all objects there, fully numbered. Consignment sheets are available at the front desk of this newspaper so that each individual can turn in something either of his own or of his next of kin. Signed, The Editors, on behalf of the grateful children.

Yet what if it wasn't like that? Then it was different. It was. Who can say how it was? The dead! They say it. They are asked to bear witness. You must preserve justice. The judge summons all to lift themselves out of the rubbish and answer him without fear. How did this happen? Two sisters. One stayed, one left. Both died. Because they hid separately. One crawled into the piano and the lid fell upon her. The song was over. Her parents scolded her because the boy with the goose had been tipped over. The goose was broken off. The figure was not made of alabaster. It was only made of plaster, white dust, powder, and nothing more. The boy pulling the thorn, however, made it through. He was made of real stone. He continues as ever to pull the thorn from his Achilles' heel and can never finish the task. He dies without ever ceasing. He could have saved himself the trouble if only he had bought some shoes. The parents can scold all they want to, but still he died and died. Otherwise there was nothing for him to do, because the times don't change, they only pass by, though the thorn of rubbish lasts through all times.

No, that can't be possible. If one has good intentions, nothing can happen. Our trains, for instance. Their safety coefficient. At least before the war. It was murder. Ida was pulled off the train. Then everyone stood there. The people on the left, the luggage on the right. The people were finished off, the suitcase was sent to the museum. One could not allow technological progress to be halted, but one also had to preserve its story as well. That's why the people were killed, there being no need to collect their ashes. They died and dissolved into the earth. Against such treatment all people need to protest: We won't do it! We don't want any luggage, we want our life back! Someone has to force the train's engineer to go back if he won't do it on his own! First to Ruhenthal and then home! The journey back! No one is allowed to send anyone on a journey, especially to death, if he doesn't have a ticket for it as well! Schedules need to be publicly displayed, enough with secrecy, it's obvious that the connections need to be listed so that each can choose for himself! Only when one understands everything and has thought it through thoroughly does the plan for the journey come together. Then each travels as he wishes. The time doesn't change, but instead a person travels through according to his own wishes. The children, however, must not be sent to the museums, where they cry or cause mischief. Instead you should show them maps of all the countries and explain it to them in school. That way even as youngsters they can learn how to read timetables and not be afraid of trains, since for them it's free. Every child loves to play with trains. This way he or she will at last catch their train.

Travel bureaus have brought so much unhappiness to humanity because so many count on them. In this manner a travel bureau only serves people who are ready, who already know what they want. How easy it is for the uninformed to be disappointed by the many pictures and prospectuses. This happens often not only as a result of bad intentions but also carelessness and misunderstanding. The attendants share what they have in high-pitched voices, but the people hardly pay attention. Whoever doesn't know the web of the railroad lines can easily be left hanging within it. If they get caught at a junction, then everything is over. Then the spider gobbles up the travelers after having waited for them while patiently lurking in its hiding place. Too late the eyes try to decipher the names of the stations as the train passes. The night descends, the light fails, the right town is long gone before you even see it, and there's no one there to help, even if you scream and plead. Strange station attendants salute the steaming locomotive.

"It's an express transport, madam. Don't say anything to anyone else! The spider is watching. If it can, it will jump as soon as the train slows down on a bend!"

Then Ida jumped out of the moving train and lay lifeless on the tracks. Only the suitcase was found in the train car and entrusted to the museum as ownerless goods. Caroline had to go to the lost and found.

"You put my sister's things on display. Please, I'm the next of kin. Give me everything that's in the glass case! I'll pay you the assessed finder's fee."

"We're sorry, but the museum is closed. The museum belongs to the state. The state gives nothing away."

"How am I supposed to get my things? I will get a lawyer."

"Legal action is pointless. The state comes before justice. The only avenue you can pursue is an unequivocal plea for mercy to the spider. But don't get your hopes up!"

"Where can I find the spider?"

"That I don't know. But it's everywhere. It has as many legs as its web has strands. You only need to tremble and he'll show up."

"I'm trembling already."

"It only comes when it wants to suck up a meal. Then you can ask him. Yet by then it's already too late, because the spider doesn't listen once he arrives."

Caroline flees the lost and found and runs off. She sits in her room on the bed. She can't go to a spider from which one has to stay hidden. Ida's space is empty. Everything sucked away. Only the uncovered straw mattress lies there. Whatever she left behind is already tucked away into Caroline's luggage. Ida nonetheless has been put on display in the Natural History Museum. She has been laid there in spirit. No, she is in the Technology Museum. The spider has brought her there. Now the old machine is taken apart. The professionals decipher the inscription on the boiler. There stands the name of the firm that supplied the machine:

SCHWARZ, IDA—6/1/1882

It's actually not been a hundred years. One exaggerates so easily. The machine can no longer be operated. It looks to be a broken-down watch. Not even the best doctor can wind the spring. It has been ruined. The clock hand is broken off and bent. The conservator says: "I've never seen such a badly handled watch." Not even after sixty years would such a piece be so badly damaged through regular wear and tear. Naughty children must have played with it. That's the fault of a bad upbringing, one in which the younger generation never has to take piano lessons. The rhythm is lost, everyone bangs away however he wants to. It's a cultural outrage when a rheumatic timepiece is not properly handled. Now it's too late, not even an oil bath can do any good. All of the components need to be designed anew, but that would be much too expensive, and the doctors wouldn't even know what to do. The war has bankrupted everyone. Diet alone cannot accomplish very much when the intestines are already rotten. All the medicine is sold out. The director of the museum is not a cruel person, but nonetheless he adamantly shakes his head.

"We have to display the work as is. Maybe after the war we can have a specialist from America come. There the ability of watchmakers has apparently made great strides in recent years. One takes the living heart out of the machine, operates, allows artificial breathing to proceed throughout, and sets a new ruby heart back in."

"Yes, it's marvelous what the human race can accomplish. It's a stunning success and keeps going on. Now give me back my sister!"

"You mean the timepiece?"

"My sister!"

"I see, then, the watch. We don't release broken items. We have to be mindful of the firm's good name. Damaged goods would immediately draw attention and would spark the interest of the unkind press."

"I will take my sister as she is. I will not hold you responsible."

"But the papers will!"

"I swear, I will say nothing to the reporter!"

"You cannot prevent that. The reporter will find a reason to interrogate you."

"I won't speak to any of them."

"Nobody can keep his mouth shut. Pressure will be applied. Nobody is strong enough to keep silent under the pressure of a painful interrogation."

"We're not living in the Middle Ages. Torture was done away with in all civilized societies in the eighteenth century."

"You don't know reporters or states. Because of your ignorance this discussion is over. Off with you!"

"But I don't have a tram ticket."

Yet the director is already gone and does not answer, no matter how loud Caroline calls out. Only machines are there, powerful flywheels, pistons, dowels, rods, blueprints, hearts, kidneys, powder, whale bones, knights' armor, suitcases, fire pumps, medicines, artificial spiders, inlaid pianos, corkscrews, tossed-away train tickets, pendulum clocks, and a seized-up printing press from the Middle Ages. The rest of Ida is not to be found, no matter how much Caroline looks underneath all the spider webs, thinking that perhaps someone could have stowed Ida away amid the museum's junk. Then Caroline grows sad, tears run, the nose drips, the face gray and dirty, the abandoned sister grabs a handkerchief with the monogram IS on it to wipe her nose and eyes. Ida had left the handkerchief behind so that it is easier for Caroline to cry. Hopefully Ida has brought along enough handkerchiefs so that she doesn't need to borrow one while sniffling. She didn't want to take along more than a dozen. Caroline needed to send this one to her, for the needlework on it is especially beautiful. Caroline will have to ask the guard at hell's gate herself, for Paul is a clumsy ox when it comes to such things. All it will take is a little bit of money pressed into Hades' hand and before you know it the handkerchief will be dipped in the waters of Lethe. Caroline was ready to sacrifice everything for her sister.

But in fact it is much too late to help. Ida has disappeared into a coffin and the funeral is over. All of the coffins have been carried off, the funeral songs have ceased. The hearse has left, the barrier is let fall. Ida is gone, Ruhenthal has ejected her, she is hidden and gone forever. But now everything goes back to normal. Leopold is still alive and wants some bread. The clock hands turn, the spider sets twelve legs on the face of the clock, yet the hand keeps turning. The days go on, bobbing merrily along. Ida never existed. Caroline has merely dreamt her up. Everyone was dreaming, they were mistaken and now disappointed, all is lost, the song over. Ida and Leopold, Paul and Zerlina, everyone and all, and so Caroline weeps and cannot hide her feelings away any longer.

Zerlina walks fast at first, then more slowly. It's not that bad of a town, as long as one doesn't look too close. The buildings and courtyards are picturesque and bear witness that people once lived here who innocently sat in the their rooms or hurried along the streets, since nothing ever changed. Everyone went about his daily business, used to doing so without worry, for each knew he was from Ruhenthal and was born here. It was all so wholesome and reliable that each inhabitant of the city was capable of fulfilling his position in life. Each evening he stood in the middle of his open doorway, lit a pipe, looked on and observed people passing by whom he greeted and engaged in small talk. Mutsch the cat jumped up, stretched her hind legs, yawned, bent back her tail, and lithely rubbed her shoulder against a pant leg. And so the man stood there in squat fashion, content within himself as he guarded the domain he knew to be his own because it never fell from sight. Then a woman called out, whose ample backside swayed back and forth leisurely before disappearing into the darkness of the house. The owner then retreated into the safety of his cave, sitting down at his accustomed spot at the table in order to shovel food into his mouth and chew it deliberately. Meat and beets were tastefully prepared, the rewards of honest work.

Zerlina looks hard at the former occupant. He doesn't pay any attention to Zerlina because he doesn't notice her. He goes about his business as always, which only shows that, for him, the number of ghosts in Ruhenthal is undiminished to this day. Has the old man slept through these times? He must have, because he doesn't see that only the frame of his house remains, the contents having disappeared. Together with his family members he hauled them off himself. It's unimaginable that he doesn't know this and still remains here. Is he dead? No, he's breathing like anyone living. He doesn't look up when Zerlina waves at him, he smokes, even though it's forbidden here, and overall he doesn't seem disturbed that he no longer belongs in Ruhenthal. Zerlina wants to convince him that it's a mistake for him to be here. Most likely he just became greedy because he must have known what everyone knew once he had been compensated and another home had been assigned to him. He didn't leave completely of his own free will, though he still did so freely and with the help of the authorities who made the disruption and relocation easier for him. He had also solemnly signed his name on the contract with his own ink and named another place, which in the future would be his home. And thus that's where he would be, having sworn to it before witnesses, and there is where his mail is sent, there anyone can find him who is looking for him.

A heavy-duty furniture wagon pulled up in front of his house and loaded up all his belongings. Not even so much as a single broom straw remained, the bathtub was yanked out, the furnace was hauled off, the fixtures were ripped from the walls. Only doors emptied of their keys and the marred wall paintings did not abandon the place since they had more loyalty to the house than to the outcast man. The owner had also taken along his family, an old father, a wife, three children, a sister. They all carried bags, full suitcases, each of them amply fitted out. Thus they walked out the door carefree, after which the children smashed a couple of windowpanes only for the pleasure of celebrating a happy departure. The emigrants didn't climb onto the furniture wagon, but instead walked slowly to the town hall, where they turned in their house keys. Then they got onto a bus that took them straight to the train station.

Why then is the owner here again when he's had a new home for the past two years? Zerlina wants to talk to him, but though she can hear her own voice speaking clearly, the owner doesn't appear to hear her. He simply stands there and doesn't respond. It could be that he only wants to know what had happened to his house. He wants to sample the misery that has brewed here. He paces incessantly back and forth across the room, yet he speaks with no one. Is he too proud? Perhaps in the last two years he's had to move again. Zerlina tries to grab hold of his arm. Mister, mister, stand still for a moment! Are you nothing but a delusion? All too often Zerlina is deluded. In the room the old women sit, herded together on the hard edges of their bed frames. Zerlina stands before a woman who, with a needle in her hand, searchingly and worrisomely and yet without understanding looks upward. Zerlina doesn't move and whispers quietly.

"It will never be fine again, Mother. Everything is changed. Perhaps it will one day be as it once was, but not for us. We're done for. We're through."

Zerlina turns around, looks out the window at the dismal yard, and turns back again. She opens her suitcase, picks up the lute ribbons and other mementos, strokes them with her fingers, packs them once again, and closes the suitcase. She shoves it under the bed while biting her lip. Zerlina straightens up, takes a cloudy mirror from a shelf, blows on it several times, holds it up to her face out of curiosity, but then closes her eyes because she no longer recognizes herself, and lays the mirror facedown on a different shelf behind her bed. Zerlina turns around anxiously and sees again the woman with the needle in her hand. That's her mother, and next to her sits her aunt, who doesn't look up at all. What are the two women doing? They are darning stockings and whispering to each other. It's impossible to understand a single word. Zerlina wants to tell the women something, but she changes her mind because she feels the women wouldn't understand her, and so she silently leaves the room. Zerlina can smell the air that rises heavy and sweet above the rubbish heap. Zerlina stands by herself in the gloomy foyer and thinks to herself. She feels the cold sweat upon her brow and shivers. She flexes her fingers, which hurt because they are so stiff. And then Zerlina can hold back the tears no longer.

Zerlina sees Frau Lischka before her, who has just dragged herself up the steps. It's clear that she has something nasty to say and is ready to make fun of Zerlina for standing there on the stoop like an abandoned schoolgirl rather than sitting in her room as she was supposed to, like the rest of the inhabitants. Zerlina feels there is no way out. One can jump over the barrier only at the risk of one's life. Whoever tries it will be shot. Once life was radiant, Zerlina had spread her feathers, she was the young golden girl whom Frau Holle* praised, but now everything is shut down, the feathers are locked away, even though Zerlina had constantly tried to spread them. Then Frau Holle became angry and turned her into the bad girl on whom the gooey tar stuck. Gooey tar also lies on the streets, her shoes getting stuck within it. Zerlina kicks off her shoes, but even barefoot she can't move forward. Everything is so dirty, tar raining down continually. Frau Holle knows no mercy. Tar, tar, nothing but tar, the tarred eyes staring into the raven black night and seeing nothing but tar.

It is also bitter cold on the streets. The black scarf wrapped around her head is no protection against the wind and tar and cold, and it makes the face so old and ugly. The mirrors hanging on the walls have gone black, not a single stream of light beams through that the blackened mirrors could reflect. Her fingernails have grown long. They are brittle spider legs, they are wires, broom straws. Zerlina must burrow through dirt with them. The bug squirms around on the floor and is happy to do so. If Zerlina holds her breath, she hears the bug moving around. The people have run off, they cannot fend off the crawling pests. The people are not protected by a good fairy. Only an old witch sits in the corner and combs the lice out of tangled locks with the last teeth of a rusted comb. She throws the lice into the night. How can anyone believe or say that he still makes his home in Ruhenthal?

The owner has fled; nor has Mutsch the cat stuck around. She no longer purrs, she struts and snorts, she stretches her black coat and shakes herself. Then she howls and jumps over the barrier and takes off right

*Frau Holle is the title character of a Brothers Grimm tale.

behind the owner. After the leap by Mutsch the cat no other escape is possible. High walls built out of black bricks are erected around the circum-
ference of the town and are topped with spikes smeared in tar. Nobody
can get out. Full of doubt, desires rise in the darkness, fluttering on the
wings of the bat, wanting to climb higher and pass over the wall, but it's
hopeless! A thick dragnet is spread across, woven by the witch from her
own saliva. Then the delicate skin of the wings is ripped, the desires can
no longer hover, they flutter wearily and miserably in the sky trap that has
been lowered onto the city, black and impenetrable and ghostly, the witch
giggling in a voice that has a thousand cracks, shooting down the wishes
with her pea shooter, the wishes falling upon the roofs and streets, falling
and freezing. It's better, young lady, that you bury yourself. You stand at
the edge of a grave that you have dug with your long fingernails, so plop
in where it's damp and cool. Soon you will be asleep, the journey will end,
there Holle the witch will bury you.

Off in the distance one can hear the faint call: "Ruhenthal! Everyone
off!" The light in the windy train station goes out. The baggage men flee
and let the suitcases fall where they are. The stationmaster spits in anger.
The switchman sees trouble coming. The telegraph operator has lost the
connection. Those getting off fall head over heels onto the tracks and are
bloodied. Anxiously the locomotive blows its whistle, its cries asking the
night for mercy, though no mercy is given. The youngest daughter of the
stationmaster appears at the window ledge in a white nightgown with a
candle, looks at the confusion below, and begins to sing a little song:

> I've seen it, it's true,
> The long journey is through,
> The train's in the station,
> The wanderers are resting.
> Lord, let me rest,
> The signal is set,
> Look after the trains
> 'Til the end of your reign!
> Good night! Good night!
> 'Til the end of your reign
> Our thanks for the trains!

As the daughter sang, everything was still for a moment, but now she's gone, having taken the candlelight with her. The air is thick and sooty. There's hardly any air to breathe. Only sharp, monstrous tears full of coal dust fill the entire world. The witch doesn't giggle, she laughs.

You are alive in a flowing stream, surrounded by black reeds and black algae. Fishhooks also dangle in the thick foam. You can feel them distinctly when they pass nearby and come too close. But anyone who is hooked by them is also not saved. You are only made to squirm unmercifully. If you are nonetheless hauled out, then no amount of pleading helps, the fish will never again be let go, Frau Ilsebill* simply won't allow it, and the most helpless creature is addressed with the scornful words of the standard verdict against those forbidden to live within the fatherland. Then they cart you off and pull you through the tar and then feather you, and then drag you to the gallows. There the verdict is read again, the fisherman having to do as Frau Ilsebill has ordered, as he reads out:

"In the name of the law, bow down! You have violated the station platform and have falsely set foot upon it when my fishhook took mercy on you. With some effort I have yanked you from the black waters because you begged me to and lied by saying that you could fulfill all my wishes. Not a single word of that was true. You misled the authorities, you attempted to deceive them. You are no goldfish. You're not even a fish. You are nothing more than the dirty little girl from the lake who must die."

Zerlina listens to what the horrible fisherman says to her. Zerlina has to agree that she is not a fish, as she had hoped. She knows that she must relinquish her young life; she must cease. She can no longer live. She is a bit of madness who happens to have a name.

"Zerlina Lustig, former daughter of Leopold Lustig and Caroline, née Schmerzenreich!"

"Here! . . . No! I'm not here! I don't know her, nobody knows her, she never existed, at least not in my life! She didn't come, nor get on the train! Since her death she's been sick! I can swear to it, Herr Fisherman and Frau Ilsebill!"

But no one believes her. Frau Ilsebill shakes with laughter. Why

*Frau Ilsebill is the name of the wife in the Brothers Grimm tale "The Fisherman and His Wife."

should anyone believe anyone when all that is said is a lie? There is no truth. Herr Nussbaum in the Technology Museum removed it from the luggage. Whoever smuggles the truth into the final destination of the journey will have to answer to the severest measures of the state police and will be hanged three times over! Thus had Cross-Eyes yelled out to everyone when he discovered a tiny piece of truth tucked away in a purse. There is however none anywhere, for it is only an illusion. If there is any at all, it is only what has been. The apartment house is suddenly no more. There appears to be a foot scraper that wants to suck in the dirt, but then you fall helplessly into the barrel of tar. Frau Ilsebill opens up her beak, snaps up the stationmaster's daughter, and flies off with her.

Did they kill your father? He loved little Bunny so much, that fat dog! No, the old man croaked peacefully like a dog, a natural death. Dr. Plato swears on bended knee that the fleas bit him in the ear. The neighbor prays that the Lord has taken him. It was a peaceful end in bed, which you can be assured of yourself. The spittoon was not disturbed. There was no raspberry juice in it, only a couple of drops of water, fresh and pure. You grabbed the cold hand and pressed it lovingly to yourself. No, it was murder, he could have lived longer. They shoved half-boiled barley into him. Whoever takes measures that shorten someone's life by a single day is a murderer, and the law will hunt him down. But when will that happen? Just be patient, Frau Ilsebill, and wait for the law, for it will come sooner than you think.

Zerlina sits with the other girls and women in the workshop where boxes are assembled and glued. Simple, small boxes that will journey far and wide. Endless rows of boxes that trundle along and are stacked in towers until there are too many, after which they are picked up. The boxes are so light and airy, but the workshop stinks of glue and awful dust. It smells of bad conversations that go on endlessly for hours, rising and sinking away without ever finding an end.

"Zerlina, don't be so sad! There's no reason for such sadness. . . . Ah, forgive me, this time you have a reason. I forgot. I'm sorry, my pale Snow White. But he was old indeed."

"They murdered him. He should have lived longer."

"You yourself don't want to live anymore and you're young. How can you complain about an old man whom God has taken in order that he be spared what we all have to suffer? Look here, Zerlina, how unreasonable you're being, worse than a child!"

"You're right that I don't want to live, Vera! Everything here is wretched, hopeless! They will murder us all before they themselves are murdered. I'm tired of it all, I'm sick of it. Enough! Do you hear?"

"That's no way to talk. You have to want to go on. Whoever doesn't want to live has no hope. And whoever has no hope, he only has hell. We at least have a chance of surviving."

"No one survives hell, or at least whoever survives it only ends up living in hell again. Therefore there is no hope worth having. It's all a hoax, an illusion, which . . ."

"You're wrong, Snow White! Have you not often said yourself that in Ruhenthal we were under a spell and really just sleeping? That one day the prince's servant will come and trip over a shrub while carrying our coffins. Then the poison apple we were forced to bite will pop out of our throats. We'll lift off the coffin lids, stand up, and live once again. Come on, snap out of it! Your dear father was an old man. He could never have lived a normal life again, as you keep insisting. . . ."

"Look, Vera, that is so because you don't understand what I said to you, for there's nobody here who understands, which is why I don't want anything to do with you anymore. Life just doesn't have any point to it. I don't want to tell you any more fairy tales."

"But Snow White . . ."

"Please, enough!"

"I don't want to upset you. But Zerlina! Whoever gives up may nonetheless live, but it's much harder, because he has nothing in which to believe!"

"I'm not talking about that! My father lived so well. He was a big kid. He had no idea how badly he had been treated. But I know it. I know what's been done to us. I see it continually."

"You are so unreasonable. You should be grateful that your father still has a grip on you. What could have been better for him than a relatively peaceful death after a long life?"

Zerlina is quiet. She should never have told these stupid women such fairy tales. She hears the talk around her as nothing more than senseless noise that is melded together with the sound of work and other noises into a mountain of sound, though there is nothing peaceful about it, instead it's disturbing and unsettling, a delusion that bedecks all of the boxes with a poisonous dust. Yet the delusion contains nothing, it is only a halfhearted murky shadow that dissolves into an untraceable odor. It smells of the night, of bare trees, vermin, rubbish, the thin layer of dust left by the fog, and all of it falls into the pits. No one knows anything more about it because nobody survives. The witnesses to this destitute journey waste away as well. Only a lone black flag waves above them, the tar of misfortune, the impenetrable shadow of the heavy night, plague having broken out, against which there is no cure as it rains, the muck breaking over the banks, it being hunger, everything that happened, the father, the train station, death, the rain, the murder, the journey, and the endless hunger.

Against her will, Zerlina thinks of Vera. Maybe she was right, but only if one could fight back and actually do something. When all you had to do was to keep gluing together boxes, there's nothing more to hope for. It's better to just leave, not wait any longer, say nothing to anyone, today, right now, drop back and turn around, where there's no guard, past Herr and Frau Lischka, then quick across the courtyard and through a passage in the wall in order to arrive at more light and bricks. There you can go through, avoid the barrier without escaping, no, just through. Nobody will ask questions, because nobody asks questions when someone disappears without a word. Unhampered freedom has been guaranteed to the people since the end of slavery and serfdom. This natural right is unassailable and sacred, since it is taught in the schools, and it remains so as long as one does not relinquish it oneself. Zerlina has done nothing wrong. Therefore she is free. Each and every person in Ruhenthal is also free and has had his freedom taken away unjustly. There is no one who is not free. If someone wants to stop Zerlina, it's against the law and morally wrong. Complaints would then be made to the minister of justice. Zerlina would inform anyone what the law says. There has been no trial at all. Cruel fate is not a proper verdict. Therefore it is also not necessary to dress like a criminal on the lam.

Zerlina leaves without anyone stopping her. She sings a song about a happy wanderer. It was not right of Paul to squash all noise. Zerlina touches the wall, tapping it in hope, yet with determination. She presses at the wall with a key. The mortar is as crumbly as old cake because it is weatherworn and helpless to hold itself together. She rubs the wall with the key as the dry mixture of sand, dissolved chalk, and water crumbles away. The egg-yellow dust piles up on the earth. Soon the space in between is wide enough that the teeth of the key can fit between two bricks. The bricks themselves also give way. The key serves as a pickax as the bricks allow themselves to be taken apart.

"What are you doing there, Fräulein? You're ruining the wall, stop it!"

"I'm making a hole. I'm about to leave."

"You want to escape? That's out of the question!"

"I'm not escaping. I have no intention to do that whatsoever. I'm simply leaving as quietly as I can and am taking along anyone who wishes to come. You'll simply have to accept that, sir."

"You're crazy. Nobody leaves here. It's simply not allowed. You must remain! You must remain or end up planted in the grass!"

"But I don't want to. I've stayed here way too long already, almost two years. I've had enough of it already. I need a change of air, sir! You indeed look a bit pale to me as well. Without a change of air the plague will spread. To stay here any longer is dangerous to one's health."

"All that about the plague is nothing more than a rumor told in the latrines. I can assure you that you need not be afraid of anything. Should it happen that you come down with the plague or any other contagious disease, you will be quarantined. Then any danger will be prevented."

"You are in my way. I am leaving. I've thought about it and I know the way."

But Zerlina does not leave. The small hole that she has bored through the wall is no deeper than a finger. The wall has caused some nasty abrasions and yet stands solid and unshaken. Zerlina turns around. She lets it go for today. Tomorrow she will come back and bring along a file with which she can better bore than with the key. She will also remember to bring a hammer in order to knock out an opening that she can squeeze through. She won't be put off or stopped. Then she will march off and follow the country road that Paul has told her about up through the hills. Soon she will leave the main roads, and soon she will be in the woods and will look for a place where she can hide herself until the end of the war. She will make a camp amid the moss and cover herself with brushwood.

The fields and woods and meadows will supply her with nourishment. She will live like a little rabbit and feed on nourishing grasses and fruits. There won't be any danger of feeling lonely, but rather the threat of inclement weather. Whoever is careful can gather many riches for the heart and spirit, the time soon passing into eternal memories.

Zerlina says to herself: I was there. I lived it and survived it. There is danger everywhere, but it can be dealt with and disappears. Today, now that it's all over, it's an indestructible good. Be happy all of you who live an orderly life today, though I really pity anyone who did not share my fears, for they have missed out on one of the deepest fears. But also to know none of it is lucky. Is it possible that there exists such an ability to forget? If so, then such horror never existed, only the confused heart that strayed too far and was overcome with sinful horrors that pulled it into the abyss. There the emptiness of sleep encompassed it and covered over everything. Yet darkness protected everything. Endless grains of sand trickled into the black tar and came to rest in the soft mud of the rumbling journey. Now they attained eternal peace as the persistent flow ceased and all the grains bonded together forever. A smooth path ran above the surfaces worn smooth as a mirror. On wheels that turned easily, coaches that rode on springs glided by silently. Buried beneath were slumberers who rested on feather pillows, but who did not feel constricted, because their thoughts while sleeping were always fixed on the blissful approach of the journey's end, everything so far having been filled with a future that had no end.

Today no longer exists for Zerlina. She does not sense that things go on happening around her. She only lives for tomorrow and is free and healthy. The plague has spared her body. Left and right, everyone is sick and writhes with pain. Nurse Dora's rooms are overfull, she can do nothing, Dr. Plato no longer risks helping the sick. Ulcerating sores break open, a disgusting stream spews out of all the rooms, down the stoop and into the yard where the drains are stopped up. The city health workers show up anxiously and vainly poke away at the drains in an attempt to release the deadly stream.

"There's nothing we can do here. We're lacking the proper tools, as well as a knowledgeable leader. We need Dr. Lustig! Dr. Lustig!"

Impossible, we can't just dig him up! We did away with him. He's no longer in Ruhenthal."

"How so? Did he escape?"

"He's no longer here. He's not among us. Only his stethoscope is still here, Dr. Plato has it."

"We don't want the lifeless stethoscope. We want Dr. Lustig, but fast, before it's too late!"

"Ask at the crematorium for his ashes if it means that much to you!"

"You're joking. We don't need a heap of ashes! We need Dr. Lustig!"

"You don't want any corpses! Anyone dead is relieved of service and without further salary is placed in perpetual retirement."

"That's not possible! We need him because of this plague! We can't let anyone die!"

"You should have thought of that earlier, my friend, before he lay on his deathbed. He starved to death. Nothing but uncooked barley for his weak stomach!"

"We don't believe you! No one starves here among us! We share. We pass around. He got his measure of bread, his sugar!"

"Those who are dying are independent once they're dead. That condition may have escaped your notice. The little feather before his mouth lost all color, but did not move."

"Could the doctor have prevented it? Where was Dr. Plato? It certainly could have been prevented. The proper procedures should have been followed if something didn't suffice."

"The food! The food was useless. The patient refused to eat it. His stomach couldn't take it, his intestines wouldn't work. Everything just liquefied and was gone."

"We're holding you responsible. Bring the man back! If you had only handled things right it would have been possible to save him. It's still not too late to try!"

"Save your whining! Point a finger at yourself! Get your dirty fingernails away from me! Don't you have a nail file like cultured people with a fine upbringing? If you're going to scrape away at all the walls, the least you can do is use a hose! Rinse yourself off! Douse yourself! Work is what makes life sweet!"

Zerlina is shocked by the intense exchange in the yard and leans out of the window, but the ones who were fighting are already off and gone, nobody else is there to overhear. Lightly the rain sprinkles on the uneven earth. The water dams up in deep puddles whose surfaces tremble. Small rivulets have formed, which, at first slowly then quickly, press through the irregular stones of the pavement. Whoever walks by below dirties his shoes, which will soon begin to rot. The old leather softens and no longer keeps out the moisture. You have to go barefoot. It's miserable, however, to have the odd feeling of the muck clinging to your feet as continually pressed down mud squishes up between the toes. Mud baths are not recommended in this weather. There are no hoses available to wash away the slop, the water mains have been shut off. Also, large stoppers have been placed in everyone's throats such that nobody can swallow any longer. Because of this stoppage even bread crumbs are inedible. The mouth fills up more and more, because any attempt to gulp does not allow even the slightest bit to pass through the gullet. The husks of barley cling to the tongue and gums and stop up all the gaps between the teeth, causing the gums to burn, the mouth now infected. Yet because the soul is hungry, the hand doesn't hold back and continues to shovel another spoonful through the lips. Everything is sickness, everything is plugged up, everything is full of misfortune. The stomach is bursting and the intestines are blocked.

Help needs to be called. There must be someone who can perform an enema. The voice fails because of the catarrh on the vocal chords. The hair gets tangled in the cooked barley and hangs in the mouth in gnarled strands. The hands should try to pull it away, but they are incapable of gripping anything because they are knotted and bent in at the joints. After a great deal of effort the pewter spoon is allowed to fall, though there is not enough strength left over to grab hold of the windowsill. Zerlina can neither walk nor stand, nor sit nor lie. She cannot move at all. She is incapable of anything. The key and the nail file are not in her little purse. Did Frau Ilsebill avenge herself? Someone stuck them in the cardboard boxes. There are too many of them, Zerlina cannot open them all. Vera could help, but Zerlina fears that she will think her a laughingstock. Also, the workshop leader might take note. Right off she would call out, What's going on there! Oh no, now they're carrying off the beautiful boxes, they have to be distributed. Has Zerlina been fooled by freedom? Does salvation lie in the fact that there is no freedom? The moment the fishhook sets itself in the mouth, that's when all salvation, all freedom is gone. It amounts only to a thought, and thoughts no longer mean anything.

Cross-Eyes took away the brass ring, so therefore no wish can be fulfilled. Have people stopped having wishes? They are still there inside, viscous misfortune having completely tarred them.

Everyone has come down with consumption. The doctors are dead, nobody knows the words that will heal. Zerlina wants to find them. She wants to take the broom and sweep the room. The vermin in the cracks will be pleased. Cleanliness is half of healthiness. Lightly the broom hops over the floorboards and causes the dust to twirl in sharp little swirls. Disturbed fleas leap up in shock like the seven dwarves, seven times seventy-seven dwarves, though they know that it doesn't mean all that much, for no one will scare them away. And so they let themselves fall again and smugly wait until the broom becomes tired.

To set the whole miserable place on fire would be the only solution. Yet the stationmaster's daughter looks out her window and cries and waves and calls out. The sparks are dangerous, the woods will burn! Zerlina would not be happy about such a fire, but she would accept it in order that some good be accomplished. The railway will not be disrupted just because some sparks have set off a fire! Unfortunately the train will have to suffer the consequences. Through night and through fog, as the train rages across the countryside, its end already looms before it as the wild machine leaps off its tracks, a peal of thunder rumbles in the sky, the wagons split apart with a dull crack, dead and wounded are everywhere, covered in coats and suitcases, this the penalty for their sins, which settles the score.

Zerlina, however, saves herself. She also soon takes care of her mother and aunt. The others? That's a difficult question; everywhere there are courageous people who sacrifice themselves in order to save others, for where there's a will there's a way. Paul also wants to do what he can and not just passively succumb to his own demise. Almost every day he leaves Ruhenthal, arriving at the blossoming hillsides on the other side of the river, there in Leitenberg where it's easier to outrun the constables. There must be good people among the inhabitants, for Leitenberg is a town with a long history. Eight hundred years, which Paul had noted himself. Zerlina had once visited Leitenberg seven years earlier and had made good friends there who told her how nice it was to live there. Paul should go to them and ask their help to escape. He could do that if it wasn't for his pride. No, he cannot do it, for the friends are long gone, adrift in all directions, they no longer live there, they have ceased to exist. But Paul doesn't need such poor friends who no longer exist; he will find another way to save himself.

The guards won't notice it if Paul drops out of line, he being clever and quick, always a champion at running, and now soon disappearing into a side street, slipping around a corner, quickly, quickly, and then into a house, saying only that he'd made a mistake. He will then be greeted warmly, a chair offered to the guest before offering him some tasty food as refreshment. He will stay here, for he can also be of help, he knows his way around both a house and yard and will certainly earn his keep, they being only too happy to take him in, clothe him, and forward the colorful adventure of his escape. In such manner Paul will happily await the first day of freedom. In Leitenberg everything is as always, people live freely and hear hardly anything of the war. The houses stand bedecked and undisturbed, no one would want to destroy a small town full of retirees. In addition they will also respect the historic buildings, the tall cathedral, the splendid town hall, the famous arcade in the marketplace, the old guild-halls. A bishop's see is a consecrated place that all respect.

If everything else fails, Paul will hide out in a cloister or in a bishop's palace. People of the church demonstrate understanding when a refugee asks for help and says: *"Benedictus qui venit in nomine Dei."* A friendly *"Pax tecum"* is said in return, after which the portals to the refectory open as the song "Qui Tollis" is heard. Singing is heard everywhere, the sins of man are atoned for and forgiven in that holy place. The church is powerful, it guards the oppressed and the hunted. The great misfortune of the world will be transformed into the pure gold of charity. Thus Paul is dressed, the lay brothers' robes suit him well. The cell is indeed small, but clean and airy, the window looks onto the quiet, sunny fruit gardens, the high walls entwined with green steeply descending to the shore road, the poplars bordering the length of the embankment next to the silver-blue stream, the soft meadowlands stretching out on the other shore. And in the cell there stands a brown bed, a dish, a stool made of oak, and a small dresser. The threshold is painted white, such that no illness can cross over it. Paul will study there, but when he grows tired of that, he thinks of ideas for journeys he'll make in the future after the war, while each morning after breakfast he reads *The Leitenberg Daily.*

From the papers much can be gleaned if one understands a little of the subtext, which the bloated claims of success seek to cover up. Secrets are not allowed to be talked about in the open, yet what is implied reveals much more than sentences full of enthusiasm. The enemy slowly draws near, Leitenberg lying smack in the middle of both east and west. Because of this the prospects are good for a certain end. Even if everything is wiped out by the advance, Leitenberg will hardly suffer. Before it is conquered, the peace will be decided, and then Paul will hurry to the survivors of Ruhenthal and lead them to freedom. In the time before then he must only wait and not lose heart, nor submit blindly and without hope himself to fate, but rather remain ready. Even though the days pass slowly, they still won't last forever.

It's been several days since his father's death and many hours since the funeral took place in the mortuary. Lunch and supper were taken in between, and so the mourning period has expired. Yet life goes on, not everyone can be executed. Frau Ilsebill's executioner keeps looking for many victims, but there are others that he passes by, and so there is always someone who survives. The hope of being one of them is the right of the young, Vera had said. The greatest treasures are protected by the soul, for they are lodged where Cross-Eyes can't find them. And so the journey goes on, announcing the good news at all of the oncoming stations. The railroad workers standing there with their red signal flags await what we have to announce. They will listen and then hand us bread and flowers. Thus we will be received everywhere and *"Pax vobiscum"* will be called out, though we will reply, *"In saecula saeculorum."* Then the central train station of Stupart will approach with its two mighty halls. The train will stop with a rattle, the minister of railways will lift the baton, the band music will begin a bit loud, though the jubilant crowd won't mind. Then everyone will get out, the station platform will be covered with a white carpet strewn with countless roses. A handshake, an embrace, a single brotherhood. A rooster in a golden cage will be carried forth, a page presenting it to Zerlina.

Cock-a-doodle-doo!

Zerlina the golden maiden is here!

Yet Zerlina does not like official greetings, for they embarrass her. She only wants to fulfill her duty, and this doesn't suit her at all; the rooster should be handed to someone who after so much privation is owed sincere thanks for not having betrayed the human dignity of those in Ruhenthal. Zerlina doesn't entirely believe what she says there, but she wants to escape the bustle and do so properly, because on a day of celebration one must praise something, since praise upholds what is just more strongly than injustice and in a healthier manner than blame. Meanwhile, Zerlina manages to find a path to the next station gate. Now she can at last walk away in order to slip unnoticed by Frau Lischka into the apartment. After two years' absence the apartment has fallen into such neglect that it will be many weeks before everything is put back in order. Also all of the things that the Lustigs hid with acquaintances have to be brought back home, which will certainly take a long time, for everywhere people want to know how you really are, what really happened in Ruhenthal, and if it indeed was so bad. You are not allowed to simply say what happened, but instead you are invited to dinner, a glass of schnapps is offered, the grown-up children are marveled at, this and that is chatted about until you can safely excuse yourself, saying, We have to be off, we're so tired and have so much to do.

A homey feel has returned to the apartment again for the first time. Strangers had packed into the place like sardines and made a mess of it. Their traces have to be eradicated, the mess in the kitchen and other rooms expunged. Perhaps it would be smarter to look around for an apartment free of such problems, one that was freshly painted and that did not cast shadows consumed with hatred from every wall. If only there wasn't such a shortage of apartments after the war! But certainly it makes sense to move somewhere else, for the old apartment indeed had many problems, it being too dark and sooty, the foyer too small, the doors not thick enough. Yet these disadvantages were far outweighed by the sense of outrage that had settled in, the horror felt before the unconquerable chasm that had opened between the time when they had departed and when they had returned. Sure, their absence is forgotten, since between then and now there is nothing that one can remember, and in between nothing had happened, only a gaping emptiness, incoherent and senseless, just empty time running on, time that didn't exist, not time at all. That's why no one can say anything about it. How then can someone demand an account? Zerlina can only quietly point out that she simply didn't exist between yesterday and today, it's as if she were asleep. Yet she knows nothing of what happened, it was too dark, black as tar, and if it were indeed any different then she doesn't want to recall it.

Yet let us continue where Zerlina has stopped. The foot pedal of the sewing machine can once again be worked, for after a bit of oil it works just fine again—ka-chunk, ka-chunk, ka-chunk. Aunt Ida had always worked it so, saying, "It sounds like a train. Where would you like to travel, dear children?" Paul and Zerlina called out loudly, "To Ingelsdof, to Freiensitz." Then the sewing machine went even faster. But if the journey took too long, she told stories. Everything, everything comes right again, the days go back to normal, the pantries and the cupboards full. What does it matter if Zerlina can't quite remember everything and has to search for this and that? At night everyone will sleep, the covers pulled back, the light turned off, the clean blankets softly wrapping around, then morning, it being a little late, the milkman rings the bell, quick, out of bed, into the bathroom, the basin filled with warm water, the breakfast table set, complete with flowers, the breakfast, the honey bread, the beautiful cups filled, the opened egg in its holder, bright gold, then the washing up and clearing, it being high time, hand me my bag, there's shopping to do. Yes, shopping, the many new purchases that are now needed include clothes, furniture, the many little things that one needs daily!

Is the little flower shop run by Frau Cimera still open? She was quite old indeed, and if she died the shop will certainly be closed, because Straka the laundry man will snatch it up since he wants to expand his business. And are the streets like they once were? Do the same people walk along them? Is any of it recognizable? The times change, Zerlina knows all too well. Perhaps she won't know her way around Stupart and won't find a familiar face. Zerlina had not slept without paying a price. Sleeping Beauty held in the Ruhenthal fortress, that was not right. While under her magic spell it would have been nice for nothing to have changed, even if the spell had lasted a century, yet in Stupart time has passed, unable to be stopped; there no one believes in a return.

You were evicted, my dear Lustigs, so how can you be surprised? It never occurred to us that you would be able to come back. Gone is gone, no one complained about your leaving. But let's have a look at you! Turn left! Now right! Turn around! My goodness, it can't be you! You have no way of proving your identity. We won't let ourselves be fooled for a moment, the Lustigs looked completely different! What have you done with Dr. Lustig? As long as you cannot produce the doctor, there's no way that we can believe you. You claim that he's dead because so much time has passed. We understand. Either everyone is dead or no one is dead. Aha, it's because he was already so old, and the accommodations in Ruhenthal were not enough to prolong the life of an old man? That's quite a story, but we're not that dumb. You're a pack of swindlers, nothing but swindlers who want to take advantage of changed relations. You were taken away from here, we know, but that wasn't done in order to keep you safe throughout the war like pickles packed in a jar that one simply opens in order to happily pick you up and bring you back healthy. We never believed that for a moment. We said nothing then because we felt bad about your future. What they did to you pained us! No one should be treated like that. But rest assured, we had a pretty good idea of what would happen, even if we didn't know for sure. The newspapers made it clear enough between the lines that you were only hauled off from here in order to spare us the repulsive sight of your extermination. That's why you were neatly sucked up, as if by a vacuum cleaner, everyone straight into the dust bag, all of you off, *eins zwei!*

Curtains were drawn between you and us, everything blacked out for miles on end. Open executions no longer took place because they stirred up bad feelings. Everything was kept hidden. The papers wrote only about penalties and fines, yet the spilled blood blackened, though nothing is left of it for the public to see today. Were you just dumped somewhere? Did walls swallow you up? They provide good protection, a guarantee of society's good intentions, barbed-wire camps a demonstration of our mercy, for they don't look so bad from a distance, just obstinate fortresses, ghostly castles out of fairy tales with proud little towers and battlements and ramparts. Live well, you criminals, but not in our backyard, instead spare us through your absence! Yet you claim that you've been done an injustice? Could be, but we don't want to, nor can we look into that, for the authorities are the ones who ordered it, thus it just happened. To doubt the good of what once happened is not our way. Okay, you say that you were not stuck in some fairy-tale castle. That could also be because they didn't want to fill the noble cells of the jail in our magisterial city of Stupart in order to protect the guards from recriminations by letting you be hauled off. You should have run away and hidden! But your pursuers wouldn't have stood for that. Which is why they hauled you off and took you far away. Long was the journey, long. Don't look so ridiculous, we know it was murder and not something pleasant. But we couldn't do anything about it, that's the way of the world. Onward and onward, summer and winter, through frost and heat, back and forth, without light and air, sixty at a time or a hundred crowded into a box, packed in, sealed off, without food and water. You should have died from that, but whoever came through was yanked from the box and tossed away.

To that you have nothing else to say. Fine, for thus you are exposed, you are not what you are! Aren't you ashamed to carry the noble name of Lustig? You must leave this apartment instantly! Off with you! Try elsewhere, if you want. The possessions of the dear Lustigs? That's carrying shamelessness a bit too far! No, the lovely, lovely, expensive things, we have stored them all away, but for the real Lustigs, if they should ever return, ah, how we hope it will happen, for we were so fond of them. You can't imagine what we indeed did for them! We would have loved most of all to have saved them! They were such good people, they never did anyone any harm, we can attest to the fact that they were always so good, so upstanding, so pleasant, each of them possessed a heart of gold, especially the dear doctor, yes, you must have known him! Now, there was a man! We'll never see the likes of him again! His winter coat? His gold watch? Are you crazy? We still have to take care of their things. We're very careful with them, everything is looked after and dusted, even Frau Lustig's jewelry, those earrings that were a wedding gift, two large black pearls, big as eyes, and then the fur, which was properly cleaned, and we spread mothballs between the clothes and underwear. It all takes a good deal of effort, but we do it gladly, because it's for the dear Lustigs. Indeed, if they don't return, our hearts will simply break, there's no way to express how sad that would be! That's why we have to keep watch over their things; perhaps Albert Schwarz will show up one day, the dear nephew from America, for there is no telling that he won't someday inherit everything. If he can prove who he is, then we must turn everything over to him, every last item, just as we listed them in the records. Then everything will be gone, though thank goodness not everything, really, for after having taken care of everything for many years we will certainly have to be compensated. Indeed, all of this stuff takes up so much room that we can hardly move in our own apartment. First, the many carpets that we have to lay on top of one another since we have no vacuum cleaner, then the many paintings on the walls, almost as if it were a museum, and all the glassware, the porcelain, the boy removing the thorn in the glass case! For years us poor folks couldn't tend to our own things and had to sell some of them just to be able to take care of everything for the Lustigs.

Zerlina turns pale, all the joy of having returned now drained from her. People don't believe Zerlina, the apartment doors open only a crack, because it doesn't help that she also remembers the past, for all that was in the past and among good friends is simply forgotten. They shake their heads innocently and are sad because none of the dear Lustigs will see their home again nor learn what selfless, loyal friends they had, who spared no sacrifice to save what they could manage to save. For a stranger, however, they can do nothing, no matter how much it hurts, no matter where they have come from, since the friends already have many other responsibilities. They have to think of their own families during the dark days after the war. The country is poor, the need is like it's never been, there's hardly any bread to buy, nothing in the stores, clothes hang in rags, such poor, poor people.

Zerlina turns away out of pity. She hasn't the strength to console the righteous, who think themselves unfairly treated after having suffered so much. Zerlina knows she will encounter much bitterness in this big, strange city in which everything looks the same, but nothing is as it once was. It's a dead, destroyed city, although the stones are still stuck together. The bombs have not smashed the walls, even though Stupart has long since died, despite there being more people wandering the main streets than before the war, the same businesses showing their wares, the same red streetcars rolling on the tracks. It's no longer the city in which Zerlina was born, in which she grew up and lived. It may be the same city, still called Stupart, but it's an endless cemetery of mass graves between which Zerlina cannot find her way. Not a single recognizable tomb is here, neither familiar nor unfamiliar names, because the dear dead that once lay here have been yanked out and their bones strewn throughout the world, there being no way to bring them back together again.

Therefore, away from Stupart, away from despair and the stench of tar that piquantly yet sinisterly almost robs one's breath. The streets have been recently ripped open, their naked entrails exposed, thick, bulging cables wind their way and are operated on; they are bound and taped together, an earthworm that rests nastily in the dug-up earth, though such misery must be covered up, the assistants shoveling brown clumps on the wounds in order not to sicken the eyes of the citizens, who are pained and almost brought to tears as they turn away from pipes, wires, and drains. Tar is sprayed by the doctors from large pails, anything scandalous is covered over and sealed off, the water mains and the telephone lines, everything banished and placed under the earth in order that the healing can fully begin. Then the feet can once again feel at home on smooth ground. The dead, who give life to people, shall not be seen. As soon as anything is dug up again it's buried again right away. It's a ceaseless business that continues on. Thousands of people make their living at it, making sure the dead are protected by water mains and telephone lines. The dead praise the work of the living, which nourishes them, for it sets in motion an endless cycle of discovery and encasement upon whose continuance the condition of the earth's existence depends.

Every creature takes part in this, but except for humans the rest are happy not to be aware of it, taking it as natural and enjoying the fact that they eat and drink from the dead, as well as living off of them and uniting with them. In fact, when they see that what they handle while living is really dead, they immediately understand and unconsciously their own being goes numb. The city is sad because everything here is human; its past is not something that can easily be restrained. Wherever the eye looks or the hand is extended, they encounter nothing but the residue of human time, the tracks running in crisscross fashion and close by one another, such that no one can escape them. They are everywhere and threaten to break through the brightness of day in ghostlike manner. Everything is but a remnant of those who have disappeared, whether it be the height of the towered cathedral or just a kernel of dust that floats up from the shadows to the sunlight. The work of the living only finds itself isolated in the realm of the dead, everything else that joy can be taken from comes from hands that have long since rotted. They press at the day with all their strength in order to overcome their absence, yet they do not exist, even though they are there because they are remembered, obtrusive, and hideous, as if they were not guests who had long since departed.

Zerlina must flee, just as she fled Ruhenthal. She must bore a deep hole, deeper in the ground than the graves of men. She must be alone and alone she must dig, for she must not be discovered. She must slink away like a thief, for no one will tolerate her escape. Whoever wants to live must live in jail, guarded by the police, yet Zerlina wants only to live. No one will understand that a person no longer wants to live among people. But to be just a person, that's what she wants, to be accountable only to herself, one who proudly dares to verify the memory of her possessions. Descending the bottomless shafts of the stairwells, deeper and deeper like a princess under a spell who wants only to disappear from the human realm. Quietly she wanders down through the core of the tower, passing all the niches and arches, not looking around, just feeling her way, no torch lighting her way, but walking along in a determined manner, carefully down the length of the street until she arrives at a still moment, and then away, away, inconspicuously and quietly, away!

What salvation it would be if the police and soldiers don't notice Zerlina, and she succeeds. She wears no jewelry and only simple clothes. She calls no attention to herself, she is a little seamstress, a typist who has just finished up her workday according to plan. Now is the time when she is allowed on the street, there being no curfew for hardworking girls who need a bit of fresh air in order to recover from work. Zerlina is not Zerlina, the friends of the family have proved it. She is someone else to whom no lover turns, someone unknown whose life has been saved by someone, but all of that is indeed long over, no one dwells on it now. She is a harmless passerby who after a while has shuffled on. Other passersby also walk down the street, all of them hurrying, knowing where they have to get to. Zerlina indeed has a certain destination, even if she doesn't know it, but that doesn't matter. She still senses people everywhere, even on the edge of the city, though there are fewer now, the houses spaced out more, smaller and more modest, followed by the rubbish heaps where children run, playing and letting their kites race with the crested larks, soaring upward. Nobody pays attention to Zerlina. Zerlina isn't even aware of herself. A boy and a girl look dreamily at the sky. They don't know what they're doing, and they also have no sense of a beginning and ending.

Two men are there with alarm whistles and clubs, and they release their dog. Already he's running, charging over stones and graves, then back again and panting with his flapping tongue. All of that would have been nothing for Bunny. But here it's serious business that transpires, an anonymous, almost nonhuman occurence that continues uninterrupted, even when there are brief pauses when one might think that everything has come to a standstill and nothing is happening. But the masters praise the dog, he wags his tail and sways back and forth on his front paws and lets himself be petted. It always happens the same way, the close observer not missing the smallest detail, tiny gestures, a hand that rises and points, a head that gives a slight nod. It all takes place as usual. Then it's over. It is, certainly it is. The wind blows, no, things cause the wind to blow, finding it easy to set it in motion. Hair becomes disheveled, yet it doesn't bother the grass when a breath tests its flexibility.

Zerlina wanders. She feels no hunger, she feels nothing at all, not even the buzzing of the disoriented flies. She pushes her feet forward in alternating fashion, striding in total freedom, starting out on a new path, or a path that has already been trod by others. Here in the bosom of the landscape it does not matter that everything has happened already and is now repeated over and over. That is only a music woven out of the same sounds. It's there, it must certainly be there, for the ears are full of the pleasure of its continuance. Thus there is only discovery and pursuit, nothing new at all. Only the moment is new, which knows nothing of other moments. But there is always what has been, for it has not disappeared, but instead remains within the moment; it is there and reveals itself. Zerlina must grab hold of it again, she cannot deny it, since she also feels that everything was already fated and predetermined. Her steps will become other steps, they are meant to be taken and will be taken, according to the same law; and yet—Zerlina's journey is also a new one. Never before has she pressed so far into the unknown with such ardency, never has she trusted the path so, despite not knowing it. But so the others walked before her, at first quickly, then slowly, then creeping, shuffling, dancing, running, hopping, and jumping. Then a foot hit a root, a gross oversight that leads to stumbling, the hard fall unavoidable.

But Zerlina is tough and doesn't let such an accident scare her. Already she pulls herself together again and hurries along all the more blithely. She has left all of her fear behind her, because she is certain that no one observes her behavior. Only she herself is concerned with Zerlina. Yet she can't guarantee that she won't fall now and then. This time, she in fact falls deeper. Zerlina sits at a long, low work table. She is imprisoned in the workshop. Vera is also here, and all the other women and girls. Are they all imprisoned? Zerlina doesn't dare look around as she feels and smells the work that surrounds her, the thin brown cardboard, the hands folding it properly as it turns into a box that will be glued, the top set on it, the building now complete, ready to be moved into. How lovely are the apartments, all you need to do is open a little door cut into the side, which one can slip through, little arched windows having been cut into the top, and the box is now pleasant and comfy.

After work is done Zerlina inconspicuously stays behind, now a rabbit who hides in the box. After all that has happened today a little rest is needed. Also, no rabbit can run around forever. The dead father is of no help. He is no longer in this town, no longer in any town. He fled much earlier than Zerlina and did not want to wait for her. True, the father deserved to go first, but the father should have said good-bye, or at the least have said where he was going. Was he even able to be properly fitted out? It just isn't right that someone simply dies and leaves behind those who are called the survivors. Ah, how careless are the dead, they go off and don't ask what will happen afterward. Poor Father! Did he want to die? No, he just wanted different food. He was sick of rotten cabbage and beets. He was also disappointed with the work. He asked to practice medicine, yet they only gave him the garbage detail. His many years of practice counted for nothing, for not even once was he consulted. His offer was laughed at. ABLE WORKERS BROUGHT IN. So it said in *The Leitenberg Daily*, which Zerlina read in passing. The first sentence stated: "The demand for able workers necessitates that in the course of the next . . ." Father is no longer an able worker. He had worked far too long, and that had sapped his strength. He had only collected ashes; from that his cheeks had withered and his hands were gray.

"Hear this, all you who do not wish to believe that I am the rabbit Zerlina Lustig: The father, Herr Dr. Lustig, has disappeared into the ubiquitous tar of misfortune, the inside of a rubbish barrel having swallowed him up, making it hard on the lungs, his pilot light having gone out, the boiler no longer warm, now empty of steam. After such misfortune the others have to change trains. That is the reason why only the living are still there, for we cannot bring Father back. We cannot even show you a death notice, none was issued. Just take a look at us! We are the ones you once knew. We cannot have entirely disappeared from your consciousness just because most of us are no longer here. But not everyone is dead! Believe us! There are survivors, we are survivors. With just a little goodwill you will see for yourself. We are not shadows, nor have we donned any masks. We have just grown a bit older and perhaps look worse than we have in centuries. Ruhenthal changed us. We have been miserably undernourished and have suffered difficulties that have etched themselves into our faces. Why do you turn away? We, too, have often cursed the fact that we still exist, but since we have come through we must find the courage to befriend you! Extend your hand! Don't stand off! You should love us because we want to join you! Do you not love us because we disappoint you? Oh, don't you think we're not disappointed as well? Should we cease to be simply because you wish that we no longer existed? We stand before you humble and agree that it would be easier for you if none of us appeared before you. Take then as compensation what we left behind with you, we want neither money nor goods back again if you will only have pity upon us and look on us as your brothers. Now it so happens that we are already among you again and must live side by side with you. That's why we will not shrink away. That's why we call upon your consciousnesses as witnesses to our existence, that which was, before you allowed without protest for us to be taken away from your midst, although you knew, indeed you must have known, that bad things were in store for us. Why are you upset when we now stand before you? Now you have no reason to renounce us, because you are not guilty, you did not haul us away, you did nothing bad to us, but instead helped us as much as the poor, weak ones among you dared to. We now want nothing more from you than the complete understanding that it is *we*, that we *exist*."

"We've heard so much about how you were hunted, you dumb, bothersome rabbits! Our only doubt is whether it made more sense to just let you loose rather than load you into train cars that took you to Ruhenthal. Another kind of journey would have perhaps have been altogether better."

To this Zerlina gives in and bows her head. She shakes because she is cold. She doesn't hear anymore what her old friends say to her who are now in the right. Zerlina tucks her front feet and lets her ears hang down. How nice it is in the narrow box. There she can settle in with a cabbage leaf, which would otherwise be dropped useless in the rubbish, as well as a bowl of water. It doesn't bother Zerlina that the box is almost too small to even allow her to turn around. Zerlina can move a bit forward and backward. There is enough air, the cardboard keeps out the cold, the muffled light suits her eyes. The rabbit is undisturbed, passing quiet nights. All the old friends have already left. Only once a day a guard comes and brings food. Otherwise hardly anyone notices the animal in the box; only a stranger hurrying past is pleased to suddenly hear a quiet scraping. Then he says, Ah, a rabbit! He says it in a light and friendly way, because the rabbit is a charming creature and only smells a little if his caretaker cleans him daily. Zerlina has at last given in, for the situation has managed to bring about what her will never could, and yet it's for the best that she is pleased to quietly chew and sip and move all the sensitive muscles around her snout.

The rabbit is confident and full of hope. It does not know what will be done with it, not knowing the hour of its execution, not knowing if it will even be executed, or if the terrible idea will even occur to someone. Nobody in the world worries about such things. All it takes is a hard thump and the tiny soul vanishes. Yet since it is still alive, it's guarded by an inexhaustible peace as long as nothing happens to it, though it remains on the watch so that nobody does it any harm. The feeling of any danger is mildly distant. Should fate reach out, then it will only be a dream without any threat. Thus Zerlina lives without any fear, cheerful, thankful for each moment. Others have gotten accustomed to the animal and sometimes let it out of its box since it's tame and obedient. Then it romps around the courtyard, the children rejoice over its funny capers, which pleases Zerlina, who is so trusting and gentle. When it's gone on long enough, someone calls, "Little Zerlina! Come, little Zerlina!" Then Zerlina hops happily back into the box, where fresh food is waiting. Thus many weeks pass, the fur of the once-shy rabbit becoming soft and shiny.

Yet the authorities know nothing about this metamorphosis and continue to send many letters to the address of Fräulein Zerlina Lustig. The letters all lie unopened, because there is no one in the building to take care of them and no one who has any idea where the rabbit is. The superintendent throws the letters into the rubbish bin and laughs that the officials are such fools. Yet because the animal is so sweet, it has long since been given the name Zerlina. Finally the authorities lose all patience with the fräulein, who has not answered any of their summonses, and some emissaries are sent who are meant to check up on the disobedient fräulein. The landlord looks at the symbol on the authorities' badges and bows deeply. His building is open to their official visit. The emissaries grin slyly and want Fräulein Lustig. Yet there is no fräulein by this name. —There must be such a fräulein. —Maybe, but certainly not in this building. Then the emissaries step inside and wander up and down from the cellar to the first floor and then back outside to the courtyard. No, there really is no Fräulein Lustig, nor will you find anything forbidden. At the end the emissaries come to a corner and take a deep breath to test the air. Doesn't it smell like a horse stall here? —That's not really a stall, but there is a rabbit that the children love. —That would make for a tasty meal in the middle of the war. —Oh no, the children wouldn't have it. They love their playmate. —A soft little animal, such a smooth, brown, and innocent creature! one of the emissaries exclaims, now that any trouble has been cleared up. Still the landlord continues bowing to the end, even though the emissaries are almost out of sight and now must search for Zerlina Lustig throughout the entire country. Yet the poor rabbit's entire body trembles, because it has entirely forgotten that it once again is there and present amid a thousand horrors.

"I'm not here. I have left. Yes, I have! It's been half an hour. When I will be back, I don't know."

"You shouldn't pretend. You endanger us all by doing so. You can't always pretend to be a rabbit."

"Why not? I cannot stand your incriminating looks! I've committed suicide. You'll find me on the dissection table because that's where they wanted to ascertain what poison I used to kill myself. In fact, I only fell out of the train, but the clumsy oafs didn't see it."

"Go on, stop talking such nonsense! You're right in front of us. Anyone can see that. Little Red Riding Hood in a wolf's skin, no, that can't be true! Everyone knows you by your long nose. It's no less obvious even if you cover it so thickly with brown dust."

"I'm not wearing any wolf's skin. How can you insult a rabbit so! My lovely little nose is real and is not made of dust. Father always said so. He claimed that it was a family trait. It comes from our rabbit ancestors."

"Nobody believes your story about the rabbit. Come here and answer when someone calls you! There's no fooling around in the Technology Museum. The times are too serious for that. They want to interrogate you and examine you, Zerlina! Have you heard? A body search, not a dissection of the body. They don't do that to people, only to rabbits and baby porpoises."

"I really am . . . I am . . . Is that what you want, for me to cry? Why don't you believe me, especially when I always gave you my little paw when you called to me? I detest lies. Mother taught me not to do that as a child. She told me how nasty it was. You don't do that. Not even in the most dangerous situations. It is better to willingly accept your sure demise than to have even the width of a finger between you and God's ways."

"You've changed the subject! Now you want to teach us morals when, in fact, you are the one who is pretending."

"I have never pretended. I am only talking about how things appear to me. . . ."

All senses dissolve beneath the earth. Only out of fear of the unknown do those remaining behind stand there and tip full watering cans so that streams of water flow into the earth in order that such dissolution takes place. Graves have become outdated, because they take up too much space and are too expensive. Cemeteries need to be made smaller, not larger. Land and soil will only increase in price. The town government beats every offer and buys it all up because it wants to build apartment boxes so that the rabbits' apartment shortage can be taken care of. But they keep multiplying and begin to take over, such that soon there won't be any more cemeteries. Boxes made out of waterproof cardboard will also be set up for the dead. A rabbit will live in each. Then no one will need a coffin when he dies, because he will just be left in his box, which will then be bound up with a little bit of string, all of it so comfortable and practical, after which the box can just be carried off to the crematorium. No need for a hearse, which indeed had not been used in Ruhenthal either.

The crematorium is practical and hygienic. It's one of the nicest and most useful inventions of the modern era, something that not only is an inspiration but also the product of the refined sensitivity of a civilized heart, quickly taking care of what must be done, as well as saving the grave diggers a good deal of work. The furnance can be fueled with oil, but as a result of today's advanced research it can also run on electricity. The length of time it takes to burn the body of a grown rabbit, which is similar to the time needed for that of a full-grown man, is about ten minutes, thanks to regular improvements, which will eventually reduce the time even further. This length does not suit the sensitive yet uneconomical cremation of a single corpse, but instead can simultaneously take care of twenty to thirty customers at a time.

The natural decomposition of the body is reduced to a manageable amount of time. This indeed means no food for the worms, but they can apply at the unemployment office for a new and better profession, such as agriculture or earthworks. That will also be healthier and more morally acceptable to the worms, for whom the decomposition of corpses, to put it mildly, is unappetizing. Isn't it horrible to think of how the obsolete way of decomposition occurs? But now the flame is lit, the energy is turned on, while from a religious standpoint the departed should be ready to be welcomed. It's regrettable that this Copernican act is met with so much enmity, but it requires proper explanation in order to overcome the last reservations. Look here, Vera, this was your uncle, a little paper bag that is neatly labeled and with a couple of dry little crumbs as its contents. It's just like it happens in fairy tales! You can put it all, bag and crumbs, into a tasteful container, ranging in price from a lead box to a Greek urn, which Dr. Plato selected, an embroidered barrel of sorrow that one can hold dear and can also be stamped with ornate lettering. The ashes were born on _____ followed by a lifted torch; the ashes died on _____ followed by a lowered torch. Up and down, so and so, one and two, back and forth, left and right, one in the earth, one in the urn.

Mixing ashes is completely forbidden in our line of work. A great deal of care is taken and everything is carried out under the official eye of a sworn expert in order to expand the public awareness among the savages. The executor personally seals each box and witnesses each bag being filled. Better that babies be swapped in a maternity ward rather than ashes! In addition the urns can be buried, and thus advantages of cremation are then linked with the preference for burial. How wonderful! And cheap!

Take advantage of it today! Reduced rates for suicides! How fortunate, an enormous step forward for the culture as a whole! Check out our free prospectus about our special offers on executions! Beautifully illustrated! Informative! Special editions available for children, with text that gently helps them understand! How entertaining! The electric chair belongs in the storage room next to the iron maiden!

Also, our executions are carried out in the quickest manner in our crematoriums. After disrobing, the patients are shot from behind on marble tiles, everything done with the utmost consideration in order to avoid any undesirable mess-ups. The corpse is then placed immediately on a conveyor that feeds into the fire of the furnace such that the lifeless corpse is never touched by human hands. As a result the danger of infection is reduced to a minimum. The perfect diet! Success guaranteed! Other methods of execution that are supposedly as good can hardly compare! One's last wishes can be fulfilled on demand or denied. Spitting within the crematorium, and especially during executions, is strictly forbidden! Afterward, the personnel must rinse out their mouths with an antiseptic solution. Technical malfunctions in the shooting mechanism are also unacceptable! Should the service be faulty then full compensation will be due! The crematorium and all of its equipment are completely protected against sabotage. All extraneous agony is to be avoided. Should it occur that the delinquent willingly gives in to his fate, this artificial way of dying is far preferable than any other means of separation from life.

Nonetheless Zerlina spits because she cannot control herself. She says she is sorry. "I did it out of overwhelming disgust!" The offense is severely reprimanded by the guards on duty, though it is also greeted with a considerate smile from the indentured engineer because the orderly completion of the systematic execution has been disrupted.

At reasonable cost the ashes can be sent to your house in a simple mail packet that holds an urn carefully wrapped in wastepaper, the package addressed and insured against loss and theft. Because it is likely that only a few will want such a service, a special public depository is constructed out of concrete, lead, and glass that allows for a tasteful display of human ashes. The rows run back and forth in an amazing zigzag fashion, left and right of the main street from the town gate. It's like being in a bazaar or the terrarium of a zoological garden, everything is done to attain the most comfort for the public, which wants to behold such things in orderly fashion. In this installation the urns live one atop another in four vertical rows, one next to another, much like postal boxes, each one magnificently decorated, a jewel locked behind glass. Whoever rents a box has one key, which the crematorium makes sure that you have, while a second key remains in the administrative chambers of the enterprise itself. Thus anyone passing by can take it all in with complete comfort. Everywhere flowers decorate the little boxes, whether it be inside next to the urns or outside hung from hooks and rings, thus signifying the eternal gratitude of those left behind.

Different classes of execution can be carried out, according to the resources available to the family or the readiness of the victim himself. Allowances are happily made for individual tastes by making various choices beforehand. Zerlina has paid a great deal. She wants to hear the cinema's organ play a chorale and the national anthem. It's a moving moment that leaves not a single eye dry. It's a rare treat. One can't often afford such a splurge. The organ whimpers and whines and complains to the living that they should be bold enough to not have anything to do with executions. Suddenly a rabbit runs into the middle of the ceremony. No one knows how it got into the hall. It disrupts the somber atmosphere inside the theater, but eventually everyone is lightened by laughter because the sight is so strange. Luckily a press photographer is also there who has a flashbulb and the presence of mind to use it. A couple of snapshots calm the bedazzled little creature. This is also true for the inconsolable widow, who, bent over, has taken her seat in the first row of the parquet, and who is moved as much by the lavish flowers as by the music, but for whom nothing is better than to push back the black veil in order to have a better view of the innocent animal as it hops about the suffering hall without a care in the world.

Only the officials from the ash factory are upset and become angry, because they are afraid that such an unheard-of incident will lead to bad rumors circulating in the city. Yet the manager knows what to do. That's why he acts fast and presses the electric bell that is normally used at the end of any execution ceremony. Immediately a servant appears with a large broom. The man sweeps lightly back and forth in order to shoo away the rabbit as he pushes the broom across the smooth floor until Zerlina grasps the seriousness of the situation and is already outside without having had a chance to pluck a flower or a garland, which was her most pressing wish.

Now the execution of Dr. Kmoch, the deserving president of the Medical Board, can proceed without further disruption. The national anthem begins, the powerful tremolo chords of the cinema organ are tenderly accompanied by the melody of the lead violin. Most of the audience rise to their feet. On the brightly lit stage copper-brown doors open left and right, set in motion invisibly as the scaffold draped in black, which holds the beautifully decorated coffin, moves forward soundlessly. Slowly it moves away, as is tactfully appropriate to such an occasion, the farewell itself being somber, as is proper. Now the flower-draped box is almost to the rear of the hall as it wobbles slightly, as if timidly entering a dream, the Medical Board on its feet and standing still at the back. The copper doors close again as mysteriously as they opened. Now the organ opens all registers to send forth the rhythms of the national anthem in thick waves of sound over the ceremonial hall and outward into every corner of the crematorium, as far as the oven that runs efficiently, and then farther into the open, where the running rabbit can hear it as well.

Suddenly the instrument returns to complete silence. Everyone is moved and weeps for the nation. Still the guests look on as the black-and-brown curtain is drawn across the stage with rustling cords, signaling an end to it all. The opera is over, the audience abandoned. The performance was wonderful and has made an unforgettable impression on everyone gathered here. Everyone has forgotten the incident with the rabbit. How surprised people will be to see it tomorrow in the newspaper. But maybe that won't happen, for the crematorium has a lot of influence, maintains the most crucial ties, and won't be above employing bribery to prevent the publication of the photo. Such things cannot happen on opening night. There can be only one view of the quality of the execution. The actors have carried themselves valiantly. The staged performances were appropriate and suited the exaggerated pretensions one can make on a fine stage. The music was met with the approval of the critics and the listeners, and even if the incident with the rabbit gets out, it doesn't matter, because its entrance was charming and only demonstrated a great love of animals. All in all the production and direction were superb, the media is impressed, it greets the production with enthusiastic praise, only finding fault with the meager courtesy of the star attraction, the doctor having neglected at the end of the execution to step out from behind the curtain and acknowledge the cheers of those left behind.

Yet nobody reads the papers anymore, for none exist. The crematorium is also empty. It doesn't matter that the doctor didn't take a bow, for he is no longer behind the curtain. He has disappeared. Nor is there anybody in front of the curtain, there are no mourners there. Actors and audience have dissipated. The crematorium's curtain separates nothing from nothing, death is everywhere and there is nothing else but what once was, and that is nothing as well. It's all in the past, long gone, finished, utterly changed, outside of time, Ruhenthal now gone and Leitenberg gone. There was only the journey and that's all there still is. Yet nobody journeys anywhere, but instead they just keep traveling, from rubble to rubble, from one spot to another, the rubbish of reality all that there is, and yet not even that, because that's also the nothing that hides in the face of nothing, the grave itself, the threadbare wall, the unseen face that does not look back, the fairy tale of nothing, the fairy tale devoid of magic, betrayal that cannot betray, steps that lead nowhere and without reason and without sense, where no one gets on and no one gets off.

Locales are abandoned because no locales exist. Leaning out of the window has become even more dangerous. Nobody dares to. No one sees anything. The faces are either hidden or drowned. Nobody has a home. Everyone is in flight and keeps on the move, because there's no other choice. Not even the ground exists onto which one might collapse. If anyone still runs around, it's mere folly. The graves that exist have been torn open and then sealed again without a hand having stirred. Nothingness has set in motion its own journey and whirls along because it can do nothing else. Chopped-off hands, which used to indicate directions on signposts, lie everywhere. They don't belong to anyone, nor is anyone afraid of them. They cause no fear; they are either just a last vestige of danger or simply a new trend. Yet there is nobody there who can understand what they mean.

If an eye looks at a hand it's with an empty gaze that does not recognize it or anything else. Yet an idea is still there, itself the first moment of creation, as it looks, imagines itself, and seeks to imagine, and since it wants to look, then something is again there. It wants to know itself, and in doing so gives rise to something more than itself, a being, whether it be a being that consists of nothing or is indeed a being, an idea that dares to exist, a nascent idea. It roams around outside, it cannot remain buried. It wants to make sense of the hands that cannot be untangled, that point their fingers in no direction that can be found on any map. Yet the idea grows stronger because it is. It doesn't give up and keeps trying, finally sorting through the images before it says: "There!"

The hands also point in that direction. And whatever once was reawakens again and exists once more, a "there" that is once again where it used to be. Yet what once was meant to follow the idea no longer exists. The immense effort now appears to have been in vain, a moment of creation that led to no creation, such nothingness being immensely powerful as it threatens Being with forgetting. Uphill or downhill everything is empty. There are or there are not destroyed graves. Yet the idea does not shrink, does not give in. It wants to belong to someone and command him. It's a person. He is not happy, but the idea makes him happy. He wants to follow it, yet he is too tired, the effort too much. The body cannot do what the idea wants it to. The body is too tired, and what the chopped-off hands point to doesn't make sense. They don't point toward anything and don't connect to any idea, but are pointless direction with no end. Thus everything is senseless.

The eye focuses and then discovers names next to the hands. They once named roads. Yet now there are no roads. The names mean nothing, they are faded, the color having drained from the names, separated from the hands, which are nothing more than dust-covered stumps. And no matter how much the gaze wishes to join together the hands and the names, it still cannot figure out how they belong to each other; they are so badly injured that they no longer mean anything. The names are mixed up and cannot find their owners. Yet there are no owners, there are just Anybodys, who are not names and not hands, but rather figures that belong to no one and which creep between the hands and the names, looking for a direction in which to head, although the eye sees no direction to recommend to them. They turn this way and that, each step changing the direction, then they grow tired and appear to rest, but only for a short while, an irrepressible drive pushing them on. Yet there is no road they can take, since none exists.

Each Anybody appears to be in the same situation. Perhaps each one knows that he has never been here, but rather has been transformed here. Back then it was someplace else altogether, but he cannot recall, he does not remember the name or the direction. This one with an idea is unsure of what is Nothing or what is Something, then he chooses Something. He feels overwhelmed by a past he does not know, yet which he can sense, Something having won out after all. This grants great courage and strength to the body, allowing him to decide to act. As soon as he exists, then he can ask questions. He stops another Anybody and tries to gain his attention. That doesn't work. Anybody doesn't stop and stumbles on uncertainly, not knowing he himself is a Nobody and not even an Anybody. Yet he tries again to help this Nobody recognize Something, and indeed, he's there, he gives a start; is he in fact now an Anybody? Yet he does not know anything, but rather mumbles dark sounds from an unknown tongue, it all having been a mistake. Better to try something else. The Question asks the Question whether Anybody knows which way to go? No, Anybody doesn't know, he knows no one in these parts. There are no roads here, they are elsewhere. But there must be roads, says the answering voice. The word *road* means something. Because of it this conversation makes sense and therefore has meaning.

Now the Question grows silent and wanders off. He tries his feet, which don't betray him. Here is a wooden pole with many hands pointing outward that have not been knocked off. This crossroads is in good shape. Each hand is sure of the direction in which it points and knows the name of the town it points toward, which indeed might exist, because the hand also says how many kilometers away it is. One has to go that far in order to get there. Unkenburg is only eight kilometers away, says the hand. Clearly the outstretched finger points the way, that being the direction one can follow. One has to give the body a direction and then guide it in order that it can make the connection. From here the body must go forward, because Unkenburg is a ways off from this point. One thinks about the distance ahead, and then sets off.

What one was once capable of must also occur now. Once time is restored, the familiar and reliable exist again. Once time exists again, you must trust how long it takes to get somewhere. But what is Unkenburg? It's not recognizable, the memory of it is still lost in the brooding. It is a place, though there is no one there. Are there other names you might know? They are not to be found here. They must be farther off than these hands indicate. How many kilometers is it to Leitenberg? It doesn't say. And to Stupart? That's a large city that certainly must be known everywhere. But *Stupart* is not written down, no matter how much the eyes search for it. It's better not to keep trying to look for it, for your strength won't hold out long enough to press through the unknown. The main city of Stupart should certainly be known. But no, it's not. It was known, and through long patience perhaps it will be discovered again. You have to hold on to the known even when it is not known. And so Unkenburg. It's that way.

Yet the mouth shapes the words *Leitenberg* and *Stupart*. These old names sound sad. Eight hundred years have passed, if not more. The city must be much older. The source of the name is locked away somewhere in the realm of speech. The names of old places are lost and forgotten. At the moment it is wiser not to pretend that this city ever existed. If anyone says "Leitenberg" or "Stupart," there are immediately ears that hear it, faces that turn in the direction of the sound of the voice. Now the mouths of strangers open and slowly send back a sound of their own, one that's a little sad, dark, and incomprehensible, yet sympathetic and friendly:

"Never heard of it. No. Don't know it. Must be someplace else or it doesn't exist. So much has been destroyed. It's certainly not here."

Then the strangers' mouths say some names that the voices listen to closely, names of places they've never heard of. Each one swears it's known by another name, all of it a confusing back-and-forth, painful, bleak, buzzing, an antediluvian stammering that grows ever louder, becoming an unrecognizable scream. All the places that once existed are named, yet nobody knows them, the speakers standing there alone with their names. The moment a name is tossed into the circle, the chorus answers with this litany:

"Never heard of it. No. Don't know it."

They don't know and have no idea. Then the toothless mouths shut upon their empty questions. All of the names of the places have been ticked off and not one has been found. Only the murky voices of the chorus slip deeper and deeper into the monotone singsong.

"Don't know it—Don't know it—Don't know it—"

Gradually the muddy chorus peters out, becoming sadder and darker, a silent rain, until it can no longer be understood. But then another voice rises from the muddy depths, crying out incessantly:

"To Unkenburg! To Unkenburg!"

Is it the wise old railroad that calls out so? No railroad runs in this lost land. Only the rails stretch out ahead as they sleep in desolation on the moldy ties, though they are barely disturbed and still bend in sharply controlled curves. However, there is no longer any service on these tracks. The rails are also not lit up, their silver-gray withers and turns brown with rust. Only one question travels along the stretch and weighs down the telegraph wires, in which it remains stuck and never sees light of day. The high poles stand there starkly, barely holding up the wires. The railroad has fallen into disrepair without any attendants there, yet perhaps the tracks don't lead to the destroyed graveyards, but rather to a place that still exists, and maybe that place is Unkenburg.

This name had once been heard. A captain had once had a general's staff map on which all the names were listed. Wasn't it Captain Küpenreiter? He was from Unkenburg, for it was there that he first saw the light of the world, and his mother lives there still. So there may be hope after all. Light and the world would mean salvation. Certainly Unkenburg is small enough that the captain can be found. He will certainly be happy to have someone there who once stood with a shovel on the shooting range at Dobrunke. The captain had made an inspection and was satisfied with the job. Küpenreiter was who he was looking for, the house where his mother lived. Yet the captain was long gone, nor was the mother there. He has been taken prisoner and draws maps for the enemy. White flags, blue flags, maneuvers take place in the countryside as if for real. Küpenreiter must remember Leitenberg, for one can't forget it. Too bad they took him prisoner. Or did he get to the other shore in time so that he could take cover in the woods? One would hardly think so. He would have had to flee very quickly and leave all the maps behind. But without maps he is lost, because he knows none of the names and can't make out the coordinates. Full of sorrow he thinks of the Scharnhorst barracks, which have fallen to pieces and disappeared in the country left behind. Two thousand kilometers away. A hand had simply pointed to it and it was no more. It collapsed in the middle of the rubbish pit.

The plague memorial has survived intact. Schwind the reporter was right to wait it out there. He has dropped the camera, so no more pictures will be taken. Yet his hands are still free. He holds on with only his feet, but his hands are free and point off in many different directions. Yet nobody says which one is the best, and the reporter gives no reply no matter how often he is asked. He can't, in fact, for he gave away his voice and no one has given it back. If one looks at him more closely it becomes clear that he has no face. He's no longer alive, he only stands there and waits for the new day to dawn, though whether it will happen remains questionable. Yet to anyone who stands below him, it appears completely different; he believes the time has come and he won't settle for getting no answers. Angrily he looks up at the plague reporter and lets him know that he no longer has any patience. Then Balthazar realizes that he who waits below will not put up with any nonsense, and fears for the future of his newspaper, which he cannot afford.

Balthazar waves to him to come closer to the column and shows him the way to Unkenburg. Whoever gets there first can write an article. There *The Unkenburg Daily* is being published. The paper is looking for freelance articles and will pay for them. Normally, unsolicited contributions sent in without return postage are not considered, but right now they are making exceptions. Extraordinary measures are needed to take an unusual step forward. No one will be upset, the editors have gotten used to hearing the unthinkable and now even expect it. How can *The Unkenburg Daily* special edition be published when the team needed to produce it isn't yet there? Also, it's a paper born amid the end of the world. Indeed, the last issue reported on the end of the paper's run. Balthazar Schwind strains hard and recites from memory:

"Because of the lack of anything essential we have suspended our existence until further notice, yet we hope that the crisis will soon pass. In light of this, any reports about anything essential will be highly valued. The unforeseen circumstances force us to take the sad step of closing without knowing exactly when another issue will appear, though in the time in between we do not want to fail to face such difficulties as best we can and survive them. To this end it will obviously require the cooperative efforts of our staff in order to overcome the present emergency, and so we ask for patience on the part of our readers, since we have complete confidence that we will soon be able to restructure. For the duration of this brief suspension we request your continued faith and understanding in order that we have the necessary time to gather our resources and begin anew."

The ghost below who hears this knows that not much could have changed, but it's comforting for him nonetheless, because in the meantime he has figured out who he is. Very quietly he also confesses this to the reporter, who has gone silent again. His name is Paul and he will live, provided that no one begrudges him the time to live. He won't be writing any articles, though, as he needs to find a road home, for he doesn't want the journey to go on forever. He's also tired and wants to find someplace where a room and a bed are waiting for a wanderer to use them. Until then the newspapers will have to wait or keep putting off their reappearance. Yet Paul, who knows little about himself at the moment, will soon realize that all that's gone wrong will not release him from such confusion, for it will be some time before he will have any clarity about his journey.

Meanwhile the toads* crawl out of their holes and begin to read. At first they don't find much and have to be satisfied with the writing on their hands, but soon they have smeared these monotone prayers and pull newspapers out of their wide mouths, which they then spread out before them and quickly read as they hop upon them. They are pleased that their newspaper has not forsaken them on this day. Each toad puffs himself up with pride, because today he finds once again his own meaning, for it's right there in the paper. Not only are day-to-day affairs restored but also the future itself is on display and exists because it has been printed. Every toad can read about himself today, for they themselves are the subject of the news. The newspaper, which until now was only the mirror on the wall, is now a manifestation of the market that has materialized and is full of public sorrow. The difference between the reader and the editor has disappeared. They are both toads who await their passing and who enjoy themselves in between. Things have come full circle. Hearts are worn on sleeves. The future is suspended, insurance is no longer bought, no credit is given, business has ceased.

This is why the windows of all offices and shops are closed. The toads cannot do anything or take care of anything. They say that things are only delayed, but Paul does not believe them. He asks that they give him a sign

---

Unken means "toads" in German. Hence, Unkenburg is the "town of toads."

if things are going to happen for real. Then they run away from him in cowardly fashion. Paul doesn't know whether they take him for a fool or hightail it out of fear. It's not hard for them to hide themselves. The field of graves is endless and full of puddles in whose mud the toads can quickly disappear. Not only is the train not running, there is also no longer any traffic. It must be lucky not to have any suitcases when things are at a complete standstill like this. Possessions that cannot be shipped only weigh one down. The town in which one stands can provide no security. Paul must acknowledge that it will not be easy to get away from this hole in the wall. But whoever wants to leave must do so at his own risk. Accidents can occur, because epidemics are everywhere just waiting to explode. Deaths cannot be avoided, because of the overwhelming nature of current conditions. The editors, however, don't post any death notices. The Unkenburg Department of Health has handed over authority to Dr. Zischke, the director of the hospital, after his strong recommendations. At the last gathering of the sad survivors it was decided to not meet again, as well as to entrust the administration of the archives to Poduschka the butcher and meat smoker, as all hands rose in a unanimous decision. Sausages that wanted to practice in the future could use the stethoscope of the former health minister. Following through on the consequences of the most recent developments, the toads, as well as their next of kin, are forbidden under penalty of law to prowl around near the city crematorium.

Particularly troublesome are the unrecognizable voices that suddenly pop up from the dead. They don't care about the newspapers, but appear when they wish and refute everything that's been said. None of them can prove who he is and therefore is ignored. Paul believes there is no need to worry about not having any identity papers. It's just an accident that the reporter happened to remember who he was and used a name that he could recognize himself by, though Paul granted it no worth, for it did not certify who he was, because there was no signature on a piece of paper. It's clear that the voices are for the most part felt to be offensive to the local population, since they continually scream about revenge, although the inhabitants are completely innocent, especially since the voices cannot prove the losses they claim. The menace expressed by the voices states how their existence should be treated as harmless, as if order still prevailed. Yet the voices want revenge for what is habitual to the toads. Revenge for the bricks that still exist in other walls! Revenge for the goods that they now have! Revenge for the families that one loves and wants to protect! Revenge for the fact that anything still exists! Revenge for what exists! Revenge, revenge, revenge!

Because of these screams for revenge, anxiety has spread everywhere, senseless anxiety; everyone who lived here and still lives here simply wants to settle into the lazy feeling of their own slumbering consciousness. Why are they being bothered and not allowed to just live? They should just stay in their houses and keep the doors closed. My goodness, the cries for revenge are scaring our innocent children! We've done nothing, it wasn't us, it was the others! Off with you! Look elsewhere! Elsewhere! Everyone here in Unkenburg is good. The stench of fear travels like gangrene through the streets, and because broken windows provide no shield against it, it enters all the buildings and causes the inhabitants to choke in their rooms. Paul, however, is not afraid of revenge and wants no revenge. He doesn't understand such baseless fear, for if indeed the time has come again when one can simply be, then no one should despair any longer. Everything imaginable has already occurred, the need for revenge having long passed. The hands of ruin have made manifest their power, and they were chopped off and tossed away. The great opportunity is now here, immediately after the end and right before the beginning. Anyone who is here should come along, but not tremble with revenge and be consumed by anxiety! The new day has not dawned, it is still just a possibility, moments occur that can still dissolve, although they are fleeting and do not last, mere accidents that can indeed cause fear, but find none, for they are simply the present.

Everyone has left. The country roads are full of people, but many of them homeless who have lost nothing and smile dreamily when a shiver of horror sweeps over them. The road runs past fallow fields that are not tended by anyone. Any old stuff grows upon them, anxious plants that no one wants to eat, whether because they are the weeds sprung from vengeance or taste of the dead because they have sprouted up in the middle of the rubbish pits. Such fruits of the earth do not give rise to pangs of hunger among the locals, and the homeless turn away from them in disgust as well. Nobody steps upon the contaminated earth of the fields that simply stretch out unattended, nor do the hands point toward them, and even today nobody wants to lose his way among them. The roads are indeed free of impediments, yet in the fields the war still lurks. The homeless gather together confidently on this road as they celebrate their resurrection from death and sing little bits of long-lost songs. A great migration has begun. Weariness has not yet been overcome, yet the will is more than strong enough to move forward and forget what is behind so that the past can be sealed off and the future can open up.

"It's eight kilometers away. There's a town there that I want to go to."

"It's destroyed."

"Not completely. It can't be. Someone told me. Bricks are still standing, walls. It must still be inhabitable. In fact I can see the towers from here. Those belong to Unkenburg."

"I've just come from there. Unkenburg is no more. It no longer burns. The flames of revenge have been stifled by anxiety, though the rubble is still smoking."

"And are there no people there?"

"There are some people there, but they are strangers. They want nothing to do with us. I'm headed in the opposite direction. Come with me!"

"No, I'm going to Unkenburg, because that's what lies ahead of me. I'm not turning back, because where you're headed is where I came from. There's nothing there. Turn around! Come with me!"

"I can't turn around either. It's too painful to turn back. I have to take care of myself. I chose this direction and I don't want to back down now."

"I've chosen the other direction. I don't want to go back to where you're headed. I barely made it out alive."

"And the same was true for me at Unkenburg. I can't hang around here anymore, I have to keep going. Safe journey!"

Thus it doesn't matter. You only want not to be where you have been already. Freedom cannot be built on those places where no freedom existed. Each needs to change his place, since he can't change the time. So the wanderers move off in opposite directions in order to realize their freedom. The destination is uncertain. The only thing for sure is that it's not here, it's elsewhere, far off. These wandering voices are now the masters of the fallow fields and will found a new order. Will they really do it? Paul doubts it. They will wander and find no home in which they can transform the order of their wishes into reality. Yet was there ever any order? That's the question. There was only the attempt; vanity was the only order that really existed. All orders have collapsed, all have led to betrayal and brought no peace throughout human history. Yet isn't now a new beginning, when things will finally be better? Paul had lived through the moment of birth. He had stepped from nothing. He sensed the wounds of a new being that spread through every limb, and so being was indeed there, which he loved and yearned for. No new world can be erected as long as the old one stands, for the old must first give way, which is why its destruction is not in itself evil. Even if it were, what is left has nonetheless disappeared, and thereby a new day has begun.

The past is erected as a memorial and placed in the Technology Museum. It shouldn't be just sent away, but it must be removed from the present so that it causes no harm. In the museum it can be watched over in order that it have its proper rest with no one to disturb it. Visiting hours must be set up and observed. No touching what doesn't exist! Can this save the new world? The new world is life itself, happiness and radiance, newborn possibility in your hands, because the resurrection has occurred. It's good that no one has celebrated it. What one celebrates tends to be useless. One shouldn't make too much of the good, but rather the bad. Good wants to do what it can. Things were indeed dark and immersed in death, there was no hope, nor any expectation. In a thousand planes rested what would soon rain down, the thunder of the bombs roared around the forest camp. No hands moved there as a voice in the huts wavered and called out.

"A white flag is hanging on the gate. We're free."

The voice spoke loudly, but without emphasis or expression. There was no doubt in it, yet it also did not sound convinced. It was just said so that it could be heard if one could hear it at all. Yet it was night. Liberation is not what happened, because it was something that none could grasp. What they could grasp was the night. Thus it was a liberation without joy, even if it was repeated by every voice. Nothing was written about it in the papers. There was nothing there about what had happened day in, day out. And so it seemed endlessly long. Had it been months? Years? None could say. Nobody had entered from outside the sleep of the dead. It was dark in the huts, no one would know they were there. Why was it all over? Why was anyone free? Were you not free in order that someone could free you? Could you really be free if you had to be declared so? The voices were alone. And if they had kept on repeating that the moment had come, it would have made no sense and been an empty sound. The dead lay between the huts and reeked. Freedom had come, yet there were the dead. Didn't one have to fight for freedom first? The fighting was a ways off, two thousand kilometers away, one thousand, one hundred, twenty, eight, but nonetheless a ways off. It had not reached the forest camp. The breath of the living rattled in their throats, only the strongest had any idea of what was happening. Yet even they didn't really know, for they couldn't turn back the night. They crawled to the windows and doors and saw nothing but night. And so they looked at the night. Was that liberation? They felt what wasn't, they thought what couldn't be, they had nothing of what was. Thus they were reminded, you have to wait for the day when indeed a day can exist.

A voice called out: "The flood has not yet subsided, the waters are running high. The weather is raging as never before. The black woods are full of the rush of water. Luckily the camp walls are thick. It's best to stand inside the ark, though inside the ark it's best to stand under the protection of the plague column. The saint has protected us for eight hundred years."

They look up at the plague memorial, and yet no recognizable soul hangs from its mast. That's a good sign. The sound of gunfire can be continually heard, yet none goes off nearby. The unconsecrated cemeteries lie too near the ark. Whoever dies is dragged out from the ark. A continual stench floats about, repulsive and sweet, yet also sharp and biting. Now and then a cracking sound softly erupts, but it is only the wind in the trees. One of the voices has brought along a fresh rabbit that was killed, but which is still warm.

"You can eat the meat. I have a little salt."

"That's Zerlina."

"Who is Zerlina?"

"A girl. You can't eat that. It smells like human flesh. We have to bury the rabbit or it will be a great sin."

"Are you crazy? If you don't want to eat it, then let it be!"

"Isn't it enough that you've committed murder? Do you want to eat the body as well?"

The voices shake their heads. The white flag has turned the poor soul into an idiot. Perhaps the name he called out was that of his lover. Yet the times are not ready for love, there's too much hunger and it has to be taken care of first. If he cannot eat, nothing will help him. It's too late for him, the healing has not healed him, for he belongs to yesterday and must die. —No, he won't die, he just sees double, but perhaps he sees after all. He will eat if it's not Zerlina. —They comfort him. —Yet he begs them to be quiet. No pick and no shovel. It's also much too dark. Who can eat the animal without there being any light? Were not the hours even darker when Zerlina had to die? And indeed she was consumed, but it was not by people, but rather flames. Have they indeed all died? —We'll have to worry about that later. For the moment you have to save others because you've been saved yourself. —Was she old? —No, but her mother is. —There is no mother, they were all taken away. —But maybe she hid herself, she was so clever and had some money. —If she did not hide, the money was useless. The money was taken away and the mother too, and they laughed at her, laughed, because she was so clever. —But what if she was able to hide? —Did she manage to do so at the right time? —No, she was in Ruhenthal and had to leave. —Was she transported? —She got on the train. —Then there's no hope. Whoever was deported and was old was killed and did not travel anymore. —Yet her daughter was Zerlina. —She might have lived if she was healthy. —She was healthy, but . . .

But why are you hesitating? Was she not all that healthy? —She was healthy, yet she was very sad. —Fool, no one was killed because they were sad. She could be alive. All of life is sad. —She was also faithful. —That means something. To whom was she faithful? —To herself. —That's ridiculous, that's not dangerous. —Nonetheless, she was a sanctimonious girl. —One can't be that without doing oneself harm. —She also stood by others. —One would hope so, but that doesn't count for a lot. That means nothing in terms of life or death. —She was faithful to her mother. —Was she transported with her . . . ? —We were all transported. —And you survived it? —I don't know, though it would appear so if you are alive as well. —Then the girl might also have been saved. —And yet what if she's not with us? —Such confusion! Are there no other girls here? —No. That's obvious. —So look then! —But when we arrived . . .

You mean when you arrived here . . . ? Say more! —Well, when we arrived and got off the train it was as dark as it is now. It was continually dark, darker than it could possibly be. It was a darkness so dark that no one could see it. That's the way it was when horrible curved lamps on high poles hung there and cast out the dense darkness, the light hurting. . . .

So it wasn't dark. It was just night, but you could still see. —No, it was dark. Nobody could see, we knew nothing, we were all blended together, but in the darkness. The others could see quite well, but it's likely they did not, even when it was allowed. And so we went through the dark, a swaying hulk of tired flesh. —So were there a lot of old people with you? —Everyone was old, us as well, too old. —You weren't old! The girl was not old! —Oh yes, we were old. —You were just tired. Everyone was tired. The uncertainty after the long journey made everyone tired. —No, old, I tell you. And then a man . . .

The one who wore medals? —The one who wore medals! You should have seen him! He stood there in all his splendor and held up a hand. —Of course he had a hand. —It was a hand like no other. This hand, it pointed. —Where to? —There . . . in different directions. Toward Unkenburg, toward Leitenberg. Two different directions. A long way. Eight kilometers or more, despite this dark weariness and all these old people. —Did he point the way for you? —It pointed the way. The journey is not finished. And the mother left. The daughter left. —The girl? —The girl left. She followed the mother. —And did you know? —I knew nothing. I stood there and wanted to collapse. —And the hand? —The hand shook. It pointed way off. Elsewhere. Back to Leitenberg! —Sent back? Impossible! —No, not back, that's right; it just pointed the way. Not toward the mother, not toward the sister . . .

So not a lover. Only a sister. —Yes, a sister. Yet she fell. The mother had her on her arm. Two women: a mother, a daughter. Women with skilled hands. What chance did they have? —None. We must eat the rabbit. Join me! It will give you strength. —The daughter is the rabbit. —You're talking nonsense. Daughters are not animals. —But she was faithful, only animals are that faithful. —But not rabbits! Only dogs, dogs! —No, but our dog was also a little rabbit, his name was Bunny. A dumb name for a dog, yet that's what he was called and he was faithful. That's how he got such a dumb name. As clever as a person, yet even better. Two men. No hand to point the way and no direction. Only a tail. It pointed nowhere, especially when it wagged, left, right, there was no deciding. It was like a clock striking the hour. —Bunny. That's good. Not a rabbit after all! —Don't take it so literally. She was called that because of her innocence. —Because of her innocence? —Yes, her eyes. Because such an animal represents all victims. She sacrificed herself, and now there are no more victims. Meanwhile such animals are treated as if they are still victims. Though it is not done out of scorn. They are eaten, then they're thrown away. The daughter along with the mother. Do you want to eat the rabbit now?

Then it's quiet. Only the dead rabbit's blood still stirs. It's not a girl. Its head is different. No girl has fur like that. Anyone can see that. It's an animal that ran off, and though it took the wrong direction, it's still just an animal. It turned out to be a good direction for someone who is hungry. They are happy though somewhat sad, but it is certainly an animal. It came and was a gift, though some would call it a victim. Have some and build your strength! There's already some wood burning in the oven. The animal is dressed and cut up, it stews in its juices and knows nothing. Whoever is hungry must eat it and be thankful. Sadness will do him no good if he wants to survive. Dirty salt is sprinkled on the fresh meat. Soon the victim is finished off and is no more. Justice demands that it be split between the seven voices. The brother eats it. It's the animal that his sister loved. Had she herself not tasted its meat as well? Zerlina is gone. The length of her journey can never be measured. The hand that once showed where and how far is broken off. All of them are gone. Zerlina is with Leopold. She resides for eternity in Ruhenthal in the shadow of Leitenberg. It's far from here. There is no memorial for her, only for the victims no one is willing to eat. No reporter is ready to write about her. The secretary refuses to even write it down. "That's not appropriate for our readers. Perhaps the other newspapers in the next town . . ."

Yet in the next town the same thing happens. The secretary won't do it.

"No, no rabbit flesh. The readers have had enough of that and want something else to read about. Maybe you should do a book about it. In another town there is a man who publishes books."

The man listens to the story silently and sighs. "That's not possible. For that's the truth and not fiction. Yet my publishing house is not suited to the truth." The secretary nods. "In some other town there lives a man who deals in the truth."

This man agrees to meet and listens patiently. "That's unbelievable, too much of a fantasy. The times are different and demand the pure truth, not fiction." The secretary follows suit. "You could maybe try another town. But I wouldn't hold out much hope for this rubbish."

And in the other town no one will even listen. The secretary states loudly: "Too late, too late! That was a hundred thousand years ago. Back then was the time for it. Not now. It's something for the museum in the next town, it's not too far."

At the museum in the next town they laugh. "We're all full up with that and don't want any more, no, not even as a gift. Earlier we took in such material, although we never had much faith in it, but out of compassion we took it in and stacked it up. Nobody looked at it in the glass cases. The public protested. Now it's all stored in the basement."

"But what shall I do? It's too much stuff to constantly keep schlepping around."

"There is no other town, none," says the secretary. "None. But stay out of this town and all the others!"

In no town will anybody listen. Nobody has ears for it. The first secretary yawns, the second secretary cleans her nails. The third secretary opens the door, the porter points contemptuously at the cemetery. There it says clearly: "All graves sold out!" All that is left is rubbish. Rubbish that is tossed away.

"Please, you really shouldn't say that. Given the current conditions, suicide is complete madness. You will be seen as a complete laughingstock forever. We have to warn you about the repercussions of such a public act. What you can't help doing we recommend strongly that you do privately and with no note left behind. At most just a note about some terminal illness or something. Then you can talk about your senses being confused. But it's much better for you and future arrangements, which we will no doubt implement, if you yourself were not so proud, but instead just tossed the goods overboard. In the prevailing darkness they will simply sink away. There's no need to worry that people today will try to save lost goods. They're still here with us in the shape of empty buildings. For the moment that's not too pleasant, but mainly for the revitalization of the public authorities, with which we are already busy. Later you will get a receipt for the contents that can be redeemed at the Unkenburg police station, though it will only cover part of the damages. A commission established with the help of the former enemy has already begun work there. The empty shells of your buildings will also be cleaned until the facades gleam once again, and the necessary bricks will be set back in order so that you don't come tumbling down. Until then, don't abandon ship. We have just created a dove and given it wings. We will release it near the plague memorial. Wait a while before you return!"

Paul walks farther along the road that stretches out before him. Perhaps he should have followed the advice not to leave the ark. It smelled so awful there, however, and after the first meal he could not stay there anymore. They had gnawed on the pale bones of the animal. There was hardly anything left of Zerlina. Now only flight could save him. There was nothing to take along from the ark. Up onto the deck. It's not far to the gate, no guard stands there. The gate is open. But can you go through it? Fear only lives in the ark. Freedom is possible only to he who conquers it. Jump into the sea of graves! What are you waiting for? There are so many on the ship, you shouldn't leave it. The hand holds on to a post, the body hangs heavily from it. The bones hurt inside the belly, for they are sins, consumed sins. Are there any people out there? A foot carefully stretches out. It's cooler out there than in here. The hand lets go of the post, the road is taken. There's nothing to look at; therefore nobody looks back at you. A miracle that the feet still work. They lift up and down, and as a result move forward.

The day is cooler. On the road there are people wandering, always wandering. Among them are women. One looks so familiar. Paul speaks to her. Her name is Clarissa. Most people call here Clara, though she doesn't like it when people call her Clara. Paul wants to know whether she knows of another who looks like her. No, she didn't think so, but what was her name? Zerlina, no, I don't know any Zerlina. She must be somewhere else. One comes across so many now. Indeed he is willing to probe more, but he doesn't want to press the matter too hard. He doesn't want to look for what doesn't exist. Too often he has heard how maddening this can be. Paul had come to terms with it all; he will be alone if he is to go on at all.

He will try, if only that life go on. Paul looks up. THE GOLDEN GRAPE. The inn is undamaged; it's not located in any town, but rather outside town, and now it offers refreshments and a brief rest. The innkeeper is back, the garden itself is covered in frost. Barrels of Leitenberg beer, freshly tapped, tasting bitter after defeat. The concession has not been lost, it exists once more in peace.

"Innkeeper, I'd like to place an order!"

"The end of the war is here, but not victory. I have nothing."

"Don't make excuses! You are an inn and a coffee shop. What are you waiting for? It says it right there!"

"I'm not quite back in business yet. Also, my family hasn't returned. The barmaid had to be let go and is long gone. I have nothing."

"Everyone is coming. Some refreshments, quick! You have a ration, don't you? So bring something, innkeeper!"

"You are displaced and on your way home. You actually shouldn't be allowed to sit under these trees. But I have nothing against it if you just want to disappear again. Only wagoners can stop here."

"None of them come anymore, and I don't want to just sit. I want something to eat, but not rabbit. The bones are too sharp. The menu, please! I also want something to drink! I'll pay more than any driver."

"Don't take out your troubles on an old man! Look, the kitchen range is not working. I can't even light a fire, everything was burned by the enemy. My inn is completely ruined."

"It's the same everywhere, everything is finished!"

"Yes, yes, yes, that's it! It's all finished!"

"Yet it will come back! So bring the sausages, the cheese! Quick!"

"Nothing! I have no rations!"

"Beer and wine!"

"The empty barrels were rolled out of the cellar. They were filled with rubbish. Then they were tipped over and smashed up! The staves are busted!"

"You're not telling the truth. Get something onto this table quick, or . . . or . . ."

"Or what? Whoever has traveled a long way cannot stop. Displaced. Have you not taken note of that?"

"I haven't traveled that far on this lovely, free day. I don't have that far to go either. Yet I've been on the move a long time, though at the start I was only eight kilometers away. The hand told me that."

"I don't understand what you're saying. Free days have been postponed, perhaps all days. . . ."

"You've lost your mind, innkeeper! Or has nobody in Unkenburg told you that freedom has at last come?"

"I've never heard of Unkenburg. But that's your business, which I don't want to get into. You should know that it's still a difficult time. Unrecognizable voices appearing everywhere have made it so. My friend, if I take a look at you, I don't see a man, and all I hear is an unfamiliar voice. My wife and daughter were taken away, and you can just rest here quietly? Have you no heart at all, such that you sit here all the same when I have lost everything? Gone, gone, everything gone, yet there are those who still made plenty! Out of here, man! Out of here, you soulless creature!"

Paul is again on the road. Soon there should be the bridge, the ribbon of water, silver and deep blue, then the gate leading onto Bridge Street. It's all so confusing. There is no corporal to be found, the soldiers have all left. They were taken away so that they could not march anymore. The plague memorial has fallen. How lucky that Paul was no longer nearby. From far off he had heard the muffled thud. The ark has been blown to bits, as well as the entire crematorium. Death sentences can no longer be carried out. The innkeeper's powder keg has been drunk dry. The spittoon split in two, and Mutsch the cat has eaten all the provisions. Rubble from the plague memorial is in the cellar. It's the ark's bunker of ashes. Here everything is preserved by the lice that have been spared in the last bombing. Nurse Dora wants to take care of them, but Frau Lischka will not allow anyone down the steps because the walls could collapse. Hospital Director Zischke waves off all appeals with his hands, no, he has no beds for vermin, though he orders the schoolchildren to collect the bones. The children are excited and obey without any fuss, because it's all for a better future, and so everyone is happy to pitch in. However, one can't ask much of old Johann Pietsch. He has retired from service and turned in his broom at the high school.

Paul walks on and no longer feels tired. Bedecked vehicles travel by swiftly, the men on them waving and throwing little gifts to everyone, which tumble in the dust. Paul could bend down for these treasures, yet he worries about his knees being weak, and he wants to keep his balance. It would be too easy to lose his way and have to start all over again from the beginning. He doesn't want that. Whoever can bend over is welcome to. Many bend down and fall onto the road and begin to gather what they can, taking as much as they can into their mouths and hands, almost dizzy with excitement. They ask Paul why he doesn't take anything. It doesn't belong to him. It's been tossed onto the road, something from which one doesn't take nourishment. The road should lead to a destination, not provide treats. The innkeeper will lie in poverty in his garden if his wares lie upon the road. He should be given something, he's the one to whom it's due. Your goods are only secure if inside a building. Yet many notice how miserable this wanderer is, the one who will not bend down and is in such a hurry because he doesn't know how to get to his destination and yet wants to get there, a hopeful wanderer, who it was easy to feel sorry for. Meanwhile they hand little bits to him from the ground, which he takes and thanks them for, sticking them in his mouth and pockets, a rich man to whom everything comes effortlessly.

His feet burn, for his shoes are terrible, yet the lazy blood begins to flow. Paul is very healthy and is happy to be on his way. He should take someone's good boots while yelling at him, for that would be a bit of revenge. In swaying lines the prisoners of war move along the road, themselves forlorn and covered in dust, though wearing good leather boots. You only need to go up to one of them and not even ask any questions but rather just point with the hands imperiously and without feeling. The guy then just bends over and loosens the straps, hands over the shoes, and still has to be grateful that he's only been stripped of his boots and is at least allowed to lie there. Paul stands before a pale young boy and looks at him imploringly.

"I can't walk anymore in these shoes and I still have a long way to walk. You've had the best shoes available for the longest time, your feet don't hurt at all. Now you're almost there and can give me your boots, but I have far to go, very far to go. Come on, why don't you hand them over? I could just take them like the others do, but I don't want to just steal them."

"I won't hand over a thing that's on my body. It's all that I have left. You can get everything you need. Just go to the next armory!"

"Who are you? Where are you from?"

"My name is Robert Budil. I don't know what's happened to my parents, or my brother, who is likely dead. The entire regiment was wiped out. My brother was among them. Let me have my shoes!"

"Budil? Are you from Leitenberg?"

"Why? What do you know? Are you from Leitenberg as well?"

"No, I'm not from anywhere. But I know someone named Budil in Leitenberg."

"Where does he live?"

"On Bridge Street. He had a very strange first name: Ambrose. I always remembered it whenever I walked by his house in my miserable shoes."

"Ambrose Budil, that's my father! Is he alive? Is my mother alive? When were you there last?"

"I was there a year ago, actually two years ago. It's been a long while. I don't know what happened to your parents. Maybe they've since left there. You must know better than I do, Robert Budil. Anyone with an apartment has something, indeed, as well as a lot more, and one can write letters then too."

"For almost four months I've had no mail. Tell me what you know! Don't torture me! I'll give you my shoes if you'll tell me! What's happened to my parents?"

"Keep your shoes! I have no idea what's happened."

"I beg you! How do you know my father's name if you don't know him?"

"That's easy to explain. I was often led by his house. I was imprisoned, yet I had good eyes. That's how I got to know Leitenberg, or at least as much as it would let a stranger see. Signs large and small. On a house on Bridge Street was a small brass plate."

Robert Budil is no longer listening; the train of war prisoners had only stopped for a short while to rest. Now all have to move on, the boys moving along weak-kneed, left and . . . right and . . . Budil walks with his good shoes, yet Paul also walks on, but in the other direction, persistently onward with his lame feet. He then looks directly at the town before him, and it no longer seems to be destroyed. The tower of the Unkenburg Cathedral looms above, high and proud. It even leans, or at least appears to. It's been shot up a bit. The monstrances have been damaged and cannot support it. The danger of falling debris forbids entry into the cathedral. There's no need for a guard before the entrance, for the doorways have shrunk, everywhere there is rubble, nobody can get in.

The bishop catapults over the rooftops, unable to bring the Mass to a close. In the middle of the creed he stops. The airplanes appear out of nowhere, only at the last minute are the sirens sounded, the bishop falling in his robe upon the cathedral square. Bombs rain down right and left, the bishop recites the *Dies Irae* and bellows it loudly, though there is nobody near him who wants to hear it, the church now empty and shattered, its followers no longer children of God. The bishop continues on in haste, not much time is left him as he dances upon the air and laughs because his work no longer means anything. It's no longer tied to anything, and so he cannot do anything, rubbish is all there is, the bishop no longer holds a post. He looks around at bodies that cannot take any sacraments because they are not alive and have no grave awaiting them. They have been damned and judged by vengeance, they have been violated to the extreme, they are the devil himself. Then the bishop looks at the other bodies; they are mute and do not want his blessings. They have bowed to him so deeply that they almost fall from the ark into the mud, but the mute are tough and embittered, and because they are dead, they cling to the bloody barbed wire of the creaking ark with gnarled fingers. The bishop flies, the doves fly. They cannot give any more blessings. The useless olive branch of peace falls into the flames, the fire blazes horribly. The dove's beak is broken, the bishop's hand has buckled.

The dead, however, let their tongues dip into the holy water. They lap it up, since they are so thin and parched. They lick up the water, the bishop can do nothing to prevent it, no matter how much he cries out or warns them. It is the bitter wine of hell that will not cool your thirst, but rather will only inflame your intestines with hellfire. Yet it does not bother the dead, they do not listen and do not believe him, because they smell the soup in front of them, a sour, made-up concoction of water, salt, and moldy beet husks with algae swimming in it that is tasty and not to be turned down. Suddenly an American is standing there and looks on amazed. The bishop wants to stop him, because it's not right for him to enter the church. First one has to save the dead, the holy walls of the crypt; the living can wait. But who now are the living and who the dead? The American is matter-of-fact and wants clear instructions. The bishop is still confused and because of exhaustion can give him no information. He points toward the destroyed cathedral with dried-up stumps of fingers and then to the bloody pools of soup next to the ark and hesitantly complains.

"De profundis clamavi."

The American doesn't understand a word and doesn't want to beat around the bush. He doesn't know the language that is being spoken. Impatiently he warns the bishop that he should tell him the truth.

The bishop whispers: *"Suscipe deprecationem nostram qui tollis peccata mundi! Miserere nobis! Miserere nobis! Miserere!"*

The American wants to hear only one thing. "Living or dead? Yes or no? Answer in English or in German!"

The bishop no longer hears, and smiles. He points toward heaven and to hell. Then the American turns away from the bishop in horror. He thinks, Such a thing would never happen in America, as he looks on at the haggard people crawling blindly across the ground, their open mouths falling upon the soup. Then the American shakes his head, his cigarette falls from his mouth. Already some of the crawling people are at his feet, scuffling for the glowing butt. Then the American takes up his camera in order to try to capture what his eyes can't believe. He waves to the slurpers and with his hands he gestures for them to form a group. Even though their thirst has not been abated, and though they are free not to follow his command, they still do what he asks, perhaps out of curiosity or more so out of an old, familiar obedience inspired by just a wave of his hand. Yet the American is understanding.

"I'm not taking a picture out of curiosity. I'm taking it for the sake of the memories of the authorities who sent me here to save you. Please, relax and look natural! It will only take a second!"

"Tell me, Mr. America, I have a family member over there who is also a photographer. Do you know him?"

"Oh, America is a big country."

"He's a good photographer. His name is Albert, Albert Schwarz. A dear son. His mother was taken away. Away, Mr. America, do you understand? Ashes . . . nothing more . . . She was my aunt. Who no longer has a dear son. Tell Albert Schwarz!"

"Sorry. Please, just a moment! I want to take another. You are safe now. Snapshots. Good luck. America will help. Don't worry. Moral rearmament."

"One request, Mr. America!"

"Sure, sure. Do you have Albert Schwarz's address?"

"No, I don't have anything. I need something else. I live in the city of Stupart, Mr. America. Can you send me a picture of myself? I want to have one for my obituary. My address? You can address it to Frau Lischka."

"Well, I can't promise anything. You know that the country . . . America is immense. Have a cigarette!"

"I don't have any other evidence. No one will believe me. People will laugh. Please, send it to me!"

"Sorry, America is immense, come and see it!"

Paul has turned away. He knows that no one will believe him, even if he could show them a picture. He has to move on. He is determined above all to put everything behind him. He no longer looks at the chopped-off hands. Now he has to get to Unkenburg fast. Maybe it's better if he also just forgets about himself. The strength left in him has no room for the past. Is this not an escape? No, it's necessity. There is a road to Unkenburg, so one can get there. If only the legs could work better! The head is clear, but the body is pained by the past that still won't let go of it. If he were still afraid, he would keep on the move for sure. Yet no one is after him. Only worry presses at him, and it's that which must lend wings to his every step.

Vehicles travel by in long chains. Happy exclamations sound out everywhere, the victorious army. Has Paul won? With what has he won? For whom? For the dead? For himself? He should put a sign around himself that says he is a victor. Yet who would believe him? Does a victor look like he does? Paul would get somewhere faster if he were to ask a young soldier for a ride on his vehicle. In five minutes Paul would be in Unkenburg. Yet he doesn't stop any vehicle. He would like to do so, but his waves are misunderstood, the boys think that he's greeting them as one of the defeated, and so they wave back at him respectfully. They are telling him: Nothing will happen to you, we're not that way, we're from America, we're here to offer freedom and to not step on the enemy who is licking the dust. Whoever does penance will be forgiven.

Paul is the defeated. He has to bow down, even if it's a mild yoke. First he has to prove who he is before anyone can trust him. Is he not a victim? Victims are the defeated, even if they are alive, and especially when they are alive. Yet how can Paul prove who he is when he's so weak? Who in fact has defeated him? The victors? The defeated? Paul belongs to neither. The victors are as foreign to him as the defeated, neither will listen to a word he says. The victors and the defeated will reconcile, while he will remain lying in the dust. No, he won't lie down, he has never given up. He wanders on, indefatigable, and wants to go on. He is on the road. He has no home at all, only the road that goes on and on. Is this Beggars Way? One must submit to servitude. Yet Paul was never a servant. Instead the defeated, a captured lord. Paul is a beggar king. His realm is without location, nor does the road itself exist. He walks along it because no one prevents him from doing so, yet he has no rights to defend. With luck there is enough confusion so that no one will question him. Paul is in no-man's-land and wants to be in someone's land. But is that a good idea? Is it not better to remain amid indeterminacy? No one will let him go hungry. He can join up with anybody. Anybody can become his friend, it's easy.

Paul must flee. He must find the end of his road in order to leave it behind him. As soon as he reaches town, the road will disappear to all sides, that way, this way, clues to it everywhere. Doors will await him, behind them apartments, the features of home, little bits of security amid the brief rest found in the decorated brick boxes. Unkenburg is not the final destination, but it lies in this direction. But in what direction is that? Straight ahead. Now unknown voices begin to buzz.

"We're walking this way."

"We're walking that way."

"We're walking."

Little bundles of possessions are exchanged from hand to hand. Paul is not empty-handed; he becomes ever richer. When he fled the ark, before the doves had returned, he had nothing. Now at least he has a bundle of this and that. Paul owns something; no one will have a problem with him now. Did he buy what he has? They were gifts, though every possession is only something allotted. Paul thinks to himself, This moment was expected from the very beginning, now the moment of the birth of creation is also being born. Is it free to make of itself what it will? You must do something. Movement left or right or anywhere. That's the first step of freedom—anywhere! It's a moment without headlines or newspapers. Whoever enjoys this moment, whoever knows that he doesn't have to read about it, he is free. All demands must fall away, it can be no other way. This does not mean that anything goes, but rather it is freedom. Yet each looks for a direction to follow. Will they only lose themselves by following any direction available? Will they be able to stick to it? Will they stick to the road they've chosen? Isn't Paul himself on a road he cannot get off? Ah, such confusion! When will all this thinking cease? And when will life begin?

Paul pauses in order to stand. The dust of the road has blinded him. So keep looking around! Cast a glance at the brindled fields. They lie there damp, some of them not having experienced the war at all. They are split up so nicely and must belong to no one. It's certainly not as cold now as it was this morning. The day has cleared up, no more rain presses down. The clouds are balled up into white puffs, a good sign. They break apart and blue sky appears between. A beautiful day. Lovely weather. The sun shines on the troughs below the underbrush, the light lines thickening into wider bands of vegetation that spread over each acre. The sun disappears, a light shadow whisks away the brilliance with a cool shower of haze, but then the sun returns, then again the light is subdued as it flashes off in the distance, followed by streams of light that reach out powerfully from plumed clouds. The entire land is bathed in gold, the sun has won the day. Everywhere there is light. The last white streams up above dissolve into a light snow of blossoms that quickly blow away and disappear. The broken-up fields will for this day remain drenched with sun.

A little rest is needed. Nobody stops you from taking it, and no voice says you shouldn't. There under that slope it's nice and dry and is a welcome site to the wanderer. Little beetles are not afraid of him, because he is happy within himself. The flowers in the grass are happy to bear his weight. But why rest now? Paul rocks back and forth. Whoever separates his life from thought will not last. Whoever wishes to just wander along without thinking will meet his own death before he reaches his desired destination. By taking a step Paul had left the road, and his body followed along easily. The view that the eyes slowly take in tries to seduce him into the unknown. Another step. It could be a hundred steps or more. That way, not Unkenburg. No hand to point the way. To remain in the unknown would be a good way to simply be. No need to own anything, no need for a grave. It could be a hundred steps more or even farther. Any step could be the one to reach your destination. Just one little step more. The feet don't have to be lifted, they can just slide along on solid ground across the soft grass. Yet Paul knows well enough that none of these steps can take it easy. All of them are in a hurry. They can't worry about finding quiet and rest, for they are nothing but blind, irresolute steps that must serve him, though he himself feels ashamed. Why do you want to rest? Only the dead don't want to go any farther, only the imprisoned. Those who are free have no demands. Don't give in to your weakness, stick to your path! Yet what wouldn't you give if only you could lie upon this slope for a week? What would you have given yesterday? Nothing! You can't give anything. The question is pointless. Now that you carry along a little bundle, you don't want to give anything away, nor should you. Paul leans sleepily toward taking a break as he slides along the softened ground, his feet gliding along, yet his body bends, the right arm thrusts out ahead, the hand stretches forward, as Paul comes to a full stop. He must not fall on this day. Yet he can no longer stand. Today he might not reach Unkenburg.

He must open his eyes in order to avoid the ditch along the side of the road. Just keep moving forward. Eight kilometers, so that's how far it is. Seven kilometers, it's less and less. It can't be much farther. When Paul looks around a bit, he can make out the mud-spattered milestones. Six kilometers, four kilometers. Halfway there. It must already be less than that. The town is more and more visible. Here there are no more milestones. Does the town not want to reveal where it is? Or have the stones been gobbled up out of necessity? You shouldn't still be on this road! Why didn't you try out that bed of grass on the slope? Now look at what's happened! We need you to be elsewhere, we really need you, you have to hurry up. You're not unneeded, don't get all wrapped up in your worldly pain. What are you complaining about? Only fools keep whimpering because they can't get rid of old habits. Yet you have no more inner resources, that makes you appealing and of worth. We'll pick you up and won't ask questions for too long. It's happened to you so often that you shouldn't be at all surprised. You can trust us, it will do you good. Be grateful that we give you fair warning. With others we give no notice at all, we just pick them up and interrogate them.

I was also picked up, yet no one said much to me. What's the difference? —There is no difference, it's just the same; you just take it in stride and adapt yourself. It's always true that you will be taken away the moment you believe you can be. They just call it something else and say, You've been picked up because we simply didn't want to let you go. You shouldn't be left alone any longer. —Yet when I was picked up I was left alone and locked up. At the end of the trip we were taken out and separated. The hand was there, all hands had flown off! —Get ahold of yourself. All have traveled your path. There are many destinations and many that die on any given day. —Some die every day. —That's why you should celebrate no specific day, but rather every day. Think of birth and death. Mourn your friends and take joy in your grief. —But picked up and hauled off! —You know the truth. Protected and always in the same hands. Your future the same as all others. —The one hand . . . ! —Renounce your urge to flee! Take the hand while it is still there! It's not cut off. It points the way and all others point to it. Often it knows more than what the eyes can tell you, often it is all you have.

If we can rip tree trunks from the earth along with their roots and topple stylites, why shouldn't we be able to haul you off? Anyone can be handed over at any moment. —To whom? —Just handed over! —But there's no one to be handed over to. —He conjures it himself; now he can choose his journey. —So there's no freedom after all? —Take it easy! What the hand chooses is still free because it is chosen. Only he who cannot decide will be sought and picked up. Freedom consists of orders and coercion, judgment and fate. —The choice sets in motion the future, it lies in the future, and it gives one a direction for its own reasons. —Now be reasonable, you little corpse, which we weigh within our hands. We can do with you what we want, and we can make it seem as if it was what you yourself wanted. But we don't want to do anything. We're just part of a chain. Above us is a hand. The first connects to the last because his hand connects through other hands. It's the same throughout the world and for all times and will always be so.

Now he is close to town, two kilometers, one kilometer. It can't be much longer. Everything will be available in Unkenburg. The people have thought of hard times and prepared for them by storing up provisions in order to last out the worst of it. The fear of robbery is indeed very real, causing many to hunt for what they had hidden, yet no one bothers you if you search high and low. Paul doesn't want someone else's things, he seeks no revenge, only his own missing things. It's not stealing when you take something out of a stranger's attic. The goods become his own once they enter his own house. But is that still standing? The cracks in the walls are not dangerous, a little whitewash and they'll be just fine. The security fortress still holds a lot. In the pantry you can find treasures stored there for ages, a little state seal on every glass! Everything is still there and has been well taken care of. Frau Lischka has her shortcomings, yet she does well at watching over the building.

"So you're back, Herr Lustig! My husband has already opened a bottle of schnapps for you. But please, just carry on. The next floor up you'll find the old doors, though there's no longer a sign. But it doesn't matter, Herr Lustig. It's better this way. No one knew that you were gone."

Nobody could haul off the apartment's furnishings. Only the raspberry juice has spilled and left a nasty stain on the floor. But it's not blood; a bit of hot water and soon the floor is clean again. If only the bed were still there; a mattress would certainly help a sore back.

"Where is my family?"

"Only Bunny is here. I fed him sausage and cheese myself. That way he stayed fat and round, and he kept a lookout for you. I said to the clever beast, 'Herr Paul is such a good man, you will see him again.' Then he was happy."

"Quiet, Frau Lischka, I don't care about any dog! The others! Are they back?"

"It's a pity, they've been gone almost four years. They never sent even a single postcard. That wasn't right. I was so worried for them."

Frau Lischka would have liked to have known where their journey took them. Back then she could not see at night where the family had gone to. The streets were dark, it was almost midnight, the front door had to be closed. They had turned right, thought Frau Lischka, the right direction in which to head. A hand had pointed that way, and then there was nothing more to see. For a while you could still hear the heavy boots clomping on the hard pavement. But only for a while, just a bit, and then they were around the corner. Then everything was quiet. Then they were indeed on their way. But where were they going such that it was forbidden . . . ? Paul, didn't you run after them? It wasn't possible, his shoes weren't up to it. And so he couldn't reach his loved ones and fell. Now he is back. Yet whoever returns from the dead alone cannot be welcomed. He has no papers, for they have been taken away, having disappeared in the hand that grabbed hold of them and tossed them into the fire. It's no surprise that no one recognizes Paul. Yet since he reached the edge of town he has been lifting his hand in greeting everywhere he has gone.

The American guards examine the new arrival for a long time and are amazed that Paul could be who he is, though no suspicions are raised against him.

"Where are you headed? The town is closed and is still in a war zone."

"But I'm here and want to come into town."

"Is this your home?"

"No, it's just the first town I've come to. I have to get inside."

"Transportation is not up and running. First, order has to be restored. It's better if you don't go in. There's nothing here but hardship and misery."

"Then that's where I belong. I'm begging you, let me in, if you have a human bone in your body. I'm only looking for a roof over my head."

"Don't move! I'm warning you. Wait a bit, or better yet go on home! The war will be over soon."

"But I'm here, home is too far away! I will head for it once I've regained my strength."

"If this is not your home, I can't let you in."

"Then I will make this my home."

"Even if you do have a home here, and I don't care if you do or not, I'd still advise you to keep out of Unkenburg. It's better for anyone to just head off for parts unknown, where things are better. It will also be better for you to put some distance between yourself and here."

"Please, stop torturing me! I've already walked eight kilometers today. This is where I was headed today. I don't have a home anymore. I can't go any farther and just want to stay here where I am now. As you can see, I can't go back. I can't set foot on that ark again. The horror of it all: the rubbish, the bodies, the burning, the ashes. I had to leave! I don't want to stay long in Unkenburg, just a day, just a night, maybe a little longer, until I can go farther."

"Okay then, go on in if you must. I warned you."

Paul thanks him and quietly ventures in. How long since he had been in a city! Here is one at last; how easily it offers itself up and takes in any stranger. The first houses are still standing, their walls intact and appearing at peace. Nothing has happened here. Is it a dead city? Only a couple of strangers walk along and tread upon the street, openly astonished by this city as their steps forward an older fear and flight that cannot end and which still pursues them, although the fear has melted away. Doesn't anybody live in this place like it's their home? Hard to believe, the windows are so clean and there are flowerpots everywhere. It smells of imposed tidiness. Unkenburg is supposed to be beautiful, Paul knows, for he'd learned it in school. The city had a glorious history. The inhabitants are proud of it; the generations that followed had preserved it, the winds of war had blown through but now are gone. It was on display everywhere and a part of the city's fabric. Hands pitch in and make sure that all of it is cared for and protected. This is not Leitenberg, no, it's much nicer here, friendlier, the quality of life much higher.

Paul walks on. He's pleased to be in the city. He feels lucky to have come from the dusty road into a city that can protect him, even if it's a foreign city. It's only fitting for one who was moved from his own city, who lost it, and is not part of it any longer. He is pleased by this foreign town and will be a guest who will appreciate much more deeply the sanctity of private property as a result of the distance gained through his experience, rather than shaming himself through the conquering gesture of an outstretched hand. Each and every house is encircled by a lovely garden lit with the brilliance of spring. The sidewalks are tidy and well taken care of. Paul can walk along them, which does him good, the embrace of the city warm and feeling wonderful.

He still sees but a few people on the streets who scurry along with shy and bashful steps. Their glances avoid Paul, as if they don't want to grant such freedom to a stranger from whom they fear revenge. Paul turns somber. His terrible shoes are ashamed to walk on the pavement, his tired feet hurting more and more as they lead Paul's anxious head deeper and deeper into the city's net. The streetcars are silent, various cars are tossed about and reveal their innards. There are only heads and legs in Unkenburg, as well as, out of habit, some hands. What had Paul expected? He had been warned and it would have been smarter to avoid this city. Now it's too late. The stranger must take in what history has prepared for him, he who couldn't wait until he could leave the ark for good.

"Where does one find the city's commandant?"

"I don't know."

"Someone said police headquarters. Which way is it?"

"Sorry! I'm a stranger here, just got to Unkenburg yesterday."

"Which way? There has to be one!"

"Maybe. Ask someone else."

No one knows. Everyone is like Paul, they've just arrived. Unkenburg is just a stopping point, a way station. Again onward. No one stays. Yet questions, questions. Paul finds nobody who is from this city. Have they all been taken away? He must ask at each house, but he doesn't feel comfortable doing so, he's too shy. Perhaps it's forbidden to do so. Perhaps the buildings won't stand for his presence within them. Paul, however, is tired and wants advice. No one can give him anything but a piece of bread. He must be hungry, it's obvious. Someone hands him some sugar, another some chocolate. Now everything is available. He just needs to keep walking slowly in order to get everything he needs. There's no need to find the commandant. Here is a bottle of wine. Paul stuffs it into his bundle, thanks, he won't drink it now, maybe later. He has to keep going, time is wasting.

Paul walks on. The middle of the city must be somewhere. But as he presses on, the rubble begins to rise around him. There's a building that's been hit, the roof is caved in, the rafters protruding starkly, though the walls have not suffered much damage. There are people living in the basement. Over there another building has been hit, but the damage only looks slight. Two boys are stacking bricks. Just a bit of fresh mortar and they can be used again. People are on the move, the buildings will survive their wounds. Paul looks at other buildings that have been blinded. Or are their eyes just sick? The windows are covered over with wood and sheet metal; they will need good glasses. A little lookout remains open for the pupils. Is there someone looking out? Here is a building, only half of which still stands, the other half having toppled to the street, though it still has a roof above the exposed rooms. The table stands, and around it many household articles. A coat hook with a hat and flowery decorations, looking as if someone had carefully laid them there. A picture with a golden frame still hangs as expected on the wall. It's the parents, the father tall and stately, the mother soft and happy in her veil, a wedding picture, as anyone can see. The people in front of the building have a lot to do. They are rescuing treasures, a bureau with underwear still in it that is pitched into a basket.

Paul walks farther. Here the streets appear to not even exist anymore. But whoever, like Paul, is not afraid can keep going. Perimeter walls stand untouched, displaying their plaster covered with colored paint, little angels on each window's gable smile their protective smiles, the gutter work running the length of the walls as the rushing sound within them hurries to the ground. Everything is as it always was, only the homes that should exist behind the walls have disappeared. They have been taken away; only here and there a smokeless chimney towers, crowned by the open wind guard. Below in the cellar holes are white arrows pointing to where one must dig in order to retrieve the former inhabitants who together have gone to their salvation. Is there no point in the rescue squads trying to free them? It appears they have come at the right time, because here someone has scrawled in chalk:

WE'RE ALIVE!

The dead buildings are the identification cards of the living, even if they cannot live there any longer. Some had been taken away from the buildings and were alive; others, who were alive, saw the buildings taken away from them. Is that revenge? What is revenge? Paul didn't hear any voices. It happens, but vengeance doesn't exist, nor does Paul sense any vengeance within himself. Then he looks around, everything is silent. The city is strange, and doubly strange is its collapse. Paul reads the newspaper that hangs upon a wall word for word. "We are alive! Look for us eight streets left, then around the corner to the right, number fourteen, in the house in the back by such and such. . . ." Joy answers doubt: they're alive! Indeed taken away from here, souls carried off in thin hulls, yet stored away there, taken care of. Oh, what joy that you're alive! But who will go looking for you? Who do you expect? "We're alive, even though we're elsewhere!" The ashes have not been tamped down, nor is the fire put out. They were just too weak to carry off all the rubbish, which overpowered them. They gave up and simply crept away from one heap to another in a different street. Why didn't they leave the city and the area? Did Unkenburg put a spell on them and keep them from leaving? Isn't there a law that says there is nothing to protect you if you aren't here? You must want to live to be saved, even if it's several streets off, left and right.

Yet Paul keeps going, searching and searching, reading the newspapers posted on many walls. He cannot keep straight all the names that are posted. They are names handed down through families, legacies written on the destroyed houses instead of flowers brought to those untended graves, and by which the souls of these buildings from back then can still be remembered, the piled mounds of bricks serving as shelter for them. Paul is pleased that amid such misery these addresses have provided shelter to the names of others, even if they are not among those he is looking for. The name Küpenreiter is not among them. Fine, there are so many names; all one has to do is keep searching tirelessly through the newspaper and the truth will out. Yet not just the buildings are destroyed. The streets here are also badly wounded, the ground ripped apart, cellars yawn wide and gape open with their stench in the full light of day, rods bent, water mains exposed. Paul has to walk with caution, one step to the right, one to the left, then around the corner, then better to step back and then go around. Out of the rubble treasures left behind appear, even fragments seeming precious to whomever wants them. It doesn't take much effort, just bend down and grab hold, or just use a stick to scrape away the rubble, for there's much that's there to take. Yet Paul moves on, he doesn't have time to kill.

Paul pushes on through a tangled wilderness, which is the old part of the city. Artfully carved stones, long since weather-beaten and newly blackened, confess themselves a part of time that has died, that is no longer, though it nonetheless still lies confused and sunning itself in the clear light of the present day, which still has mercy upon what once was. It is quite warm, here it's still burning. The attack was defied, the lost fatherland still wanted to be victorious. Now real guilt suffers in secret as a result of inflicted guilt, but above such adversity stretches a sky empty of shards, full of clear air. Only little fires flicker, slowly fueling themselves. A man stands there. He warns others about something and points with his hands in senseless gestures. Not too close, best to go around, the wall that's leaning forward is pretty shaky, the stones are loose and are about to fall. "Whoever doesn't have anything to look for here should get out of here!" Paul is now a free man who doesn't allow himself to be ordered around. —What do you want? —I'm looking for the commandant! —He's not here in the rubble. —Where is the commandant? —He's not here. Everything that was alive was taken away. —Where are the others? —They will be buried later after everything has been pulled down, the chimneys still standing have to be toppled. The outer streets are much safer, Paul is told. He takes no advice, but instead walks straight ahead through the field of rubble. As long as he's going forward. Then a fallen horse. Has someone pulled it from the museum? The legs and rear are recognizable. Why doesn't anyone bury the old nag? A horse?! First come people who are still alive, then dead animals.

Paul drags himself farther. No matter how much he wants, he still can't get himself to move fast enough. The burned-out city requires caution. Here is an outlying plaza with old elms. Even the limbs are knocked off, the tree crowns destroyed and barely able to sprout. The most fashionable shops were once located here, the riches of the world displayed row upon row. What is left has been taken off to the museum, if there's anything. The businesses stand wide open, cleaned out and without any wares. The only vendors left are those who have been buried alive and who no longer have any customers. Only beautiful signs still hang there in the night, though no one comes. No one watches over the wares that are left. On a pane of glass one can still read:

HAPPY WITH YOUR PURCHASE?
PLEASE COME AGAIN

There is city hall. Only the entrance stands in undamaged splendor. The building cannot be saved, it is swept away. The officials who worked here each day have fled. Nothing is administered, the city no longer has any city fathers. Perhaps they are not far off and are hiding where walls are still standing, inside of which they still govern. The higher-ups have time and are only waiting until everything is on the mend once more. Then they can show their heads once again and nothing will happen to them. And so it happens. Honor us once again! Orders ripple through Unkenburg. The orders say what will be closed. Be patient, we will certainly be back, it's just today that we have to hide out around the corner.

Paul reaches a deserted playground, then a dormant park that is a little messy and weedy, though spring has shyly reappeared within it. Some of the trees are damaged, but others are not and are sprouting. The first branches are budding. The grass is fresh, the flowers are opening up. Nobody sits on the park benches, for there is no one who wants to. Even Paul doesn't allow himself to take a rest. In the middle of a flower bed there's a memorial that still stands, the white marble having turned gray, what was once a general. His name is pressed in gold and will last for many years. The city is grateful; three times he saved it, hunting down the enemy until it lay stretched out in the dust and demoralized, the citizens never forgetting it, fame and honor following. The general raises his saber, proudly as ever; he has lost only his head, though it lies not far off in the flower bed and looks satisfied, because victory belongs to him. Only the nose is missing from the face, but that doesn't matter. A sculptor will make a new one and set the head carefully back on the trunk. The living will fulfill their responsibility in placing the healed general once again on the decorated pedestal.

After the general, Paul doesn't look around at anything. He crosses the park, behind it towers the cathedral, a noble work of time-honored beauty, three hundred years spent on its construction. It still stands as its creator had planned, its massive weight lightened by its delicate features, a placid embodiment of the spirit of the firmament, its dimensions conveying certainty through their weight and welcoming the observer, who after having seen so much destruction can now take joy in the quiet safety of its mighty height, because it stood the test and did not collapse when all else did. This is a comfort. The residential buildings have fallen, city hall has fallen, the churning whirlpool has swept away Unkenburg, sparing this lovely building around which the city can rise once again. The enemy was honorable in sparing this treasure. Paul only looks for a short while at the wonder that for a moment grants him faith, and then he looks up. It pains his eyes. One tower still hangs above, the other is lopped off, the steep, bright slate roof now caved in, the delicate high windows smashed, the great rose window over the portal now blind. Not even the cathedral is sacred. Away from here!

Paul hears music, singing and instruments, none of it can be too far away. So there must still be happy people here. They are lucky to have a long building that's still intact and with a large courtyard. Paul hurries inside, they welcome him with slaps on the back and chuckling comments, arms encircling him as they walk into the house and into a cluttered room. The celebration pains him. They offer him a chair. The celebration of freedom. Paul forgets for a moment, because the drum beats so loudly. Paul is a victor, and victors celebrate. Soon they'll be going home. This Unkenburg, who cares about it! What happened, there's no need to talk about it, it's all in the past. The city is destroyed. Who can be sad about that? It's only right, it's pure revenge. The cathedral there, a couple of hundred steps away. A cathedral? They'll rebuild it. But people! Taken away! Taken away! At least there's peace again. Time heals all wounds. Only life matters, lovely freedom and all of its revenge, the overflow of riches showering down on all. . . . Paul no longer listens, the voices blend into one another such that none can be heard. The tired spirit cannot hold together what is being torn apart here by many voices crumbling, and what a sound, each one singing a different song.

Paul squats with his back bent and sinks into himself. They bring wine, they bring bread and butter, a plate full of apples. They offer him sweets. He should take some more. They bring good shoes; it doesn't matter that they're not completely new. His feet are pleased, Paul is satisfied, even if one is bigger than the other, the pliant leather rubbed with whale oil. One of them ties Paul's shoes and strokes them with his fingers as if blessing them. They bring him a dark green woolen coat. It's soft and smells clean. The people say that they will soon leave Unkenburg, most likely in the next few days, in a week at the latest. He should stay with them, there's a bed free in the hallway, he can have two blankets, a feather pillow, and a mattress that's been filled with fresh straw. Paul is not from their country. He has to leave. —Where are you going? Paul doesn't know, maybe to Stupart, maybe not. The new friends press him to stay, they will make him comfortable and take care of him, they will take him along to their country, there it's beautiful, there he will be free, he will have a new home. Paul is touched and thanks them, yet he says sadly that he knows nobody in that country. —What do you mean you don't know anyone? You indeed know everyone who is here, and everyone there is just like everyone here. —No, Paul has to go back to the country from which he came. —They tell him that the war is still on there, even though it won't last much longer. He should wait until it's over before he returns. Meanwhile they invite him to travel with them. If he still wants to go back later, then he can go on his own to Stupart. Paul thanks them again but says no, he has to get to the commandant. They hardly pay attention to what he says and continue talking. Yet one of them knows that the commandant is at the other end of the city, not far from the train station. —Police headquarters? —Yes, that's it. They explain it to him, first take a right, then straight on. Paul says good-bye in his new shoes and new coat and is once again on his way.

Paul can't make any headway. He asks once again for the building he's looking for. Most have no idea. Some point him in the right direction, others lead him astray, but slowly he presses on. At one intersection he remains standing and recognizes the theater. It looks a lot like the one in Stupart. About half of it is still standing, namely the stage with its protective iron curtain that has been scorched by heat and shot through by bullets. The prompter's stall has survived intact. Maybe the prompter still sits inside it and whispers his prompts so that the show isn't interrupted. Yet nobody makes a sound, the actors have gone off. Strands of fabric onstage sway in the wind. Isn't there a rabbit squatting there who is waiting for the show to start? The music plays on merrily, yet so quietly that Paul cannot hear it. The coffin has already disappeared, soon the burning will occur, which the public never sees. One cannot even demand the producers show it, for no one has been charged an entrance fee. Nonetheless some would steal a glance at the stage, though no one remains, there being no proper audience left. The public is denied the sight, though in fact it's never even presented on stage. The spectators have been taken away, their most important role has disappeared. Paul knows for sure that the time of the spectator is over. Whoever does not want to act for himself now is lost, for he does not exist, he no longer even has an apartment in which to live. Will guest performers still be allowed to make an appearance? If the trapdoor has not been destroyed, there's still hope. Whatever is still a part of the theater can be rebuilt. The onlookers will gather before time's stage. Then the present will dawn again.

Paul quietly says to himself: "You're still a part of this. You are on the road with your companions and friends, you stand, you walk, you fall, and you die. The image of the journey. Memory that is ever drawn to wandering. There is a center that is the original beginning and final destination of the journey. Have I reached the destination? Am I now a guest? Am I the innkeeper of The Golden Grape who plays his role before his guests? I'm standing on the stage, like a dead man fleeing a specter." Paul stops short and ceases whispering the moment he senses someone nearby. Paul laughs, trying to pull himself together as he is spoken to.

"You're not from Unkenburg, are you?"

"No."

"I thought not. But a theater lover nonetheless?"

"The hand. The wrong way. The crematorium."

"Excuse me?"

"I'm sorry, I know. You mean the theater?"

"Yes, the theater. I'm from Unkenburg."

"You're from Unkenburg. That was the stage. I can see it. That means the stage is still standing. Everything is there. One can still play a part."

"Unfortunately that's not possible. But I thought the same thing. You were just talking as if you were onstage!"

"And you understood what I said?"

"No, I didn't. It was too soft. Are you a professional? Pardon me, a friend of the muses?"

"I'm not a professional actor, and yet I am. It's kind of a joke."

"Excuse me?"

"I mean that I'm not at all from the theater. I only act in a certain way, not for real. I don't want to disappoint you. Instead I'm from the museum. I am from the Technology Museum in my hometown."

"So then a theater lover. Pardon me, but you seem somewhat upset. I don't want to bother you."

"What do you mean!"

"I see that you've had nearly as hard a time of it as me. Any sensible person today can't help lamenting any destruction that occurs. Whether it has to do with a theater or with a museum, there's really not that much difference."

"Or people, the many, many people? If it has to do with a crematorium? . . . The difference, perhaps one can only flee the specter, no rest . . . the journey . . . taken away . . . rubbish, rubble everywhere . . . Forgive me . . . !"

"Are you all right?"

"I already said, forgive me! I'm tired. I have traveled too far. The image of the dead stage got to me."

"I had a subscription."

"Really? Tell me about this theater."

"Even in the last year of the war the best plays were still staged in Unkenburg. Then came the tragedy—everything destroyed. You can see for yourself!"

"I do see! And yet you had a subscription?"

"As you can imagine, I was well off. But you have to bear what you have to bear."

"Yes, yes, you have to bear it! It's terrible! Everything is terrible! Please, just keep talking! Did anyone take a bow after the dead waltzed across the stage in their own blood? Was there a lot of applause? Were people moved?"

"My friend, you're talking crazy! Theater is not reality, theater is art. What's wrong with you? Are you sick?"

"No, no! But the applause? Was there any applause for the actors as soon as the curtain fell?"

"Yes, it was often wonderful! It really released tension, then people settled down."

"Did you settle down?"

"Yes, of course I did. You should also settle down. You have to be able to forget. Only the exalted remains. It above all has to remain. One must seek out refinement, not rawness, which is served up today. Please, pull yourself together!"

"I am together. And haven't you nonetheless settled down? Forgotten as well?"

"One has to! It's the responsibility to do so that art demands. Only then will life be life once again. The ideal raises us out of the everyday, the pure joy found in the highest things."

"Enough of that! The horror is still afoot. The voices call out. A hand points into the abyss. The long road. There are the refugees who stream out of the ark. They don't want anything more to do with the theater."

"I can't make sense of what you're saying."

"I'm talking about rubble. It's everywhere."

"Ah, what does this have to do with rubble! The rubble will be whisked away. The need to rebuild is what matters."

"My friend, the rubble, the rubble! You will not make a dent in it with picks and shovels. It stands in the way and will trip you up."

"Bewilderment will get us nowhere. But we can deal with it. You can be sure of that."

"No, that's not the way it is. But I don't want to quarrel with you. And the crematorium? I mean, the theater?"

"That will also be taken care of with time, at least I hope it will."

"You mean the theater?"

"Certainly! That's what you were asking about?"

"We're still talking about that?"

"What else is there?"

"I'm talking about rubble."

"I'm talking about the theater. I'm happy to talk about everything, but first things first."

"You mean rubble, at last I understand. Theater or rubble, there's no longer any difference."

"You talk strange. It's perhaps better if we don't talk about this anymore."

"It's hopeless. I know that one of us is dead."

"Forgive me, but aren't you the one who is acting now?"

"I'm not acting. I see only the rubble of Unkenburg. I'm sorry, I don't want to disturb you."

"No, no, it's fine. Is there anything I can do for you?"

"How do I find police headquarters?"

Paul moves on and doesn't look back. He passes other buildings, many of them without any damage. What would happen if he entered one? It doesn't take him long to decide before his hand is already on a door handle. It gives way, the door is unlocked. The stairway is clean, the steps gleaming. People must still live here. Nothing at all has happened, on each door there is a nameplate. These are displayed in the usual manner. None of the names is familiar, but they are names that sound pleasant. Here nobody was taken away, time has stood still and has not been torn in two. People were not disturbed and walked in and out freely. They only had to put up with little raids, then they went back to their routine affairs. Maybe someone lives here who can help lift someone else from the rubble if you ask him to do so in a reasonable way. Paul adjusts his coat and wipes a hand across his face so that he looks refreshed and a bit better. He doesn't want to frighten anyone, he is neither a beggar nor the bearer of bad news. He has only one wish, he wants to see the inside of an apartment, if indeed one really exists. On this nameplate is the name Wildenschwert. That's as good a name as any, and so the address has at last been found. No need to walk the length of eight streets and around the corner. Here is the final destination, here lives someone who lives in his own home. He also has a doorbell, so he must get visitors. He cannot be completely surprised that someone should show up. There are many who come and don't even attempt to ring the bell. One certainly opens the door for them. What need then for doors at all?

Paul presses the button and it rings. Someone is in the apartment. After a while Paul hears footsteps. The door is cautiously cracked open, the eyes of a woman look out, as a strong voice asks what the stranger wants, there's nothing here to take. —Just a simple request, no need to be afraid. Just to see the apartment, nothing more. —There is nobody here, it's not even my apartment. —Yes, but he wants to see it, he isn't armed. —What a strange request. What's the meaning of this? —Nothing really, just to come in for a little while, no, not to move in completely. Just a visit, in and then out. Not to confiscate anything or to steal anything. —There are so many who show up now who want something, all of it out of revenge, though that means you have nothing for yourself. —Paul shows her his empty hands and says imploringly that he wants to see an apartment, just to look, nothing but look at an intact apartment, an apartment free of rubble, if such a thing still exists. It's been four years since the stranger has seen an apartment.

The woman decides to trust him and no longer denies entry to her unknown guest. Once she opens the door, Paul takes a step back in surprise, then gathers himself and staggers clumsily over the threshold. He is blinded and can see nothing and asks if a light can be turned on in the foyer. —No, unfortunately that's not possible, for even though the electricity is still on in the building, there are no lightbulbs, there are none to be bought. The woman opens the door to the living room. Paul realizes he should walk in. The dog is tame, he doesn't even bark once. He strokes the pant leg of the guest with his snout. He's a good dog. What, Bunny? No, he's not called that. That would be a strange name for a grown wolfhound. Two boys are there, whom Paul at first doesn't notice; they stand there with mouths open. The children shouldn't be afraid, he's not a bad man. Big boys shouldn't be afraid. The guest won't be staying long and he likes children.

Would he like to sit down? He'd love to, he's a little tired, but he'll wait until later to sit, if that would be all right. His heart pounds loudly, he feels hot, he's come a long way and at the end had climbed the stairs, which was a strain. That's certainly the sitting room, but it's been cleaned out, a bed put there instead. A refugee lives here, but luckily not a foreigner. It's important to have someone you know when you take in people these days; the foreigners are so careless, the things they use here are not theirs, and so they ruin them, and nothing can be replaced anymore.

The woman talks on, but Paul hardly listens to her; he is transfixed by the sight of the apartment and wants to press it into his consciousness: a room with furniture, a room where everything is intact. There is the bed where the refugee sleeps, a tasseled blanket thrown over the bed that's not new, but smoothed out so that it looks nicer. Each morning the bed needs to be made in order that the room remain pleasant. At night the blanket is lifted and folded back carefully, underneath it are the white sheets. Paul would love to grab hold of the blanket; underneath there must be a mountain of sheets as white as blossoms. The wood is brown and gleams with polish, the woman having wiped it with a dust cloth. Emmy had done it once a week. The furniture also is not new, yet it is well taken care of. It had been purchased in the hope that it would last a long while. The children are well brought up, they don't kick the paneling with their shoes. There stands the vitrine, the family's treasures, their inheri-

tance and memories. Paul bends forward and sees a lot of glass and porcelain. Something one has but doesn't need, it's just beautiful, because gifts
are always beautiful, though pointless. Yes, they are souvenirs, the woman
confirms with a smile. Most likely she is pleased that such things interest
her guest. Not a bit of dust mars the view, she is a good housewife. That
one belonged to her grandfather. He had indeed smoked this pipe, it's
made of real meerschaum. Today nobody smokes such a pipe, there's no
tobacco. There's also a plaster figurine there, it's the boy who is pulling a
thorn out of his foot. They had the very same figurine back home, just a
bit bigger. Paul said that his mother had taken it when her parents' household things were divided up. It stood there on the piano. Paul can recall
when his mother had brought it home. There had also been a lute just like
this one on the wall, though it didn't have as many strings and was made
of lighter-colored wood, more yellow than brown. His sister had played
it when she sang, though sometimes she played it quietly without singing, plucking lightly at the strings. Now the lute is gone. —Why? —It's
broken. —How did that happen? —Don't ask, it's too sad to tell.

"Will you go home now?"

Paul hesitates. He should not have intruded. Frau Wildenschwert
doesn't mean to press him, she is just curious and talks and talks without
end. He doesn't want to talk about himself.

"You're one of those people that was set free, right?"

Paul can't disagree. But "set free"? Who had set him free? Nobody he
knew. He left. Nobody had tried to stop him. The ark was forgotten on
the beach. He walked eight kilometers, and back and forth throughout
Unkenburg.

"Yes, I was one of them. But that's all over now."

"Was it really so horrible? There have been so many lies. Indeed, no
offense, but at the very least it doesn't appear that respectable people were
taken away."

Paul listens with burning ears. He doesn't want to say anything that
he's thinking. Perhaps it hadn't involved respectable people. But what
does that mean? And where are the respectable people now? Respect?
What respect is there left? Respect had disappeared from the world.
Whatever happened outside as the ark sailed on and whatever rotted

within it—all of it had rotted to the core. Yet no one today can slander those taken away, those who were gathered behind barbed wire and left to die.

"I lost everything. Father, mother, sister, my name, apartment, possessions, and home. If I make it home, I will not be at home. I am your guest and don't want to bother you."

Frau Wildenschwert says she is sorry. She can't do for her guest what he deserves, but she can offer him some coffee, there's also a bit of schnapps in the house. Paul won't allow himself to be bought off through gifts. He goes along with it, for he needs it, but he's not a guest who was expected. An intruder is usually an official with a task at hand and thus someone who needs to handle matters appropriately. The orders are gone through carefully and not simply carried out haphazardly, like when Herr Nussbaum's messengers hunted down their victims in the middle of the night while desecrating the apartment. Yet Paul has no orders from a government office, not even a bogus office; his appearance here is inexcusable. The disturber of the peace in the best room, his presence detestable since he has no right to be here. The best thing to do would be to say a sincere thank-you, turn around quickly, and hurry out of there with his tail between his legs. But Paul has no control over himself, he has lost all his strength. Because of his weariness his gaze remains fixed on a painting. It's a medium-size oil painting that shows the Unkenburg Cathedral, still intact, in bright light, the sun beaming down too strongly, though the colors are not too bad, just a bit overdone, too much that's too pretty for an aged cathedral.

"Yes, that was our cathedral. Before the enemy, excuse me, America . . ."

"It's nicely painted. It's not entirely destroyed. Just the one tower is broken off, the slate roof done in. It can all be repaired."

"Not inside, it's completely gutted! Barbaric! The marvelous remnants of our glorious past! Not even the stones are spared! And they're supposed to be human beings?"

"The theater is much worse off. I saw it. Only the stage is left."

"The theater . . . that's right. But the cathedral! Have another schnapps! It seems to suit you. It was in the middle of the High Mass when the sirens went off. What did the faithful do to deserve that? With effort the bishop escaped without being wounded. It was almost a miracle. What is it that we've done that allows our city to be laid to waste? We were peaceful people and wanted only to live in peace with the world! A country of justice and order! A prosperity achieved through the fruits of labor! We've been hounded by envy and hate. What took us a thousand years to build was swept away in an hour! Rubble like sand castles that children build and then destroy. What right do they have to do that? Everything, everything taken away from us! Before the war we had a lot of tourists, even Americans. They couldn't believe the beauty of Unkenburg. Now what can they look at? Have another schnapps!"

"Thanks. Please, no more, really. I'm not used to it. My legs will get too heavy. The velvet on your chair is wonderful, so soft and comfortable. You've lived here a long time?"

"It's our home. Two years before the war started was when it was finished. We've lived here eight years. That is, until my husband . . ."

"Where is your husband?"

"Drafted. They took him away. He's been gone five years already. I haven't had a word from him in over a year. I can only hope that he was captured. I still believe he'll come back; one has to have faith when you have children."

Paul can no longer remain sitting. He paces back and forth in the room. The master of the house is missing, but his home is still there, the apartment is in order. No doubt that's his picture in the frame. Herr Wildenschwert looks on solemnly. Why did he go to war when he had such a nice apartment? When one goes away, the family cannot stay in the apartment. What kind of loyalty is that? Everyone must have gone to Ruhenthal of their own free will. The couple were married in the cathedral, and the bond that was sealed in the cathedral cannot be broken by the hand of man. The train takes everyone away. The hand pointed in the wrong direction. Anyone who allowed himself to be led in that direction was a fool, or so they say, they who sit here lamenting inside an undamaged building. His picture is no substitute for him when his children look at it every morning. The moment he leaves, the country ceases to exist. The children can leave, Herr Budil, that's okay, but not the parents; they must spoon out soup when the table is set. Today there is sausage; Herr Poduschka made some extra. Does one braise rabbit in the Wildenschwert household? There are so many ways to prepare it. Fresh out of the box is the best. The lid opens, Snow White can now leave Ruhenthal. All the others there are now also free, and so they leave on freshly cut crutches, Herr Wildenschwert also is there with a fresh crown of nettles resting on his pale penitent's head, two legs and a nose, left and right, the last broom thrown onto the rubbish heap and never, ever, ever seen again.

"You won't have to suffer any longer once your husband is back, will you? Prisoners are being set free everywhere."

"I hope so. One hears bad things about the prison camps. The people are fed badly. It's horrible."

"That's right. Only soup. Nothing in it. Not even nettles. Nothing floating in it at all. But you can eat it if you have to. No, no thank you, no more schnapps!"

"Oh, come now . . . !"

"You're still alive, Frau Wildenschwert. When your husband returns, then his journey will have arrived at a happy end. Two healthy sons await him. That's lucky for you, two lively boys!"

"Only Herbert is ours, the younger one. The other is my nephew, Ludwig. His name is only fitting for this awful time, Ludwig Schmerzen-reich."

"Your nephew is named Ludwig Schmerzenreich? What a name!"

"I'm serious! It's my parents' name, my brother's. What's wrong?"

"It's my mother's maiden name, Caroline Schmerzenreich."

"What a coincidence! Is your mother still alive?"

"Didn't you hear what I said? I already told you, lost, everything lost! She followed the wrong hand. She had to. My sister also had to."

"The wrong hand?"

"The wrong hand! There the tall man stood in the cool glimmer of night. His face was pale, and his hand pointed unconsciously, for there wasn't much time. Don't you understand?"

"How can I understand? Your mother, your sister, they're women! They don't assent to what any man says!"

"They were women . . . they were! And as for assenting? They were hauled out of the house along with me, with my old father, with my sick aunt. All of us were taken away from the home in which we lived. There we had all of our things. . . . We had them just like you have them here. . . .

Our things, the things in our apartment, where you could look around, all of it, all of it! We were taken away without any questions asked. It was at night. We had to leave. That was four years ago."

"I don't understand."

"You don't have to understand. There's nothing to understand. You only have to know it because it's simply what happened. We were no longer allowed to exist, and now my dearest ones are dead! Gone! Gone! That's all you have to understand!"

"Have mercy on the children! Not another word! It can't be true!"

"Why not?"

"It can't be! Have another schnapps! It will give you strength. I have some cake. Unfortunately there are no eggs in it, yet there is real sugar. It will taste good! I also have some raspberry juice. The son of a Schmerzen-reich . . . maybe we are related?"

"We most certainly are not! But thank you. At last I have seen an apartment again. That's all I wanted. It's very beautiful. My dear lady, that means a lot. It's certainly well-swept. You've been very kind."

"Wouldn't you like to rest a little while longer? Make yourself comfortable, just like at home!"

"No thanks. Maybe I'll stop by again in the coming days, should I want to see an apartment again. Maybe, if that's all right with you. An apartment where everything is still . . ."

"You can stay! It's nice to have you. You can stop by whenever you want to! Or is there anything you need? Maybe a shirt? My husband still has many shirts here, or a tie! You don't seem to have one."

"Please, let me be on my way. Perhaps you could be good enough to tell me the way to police headquarters."

"Do you know the city?"

"No. I just arrived today. Twenty-four hours ago I was still a prisoner."

"Ludwig will show you the way."

Paul is already outside on the stairway. He holds on to the railing, for it's a building with strong walls that has not been harmed. The stairwell smells of strangers. It's better not to be here, but it's hard to leave this place. Paul is happy that Frau Wildenschwert has at last closed the door. He doesn't want to see her again, nor hear her sharp-edged voice again.

Every word was painful. The layout of the apartment seemed stuffy and musty. The air was much too heavy, it was like mildew, somewhat dank and cold, sort of like the sweet schnapps that Paul should not have had. How can he at last get free of this building? Ludwig might be big enough to help. Paul only has to whisper a word to the boy and he would do what he was asked. The boy's tousled head stands boldly at the ready; this little Schmerzenreich is not afraid of Paul, but Paul moves on silently and motions with his hand that he wants to go soon. Ludwig understands right away; there is no need of a sign, because it only takes two steps down the stairs before he comes to a dead stop in order to figure out if the stranger is going to follow him or not. Thus they slowly reach the exit, and Paul is happy when Ludwig closes the door behind him with a clink.

Judging by the light, it must be early afternoon. Paul has no more time to lose if he wants to reach the commandant, though he doesn't have to spur Ludwig on, for the boy walks along and keeps up with Paul's every step. Nothing happens fast, however; Paul can hardly feel his legs, but he keeps them on the move and marches on like a soldier whose new boots fall hard and loud on the pavement. It's a way of walking that Paul once knew. It's not how he walked as a free man, nor as a prisoner; it's rather a pace by which everything is forgotten and yet at the same time also reflected upon. Paul feels the weight that he has carried without having to bear it any longer. He wonders why such a pace is maintained if indeed the answer has come to him already. Paul would be happy to renounce this path, and yet he had planned it out just that morning as he set out on the road. He felt it was his responsibility to get help for those still at risk inside the ark. He wanted to find someone he could trust to tell all of the details of his journey. Since Paul knew no one in this country, he decided to head to the nearest city he could find in the hope of getting the commandant of the victors to listen to him.

During Paul's visit with Frau Wildenschwert he first began to doubt what good it would do to approach such a stranger just because he had been granted a certain power and was responsible for the fate of a conquered part of the country, for no doubt he would have no time for homeless visitors. To maintain command amid the rubble was the mission of the foreigner. What could Paul expect, what kind of complaint could he raise when there were a hundred thousand people who were powerless and without hope and forced to play the part of victims? What could Paul say, as someone unknown who would make real his own suffering, to the man who only allowed an unintelligible and senseless word of thanks to be paid? What should Paul ask the commandant for? A train ticket to Stupart? Should the commandant make a special offer for Paul to be led off to a city with a secure detail, something that wasn't even within the powers of the commandant to order? The only reason Paul had said he had to get to police headquarters was to get away from Frau Wildenschwert. He regretted asking which way it was and taking on the young Schmerzenreich as a guide. If Paul had gone off on his own, nothing would have prevented him from choosing which way to go himself. He might even head back to the friendly men who made music in their hallway while feeding Paul and showering him with gifts. Now it was too late to think about. Ludwig should not be insulted, especially after so willingly remaining at his side, nor should he get the idea that Paul was a liar who, he would say back at home, had only talked a lot along the way as he hurried toward police headquarters.

They neared a large office building that had hardly been damaged during the war. Paul did not have to wait for Ludwig's advice. From afar he recognized that he had reached the wrong destination. Many people stood around there, both locals and foreigners, who had divided up into tight little cliques. Some stared up at the stars and stripes that stretched out above the gate, the bright banner of those in control. A row of military vehicles stood along the street, crusted over with mud. Noticeable was the way the victors hurried about, the pride they displayed, and the utter foreignness of their manner. Two soldiers stood watch before the entrance, and though they were armed, they stood there harmless and peaceful, as if it had been their job for years to guard the main police headquarters in Unkenburg. Paul thanked the young Schmerzenreich for his help, wanting to hand him a little something in the way one tips a guide. Out of habit he searched his pockets but found no coins there. Paul was ashamed and had to smile. He gave up and stroked the strange boy's head. What was it about this boy who proudly and defiantly held his head high and shook it in order to toss a stubborn strand of hair to the side? Ludwig was certainly pleased to have fulfilled his assignment. Once he saw that the thank-yous and good-byes were over, the boy turned and ran back as fast as he could.

Paul sees the open steps in front of him and starts to climb them. He sees the writing on the buildings that announces a great many things. Perhaps there was something there he would want to read. Yet a glance confirms there's nothing for him, it all has to do with people from Unkenburg: they must obey orders, they are warned, they will be instructed and it will be expected. Paul cannot read everything that is being announced here, but certainly it has nothing to do with him. Paul stands before the gate, the soldiers look at him. Should Paul turn back? Is it forbidden to enter? Must one have a pass? Who is allowed? How can he get in? Paul grows anxious and breaks out in a sweat, his heart beats loudly. The amount of power housed here is awesome and will kill anyone who is not allowed to enter. Paul is not allowed, he had signed papers from Stupart. If they ask, what should he stammer on about? He has no reason to be here, he stands inside a vacuum, under no one's command. This would be a good time to climb back down the steps, yet maybe that would cause more trouble, for it would only show that Paul did not belong in Unkenburg. And yet he stands there in the magic circle of foreign power and cannot hide, it is much too late to do so, and yet to Paul's amazement no questions are asked. Others go into the building and are not asked, others come out of the door and are not questioned. The soldiers only appear to keep guard without being concerned about the continual traffic in and out. Why a guard is even posted here is hard to understand. Paul imagines that perhaps their watch ended long ago; the soldiers only stand there because they have forgotten that their duty is over.

Paul finally pushes through and is in the hallway. There are no hands here, only arrows pointing this way and that. People are everywhere, weaving back and forth as if they know the point to and reason for existence, it having been revealed to them here. Everyone hurries along and is busy, keeps talking and has something to do, it's a miracle that it all just goes on and on by itself. Paul can also move along any of the hallways without hindrance, reading the inscriptions on the many doors. On one it reads, OFFICE FOR REFUGEES. Soon Paul finds himself in a large room where many people are waiting. They are all tired and have knapsacks and boxes with them and look like they have no idea what to do. A couple of kids keep on making noise with no one there to reign them in, no one can get them to quiet down. Paul considers how long he wants to wait, for it looks like things are unfolding here quite slowly, and he isn't a refugee any longer. Where is he fleeing from? He is with himself, and his home is with him wherever he plants his feet. The people are given little slips with numbers so that those who are impatient won't fight with one another about whose turn it is. As Paul considers whether or not he wants to stay, he tells the person in charge of keeping order that he does not want to take a number. Yet he takes one anyway, mumbling a couple of words of apology before he says that it looks like it will certainly be a while, so therefore he will wait outside in the hall.

Paul throws away his number once he is outside the door and laughs at himself for being so foolish to look for an office that meant nothing to him. He then comes to another door, where he sees faces that are familiar—dull, gloomy souls whose gazes are dead, yet full of hunger, then cast to the ground, full of anxiety and pain, unbearable, the smell of death, the burning cold odor of the horror of the hacked-off hands in front of the ark, voices without names that are suddenly there and then again not. Paul isn't certain, although they greet him in a friendly and trusting manner, but yes, here was the right place for reparations, each would get something, just be patient, it wouldn't be much longer, because here is the Office for Former Prisoners. Yet that is not for Paul, he is not a "former" prisoner. Paul wants to have an official designation for himself in the present, not an honor granted to the past. He shuffles farther along. Then up to another floor. There someone stops him. Only Americans are allowed here, or people who have business here. Paul has business here, he says quickly and forcefully, he needs to speak with the commandant, the situation can't wait. The commandant is unavailable, it will be at least two hours, he learns, since right now he's in a meeting where they're discussing the temporary governance of Unkenburg. Paul doesn't let himself be dissuaded. Eight kilometers, four years, right and left, then across the entire city, that's too much; there has to be at least a deputy to whom he can talk. —Perhaps Captain Dudley. —Okay, fine, it doesn't matter, Captain Dudley it is.

Paul is announced and doesn't have to wait long. There sits the young

Captain Dudley at a desk, smoking like a chimney. Paul is no longer used to such smoky air, so it's uncomfortable for him and he has to cough. The captain, however, already has company. Someone from Unkenburg stands hunched over before him. What can he do for him? He has brought a small box with him whose contents he unpacks on the table. The captain is very interested. He collects medals of the defeated. He'd be pleased to have all of them, the many lead shields in all their colors. He'll give a hundred cigarettes for them. Is there any chance of getting more of them? —Yes, certainly, but it's not easy now to get such loot, but the man from Unkenburg will come back again tomorrow, and not empty-handed. —He just needs to be on time, it's important, the collection is not yet complete. Duplicates don't hurt either. The captain is happy to pay, he's not cheap, yes, cigarettes. Paul keeps waiting, he is exhausted and asks the captain whether he can sit down. Captain Dudley shakes his head. Paul doesn't know whether that means yes or no, yet he sits down nonetheless and continues waiting.

The captain doesn't stop admiring the treasures before him. He lifts up piece after piece, turns them in his hand and holds them before his eyes. He's not ashamed to do so in front of Paul, at whom he glances impatiently. Paul, however, does not shrink away from the captain's blue-eyed gaze, though now and then he looks around and stares at the pendulum clock that oddly hangs upon the wall, assiduously swinging back and forth. The droning clock was now striking the quarter hour. "Two hundred cigarettes, but make sure you bring them!" A half hour has passed. The clock has croaked it out with its rude little hammer. Will the deal take place? The assistant comes in and announces other visitors. Dudley gives a short wave, okay, well look at these, just a . . . just a couple of minutes, not too bad. The new guest also arrives like a train rattling along its tracks, to and fro. He is also American and has a uniform and a cigarette, a Lucky Strike. Therefore he doesn't have to wait. That would be silly. He talks as fast as the mighty pendulum. Is the hour up? The captain can do nothing but listen to his countryman. His hands are hard, the table is silent. He doesn't pay attention to Paul, who simply sits on his chair inside the pendulum clock, feeling like a fool. The captain shows the many new medals to his visitor. He picks one up that is bent, then he picks up another, turning it slowly back and forth. With a quick wave he snaps: "How terrific! Aren't these things terrific?" The hunchback from Unkenburg rubs his hump, pleased and yet submissive, well, well, well, sure, he can also bring some for the other man, always something, every day. The deafening clock strikes three-quarters past inside its dusty glass chamber. He doesn't want to be paid in currency. For God and the liberators he will do it for nothing, just Zig-Zag cigarettes, no-frills compensation. No, the other one says, it will be American cigarettes when you come back, not just nothing. Then Paul can be silent no longer. He jumps excitedly out of the chamber of his clock, his knees wobbling because his legs have gone to sleep. Paul yells out:

"Herr Captain, are you not done yet? Or do you finally have some time for me?"

"Sure, just a minute. As you can see, I'm busy. It's important."

"What? Busy with your medals?"

"So you also have some medals? Great."

"No medals! I need to talk to you!"

"Can't you wait a bit? You can see that I'm busy. I can't take on every single case."

"You're not taking on any case while playing with medals! I see what you're up to!"

"What's it to you?"

"Nothing. It's about many others, me even, and perhaps even you."

"Okay, if it's that important to you, talk!"

"I won't say anything in front of this man."

"Who? Who are you talking about?"

"This one here! You know who I mean! The one with the medals!"

Captain Dudley grows angry and jumps up. The cigarette falls out of the corner of his mouth. He is at least ten years younger than Paul, whose look he doesn't like. He's cold to him. The captain waves at the hunchback, who gathers up his little box and offers a submissive good-bye. At last he is gone.

"What do you want? Make it quick!"

"I wanted to see the commandant, yet someone steered me toward you. I've come from the forest camp, which needs help."

"Where is this forest camp?"

"It's hidden. Eight kilometers away on the main road and then twenty minutes through the valley, then a path leads through the woods."

"That's too far. We're only responsible for Unkenburg. Who sent you here?"

"I came on my own. But they really need help. There are more than a thousand sick people. Something has to be done!"

"We already know about the camp. You don't have to worry. I'll make a note of it. Everything will be taken care of. They'll pick up the sick."

"Herr Captain . . ."

"Yes, what now?"

"What is going to happen? I'm standing before you . . ."

"Go to the Office for Former Prisoners! Take your problems there! Not everyone can come to me. I have much too much to do. Did you hear me? Get out!"

"Can you verify the present? Can you verify that I exist?"

"What? Say it again, but in English!"

"Excuse me, I made a mistake! I was looking for a human being. I knocked on the wrong door."

Both Americans smile and say something to each other in English, but Paul closes the door and listens no longer. He's ashamed of having complained about something that he should have taken care of himself. What was he asking for there? Why didn't he get out of there ages ago? Captain Dudley is not the kind of man that you go to and simply talk to, especially when you have no orders to do so. Paul has not found the right means and has only managed to arrange a visit that is senseless and pointless. It's not that easy to go back to how things were. One must begin more slowly, from the bottom up. One shouldn't go to important men first. Paul should have known better. Aren't there unfamiliar faces pressing against the door of the Office for Former Prisoners? Have they not already said what is necessary to do themselves? Everyone needs something, yet nobody exists for real. Paul has no duty here, he can and should think of himself. He is liberated, things will go on as they will.

Paul sits down on a bench in the hall and looks at the many people passing by him. They are all strangers: people from Unkenburg, people from this country, people from far-off countries; nothing but strangers caught up in incomprehensible affairs. No matter how much Paul tries to find an entry into this world, nothing works. Is he too wounded? Have the others not lost as much, such that they know right off what they need to do? Even if they have their own worries, they appear to be satisfied; they indeed have *their* worries and can think about them, namely what to do and what to leave for later. Everything to them is self-evident. Certainly none of them goes to the commandant without a clear reason. Silly matters or ancient history are not what they'd present, when instead there are more important concerns. Is it so difficult to find the right approach? For Paul it's difficult. Maybe it was good that he stopped off at that strange apartment earlier, but even there he should have recognized that each is caught within his own circle and that you can't expect secrets to be easily shared with the secrets of others, or even demand that they be. Whoever follows only his own inner needs is selfish, but he at least won't be easily derailed. Paul has been derailed and can't find a track, be it good or bad. Any road that he chooses today leads into emptiness. He suffers states of awareness without any ties to reality. Is there any way to begin anew? Right now all he wants to do is wait. He had rushed himself and yet had only ended up chasing something mad, his steps unconscious, weak and powerless, heading in an unknown direction. Others hitch a ride with the victors on their vehicles and travel along without worry. They were simply asked where they wanted to go; then many simply expressed their wishes as if they were orders. Such travelers could get an appointment with the commandant, but not Paul.

Paul doesn't know what he should do. He can't stay at police headquarters. He doesn't want any help from the Office for Former Prisoners. After four years of not living in an apartment, he doesn't want to be crammed into crowded group quarters, not even for one night, no not at all. Should he impose upon Frau Wildenschwert or knock on the door of a different building and ask to be taken in where no doubt refugees will already be sweating and freezing in each of the rooms? Walk on ahead for so many streets, then left, then again right, then around one corner more and down into a cellar where the bombed-out names squat? Paul has had enough and wants just to be on his own.

For a while Paul doesn't perceive that a stranger is standing before him. It's a man from Unkenburg. Only someone who is from this city can give such a look. Half asleep, Paul takes his advice. On top of Kanonenberg on the other side of the city there's an empty barracks. Paul listens in amazement, could it be the Scharnhorst barracks? They have hardly been damaged, despite the destruction of Unkenburg. If Paul would like to go there the stranger is willing to take him. Paul accepts his offer and thanks him, the man from Unkenburg helps him up. Paul walks on almost blind, without thinking, shutting down his overexcited gaze and half closing his eyes. He hardly listens to what the other man says to him, and walks and walks, the stage swimming before him, then the cathedral, the general in the park, as once more they pass through the burned-out center of the city and its rubble. Paul doesn't pay attention to anything and doesn't know where he is, though he feels that he must be getting close to the place where he first entered the city that morning. The stranger leads him to the open gates of the barracks. It consists of many individual buildings with little lawns in front of them and bordering on a large courtyard on whose edges stand freshly blooming linden trees. The stranger tells him that the barracks are now empty, any of the doors can be opened. The man from Unkenburg says something else, but Paul just nods his head and understands none of it, he is too tired, he says a sleepy thank-you, the stranger is gone already.

Paul hesitates for a while. He has no pass, he shouldn't be here. The guards might suddenly show up. What is he doing here? It's so quiet, the late afternoon is clear and silent. Paul could be arrested for making himself comfortable in a strange building where he has no right to stay. Yet the weariness that sets in with twilight dampens such anxious thoughts. The gate has already been snuck through silently and surreptitiously; soldiers don't bother the intruder who walks across the smooth, spread-out sand. The yard is wide and yet unviolated by a single step, a gathering field of undisturbed peace. Only one building has been hit and its roof collapsed, the others have survived all the horror. Now Paul hesitates no longer as he moves unconsciously; a door stands open, Paul doesn't take long to decide. Already he has stepped inside, trusting his feet more than his eyes as he clomps heavily up the steps and enters a long hallway. All the rooms are open. It looks quite welcoming. The soldiers have left behind what there is. Beds, tables, stools, cupboards, stoves stand there quietly. Paul selects what for him is a dream of a room, one that must have belonged to an officer. A bed lies here with clean sheets. Paul needs nothing more, and so he turns the key from the inside, takes off his shoes, the dark green coat, the pants, everything, as he tries to find a window, hears something fall, then it's dark. Paul shuffles back, bumps into something, keels over, and is already lying in the commandant's bed fast asleep.

At one point Paul wakes up. He feels sick and miserable. He has lost everything, though it could also be that he himself has been lost. Afraid, Paul yells out, "Where am I?" Yet no answer is offered in return. Indeed the question could not have been heard, his voice was not there, it's spent. Paul has no voice. He has no idea whether it's night or a new day. Curtains hang all around, which don't allow in the slightest light, making it impossible to figure out what time of day it is while in bed, requiring the desire and ability to get up. Paul also doesn't know if there's a window. He only hopes so, as he hopes also that he can find a door, a switch in order to have some light in the room, or at least a candle and matches. Yet that's asking too much. Everything is thickly tarred with misfortune, the viscous slime having hardened so that it is impenetrable. He seeks nothing but peace in the grave. There you can relax because you are forgotten and don't have to remember anything. Paul is surprised to find that the grave could feel so soft and comfortable. His limbs are not held in, he can move them, even if just slowly. Whatever happened, it's fortunate that Paul has been allowed to remain alive in his body and not been reduced to ashes. It was a huge cathedral with two towers and a colorful slate roof, the high building having collapsed, dissolved into one's consciousness, and that was for the best. Then there was nothing more, the worries faded, no hunger pangs, and no thirst. The high office that had been held had indeed been brought down, the blessing could no longer be given, yet from now on was one continuous holiday, because time had been done away with as well.

The journey is over, and there is no one who can do evil. The judgment of blind hatred that drools with revenge remains unimposed. The recent peace has been much too short to justify having such horrors consume the heart with overwhelming force. The crypt in the basement of the cathedral is the best grave. Nobody comes there and nobody is disturbed. The other dead ones had it a little better. Did they have a different hand directing them there? There is no longer any hand, none whatsoever points into such darkness. The direction has been lost, any way forward leads only to nothing, which is why nothing moves forward; not a step can be taken, neither left nor right. Even if the feet want to, there's no going forward. No orders can be given where every command is ignored. That's why it's better to get used to being dead and not to look for any way out. Seek nothing. That's at least a pure goal, to remain distant from everyone and solitary, but without any pain, just a feeling that rises within oneself. All desire is also extinguished. Not even freedom is longed for or thought about. When everything exists, even that which does not, but nonetheless is, then joy is attained, one that no striking of the hour can disturb. Every effort has withered away. All knowledge striven for now means nothing. The next moment can't even occur, for it will not happen, it will not pass, it's severed itself from all Being, because every moment is now eradicated. No other existence is possible, it doesn't even attempt to assert itself; what is not itself is eradicated, done away with, no longer accepted, for it cannot be withstood; it is tossed away. The hand now dipped into the darkness, perhaps closed, perhaps open, yet without any fingers, no way to point and no meaning.

How wonderful that one can breathe freely in a grave. Paul feels the soft, warm air that doesn't stir, a sweet, dark honey that moves through the tomb. Honey, and not the tar of misfortune. Does Paul still have hands? Do the dead have hands? If there can still be horrors inside the grave, that would be one; but Paul is calm because all around him the stillness remains unchanged. He can still risk believing in himself; what he is seeking is not a bad thing and will not hurt anyone else, nor disturb anyone. He can do what he wants in the grave, and thus not be called upon to bear witness or hear confessions. The hem of justice, which everyone seeks in the end, is like a shadow; but where is there room for injustice? The desire for punishment has faded from the body, for a blesséd compassion does not assert guilt, and is not guilty. If there is any thought of pursuing such a thing now, it is dismissed outright, especially when a world outside continues to exist that could put fear even into the dead. Yet nothing is outside, nothing has remained in the past, but what comes from within has nothing to do with creation and means nothing, has no reason to be and no content. No protest holds sway; yet because there is something that can still assert its strength, so the unburdened spirit arises, it comes to its senses, it lifts itself up and it sinks down, it collapses upon itself in order to rest quietly, as it falls back upon itself before it rises out of itself again.

That one can be happy in the grave is an unexpected wonder worth pursuing, because there is no risk of failure. Thus contentment as well as joy are encouraged and constantly approved of; it helps lull one into a feeling of certainty. The wrappings protect you lightly and flexibly, applying a slight pressure. A grave is large as soon as one does away with the coffin. There was no time to box up the corpse. It's relaxed and not stiff. Paul is surprised that he knows nothing more of the other dead ones. He thought he was tied to all who once lived, but it was not so. Paul gathers himself to call out a name, but none occurs to him, thus making him all the more acutely aware that the dead know no other names than their own. What the newly dead imagine as possibly being outside cannot be imagined, which is why everything is placed within the grave, whatever was and could be given. Death is the great remover that doesn't miss a thing. Its realm contains no borders. If Paul feels inhibited, perhaps this is only the beginning of death. But soon he will not feel inhibited. Wherever he feels constricted, death has not yet taken hold.

Paul lets himself fall deeper and deeper in order to attain this outward condition, yet he is surprised to find that nothing happens, no matter how much he's willing to let go. Since he is not lying down, he floats. He floats within himself, closed off from all else. Yet if death itself was afloat, then he himself should be able to climb onto it or sink. There is no need for death to risk being so shy. Whatever happens will be gentle, he will not be eaten by bugs. Paul finds it easy to begin. He lifts the limbs that were once his arms. They obey without weakness or anger. They are still arms, they burst through the inner wrappings of the grave and reach the outer wrapping, which was not at all expected, it appearing to go on as eternally as eternity itself, which is what it encased to begin with. But then Paul was reassured that he would not be wounded in death; the incident that had allowed him to die had not at all changed the body that felt life within. Nothing is rotted or dried up; the bones are intact and covered with warm flesh, healthy skin protects them both.

Paul lifts himself up to sit, first his head, then his back; he listens without straining. The eternity inside him has suddenly fallen away, it becomes a bit cooler, yet not cold, just fresher. It would now require a second game of chance to get the legs going, this being a fantastic grave in which one is free and certain that he is allowed to stand on his own two feet. And yet it's a success, a yearning is coupled with energetic strength, the legs lift and carry the dead man straight up from the grave, he himself grateful that he died in such good shape. Paul is excited, he wants to try taking a step, yet he's careful not to let his eagerness get ahead of him. It's fine to be eager, but overconfident will not do. Paul sits down, he wants to check his legs, to touch them. He thinks anxiously whether that's possible without any hands. A dead man wants to have all of his limbs, but he's not allowed to have hands since hands are sinful. Yet as the dead man reaches down, his arms split open, meaning there must be hands with fingers that spread and feel like they are supposed to.

At last Paul realizes that he is awake. If death is this easy then it's not death at all but rather life itself that has arisen out of death and yet has nothing more to fear than the ever-present grave. All that needs to be overcome is the fact of having been buried alive, yet the hands are there, whose strength will not fail in clearing everything away that separates them from daylight. The first thing to do is to feel where the border is that demarcates the realm of the grave. Paul thrusts his legs forward carefully, one after the other. He lets one leg dip down into the depths, it trembles from a deep exhaustion, yet there is reason to feel, with caution, that he can stand. The foot sets itself on the ground, the other leg follows, the second foot soon securing a firm position. Now just to stand. It's done.

The eyes find a small bit of light, which provides a direction Paul wants to trust. Then the doubt that had a hold of Paul begins to fade. No, it was not doubt, because Paul had not swayed. He simply was; without doubt, without pain the change had occurred, an easy, blesséd passage through which death was carried into life. Paul is alive, he cannot be dead, he has a direction that can be followed, and he remembers that he is in a room and is not decaying. Yet now he wants to know where he is. He knows that there was a yesterday during which he felt more exhausted than he had ever felt before in his life, so exhausted that he cannot recall just where he had found a place to get some sleep. It must already be day, the middle of the day, a time Paul did not need to be afraid of, yet certainly a day in which he needed to seek out others. He could not hesitate any longer, hunger stirred, a desire for things rose higher and higher, just small things, yet they were nonetheless irrepressible desires that needed to soon be fulfilled. Since Paul still does not recognize the room, he carefully feels his way with hands and feet toward the glow.

He reaches the curtain, the fingers feel rough cloth, which has kept

Paul protected during the night. It takes a while before he succeeds at lifting the curtain, which hangs down tightly wound up and ends in a roll. Then there is light. Paul squeezes between the curtain and the window because he is not able to push away the heavy fabric. Before him stretches a huge, broad yard, which causes him to remember. He feels like he is back in the Scharnhorst barracks, but this does not make him anxious, for it is all so different than before, it's now freedom's camp. Paul smiles, aware of the contradiction between the barracks and freedom. Outside a bit of life stirs. It's morning, though Paul is uncertain of the hour, nor is there any clock in sight. Paul is embarrassed to look around at the room that late yesterday afternoon fell to him with hardly any effort. He then turns back to the view outside. Nothing special is noticeable, but Paul is at peace because the broad yard calms him. Here and there he can see a person who casually moves about as if there were no other world but this one. Will Paul be able to move about in the same manner? There is still time to answer that question. Paul turns away from the window.

Paul is happy to have his own room that no one will hassle him about, at least for the next few days. It's good that such a refuge exists in which one can prepare for the resurrection of the world. He looks around the room. Without avarice, without shyness, he feels the room is a gift. Whoever lived here before had left nearly everything behind, even his toiletries, a good bar of soap, a new toothbrush still in its case like it just came from a shop. Paul finds many little everyday objects, looking over them piece by piece, picking them up and then laying them back down. He's as happy as a child and is grateful.

Paul catches a side view of himself in the mirror and stands there transfixed. An old, dirty man appears in the glass, older than Leopold on his deathbed and almost as used up. Paul lets out a scream then he quickly shuts up. Should he close his eyes? Should he look away? Throw the mirror out the window? No, don't be a coward! Paul is spellbound, he can't help but look. Even old women look into their mirrors and with great tact manage to console themselves. His eyes are set deep and look wild and confused, the mouth is small and bitter, the lips awfully pale, the skin dull and gray, the cheeks sunken, the brow wrinkled, the throat a ridiculous pole that can bow and nod. Paul wants to flee this wretched image, yet his gaze is completely spellbound, something bothers him about it, he doesn't really know why and feels ashamed, though he cannot resist, nor can he prevent himself from sobbing constantly and crying helplessly and watching his own tears fall. Is it possible for an old man to lose control amid his own tears? Is he allowed to cry? Who is he crying for? What's he crying about? Is Paul missing or is he what he used to be, has he been taken away or is he standing here alive? No, it's not an old man, it's not a child who is crying. It's a silent, unstoppable weeping, an infinite sadness that has no reason at all and cannot cease.

Paul tries hard, feeling as if he must remember everything, although he remembers nothing; his consciousness remains empty, no matter how hard he tries. Does nothing make sense, such that he cannot find the key to unlock the secrets into which each day he had newly and unmercifully been initiated for years? Perhaps everything has been too deeply repressed, such that it won't allow itself to resurface, so deep in fact that it has now become a part of himself, no amount of courageous will capable of bringing it out once more. Everything has collected in an abyss that no gaze can penetrate. There it is sealed like iron and incapable of being moved, nor can it be changed; it simply must be borne, it is the fruits of evil that fall to one's lot because the weapon of wisdom was not forged in time. But now that Paul is free of the ark of affliction, how will he in fact free himself completely so that he can step away from the mirror once more, though not just from the mirror, but from the room, not just by looking out the window, but by heading out the door, down an unknown hallway, where the way is at last discovered that leads to an exit and then farther across the yard and out of the camp and into the city, whose suffering had just begun and which Paul now has to leave behind?

Now Paul can recall clearly the events of recent days, the tears swimming into the light and emptying out the past. Such sickness cannot be healed by any means, it can only be cried out in front of the mirror, which is why Paul doesn't hold back any longer, the fruits of evil have burst open. The mirror once again stands open to the observer. Paul feels the glass with the tips of his fingers. He wants the mirror in front of his eyes constantly in order to touch it and recognize himself. Soon the face quietly becomes more real, a sense of safety making it possible to feel that a new era is about to begin. Years ago Paul had not liked mirrors and had avoided them. He doesn't like the way his gaze is trapped here as well, but he will take this mirror along with him when he leaves this room. Then a decision begins to dawn inside him. Paul will not stay in Unkenburg any longer than he has to. He wants only to regain his strength and his wits before he prepares for the onward journey. The journey will have to take him back to where he was hauled off against his will. Nonetheless, Stupart is not the only destination. Paul wants to go farther, yet he knows he has to travel to Stupart, because only there will he find what was taken away from him on this journey. Finally conquering the storm of tears, Paul smiles at himself. It's not a happy smile, but rather an end to this keening.

Now Paul finds his bearings in the room, finding as well what he is looking for, as if he has known this room for years. Every board and nail reconfirms the fact that he is safe and free to roam between the window and the door at will. Paul opens cupboards and drawers; the goods lie openly within them, everything just waiting to be picked up and made use of. Paul is the master of the day here; he knows how to treat as his own everything brought here and arranged by someone else. The strange is not strange if it can be of service to Paul; in his hands it will become something he owns and no one else's. Paul reaches for a new shirt and his pants; he dresses absentmindedly and the moment he reaches the hall is ready to run off. Where can he find some water?

Paul goes from door to door, all of them are unlocked. Most of them are to living quarters where there are a lot of things lying about, some of which he can use. A few things are gathered together, for Paul doesn't want any shortage of things. He's living in the barracks now in order to avoid further hardship. Out of a bunch of ownerless goods he gathers together an impressive collection. He finds a good knapsack, a blue cap that fits him well, a beautiful silk handkerchief and long gray socks of soft wool. Once Paul's hands are full, he hurries back to his room and dumps everything. He discovers an office where everything has been turned upside down, a nicely sharpened pencil points to a list of obsolete words, a ream of fresh writing paper awaits dictation, in a drawer there rattles a heap of bent metals, the kind that Captain Dudley collects with such zeal, while books also lie around that teach one how to slaughter, and which are signed with a dedication complete with a snakelike signature, as maps remain heaped up in thick piles, military leaders staring out awkwardly from behind framed glass amid such devastation. Paul does not touch most of it and smiles to himself. Useless, completely useless, nothing but rubbish.

In one room Paul comes upon an old man who has also collected a number of things. The stranger is frightened when Paul appears, but soon he settles down and asks Paul's pardon for keeping on the lookout for things, since his household has been destroyed by enemy hands and is scattered all about. Paul laughs at this, he can well understand it, not everyone can have come through as easily as did Frau Wildenschwert. He asks if the man is from Unkenburg. —No, he's not from this city, he has fled here from far off, but he has been lucky, his wife and children had also been saved. Then he asks Paul how things are with him; he must also be a refugee, for no one from Unkenburg looked the way he did. —No, Paul confirms, he is not from Unkenburg, but he has not been so lucky, yet he is still happy that he had neither a wife nor a child to lose. —It's a huge advantage to be in this mess without anyone depending on you, for then at least you only had yourself to worry about. Paul doesn't say anything in reply, he has vowed not to speak about his fate, at least for a good while. He recalls his crazy visit with Captain Dudley, thinks about the thoughtless conversation in front of the theater, the hesitant intrusion among strange people in those rooms. Such false steps cannot happen again. Paul says he had drifted here and there, a prisoner who survived it all, something he can't hide after all, though the hard times are now over.

The man replies that for Paul everything is simple, he will be taken care of, soon he can go home or wherever he wants to go. Whoever attaches himself to the victors will be well taken care of, his worries are over, something that for the man had just begun. This war had lasted so long, and yet it had all come to this! If his people had only been victorious, then everything would be different. The world could have done nothing about it, for nothing could be done against a mighty victor. —Paul should have kept silent, but he doesn't and instead expresses his own doubts. —Indeed, he should have known. Now he can be happy! Hopefully he is more decent than the many others who, with no reason at all, scream for revenge instead of being grateful they had been so well taken care of. He should be fair and tell the truth back in his country, namely that no one who was imprisoned had to worry about a hair on his head as long as he worked. —Paul promises to never speak anything but the truth. —Then the man is relieved and pleased to find that among the victors a reasonable man still exists.

Paul asks him where he is from. —Oh, a little town that nobody here knows, yet it was a lovely town. Too bad that he can't show it to him! There he had his own house, a villa with six rooms, in which the victor would be welcome if he ever had a chance to make the trip. Yet it's all gone, even if the house itself were still standing. It was an old town, much smaller than Unkenburg, but certainly just as beautiful, the countryside lovely around it. Paul hears the name, Leitenberg, an episcopal see, a cathedral, a town hall, old arcades, the guildhalls, and in the middle of the plaza a column dedicated to Saint Rochus. Beside the town there flowed a river, which was deep blue and sometimes looked silver.

Paul asked about the opposite shore, whether there was a town there as well, smaller than Leitenberg and not as pretty. Yes, said the man, there was a town there, quite generously it had been cleared of its native inhabitants, the higher-ups having done so for the prisoners in order to help them. You couldn't help but appreciate what an act of kindness that was, an entire town for prisoners, such that they could live there undisturbed and provide for themselves, no one to bother them, almost as if they were free, themselves feeling completely at home. The enemy had never done anything that honorable, but today there's isn't even a hint of thanks for those who have suffered so much, since all there is now is slander and lies taken as truth. The enemy's newspapers write what they want, they are unmerciful. —Paul asks if this town was called Ruhenthal, an old fortress, dirty and unhealthy? —Ruhenthal, that's right, but dirty and unhealthy? That's not true! Certainly pleasant and simple, yet nice and clean. That the prisoners were not happy there, that could be, for that's the way prisoners are, they can't stand living with one another and are often dirty. But that's their fault. —Had he known any of the people who lived in Ruhenthal? —Yes, he had seen many of them himself; many of them had worked in Leitenberg, a group of them walked leisurely each morning and evening through town, almost as if they were free; handsome men they were, who looked well fed. One noticed how pleased they were that nothing bad had happened to them.

Paul is on the brink of setting the man straight, yet he doesn't do so. He'd like very much to ask him whether he himself ever went to Ruhenthal, and whether he saw that funeral wagons were provided to the living, but for the dead there were none. And whether he had looked into the narrow rooms and saw the old people, crammed together and helpless, living upon what was left of their possessions? Whether he had seen the sick who were left untended and for whom there was no care available? Whether he had seen the hunger that ravaged faces, wasting away the living, erasing them? There was a lot he'd like to ask about, for Paul could see no end to it, yet he is now so far away from Ruhenthal, such that so much else had come between him and what no amount of questioning could ever touch upon. There is something today that is also omnipresent, something that years ago was only known as corrupt and unjust; now the entire country is a wasteland, and all countries have been laid waste along with it, suffering having broken out among all of those imprisoned, a plunge into the rubbish heap, a lone ark floating above like a wretched home, though it is leaky and gurgles as it sinks in the bubbling mud. Paul doesn't ask a thing, he wants to leave the man to himself. No one can hear and feel what has happened to another, just as another's guilt cannot be taken on. Only he who wishes to feel guilty will embrace guilt, yet it cannot be allotted. Perhaps this man from Leitenberg really is innocent and barely reaps expiation, as all men are implicated in the work and deeds of their brothers.

He is a guest in the barracks just like Paul, and so he plunders ownerless goods, which for Paul is loot that he takes from strangers, since they took everything from him, though for the man it feels like robbing his own people in Leitenberg. No, that's unfair. There is no difference between them: everyone robs his neighbor, whether it's his friend or foe. No one has anything, that's why everyone takes something. The man from Leitenberg had to leave behind his belongings, just like Paul. Both of them were now refugees, so there was no distinguishing between them; one leaves because he cannot stay, the other is taken out of his house because he is not allowed to stay, but everyone has to leave. Whoever among those still alive is unwilling to beg has to take something when it lies there ready and in the open. Even the soldiers have to flee the barracks without having enough time to take the pictures of their loved ones down from the walls, the books they were reading from lying open on the table, the plates from which they ate left behind unwashed, knives, forks, spoons, and glasses left unattended, there to save the lives to whom all these goods have been sacrificed. Paul is amazed that more people don't arrive to take advantage of such a respite. Certainly that will happen soon. Most people in the city are still paralyzed; the inhabitants of Unkenburg move through the destroyed streets and look for their family members and what can be gathered of their goods among the rubble; thus the salvation of rubbish as it becomes goods once again.

The man from Leitenberg starts to speak again, Paul's silence has gotten to him. He wouldn't want him to think . . . —No, Paul wasn't thinking anything, there is nothing more that one can think. The man from Leitenberg had lived well, one could see it by looking at him. He had said so himself. Paul wants to know from him what he was? —The man from Leitenberg drew himself up. Would the victor believe him? He was the mayor of Leitenberg. He had run the town and sat in the town hall. Now he stands amid a hostile wilderness, a beggar in a strange town, which doesn't have a mayor of its own either. What is it like now in Leitenberg without a proper town government to run things? It's hard to imagine. No one knows who is leaving, who is staying. No news gets through at all. The people who used to live together have been separated and so scattered that no one can bring them together again. No one knows for sure how many are dead. There is no one in charge of the country, there are no leaders, everything is destroyed, it's terrible! Nor is there any leadership whatsoever. It's all done with and gone.

Paul says that Unkenburg already has a commandant and that order has been restored. The former rulers are not completely gone. Many officials are still alive, they have only ducked around the corner and will soon return, looking for their old desks. —Yet if everyone flees? You fled, otherwise the air raids would have done you in! —Doesn't matter, there will be others there, the seat of government is still there. Someone will claim it when it's time to do so. —Even in Leitenberg? —Even there it will be the same. There will be someone there to take power, the government never disappeared entirely. —But the mayor of Leitenberg no longer has a position. In Unkenburg no one needs him, no one here would even give him the time of day. They would laugh in his face. —If he is not needed here, then there are other positions elsewhere. In any case there is no need to stay in politics, there are other professions. —But when one is born to govern? —What do you mean born to? There's no such thing.

The man from Leitenberg means that it doesn't matter for the victor, for *he* will go home, he will arrive in a city where he belongs, where he has his rights. There's no chance of that for the mayor. He has been taken away and has been banished for good, he cannot go back to Leitenberg, at least not for long, he wouldn't survive it, or at least the mayor cannot expect that any such miracle can occur. He no longer has a home, Unkenburg is no home at all, nor can there be one anywhere. He doesn't even know if he will be allowed to stay here. He is the last mayor in a long line of mayors, for eight hundred and two years they had held office. Two years before the mayor had spoken at the eight-hundredth anniversary of Leitenberg. The festivities were somewhat curtailed, it was the fourth year of the war. Back before the war everything had been planned, there had been an organizing committee. So much more had been planned, visitors from near and far were expected, tourists, special trains, renovations of the guesthouses, overnight stays arranged for with community members, the laying of a cornerstone for the new hospital, the Leitenberg archivist and the principal of the school thought big and composed a festival play in which the historic rise of Leitenberg from the darkness of the Middle Ages up until the brightness of the present was supposed to be depicted, the Beautification Association was supposed to take care of so much, old frescoes were to be uncovered, benches installed, the castle park behind the bishop's palace was supposed to be connected to the docks on the shore by a new set of stairs, a broad expanse on the edges of the town that was more than just an adornment—it had been a dump full of dirt and ashes for many years—had been envisioned to be developed into an open park, drawings for which still existed in the Planning Commission of the town hall. The clearing had begun when the war broke out. The work had to be stopped, but one hoped for a quick victory, for then most of it would have been finished. Yet it was not to be. And so the celebration was a bit scanty. Because of the blackout, the torch parade that the children had been so excited about had to be canceled at the last minute. A couple of speeches were given with great vigor, a special edition of *The Leitenberg Daily* was issued with eight pages, rather than the hundred that would

have been published in peacetime. In the schools the students were told
about their history and the future. A gathering on the main square in front
of the plague column was canceled, only a High Mass was celebrated in
the cathedral. That was all.

Now there will be nothing more. Who will celebrate a nine-
hundredth anniversary of Leitenberg?

"Such thoughts are superfluous today, Herr Viereckl. Perhaps the
grandchildren."

The mayor is taken aback and somewhat disturbed. How does the
stranger know his name?

"Is the mayor's name not Viereckl? If that's the last mayor of Leitenberg, then that has to be the right name."

Yet Paul has had enough of this talk. He turns toward the door and
wants to look for a washroom. The mayor doesn't want to let Paul go, but
the latter doesn't want to hear anything more. He turns back once again.

"Enough, Herr Viereckl, I know the town you're from."

Paul looks around and finds a faucet, but no water runs from it. He
runs back to his room, gets a bucket, and goes to the pump in the yard.
The handle is too heavy, Paul can't lift it. Someone notices how weak he
is, hurries over, and helps him pump. Paul thanks him and wearily carries
back the bucket of water. Along the way he has to stop now and then to
catch his breath. At last Paul is back in his room with his load. He's happy
to have a key and loves to turn it in the lock. Paul is at last his own master,
he can now perceive the border between himself and the world. He has an
address at which others can visit him. He will put his name on the door
outside. Here lives Paul Lustig, please knock! Paul Lustig, resident of the
Scharnhorst barracks here on the Kanonenberg in Unkenburg; that has a
certain ring to it. The master of the house decides whether he will answer
the door or not. No one who is not welcome here can darken this
doorstep. This is private property, and it belongs to him. Whoever damages it will have to answer to the law. Now the barrier is once again
erected that should stand between oneself and all others. A path can run
between the two that is acknowledged by all, yet no one is allowed at the
table who has not been invited.

Paul then cleans himself up. He washes himself a long time and scrubs
his arms and legs. He has the best soap he can find and a soft washcloth,

which is easy on his skin. Paul shaves off his disheveled beard in front of the mirror, before which he no longer cries. He laughs at seeing his face covered up with white foam. The brush is useless, for the brush hairs fall out and end up stuck to his cheeks and feel ticklish. The blade needs to be sharper. At last his skin is almost smooth, only the throat is still a little raw. Paul applies some powder, something he never would have used before. He will have to look for some new blades, there have to be some somewhere in the barracks. Paul chooses a pair of pants that pleases him; they fit once he uses a leather belt tightened halfway. He throws the old pair of pants out the window. He also dumps the water into the yard. Other shabby items are thrown out as well. There is no order to it, but it's simple, the most direct route to the rubbish heap. Perhaps someone else will need what Paul throws away. It's fun to get rid of so many unwanted things; they fly out the window one after another.

At last, after nearly four years, Paul finally looks good enough to once again appear on the street. Except for his shoes, everything he was wearing had not belonged to him the day before. He doesn't even want the dark green coat anymore. Yesterday the soft fleece still seemed splendid, but today it appeared as if moths had gotten to it. Paul is now an officer, but more presentable than Captain Küpenreiter; the clothes provide him with a certain air. Only the silver insignia of the defeated officer looks ridiculous. It should go to Dudley, if he wants it. Paul takes off the coat once again and cuts off the shoulder insignia. He has resigned, he doesn't want to command an army. Throw the weapons onto the rubbish heap, away with them! The soldiers have been granted permanent leave. They have deserted, but Paul won't chase after them. They should just scatter, left and right and around the corner. No need to march in line anymore. Regulations are meaningless to those in chains. The war is over, the army is discharged, it has crawled under the earth, defeated. Paul looks once more into the mirror and salutes. The mirror salutes back. The two are very courteous to each other. Paul is grateful to the mirror, it has done a splendid job. Now the mirror can take its rest, for Paul is leaving, he wants some breakfast.

Paul turns the key, steps out, and locks the door behind him. Then he thinks to himself that strangers might come who wouldn't know that this is someone's apartment. He wants to put up a sign. And so he goes back inside again. He's already written his name, but it won't mean anything to a stranger, so Paul adds FROM STUPART and DO NOT DISTURB! Now it's in order; the sign is put up, he can go now. The yard stretches out in front of him, it is warmer today than yesterday with everything drenched in sunlight. It must be nearly noon. It doesn't hurt him at all to walk, and soon he is at the front gate. The city greets the old officer who has resigned all of his commissions. A good commandant who now only gives orders to himself. He is a wanderer in search of his own nourishment. Paul doesn't have to wander for long. He finds a soup kitchen. He doesn't ask, he doesn't plead, he simply goes in. Earlier this was a school. Now full kettles say that not much learning goes on here any longer.

People stand there in long rows, shying away from Paul when he enters. Such is their feeling still toward an officer. Paul won't have any of it and thus makes it clear that he's not an officer. Then they laugh, for of course there are no officers, they are either imprisoned or have fled. Anyone dressed like Paul would not be allowed to stick around. So they give him a full bowl and utensils. Others sit around. On one side are the so-called officers, on the other a lot of people press together. The warm food makes Paul happy, he savors every bit. Yet he's still not full. He should go back to the counter. He goes back, he goes back, he goes back once again. He keeps going back until he is full. He doesn't ask about the check, yet nobody asks him if he's going to pay either. He is a guest and thus deserves such treatment. He just needs to keep coming back until he regains his strength.

Paul walks along the streets again. Some people greet him, and he learns that he has other rights as well. Notes and cards are pressed into his hands. Paul takes on all the rights he desires. The day passes full of rights that are granted to him. All Paul has to do is walk down the street, picking them up or discarding them at his will. His pockets are full, there is no more hunger. Even breakfast is served to him because he has a right to it. And the time? When someone gives him the time it seems much too early. Yet Paul is well provided for and can now have his dinner in his own room. He walks through each district, each person shies away from him the moment they think he's there to demand his rights. Then there's even money in his hands, though he doesn't know who gave it to him. Finally he grows tired and thinks of heading home. He wants to check on his rights, to see himself in the mirror again. Paul climbs the streets toward Kanonenberg, soon the officer is in front of the familiar gate, the master of the house steps through it with his rights intact, so quickly does everything revert back to normalcy, the yard, the steps. There appear to be a lot more people in the camp than there were at noon. They have all attained their rights, many rooms are now occupied. There are names on the doors, and Paul now has a neighbor, while across from him there are three people living in a room. Paul is pleased that he had first choice. He has a place to himself, alone and undisturbed in his room, everything like it used to be long ago, just needing a little tidying up so that it looks nice, though Paul is already so tired as it grows dark, the curtains are closed, it's night once again.

Paul has turned into an Unkenburger able to find his way through every part of the destroyed city. He knows the parks that surround it, the forests nearby. He knows certain corners that he loves. He has people he knows and looks up and who hide nothing from him. He has become friends early on with Herr Brantel. Hungry, he had broken into a half-destroyed villa in which there was a lot to eat. He hadn't asked if he could, but instead stole what he needed under the same right by which others had stolen from him when not allowing him enough food for years at a time. He wasn't at all ashamed of what he'd done, nor would he ever regret it. The rightful owner arrived and saw Paul and other looters taking things from ample stocks that had been broken into. The owner said little, for quickly Paul's look reduced him to silence. The owner just looked on and took in what was happening. Then they smoked cigarettes and left together. They walked along for many hours, Herr Brantel listening and not interrupting Paul's talk. At the end Brantel asked him a question.

"Didn't I see you sitting on a bench at police headquarters the day after the troops entered the city?"

Paul at first can't remember, but then he realizes this was the stranger who had led him toward Kanonenberg. Now they are good friends. The Brantel family had found refuge among their relatives. Now Paul is often their guest. Wine is served that has been waiting for him to taste. He is asked to tell about what happened, so Paul talks about the journey. At last he can say what it was like. He quietly talks about it without emotion. It feels different than when he was with Frau Wildenschwert, whom he no longer visits. People listen and are quiet.

Once there had been a family. They had an apartment in a building. You went there and it was as it always was. Everything stood at the ready. When the clock struck, things were set in motion. The table was set. Each plate was familiar. Emmy, the maid, was spotless when she carried out the food. The food tasted good. Often the father was not there. Emmy had to keep the oven warm in the kitchen so that his food would be ready for him at any time. A doctor had his responsibilities, not just his rights. Everything was so similar to how it was in Unkenburg, there was nothing to fear. Clothes hung in the closets, Emmy ironed and cleaned. The sister's name was Zerlina, she loved fairy tales. She sang songs out loud. She made beautiful little things, loved to paint, and had a good sense of tone. She made boxes for gifts out of leather or parchment, and they were lovely. This silver case lying here on the tablecloth would have really pleased her. Her mother was different, she loved to talk and have visitors, a lively woman who danced wonderfully, that was what she loved most. Yet the father had no feel for such things. The mother loved trinkets, she always had to have something new. Inside she was really a child. She seemed a lot different than she really was. She always kept something hidden inside. Zerlina, who looked like her, was not that way. She was simply an open book, perhaps too open. The father was the same way, but much simpler. He didn't waste his time with brooding questions. He lived for medicine and was a good doctor who cared about nothing more than the care of his patients. Then came a wife and children. There was hardly ever much of a family life, and yet, between the four walls, it was a pleasant household full of an intimate yet subdued exchange. Then the mother's sister came, a widow who had a good son who is perhaps still alive. He went to America to be a photographer. The aunt had a light touch and always smoothed out any differences between the others. Thus the fabric of everyday life in Stupart was probably no different than what it was in Unkenburg.

But alas, Unknenburg is just a shadow in comparison, Paul should have realized earlier. There is simply no comparing it to Stupart, though one could be happy living here. The song is over. In a hundred years the residue of the war will still be present. City hall cannot be rebuilt, even if they had the original plans for it. —Paul agrees. But the citizens have not suffered that badly despite the destruction, their families were not torn apart and will soon be reunited again. —Did Paul have any hope at all? What happened to his cousin? —My cousin? He must be somewhere, though Paul doesn't want to talk about him. Even if the hand had pointed toward somewhere, there was no hope. It's even doubtful whether Stupart came through it all intact. Paul had no idea, there still are no newspapers. There is nobody he could ask either. —Maybe there is. Someone said that two girls had recently shown up from there. They had fled early on. —What did they have to say? —The city had not suffered. All the buildings were still standing. The citizens had risen up and driven away the foreigners, but otherwise everything is still the same.

Thus it's time to head home. Paul only has to wait a couple of more days until the trains are running once again. One still had to walk a ways in order to catch a ride on a train. For that Paul would wait. He has already recovered, the mirror tells him so. People no longer draw back from him. The children don't run away when he talks to them.

Paul roams through the surrounding area. He remembers how often on the march from Ruhenthal to Dobrunke he had wanted to peel away from the road and run freely through the trees in the forest. Now he could do that, there are no guards to prevent him. Nothing has happened here. Now and then he bumps into someone who also wants to be on his own. They look at each other then hurry off in opposite directions. The days are lovely and warm. Innumerable paths lead through the bushes and have no idea how close the destroyed city is. So lightly have the footsteps pressed into the countryside, they are only aware of themselves and they know nothing of the refugees either. There is fresh moss growing on the summit. There a strand of sunlight beams down and a pair of butterflies flutters. Logs lie across the path, the peeled-away bark shines red and smells fragrant. Is there nobody who needs wood in Unkenburg?

Paul should not go back to the strange city. He has stayed there too long; he might be too tempted by what it is best to avoid. It had been a mistake to talk to so many people there, to let just anyone in, yet it was an attempt to once again live in the world in order to figure out whether such talk would be allowed and bearable to others. Once he found that he could speak freely, that was enough. The country promised loneliness, its people too much to take; it would not work to remain here even among such kind strangers.

It could be that this road is forbidden, for a sign warned about something and threatened penalties, though the commands no longer mean anything. Paul is not worried about having to answer to some forest ranger. He walks on wherever he wants. He slips around a corner, turns around, stands there, closes his eyes, walks on for a bit, looks up at the sky, smells a leaf, a blossom, stops, closes his eyes again, blinks, then opens them again, feels the sun warm his back, enjoys the kind embrace of a bench, then jumps up again, reaches a fence whose boards hang loose and are painted honey yellow, walks past and sees tender saplings growing, the forest nursery, where the hand of the forester makes—once again a hand. Paul smiles, turns around quickly, and slips out of the nursery.

Then he climbs a hill. He wants to get to the top quickly, but he loses his breath, the steep incline requiring repeated stops to rest. On the top there stands a small viewing tower. A price is written down, which the curious wanderer is supposed to pay, though there is nobody there to worry about the deserted tower, the owner and the guard have left it. Had they been taken away and imprisoned? Or did no one else come who wanted to pay money to enjoy the view? The tower is unlocked. Paul feels free to enter; slowly he climbs each step and counts out loud. The stairs rise in a tight circle, and he counts eighty steps. The climb was hardly worth it, down below the view was better, though Paul can see Unkenburg again from above. The city is far enough away that one can't see all the destruction. The intact outskirts of the city and its parks have not suffered any damage. The red roofs of the Kanonenberg barracks shine between the trees. The old part of the city is deeply embedded and hides its wounds, the cathedral appearing hardly touched at all.

Paul looks at everything matter-of-factly. He feels like a reporter who shares what he has to say free of any emotion. Yet to whom should Paul report? The Unkenburgers know all about it already and are not waiting for his story. The rest of the world has its own destroyed cities and doesn't care about Unkenburg. Everyone has had enough of the news and doesn't want to know anything about any journeys that might be offered up by a journalist to his readers. Paul no longer looks off into the distance, no longer at the city, but rather in front of him at the balustrade. It is made of wood, letters and names have been carved into it, along with dates. Was there ever anyone here whom Paul knew? He doesn't think so, for the names seem strange, the dates don't mean anything. Then he thinks of the names of his new friends in Unkenburg, though none of them have immortalized themselves here. Nor is the name Küpenreiter scratched in. The captain didn't write anything either, he only saw the tower amid the battle and thought only about defenses and fighting and victory. Now Paul has won the tower, having taken it without a weapon in his hand.

Should Paul also lend his name to this tower? He has no knife with him, only a pencil; any trace of it would soon disappear. Paul plays with the pencil in his pocket but doesn't take it out. Paul has paid no entry fee, the tower won't allow his memory to be preserved. Paul has already started back down the stairs and then hurries away as fast as he can. He wants to go home to the Scharnhorst barracks. The day has shown him that he doesn't want to stay in Unkenburg any longer. Life among complete strangers is much too easy. He can say whatever he wants, he can lie, he can inspire sympathy and friendship, he can experience this and that, yet have no responsibilities, no ties, be free of it all, always on the fly, and no price to pay. Paul knows many names that have been written down in a notebook. They are hoping that he will let them hear how he is sometime, and they will write back as well. But Paul will not write. They are just empty gestures that one exchanges, but soon they are forgotten. The road had caused their lives to come in contact with one another, then they had all gone their separate ways back to different countries, the ties between them dissolving amid all the changes.

Paul has gathered a small bouquet and wants to place it next to the mirror, which could not hold just Paul's face alone forever. After an hour he arrives at the barracks and can see from afar that something has happened. The inhabitants are amazed that he has heard nothing, for everyone else already knew about it that morning. —Paul had not been there the entire day. —Then it was high time that he find out, because in three days prisoners will arrive at the barracks, both healthy ones and sick. Anyone who has set up house here on his own has to leave tomorrow or the day after tomorrow. Some have moved fast and are already gone. Others are still searching for a place to go, some wanting to go to the collection camp, where they will be taken care of. Paul is sad and out of sorts, though he pulls himself together and only says: "That seems kind of sudden!"

Someone asks, "Is this the first time in your life you've had something happen to you suddenly?"

Paul has to laugh, he was right: it's always sudden. He knew enough people in order to find a place to stay for a couple of nights. But it would no longer be necessary. Paul decides to leave Unkenburg by the day after tomorrow, perhaps even tomorrow. The few things that will be of use for his trip he will pack in the morning. There isn't much: a knapsack, a satchel, a small suitcase. If the suitcase is too heavy then he can leave it behind. The journey beckons, it is sure to happen. Today the first trains left. Paul has no idea at all how far they will travel, the main thing is that they are running. People warn that they are too full. Paul has no fear of that as long as he can leave Unkenburg. Already today he decides to go to the train station. There is no schedule, yet every day some trains arrive. They move slowly. Departure times cannot be given. The best thing to do is show up at the station early in the morning. One has to be patient, for it could take a couple of hours.

Paul decides to leave the day after tomorrow. He then heads into the barracks. He's tired from the short hike today, yet he's happy, for soon he will travel the way that he wants to. Paul prepares a good dinner out of his provisions and chooses to have the best bits that he's been saving until now. Otherwise he won't be able to take everything with him. He prepares everything and sets the table as if he were expecting a guest. Never had Paul gone to such lengths before. The flowers he'd gathered were placed in a little pitcher on the white tablecloth, along with a wineglass and a genuine silver spoon for the stewed fruit. Paul enjoys his dinner immensely. Even though it isn't dark yet outside, he lights a candle. Is it someone's birthday? No one sees any of it, for Paul has locked the door in order not to be surprised by anyone. He could have propped up the mirror on the other side of the table, but he had not invited that fellow to dinner. He needs no witness to confirm that he has become a person again. He has granted himself the highest honor, which no one else can give him.

In his pocket he carries the folded-up identification papers that he had asked the Unkenburg city officials to grant him. The wording is nicely put and requests the assistance of anyone to whom the letter is presented. When Paul went to the office, where everyone sought the affirmation of their existence through official channels, he simply gave them the name that he had always gone by. The helpful attendant asked whether he had any other papers that would attest to the accuracy and truth of the name he'd given. No, he had no such papers; the lack of them was the very reason Paul was here. The attendant was already used to hearing this, though he still asked, half out of protocol, if he had any witnesses. Paul had no one he could present, a stranger among strangers has no witnesses, the best he could do would be to ask someone to say, yes, that's Paul Lustig, but none could say they had known him for a long time. The civil servant just waved away any such need, and Paul was deeply grateful for his courtesy and understanding. He said his real name, he stepped out of his solitude and reentered the world, all of it carried out on a typewriter, where those who had been taken away were taken back into existence and not asked a penny for the privilege. The civil servant wrote and wrote what he was instructed to write, making sure not to note his own name anywhere, for he was indeed an official, a dispenser of verified existence by virtue of an imposed order, a man who is authorized to do so and who wields a stamp, there in his position where he serves the needs of justice. Paul told him his date of birth, told him the name of his hometown was Stupart, handing over all such information out of a deep desire to acquire a name, and then the miracle happened, one granted by the authorities, who had been appealed to, but about which no more questions were asked. In order to conclude the transaction, Paul took the pen that the official offered him.

"Here, take my pen. Sign here, but legibly, please!"

Paul hesitated only for a second, then he did as he had been instructed. With thanks he said good-bye, able now to convince anyone that he is alive and is official. The name he signed verifies that Paul can exist. He looks fondly at the piece of paper and thinks, Look, I have found myself again. What others wanted to eradicate when my life was no more than a nameless nothing, this official has restored only because I wanted him to. It's the greatest victory I have accomplished. A small victory. A victory that thousands who show up before the officials in order to let their reality be put in order will attain. Yet a victory, a genuine victory.

Now there's no longer any need for such assurance. Paul celebrates the birth of his own freedom, something no official can certify. The dinner comes to a tidy close, Paul gives thanks with a deep bow of his head.

He gets up from the table and bows once again. His extreme behavior is unusual, this he knows, but no one would dare laugh at him. Paul lifts his hands before him. A current flows through them, Paul can feel a deep warmth. He no longer walks stooped over, he is sound and can feel the strength within himself. Decisions are now more likely than promises. Paul wants to leave because that was his plan. According to the Office for Former Prisoners, he could indeed travel soon. In some countries, large groups of people have already left. Paul, however, is too proud. He won't go to any collection point, and he won't let himself be loaded up according to some train schedule that is completely unknown. He doesn't wait around to be told to be patient or to be granted patience when he finds himself at some meeting point. Such journeys horrify him, ones where he is suddenly whisked off and has no time to decide for himself what he'd like to do. When he wants to start out on his journey, he will arrange it for himself. Certainly he can't do it all by himself, for there are only so many opportunities, but among them he will make the choices that he can. He lives by his own laws now; it's the only way possible if what he wants is more than to be called by just any name like all the others.

Paul clears the table and makes the bed. He wants it to be nice for the chosen guest who will soon move in today. He folds the nightshirt and lays it carefully on the pillow. He pulls up the blankets and smooths them out. When the master of the house returns home he should feel cozy. Then Paul leaves. He wants to tell some acquaintances that he has decided to go away. Many would be happy for him to stay in Unkenburg. Paul had so often confirmed that nowhere in the world did anything special await his return, that he had no one upon this Earth, though he didn't really count the cousin in America. Why then does Paul not want to stay? It would not be that difficult to begin a new life here.

Paul thanks them, but it's too late, he has decided to go away. He must hold to the conviction that has grown within him. He must see the world and most of all the country that he had been taken from and from which he was set upon his journey. He would not stay in Unkenburg, for a month would pass, or maybe two, but he wouldn't be able to bear any longer than that. Paul didn't want to wait around for that. He wants to make the departure from Unkenburg as easy as the entry was difficult. He thanks them for all the kindness and friendship that has been extended to him here.

Then he says good-bye, for his time has come. These days, whoever has a chance to leave is wise not to worry about parting. Thus Paul takes leave of his acquaintances. In reply to the question about whether he will ever come back, he simply shakes his head.

"I will leave tomorrow, if I can get a train. I wanted to leave the day after tomorrow. I think, however, that it will be better if I leave the city tomorrow. The day after tomorrow the Kanonenberg barracks will have to be cleaned out because prisoners of war will be brought there."

"Is that the reason you're leaving so soon? Stay with us and travel in a week's time!"

"No, I will leave tomorrow, if I can. I don't want to rest a moment longer."

That's how Paul feels. He wants to lose himself amid new contingencies in order to leave behind this haphazard life that he has just survived. It is a blessing to have only yourself to worry about and to figure out on your own which way to go, but the moment one destination is reached, this feeling would disappear if he were to rest there any longer. Any pause that jeopardized moving on would be painful and would undermine the freedom that only exists when the heart isn't lost to its own desires, but rather chooses its own path, even if all the promises made, which would hold one back, are not kept. Paul explains this to his acquaintances as well as he can, because he doesn't want to hurt them, for they have taken care of him and were happy to see how he was able to come back from the wilderness and regain his strength. They ask if there is anything else they can do for him, yet there is nothing that Paul needs, everything that he will need in the next weeks has been taken care of, it being senseless to think any further ahead than that. It's also possible that the train will not take him as far as he hopes, and then he will have to walk a long ways. Paul was not afraid of long marches, but too many bags would be a problem. And so his friends didn't weigh him down with anything else and simply wished him well. Herr Brantel asks Paul to just remember that in the country whose people had robbed him of everything precious and dear there were still decent people. Paul promises to keep that in his thoughts. Then he is ready to go, though Herr Brantel says there's no hurry and brings in a bottle of wine.

"Some thirty years ago I brought home four bottles of wine. This is the last one. I wanted to save it for a special occasion. Now is the right moment. I had thought it would be different. My daughter was engaged. The war has claimed the groom. He was taken away even before his wounds had completely healed. He never came back at all. The wine was for the young wedding couple. Please, don't think twice and give us the pleasure of drinking this wine with us!"

The old bottle's cork creaks, the wine is dark red. The glasses clink with a silvery ring, everyone drinks slowly. They are silent, three people from Unkenburg—father, mother, daughter. The stranger from Stupart sits almost motionless and studies them thoughtfully. He was often a guest here, they were wonderful times. They had never asked a thing, but had only listened, nor had Paul ever left empty-handed. Now it is silent. It has not been this silent in years, so still. The man from Stupart remembers nothing. Is that what peace is? More wine is poured, the bottle is emptied. The empty glasses cast a dull light. The last drop is enjoyed. Paul gets up. The friends are upset, yet warm and subdued; they know that he is leaving, the looter, the one who came searching for booty among the blown-apart bricks of their building. Paul looks at the girl. What are her hands searching for and why is she trembling? The groom will never come again. What else is it? Hands reach out, hands are taken. Maybe this is where Paul should embrace his happiness. Perhaps at last the daughter of this house, too. What a bold proposal! Is it the last possible sin among the rubble that has fallen? An old grandfather's clock announces the time in low tones, striking three-quarters past the hour before falling silent. Paul looks away. He doesn't say much, but instead turns toward the door with half-closed eyes. Frau Brantel and her daughter are bent over, weeping quietly. He can hardly hear them. He takes hold of their hands and feels the magic pass between them.

"What we cannot hold are the hands of our neighbors. The journey calls, each of us is called to take it. I thank you all for the kindness you have shown me. I leave your house wholly recovered."

Herr Brantel accompanies his guest down the stairs, clinging to a candle along the way. With his free hand he protects the flickering light. The stairwell is quiet, but the steps echo loud and strong. Paul is not anxious, yet he feels himself descending into darkness as if encountering the arches of a crypt that holds the past. But then mockingly and with a smile the door is opened, the air heavy with the scent of lilacs, the clear spring night feeling contemplative and unusually warm.

"I can walk along with you for a ways."

"You should go back to your wife and daughter."

"Just to the next corner. I can't go very far. It's a quarter to eleven. It's almost curfew."

"You don't have an overcoat?"

"On a night like this?"

"You want to accompany me just like you did then on that first afternoon when I was dumb enough to speak to Captain Dudley so stupidly."

"Captain Dudley? He was transferred out of Unkenburg yesterday. I thought you'd like to know."

"That's all behind me. Everything in this town, everything in these past few years is behind me. Herr Brantel, what do you want with a stranger whom you will not see again? He drank the wine for your daughter's wedding."

"It was the wine of friendship that we shared. The journey will not separate us."

"Hasn't too much happened? Still, I think joy is still possible. I feel perhaps a bit too unburdened, more than is right to feel, yet I'm an old man. I can be forgiven somewhat. The official who filled out my papers couldn't believe how young I was."

"Anyone who remains committed to such a journey and is impatient and wants to complete it as fast as possible is still young and cannot be broken. You have a lot ahead of you. Perhaps it won't be easy, most likely not, I don't want to lie to you. I've gotten to know you enough such that I can understand the path that lies ahead of you and know how long it is. But it will continue. It will continue for you, for us, for everyone. That you can count on, something that for most is a terrible thing and even more terrible than sheer despair. In our time there exists a race that has a propensity for the negative. At first this world degenerated into lovelessness and then into madness; it was destroyed and made uninhabitable, which only brought satisfaction and joy in the downfall that was served in turn. Maybe you are right, or at least for yourself, when you claim that no one has a home anymore. I can't conceive of that, though I have to say I respect what you say. Yet homelessness must not lead to nothingness."

"You don't have to worry about that with me. I have goals, many goals. Someone like me, who was swept away and no longer knew whether he belonged to the living or the dead, cannot be held back for long. I, too, despair. Despair can be like a warm bath, something that I wish more people could experience. It can exist without enmity. But I think I already see things in a similar way as you do. There are too many in the world who, because of fear and vanity, fall into despair; fear, because there's no stability, vanity, because they don't want any stability. One should despair *for* something, not *about* something. Do you understand?"

"I think so. One must have a center, an unshakable quiet space that one clings to vigorously, even when one is in the middle of the journey, the unavoidable journey . . . an unmuddied sensibility free of rubbish, no left, no right, only the center, a constancy that does not change for the better or for the worse. I don't mean it strictly in a spatial sense. I mean it instead as a circuit, one that travels from hand to hand, from heart to heart and really exists."

"The immutable amid the journey. Free of sin and the fall from grace. I see what you mean. Despair is our fall from grace, here amid the rubble, our confiscated stolen property, our transmutable and disputable names, the heart's home, but not the heart—in short, everything that could be taken from us. The center, if I understand correctly, cannot be taken away from us. It travels with us and lifts us up from sin, from the rubble."

"I think we understand each other. We must bring everyone that we can into the circuit, no matter how young. One's potential growth is only the very same transformation that vanity and fear latch onto when transforming true freedom into an impediment. The conditions are such that, in regards to this circuit, most likely it is quite small. When other people look into our faces, we have to try to reach out to them. I know myself how hard that is, for who wants to stand in someone else's shoes?"

"Hardly anyone. But there's always somebody. One has to trust that it will happen."

"One can trust. Now one will not only be taken from, but also given to. That is the grace amid which creation is woven and renewed. Without such grace it will not happen."

"The moment of creation is perhaps only a matter of a reawakened will; creation itself is a result of such grace. And grace is the journey. The dead must rest and possess a grace that, presumably, comes from the human masses and is not the journey. The first night I slept in this city, when you forgave my way of speaking, I experienced for the first time the grace of death. It was a feeling separate from the journey. It was without question something in and of itself and yet a spirit that moved, no, actually, it was the center that is within us all."

"It's already late, my dear friend. I thank you for everything. You have helped me so much. Neither of us will forget this day. A day lived in the center, not the middle of the night. . . . Take care of yourself, and safe journey!"

"Safe journey to you as well! You know what I mean, don't you? And please greet your loved ones from me!"

Paul looks around, but his friend, whose hand he could still feel, has slipped around the corner, and Paul has to hurry in order to get back to his barracks on Kanonenberg. Paul is not happy, but rather in high spirits and sustained by a deep current of feeling, thoughts swimming clearly and in relaxed streams through his satisfied consciousness amid a fertile quiet. So feels the wanderer, and he had never known such a feeling before, how deep his memories stirred and how far back they reached. To walk along as light as a feather was no longer hard for Paul. He could not have stood to hurry so just a week ago. Now he moves on ahead with ease, even uphill, his breath supporting his relaxed gait. He tells himself with confidence that he will make it through the journey, he doesn't have to worry about whatever trouble lies ahead. It will happen! It will happen! I will be on my way! The road beckons. Someone should rouse the late sleeper, he should hurry, it's almost eleven, the time is here for the rabble, a whistle blows and rattles, a smile of derision rains down from behind, go on home, off with you, go on home!

"I'm already home! I leave tomorrow!"

The American shines a bright flashlight on the idiot who shouldn't be out on the streets, wondering what kind of guy he's dealing with. He cackles out an order in English as a well-meaning joke, then he is quiet. Paul no longer listens; he's a long way off from being asked to do anything today. Paul is already in the yard, his steps slowing. He climbs the couple of steps and then for the last time is a guest in the officer's room. He is happy that there is no longer blackout, at last the light can shine freely through the window. Quickly he readies his things for the morning. Then he goes to sleep.

Paul is glad that he has everything in order; now everything will be as easy as the first night he was in Unkenburg, but without any feeling of death. The image of Zerlina enters his thoughts without sadness, his parents also arrive and look peaceful. Paul bows his head before them and without any shyness considers the dead who are there with him. He is confident that he will not feel ashamed before them anymore, that he will venture forth on the journey, and that the hand of life has been extended to him. Onward! He senses that, as long as he remains here, his longing will diminish and dissipate. He must no longer cling to things with such intensity and can now pull himself away from the column that he was chained to until earlier that day. Paul can still hear the time strike in the middle of his sleep, a quarter after, half past, patiently on and on. Then he no longer noticed how the night grew ever deeper and embraced him more and more and let the quarter hours continue to strike.

When Paul awakens it is early morning. Yesterday has flowed into today, as if today were still yesterday. Paul has no time to waste. He gets up and thanks the bed that has taken him in. He folds a blanket and attaches it firmly to the knapsack. After washing he quickly packs. When he's done he takes the mirror off the wall, wipes it clean, covers it with a clean hand towel, and buries it in between some underwear. Then he closes the knapsack. After a little meal, Paul grabs the satchel, then he lifts the knapsack and puts his arms through the straps, lifting his suitcase meanwhile with his left hand. Paul thanks the room that has put him up so well. Already he is in the hall; he doesn't leave his name on the door, but rather rips up the note and throws it away, leaving the door open.

Paul crosses the yard and thanks the barracks, thanks Kanonenberg as well. Now he follows the road down the hill, once more through the city, the little park in full bloom, the general's statue without a head, the extinguished cathedral, the picked-over rubble of the old city already partially swept away, paths in between having been shoveled clear. Paul sees again the theater's wreckage, its decay even further advanced, the walls perhaps ready to collapse. Then comes the house where Frau Wildenschwert lives, then the long street, and before long he passes police headquarters. Finally Paul is at the station.

"They're readying a train."

The man in the red cap assured him it was so. Paul should stand in line with the others who are waiting. The crowd grants him a spot. Paul says thank you and shoves his suitcase forward, his free hand already clutching the cool railing. Perhaps the people understand why he's in such a hurry. He thinks he sees them waving, wishing him a safe journey, the rubbish and the rubble vanquished at last.

Afterword

ONLY THOSE WHO RISK THE JOURNEY
FIND THEIR WAY HOME

Jeremy Adler

THE JOURNEY TELLS THE STORY OF PEOPLE WHO WERE FORBIDDEN. ORDINary people with hopes and fears like the Lustig family. In the middle of their everyday life they receive the latest commandment, "Thou shalt not dwell among us!" and this simple sentence is the start of ever more monstrous decrees. "The entire world" has turned into "the forbidden." The victims know it themselves: "We are all forbidden." Such declarations reverse all normal conceptions, transforming a free society into a slave society with inverted institutions whose purpose it is to make life impossible. Thus we learn: "In the name of justice, injustice is installed." Even though innocent people "invoke the need for justice," what we hear is "Oh, what crazy ideas you get, still thinking about justice, as if you were never told that it's already fit and just that inevitably you are ordered about and told to do things that only to you do not seem right." Nothing remains as it was, and even the reader must find his way—led by the narrative voice—on a blind "journey" in a senseless world in which "all experience is betrayed," where all words cease to exist, since in the end names "no longer mean anything." In order to still try to evoke the unspeakable, the narrative voice chooses "the image of the journey." Initially the "fleeting journey" simply serves as the image of fate, or in other words as a timeless metaphor for the plight of the people who have been forbidden. In addition, however, as is made clear at the start of the tale, the metaphor represents "memory itself, which sets out on the journey and is also dragged along through constant wandering." Thus the novel creates the possibility of memory, by pursuing the path of the forbidden people through their own hopes and memories, in order to bear witness to the compassionate memory of the victims for posterity, and thus the simultaneous journey of the narrative voice itself. Elias Canetti recognized the groundbreaking aspect of this work: "It will become the classic book about this kind of 'journey,' no matter who is displaced or devastated, no matter to whom it happens."

Born on July 2, 1910, in Prague, Hans Günther Adler grew up in a middle-class family, studied music, literature, philosophy, and psychology, and wrote a dissertation on "Klopstock and Music." He experienced firsthand Hitler's seizure of power while researching in archives in Berlin. He aspired to a career as an academic while seeking at the same time to establish himself as a writer. His hopes for each were destroyed in 1933. He then began work as a secretary in a Prague school for continuing education. By 1938 he had plans to emigrate. Unfortunately, these fell through. He remained in Prague and was intensely caught up in the confusion of the times. In 1941 he was put to work as a slave laborer building railroads. Then, in 1942, there followed his deportation to Theresienstadt along with his wife, the doctor Gertrud Klepetar, and her family. Gertrud's father died there. Her aunt was transported east. Hans Günther and Gertrud Adler-Klepetar were deported to Auschwitz in 1944. There on the "ramp," Gertrud chose to join her mother on "the bad side" in order that she should not die alone. After two weeks my father was transported to Niederorschel, an outlying camp of Buchenwald, and then to the underground factory at Langenstein, where he was finally liberated by American troops in April 1945.

Next he wandered—exhausted and sick—to Halberstadt, from where he began the adventurous return to Prague. He hardly had the strength to climb the stairs to the first floor when he got there, and for years he suffered from sudden spells of weakness. Nonetheless he managed to start a new life. He dedicated himself to the memory of the "precious dead" and found his vocation as a "witness to truth." This gave him a new, in fact the sole, purpose for his life. In 1947 he fled the arrival of the Communist regime, leaving his native Prague for London. There he remained an exile, describing himself as a freelance writer "at home in exile," though he was able to establish himself neither as a poet nor as a teacher. Eventually he found a footing as a writer in Germany, Austria, and Switzerland, as well as in Israel and the United States. As his first biographer, Jürgen Serke, remarked, when he died in London on August 21, 1988, H. G. Adler left behind an unparalleled *"Gesamtkunstwerk"* made up of poems, stories, novels, scholarly studies, and essays. Among these *The Journey* holds a special place. It is his most tender, most moving book.

After he finished the first draft of his groundbreaking monograph *Theresienstadt 1941–1945: The Face of a Slave Society*, which he wrote between 1945 and 1948, with an unbelievable outburst of the energy that had been chained up in the camps, my father quickly produced five novels, including the novel of his formative years, *Panorama* (written in 1948 and published in 1968), and *The Invisible Wall* (written from 1954 to 1956 and published in 1989). *The Journey*, written in 1950–51, is the centerpiece of this unique confrontation with *l'univers concentrationnaire*, to use David Rousset's term. Like many of the works from the early part of his career, the novel remained unpublished for a long while. For one thing, his reputation as a scholar after the publication of his Theresienstadt book in 1955 overshadowed his literary efforts. For another, the time was not yet ripe for a former prisoner to present his years in the camps in literary rather than documentary fashion. Moreover, the members of the Prague School that had shaped Adler's writing had either been expelled or exterminated, and with them his works' ideal readers.

Only gradually and through the repeated assays that have been made over the years are we able to comprehend the scale of the terror between 1933 and 1945. Memory fails in the face of facts. One needs only to think of how long it took for Primo Levi's moving portrait of his life in Auschwitz to become widely known in order to recognize how difficult it has been to make the Shoah known in the world. Simply reporting events was in no way enough to develop awareness or to shape memory, and thereby enable readers to enter into the world of the camps. For the public at large, the decisive turning points were the Nuremberg trials, the Auschwitz trial in Frankfurt, and the Eichmann trial in Jerusalem. Outrage at the perpetrators who were still alive rekindled the memory of their victims. After that there was no looking away. Understanding still depends, however, on the perspective from which one views the events, with what degree of sincerity, and whether one accepts the truth. Whoever wants to look away has to ask himself in what direction he will turn his gaze. In *The Journey* this means: "The truth is merciless, and it is always victorious, always to people's surprise, for nothing is as deeply mocked as the final victory of truth, even when its story involves countless insults, though never a final defeat. The truth is most terrible for those who never risk it. . . . Truth allows no escape . . . but it is never cruel." People, so it seems, were simply not ready to listen to this kind of "truth" in a novel in the 1950s.

Although there were a number of voices at the time that spoke in support of *The Journey*, the book faced stiff opposition from several influential people. In England a well-known publisher advised H. G. Adler to take Norman Mailer's *The Naked and the Dead* as a model of how to tackle a novel about Auschwitz. In Germany, Peter Suhrkamp reacted with outrage: "As long as I live, this book will not be printed in Germany." That is just what happened. Only after Suhrkamp's death did the book find an independent spirit, Knut Erichson, who decided to publish *The Journey* in his Bonn publishing house, bibliotheca christiana, in 1962. "I'm not the publisher for you," he explained to the author, "but I'll publish the book because no one else will." The notable typographer Hermann Zapf did the design, and so the book first appeared in a suitably elegant form. However, the publisher did not have the means to gain widespread attention for the work. Despite important reviews that should have helped the book to break through, it didn't happen. *The Journey* remained a well-kept secret.

The original title was *Die Reise: Eine Ballade*, yet for reasons of copyright Erichson chose *Eine Reise*, and he advised the author to drop the unusual subtitle, *Eine Ballade*. But since in Adler's eyes the book was not a "novel," which in his opinion is a genre that captures "an entire world," he chose the more modest subtitle *Eine Erzählung*, or *A Tale*. This confusing, somewhat lightweight subtitle is another reason the book was rarely noticed. In his review, Heimito von Doderer acknowledged the problem with the genre: "The author calls this book 'A Tale.' Yet it's a novel. Not because of its length, but rather because of its universal reach." Then came the concession: "Yet the work is really a ballad." Doderer went on to explain his view: "A ballad does not accuse, it does not excuse. It is a crystalline form." The ballad of *The Journey* is "liberating," "it makes the subject, be it as it may (and here the case borders on the unbelievable), weightless and floating, without relinquishing any of its weight. A whole mountain of horror is turned into song." Though Doderer was right to draw the analogy between the lyrical nature of *The Journey* and the ballad form, the term also makes sense on other levels, for in a ballad, according to Goethe's definition, lyrical, dramatic, and narrative moments join together. These three forms of expression are bound together elaborately in *The Journey*. The polyphonic stream of consciousness leads us continually from one point of view to another. The reader often no longer knows who is speaking before the next voice enters. In this manner, the narrative stream runs from Paul's thoughts to his mother's feelings without our noticing a break, or the narrator's reflections into the sister's fears. As with a ballad, the book contains the refrainlike repetition of numerous central motifs. Thus the form of the ballad does not harken here to a traditional genre, but rather creates a new narrative form, one that can be placed somewhere among Joyce, Woolf, and Faulkner. *The Journey* appeared almost at the same time as Faulkner's great memoir of World War I, *A Fable*, and there are also parallels with *Ulysses* and *Between the Acts*, Ilse Aichinger's *Herod's Children* being another important point of reference. In the end, however, like Doderer, I am at a loss when it comes to finding suitable literary comparisons for *The Journey*. Roland H. Wiegenstein came to the most radical conclusion on this point in his review in *Merkur*: "The book belongs to no literary category whatsoever."

The book is dedicated to Adler's friends Elias and Veza Canetti. Soon after it was completed, Canetti formed a clear judgment: *The Journey* was "a masterpiece, written in an especially beautiful and clear prose, beyond rancour or bitterness." Canetti went on to elaborate his view, using his own characteristic idiom: "I believe that your experience . . . has here met with a complete poetic transformation, one that has never before been

achieved." Since Canetti considered a writer to be the "guardian of transformation," we can assume that he was choosing his words most precisely,
and that *The Journey* matched his own illuminating criteria for successful
imaginative literature. The magic word *transformation* recalls the continual movement of *The Journey*, its overwhelming linguistic richness, that
"boundlessness that tolerates no limit," which the narrative voice invokes
right from the start: "You travel many roads, and in many towns you appear with your relatives and friends; you stand, you walk, you fall and die."
That which Canetti called the mythic is found in the images that are
continually transformed and used as leitmotifs, as well as in the various
fairy-tale figures. Finally, Canetti was the first to arrive at what the novel
meant for modernity. In the quality of the novel, which Canetti particularly stressed, we recognize its lasting relevance: "The most terrible things
that could possibly happen to human beings are presented here as if they
were weightless, delicate, and easily withstood, as if they could not harm
the human core." When the book appeared, Veza Canetti wrote to thank
the author with a postcard from the British Museum that depicts the torso
of Pallas Athene together with its head, from which the face has been broken off. "The book is *too beautiful* for words and too sad. We are proud of
the dedication."

The novel transposes the experience of the author, "estranging" it as Adler
was wont to say, and removes it from the realm of the personal. Casting
himself in the form of Paul Lustig, the writer transforms himself into the
brother of his first wife, Gertrud Klepetar, to create a family unit. My father called Gertrud "Geraldine." Here she is transfigured as Zerlina. Her
parents, Dr. David and Elisabeth Klepetar, appear as Dr. Leopold and
Caroline Lustig. Gertrud's aunt, her mother's sister, is portrayed as Ida
Schwarz. In this way the family represents a sociological unit, a social
atom whose very nucleus is annihilated by the destructive force imposed
on them by history. This small group symbolizes the innumerable number
of their fellow victims in suffering. The family name of the two sisters—
Schmerzenreich—evokes the fate of this whole community bound together by a common fate. Their valley of tears is a realm of pain. "Lyrical
irony" was what H. G. Adler called the style of the book, referring to the

lyricism of the language as well as to the ever-present use of irony that accuses but does not offend, that laments but does not complain, granting a lightness of tone to such appalling events without lessening the grief or shrinking away from the horror, and enveloping the victims themselves with the love that is due to them even in the moment of their downfall. The narrative voice speaks gently, a secret love suffuses the novel like the spirit of the ineffable in a lyric poem. At the outset we are told: "You were rounded up and not one kind word was spoken." Right from the start, one senses the presence of the goodness that is absent from the events themselves. When Ida Schwarz begins her last journey, the narrator evokes the hour of her birth. We hear the midwife, "a capable woman," inform the mother: "It's a girl, Frau Schmerzenreich!" Here again a certain tenderness can be heard. We measure death against birth, compare things as they are with the circumstances that would be more appropriate to them. The incalculable horrors are measured against missing values. In this ironic context, pleasant words seem like satire. The executioners appear in the novel just as they themselves wish to be regarded. They are simply called "heroes." Their method of execution, as attested by many to this very day, is hygienic. Everything is undertaken "with the utmost consideration." In the play of values—which is also still relevant today—we also recognize the shared responsibility of economy and society, culture and the press. Through their own words, the fellow citizens, who actually know what is happening, judge themselves.

And so we wander on this *Journey* that moves with lyrical irony between concepts like "justice" and "faith" and symbolic images like "the journey" and "rubbish"—as Heinrich Böll noted—in a narrative that constantly returns to everyday matters and activities. "It only takes someone like Adler," said Böll in characterizing the effect of this multivoiced dialectic in his *Frankfurt Lectures on Poetics*, "to describe something as seemingly harmless as rubbish collecting in order to reveal the uncanny." We are led through the various stations of the novel almost unnoticeably, moving from Stupart to Leitenberg, then on to Ruhenthal and Unkenburg. Behind the names lie Prague (one thinks of Stupartgasse, around the corner from the Old Town Square), Leitmeritz, Theresienstadt, and Halberstadt. But the many strands of memory do not run in a straight line. The principles that the horror, the madness, the traumas, and the mourning obey cause the course of this journey to run in ever-new directions until finally the narrator exhausts every path. Memory is a burning ember that defines the theme as well as the style. We experience from within how everything began: "The sickness had crept out of nowhere without a sign to alert the medical world before suddenly everyone fell sick. It was the first epidemic of mental illness." In Ruhenthal the father dies. Then the aunt begins her journey to an unnamed place. Finally we follow Zerlina on her last journey. Everything resists this journey. Zerlina cannot admit to herself where she is headed. The narrator cannot follow her, can only try to find different ways to approach it. The ultimate place of terror, whose name today is on everyone's lips as a symbol of these events, remains nameless. In the same way, the narrative voice refuses to name religions or nationalities. It was the very polarization of such groups that led into the abyss, and hence their concepts are of no use for the narrative. In this all-encompassing anonymity we see once again the power of the ballad, which transmutes the particular into the general. It is about people as such: "There are no roads. The names mean nothing." Paul escapes the unnameable place, reaches Unkenburg, spends some time there, makes new friends, and then begins a new journey. The tale ends on a fitting note. In a dedication copy, the author one day wrote: "Only those who risk the journey find their way home."

Born in Prague in 1910, H. G. Adler spent two and a half years in Theresienstadt before being deported to Auschwitz, Buchenwald, and Langenstein, where he was liberated in April 1945. Leaving Prague for London in 1947, Adler worked as a freelance teacher and writer until his death in 1988. The author of twenty-six books of fiction, stories, poems, history, philosophy, and religion, he is best known for his monograph *Theresienstadt 1941–1945*, for which he received the Leo Baeck Prize in 1958. *The Journey* is the first of Adler's six novels to be translated into English.

About the Translator

Peter Filkins is a poet and translator. He is the recipient of a 2007 Distinguished Translation Award from the Austrian Ministry for Education, Arts, and Culture, a 2005 Berlin Prize from the American Academy in Berlin, and a past recipient of an Outstanding Translation Award from the American Literary Translators Association. He teaches literature and writing at Bard College at Simon's Rock.

About the Type

The text of this book was set in Janson, a misnamed typeface designed in about 1690 by Nicholas Kis, a Hungarian in Amsterdam. In 1919 the matrices became the property of the Stempel Foundry in Frankfurt. It is an old-style book face of excellent clarity and sharpness. Janson serifs are concave and splayed; the contrast between thick and thin strokes is marked.

Modern Library is online at
www.modernlibrary.com

MODERN LIBRARY ONLINE IS YOUR GUIDE
TO CLASSIC LITERATURE ON THE WEB

THE MODERN LIBRARY E-NEWSLETTER

Our free e-mail newsletter is sent to subscribers, and features sample chapters, interviews with and essays by our authors, upcoming books, special promotions, announcements, and news. To subscribe to the Modern Library e-newsletter, visit **www.modernlibrary.com**

THE MODERN LIBRARY WEBSITE

Check out the Modern Library website at
www.modernlibrary.com for:

- The Modern Library e-newsletter
- A list of our current and upcoming titles and series
- Reading Group Guides and exclusive author spotlights
- Special features with information on the classics and
  other paperback series
- Excerpts from new releases and other titles
- A list of our e-books and information on where to buy them
- The Modern Library Editorial Board's 100 Best Novels and
  100 Best Nonfiction Books of the Twentieth Century written in
  the English language
- News and announcements

Questions? E-mail us at **modernlibrary@randomhouse.com**.
For questions about examination or desk copies, please visit
the Random House Academic Resources site at
www.randomhouse.com/academic.